RISE OF THE
DRAGON QUEEN

DARRAH STEFFEN

Rise of the Dragon Queen

Cover by Marta Dec

ISBN (print): 978-1-7364190-0-7
ISBN (ebook): 978-1-7364190-1-4

First edition 2021

Published by DSquared Publishing
Dickinson, ND

For the teachers along the way who encouraged my love of writing.

PROLOGUE

*I*n times of peace, people readily discard the truth. They stubbornly hold to what they know. Sometimes, the most stubbornly held logic is furthest from the truth. Throw out your logic now, my dear listeners. Listen to what I have to say.

People say that the myth of Queen Sammaria's rise to the throne is just that: a myth. They say that Olo Hamwich, the Prime Minister at the time, had simply made up the story to justify Dragonia's fall. Now we…"

The door opened, causing the young woman to break off. The light of the two moons shone into the small room. The small yellow moon, Dainia, sat low in the east. Its twin, Thenia, glowed blue in the west.

She looked at the young man who walked in. He said, "Telling that tale again, ma'am?"

"Why yes. I am."

He asked, "You do know that is only a story, right?"

The children at the young woman's feet looked up at her with pleading eyes, begging for the truth.

The storyteller looked down at them. She said, "Sir, sit and listen to the story. This is not the legend that has been told by your friends and family. This is the real story of Queen Sammaria."

The young man rolled his eyes but sat before the storyteller. A little girl with blonde hair crawled into his lap. The young woman closed her eyes for a moment and then said, "Settle in. Listen to the story. This is the truth."

Amid the war between the O'rult and the Elvateth,

King Delfan used what little influence he possessed to force the creatures of old, the Grumpices and the Hawkaties, to destroy their serpentine invaders. As a result, the dragons after which this country was named were eliminated. The Grumpices disappeared into their colonies in the earth. The Hawkaties disappeared from the planet entirely. Before vanishing, the Hawkaties presented the Elvateth with one last prophecy.

As long as the Dragonian throne held a king, the creatures of old would never answer a call for aid.

King Delfan took this as a good sign. He believed peace would come to the land. He did not realize until he was deep in battle that it meant he would call, and his once allies would not answer. He never learned the second half of the prophecy. They would only answer the call of the Dragon Queen.

Kiro, the Ultimate Protector, sent three lockets to Ethota. No one was to know about these lockets apart from the three who were to use them. They were to be a form of silent protection.

As time passed, however, the lockets began to surface. The Elvateth did not know the purpose of these seemingly meaningless trinkets. It was rumored that the lockets held the Power of the Hawkaties and the Grumpices. One person was rumored to be able to hold the Power of Three – the power of the gods. She would be called the Dragon Queen.

Death came to many in their quest for power, and none succeeded. Those seeking this power vanished along with all trace of the lockets. Slowly, the lockets faded into myth.

This is where the tale begins. The destruction of the O'rult was over one thousand years past, and Enchardo had taken the throne.

There had always been trouble with the people of the neighboring country of Pilleetain. Dragonia and Pilleetain had warred from the beginning. Dragonia had always been known as a haven for all magical beings. Pilleetain, however, had often tried to eradicate magic from their breed. Slowly, the mindset in Dragonia had been changing. Fear had been growing throughout the land. The actions of the commoners had shown influence from the Pilleetain culture.

People murdered their magic bearing children. Magic was considered dirty and threatened the good of their society. The hysteria that had been kept under control for generations was slowly creeping into the magical haven.

Under the rule of King Enchardo, the battle to keep Dragonia pure began. While he was beginning to let uneasiness seep into his heart, he knew that he would be taking in more than the Gabvand refugees. He would lose his country to these new people's ideals if he did not fight. As Dragonia pushed against the warring country, Gabvand called upon their small but powerful ally, the country of Ancefra.

The Ancefran forces raided land along their border with Dragonia. They burned villages and killed civilians. From a village along the coast, the Ancefran army kidnapped over two hundred citizens. Enchardo led a massive campaign to free them.

The King was foolish in his actions, but he was able to save the citizens. As he helped pull the citizens from their dungeon prison, he met a most beautiful girl with eyes so light they appeared to be the milky white of a blind man. Her beauty haunted him. He brought her back to the palace with him, and soon they fell in love. Her name was

Milamare Deswayze and, while she was a commoner, King Enchardo married her.

Fourteen years of uneasy peace followed the conflict. As King, Enchardo was briefed with all secret and important information. He believed, without doubt, that the intelligence was mistaken.

Enchardo could not face the truth of the intelligence. O'rult had been seen roaming the land in Gabvand once more. Someone had to be creating these hybrid creatures. Rumors pointed to a necromancer named Trydexzi. The O'rult were biding their time, waiting for the right moment to strike. It appeared Dragonia was their next target.

Dismissing the growing danger to their country, Enchardo and Milamare were expecting a son, heir to the throne of Dragonia. One could not find a more festive time in the country. Everyone was celebrating the upcoming birth of a new royal child.

Flowers and banners decorated every road within the capitol city of Mestchester, for the queen was adored by all. Milamare was admired for her sympathetic nature and love for her people. Though she was heavy with pregnancy, Milamare went out every day and met with the people. She was fair but stern, hardheaded but openminded, strong but gentle. She related to the people better than many queens, for she understood their needs. Dragonia rejoiced for this birth.

The strong queen gave her life when, much to everyone's surprise, two girls were born. She touched the eldest girl with blonde hair and amber eyes, "Sammaria."

She brushed the dark hair off the younger girl's forehead. The little girl turned her deep blue eyes on her mother. The Queen smiled weakly, "Jennica."

She handed the small babies to the nurses that were

attending her. She said, "My daughters, may the gods look pleasingly on you."

Before she closed her eyes, she pressed a trinket into her young attendant's hand. She said, "Give this to them when they are ready. Them and only them."

The young attendant's mother did everything she could to save the queen. Alas, the queen left them.

The young girl ran for the King. He was pacing outside of her room. The girl ran into him and went sprawling to the ground. The locket went skittering across the floor. The King looked after it as he helped the girl, Diana, up. He asked, "What news?"

Diana opened the door for him. He rushed to his wife's side. The King was devastated by his wife's death. He looked at his daughters but turned away from them in disgust. They were not what he wanted. The King changed that day. His once clear mind became clouded. His decisions placed Dragonia and himself in harm's way. He seemed to want the world to end as his did.

As the girls grew, they held all the traits of their mother and were taught by a monk of the Dregon religion. Mystery surrounded them, but they did their best to relate to the people of their country.

"People knew things were changing. They could see it in the sky, smell it in the air. People both feared and adored the girls. If anything were to happen to them, all the rage of the god of death would break loose."

At age sixteen, the twins were still learning what it meant to be a princess of their country. They secretly studied with Brother Orlten to learn to control the Power with which their mother had graced them. Sammaria was gifted with the powerful and mysterious Power of Fire. Jennica, the soothing and healing Power of Water.

Under the rule of King Enchardo, the once magical haven of Dragonia turned. Magic users were hunted and killed. There were rumors of people with Power simply disappearing. Some say that guards came one day and took them away. They were never heard from again. Jennica and Sammaria began to fear what was happening in their country.

CHAPTER I

Jennica looked out her window, waiting for her father's return. The sun was rising above the babbling brook that flowed on the eastern horizon. She turned as the door opened and saw Sammaria standing there. Sammaria asked, "What are you thinking? You seem distant."

Jennica got up from the window seat and walked to the shelf that held her Seeing Stone. She took it out of its velvet case and turned it over in her hands. Sammaria asked, "Does this have anything to do with Prince Morlyn?"

Jennica shrugged and said, "Yes! We don't even know this man! How can he expect you to marry him? He is not even the same prince they originally agreed on! I just … I just hate him sometimes."

She collapsed onto the bed. Her energy spent. How could she say that about her father?

Sammaria said, "I know, but what can we do? He's the King and our father. There's nothing we can do."

"Yes, there is. You are the future queen. You can change the world. People love you. They listen to you. If you say no, they look to see what is wrong. If you laugh, they try to find what is funny. They'd do anything to please you. Just fight him. You will win."

Sammaria watched as Jennica whispered something to her Seeing Stone. "What in all the heavens and earth are you talking about?"

Jennica handed Sammaria the stone when it illuminated. She saw herself standing before the whole Kingdom as a beloved queen. The stone showed a woman accept a baby from Diana. She heard the stone say, "You will be great someday, Endellion."

It was Sammaria - the Seeing Stone Sammaria. The stone dulled to its normal state.

Sammaria said, "I don't understand."

Jennica snatched the stone back and said, "That's your fate. You are not going to marry that foreigner. You'll do whatever you wish. You'll be a great queen. Sammaria, look at your fate. You are destined to change the world."

Sammaria said, "Well, what about your fate? Hmm? I've seen the world fall at your feet as well."

"No, you haven't. At least not in the way they do for you. They use me to get to you. It's ever so important to be the heir. Not just her sister. My fate is not so glamorous."

Sammaria replied, "What?"

Jennica shrugged saying, "Luenta futura."

The stone stayed blank. Sammaria shook it. She repeated the words Jennica said. Nothing happened. She invoked the name of Mokana. She asked, "What does that mean?"

Jennica shook her head, "I don't know. I've never had that happen before."

She let her words hang in the air. Sammaria stared at the stone.

"Jennica, are you not always saying that the future changes constantly? That it is never the same?"

Jennica said, "Yes, I know, but I've been checking. It's always the same. I have this great sense of foreboding that something horrible is going to happen. I don't know what, but I am certain it's connected to Morlyn. I'm worried."

The sky had grown lighter as Sammaria looked past Jennica and out the window. She said, "Jennica, nothing is going to happen. I'll make sure of it."

Jennica looked gravely at her, "What if it's beyond your control?"

Sammaria said, "You worry too much. This is why normal people don't see the future. It'll be fine."

Sammaria squeezed Jennica's shoulder as she left. Jennica took a deep breath, pushing the thoughts of the future from her mind. It made her feel somewhat better. She thought, "If I only live for a few more years, I shan't live in fear."

She stood up, stretching, and began to run a brush through her long dark hair. The familiar movement seemed to calm her some. She set the brush down and pulled on a robe. Idly, she hummed a small tune.

She picked up a book and opened it to the place she had marked. It was a history text from the palace library's restricted section. She had begged Brother Orlten to get it for her. She settled in for a relaxing read.

Jennica jumped as she heard a loud galloping on the front path. She ran from the antechamber to the balcony, dropping the book. It fell open onto the floor.

Jennica looked down at the arriving caravan and saw her father riding to the stables. He looked toward her and waved. She smiled, waving back vigorously. Even though she was upset with him, she still loved his homecoming. She loved to hear the stories of his travels and see the gifts he brought back to her.

She saw one of the other men staring at her and she remembered she was simply in her dressing robe. She turned, fleeing into her room to change.

Jennica dismissed the Brother before slipping out of her bedclothes. She fidgeted the whole time Diana tied up the back of her plain brown riding dress. After Jennica's hair was plaited with a green ribbon, she raced to Sammaria's room.

The King and his men rode around to the other side of the castle below Sammaria's room. Sammaria's window faced the western sky, opposite from Jennica's, as she had wanted the view of the dying sun at the end of each day.

Some of the men were whistling at her. Sammaria's friend Antien asked, "Why don't you come down and show…"

He trailed off at a glance from one of his elders.

Sammaria looked down at them. She was wearing a simple white dress with a V-neck and Nyma, her falcon, was perched on her shoulder. Her golden blonde hair flowed unrestrained in the wind. She was standing on the ledge of her balcony in perfect balance. She noticed her father's look and climbed down.

Jennica ran up behind Sammaria and yell down, "Welcome home, Father!"

Sammaria waved. Jennica took a hold of Sammaria's hand and they ran back into the room.

As Jennica and Sammaria reached the stairs, Sammaria pulled her hand out of her sister's. Jennica turned around, confused. She asked, "What's wrong?"

Sammaria rubbed her arms as if she were cold. She said, "It's Father. This whole ordeal with Morlyn. Do you think I should fight him?"

Jennica said, "Yes. Absolutely. If you are to be truly happy."

Sammaria frowned, "But …"

Jennica frowned back, "If you are unsure, wait until you meet him."

Jennica stepped onto the first step. Sammaria followed. They gave each other a look before racing down the stairs.

Sammaria and Jennica ran to the stable. Antien brushed Sammaria's hand as they ran by him. She looked back, and he gave her a quick smile.

The girls ran to their father's side. He was rubbing his shoulder. Jennica hugged him then took her place beside Sammaria. King Enchardo nodded to the girls and said, "Sammaria. Jennica. I would like to…"

He did not finish. Enchardo doubled over and fell to the ground.

Jennica cried out, "Father!"

He looked up at her face and said, "Darling, I'm fine."

Walking toward Sammaria, Antien said, "Sire, you should go see a healer."

The others agreed. King Enchardo sat up and looked at Antien standing close to Sammaria but not quite touching her.

He frowned saying, "Isn't my oldest daughter going to hug her old father?"

Sammaria forced a smile and walked over to hug him.

"Sammaria was weary of her father's several reassurances of love. They were usually followed with an order to stay away from someone or a request to do something she did not want to do. This time, however, he gave no orders. Sammaria had not been close to her father for about a year now. She saw a change in him though she could not put her finger on exactly what had changed.

You see children, Sammaria was weary because her father seemed to resent her. She attributed it to her being next in line, and he knew she had Power. He was trying to control her in a way that did not fit a King. She rebelled in small ways. Her friendship with Antien stemmed from that."

Enchardo was ushered away from the twins. After he had gotten a short distance away, Antien grabbed Sammaria's wrist. He pulled her behind the stable door. Jennica gave her a worried look. Sammaria waved her on.

Antien said, "Morlyn will be dangerous. Be careful of what you do around him."

Sammaria said, extracting her arm, "How do you know? Why are we hiding?"

Antien did not answer. He leaned in as if he was going to kiss her. Sammaria stood stock still. He said, "People are not as loyal as they seem. They would not keep this conversation secret."

Sammaria sighed and leaned her head on his shoulder, "I don't want to marry him."

"I know."

"You know me better than I do sometimes."

"Be careful, Samma. Try not to need me for a while."

Sammaria cringed at the nickname. She didn't say anything. There were more pressing matters at hand, "You're going? So soon?"

Someone called Antien's name outside of the stable. He said, "No time to explain. I'll find you."

Sammaria stepped out of the stall. She looked back at Antien. He was brushing her father's gelding.

She joined Jennica outside their father's room. The healer was having a serious talk with the King's advisors. They raised their voices now and then. Sammaria and Jennica heard bits and pieces like, "A spell cast upon him… Couldn't undo… Wouldn't let us… Could kill."

The doctors looked back at the girls. One walked over to them and said, "The ride was rough, and the food he ate while traveling was not fresh. He shall be all right, but he will have stomach pains for a while."

Sammaria noted the way the doctor's eyes shifted away from them as he spoke. She nodded, "Thank you, sir. I'm sure your recommendation will do him wonders."

He smiled, bowed, and left.

As he retreated, Sammaria whispered to Jennica, "They are lying."

Jennica nodded in reply. She had seen the shifting eyes as well.

They went over to their father's bed. He smiled. Jennica could see from the way his mouth turned up that it was forced. She said, "How are you, Father?"

He said, "Fine. Just fine. Now, back to business. Jennica, I have had a new dress placed in your chamber. Dress and I will escort you to meet someone. We shall have a feast."

"Who?" asked Jennica perplexed, "You didn't say anything about marriage for me. You ..."

"Jennica. Stop this. He is a knight. He has returned to Mestchester after many years. I would like you to entertain him while he is here."

"Father, please. Can someone else do it?"

The King looked contemptuously at his youngest daughter, "No. Do your duty. Now, go get changed."

Sullenly, Jennica stayed silent. She crossed her arms and refused to look at him. He said, "Jennica?"

She said finally, "Are we not unpacking?"

"Unpacking? Are we commoners?" asked Enchardo insulted.

"We always help you unpack. Do you not remember?" asked Sammaria.

The King said, "Ah, yes. Well, I thought, given the circumstances, we would leave that. However, since it is so important to you. Let me rest for a time. Meet me back here in a couple hours."

The girls agreed with the arrangement and left him.

Jennica fumed, "How could I have not seen this coming? You knew about this, didn't you? He is going to try to marry me to this knight now."

Sammaria said, "I had my suspicions."

"Do your duty," she mocked, "I'm not the heir."

Sammaria said, "Can we drop it, please?"

Jennica softened, "Oh, I'm sorry. Now I understand what you've been going through the past few weeks."

Sammaria changed the subject, "I don't like what those doctors were saying."

Jennica replied, "I know. What did they mean by a spell?"

Sammaria shook her head, "I'm not sure, but it's addled Father. He's acting odd."

Jennica agreed, "This isn't the first time. He keeps forgetting things that he should know."

Sammaria stopped as she heard Pranshey talking with another of her father's advisors, hearing her name in whispered tones.

Pranshey had been the King's most loyal advisor for as long as she could remember. Enchardo had trusted no opinion more than Pranshey's.

Pranshey was of slight build with a face Sammaria did not trust. He had foxlike features and seemed to slink around the palace. Even with his slight fiendish air, Pranshey was trusted. That was until he and the King had a falling out. Enchardo had not dismissed the strange advisor, but he no longer sought Pranshey's opinion as he once had.

Pranshey made her uncomfortable. She did not particularly want to announce her presence to him. He was saying, "It's a shame Sammaria and Jennica have forgotten him."

The other said, "He was much older than them. He was to be married. The Princesses were just younglings."

Pranshey replied, "Still, Einar loved those girls. He was a second father for them."

The name stirred something in Sammaria. Who was this Einar character? Why did she feel her heart smile as she heard his name? As far as she knew, there was never an Einar in her life.

The other advisor agreed, "And with that dreadful business with Mersaya. Then what happened with Duchess Lilliana Krulle. He was to marry her, you know? It's no wonder the King forbade mention of it to him and his court."

Pranshey nodded, "And yet it seems cruel not to speak of it to the Princesses. He was, after all, their flesh and blood."

Sammaria gasped. Why was he forbidden in the castle? Who could he possibly be? A nobleman if he was living in the palace and was to marry a Duchess.

Sammaria heard footsteps coming down the hall. She backed and tried to make it seem like she was just coming out of the nearest door. She ran straight into Pranshey. He looked at her, surprised. He bowed with a slight sneer, "Your Highness, forgive my inattentiveness."

Sammaria nodded, "All is forgiven."

Pranshey said, "You are too kind, my Lady."

Sammaria nodded again. Pranshey left her. He said as they parted, "Your Highness?"

Sammaria turned to look at him. His eyes glittered with danger. She said, "Yes?"

He said, "Be careful on which conversations you eavesdrop. You might find out something that is dangerous to know."

Sammaria's eyes narrowed. She did not speak but registered the advice. Pranshey turned and left. Sammaria continued on her way, stunned. She wanted so badly to talk to her sister about it, but, after all, she *was* eavesdropping. Still, Jennica had Sight. Pranshey said they had forgotten him. The gift of Sight made one more mentally aware. Maybe Jennica could recall something.

Sammaria decided against it. Jennica was already preoccupied with worry for their father and her troubling future. Sammaria did not know what to make of that. Seeing Stones were quartz crystals with a spell cast upon them. The spell allowed one to see only a few hours into the future. The Stones were dangerous. Not many people had them anymore.

Enchardo had banned them after people began to use them to manipulate their lives and the future. Most of the Stones were gathered and destroyed. There were only a few left in existence.

Yet, Jennica's was different. She could see years into the future. While most stones only lasted a few months, Jennica's had lasted years. The Stones were rumored to die when the spell wore off, and many people saw death around the time their Stone died.

Jennica was not always sure what she was looking at when she searched into the Stone. She usually looked for markers she recognized, but there were times when there were none. Sammaria believed Jennica's natural ability amplified the power of stone. The stone allowed her to enter Sight State without being fully in the state.

Sammaria wondered if Jennica remembered Einar. It might explain her visions. Still, Sammaria was not convinced. Jennica was not the kind to be worked up over a Seeing Stone. It had to be something more.

Sammaria walked into her rooms' antechamber. She looked at the drawing on the wall. It was of a giant dragon, one of the first to allow a non-Draigar to ride it. The Draigar were god-like creatures with the ability to control Water, Earth, and Air. They had been a peaceful tribe native to the Dragonian frontier.

Sammaria had always thought the story of how the Elvateth came to Dragonia was sad. The Elvateth came from across the ocean. At the time, Fire was gifted to all of the Elvateth race. They wielded it foolishly. The Elvateth wanted control over the land and they quickly took to the extermination of the native Draigar.

Capturing the Draigar, however, was a difficult feat. The Draigar moved around stealthily. They seemed to disappear into the land and reappear miles away. The Elvateth eventually overtook the land and pushed the remaining Draigar into a small pocket of land on the border of Dragonia and Illicus. As punishment, the Draigar bound all Elvateth magic.

Over time few Elvateth proved their worthiness. Dragon furies bound themselves to these people. They returned their abilites to them. The bond furthered resentment in the land. Magic users were shunned and killed. That is until the half Draigar- Elvateth bonded to a dragon elder, Mestchina, restored peace and established Dragonia as a place of magical freedom.

Sammaria and Jennica had always scoffed at the irony that Dragonia was supposed to be free for magic users like them, and yet they were forced to hide their Power from their father, their friends, and the world. Sammaria vowed she would undo what hundreds of years of magic intolerance had done. She would set Dragonia right.

She moved back into her room and lay down on her bed. Everything she had heard that day took turns crowding her thoughts. She had no desire to go unpack with her father. It would only cause her further stress. He would treat her as if she were a servant. She was never his daughter, just another rival, someone he believed was out to destroy him. She was like one of the Draigar. A Pilleetain. An enemy.

Jennica still clung to the hope he would return to his normal self. She loved him but knew he was probably going mad. Still, she stayed patient with him and calmly reminded him of the forgotten memories. Sammaria wished she had that kind of patience.

Sammaria ignored the servants bustling around her room as she contemplated. A knock came to her door. It was a messenger. He handed her two envelopes. One was large with a seal stamped into the hot wax. The other was small. The writing on the front was large and heavy. Sammaria set it aside even though it intrigued her. She figured the other, sealed letter was the more important of the two.

She opened it. The letter was written in a fine hand. She quickly read the letter:

Your Royal Highness Princess Sammaria,
I deeply regret not being able to join your father. There are responsibilities I must attend to before joining you. Surely, you understand this as a Crown Princess. I am pleased that our long betrothal is finally moving forward. I know that this is strange, marrying a man you have never met. It is strange for me as well. I do wish to know you before our wedding in the fall.
Morlyn Agnaldo de'Jenginald

Sammaria rolled her eyes as she put the note aside. He sounded so impersonal in the note. There was a small attempt with the comment on the tour she was supposed to give him.

Sammaria frowned. She wanted to be given the chance to choose a suitor herself. She sighed. What did it matter? He was her future. She might as well get used to it.

Sammaria picked up the other note. She looked at it. The writing was coarse. It was none that she recognized. It certainly was not from Antien as she had expected. She ripped open the seal and pulled the note out.

She looked around making certain the servants had left. The only one remaining was her chambermaid, Narcissi. Sammaria took care to shield the note from her. Sammaria slowly unfolded the note. There were only eight words, but they set her heart beating with mystery and intrigue:

The information you seek is to the east.

Sammaria looked at Narcissi. She was waiting with her head bowed for an order. Sammaria asked, "Do you know who sent the second note? There is no signature."

Narcissi replied, "No, madam. It was left with your messenger. Would you like me to find out?"

Sammaria nodded, "No, that is all."

Narcissi bowed and left the chamber. Sammaria turned her attention back to the note. Who could it have been? And to the east? What did that mean?

Sammaria slipped it into her pocket. It was time for her to meet her sister.

Jennica looked up as Sammaria walked around the corner. She asked, "Where have you been?"

Sammaria dismissed her with a wave of her hand. She said, "I'm here now. What have you heard?"

Jennica replied, "Father is talking to some woman. Except I don't think anyone else is in his room. He might be using some magic communication charm, but I don't know where he would get it. They are arguing over the date of something. They keep talking about the Meyeah moon."

"Our birthday?" Sammaria asked.

Jennica retorted, "The day it's legal for you to rule sovereign."

Sammaria glanced at her younger sister. She was not being tart. That was how she marked that birthday. Sammaria said, "Whatever."

Jennica hushed her. Their father was saying something about them. The words were muffled. They could not make it out. Jennica said, "I think I heard something about an unpleasant surprise."

Sammaria said, "That's strange. Did you hear anything about his pain?"

"When I first arrived here, he was cursing magic. I do not know if it had anything to do with his pain or not. Father hates magic."

Sammaria nodded, "I know. Why -"

A chambermaid opened the door. She bowed her head and stepped aside for Jennica and Sammaria to enter. Jennica gave Sammaria a look that sent shivers down her spine. It was as if she felt they were entering the dragon's keep.

CHAPTER II

Jennica took out the dusty clothes. She placed them on the bench at the end of the King's bed. She had always enjoyed this tradition. However, this time it did not feel the same. There was a melancholy tone to the room. Usually, their father would joke and laugh as he told them of his grand adventures in far off lands. Today, he was simply handing the items to the girls as if to appease them. He sometimes chatted about something he saw, nowhere near the wild stories he had made up when they were young.

Jennica unwrapped his jewelry, ears perking up as her father mentioned the infamous Donichello's name. Enchardo spoke of his hometown of Likenton. The city was slightly smaller than Mestchester. However, Donichello's family controlled the Myhadry Peninsula from Likenton. Jennica frowned as she recalled a dark-haired man telling her of the great city.

Enchardo said, "Lord Donichello hasn't been here in Mestchester for many years. Society has always kept him abroad or near his home. Still, he seems quite taken with you, Jennica. He claims to have met you in Likenton once. I am afraid I do not recall the meeting."

Jennica could not recall a meeting with him either. She remembered going to Likenton when she was young. That had been fun. She had to prove to the other children she was just one of them. She played with them and Diana until someone squealed that the princess was playing with commoners and she was taken away.

Her father continued, "Maybe you could give him a tour of Mestchester."

Jennica did not reply for the longest time, "Yeah, maybe."

King Enchardo never noticed the lack of enthusiasm in his daughter's voice. He began speaking to Sammaria about Prince Morlyn. He told them of Morlyn's military prowess. Jennica did not care. She hoped that was not the only thing Morlyn cared about. She wondered if he was kind.

Sammaria asked, "What is Ancefra like?"

King Enchardo said, "The grass is always green it is said. However, the standard of living could be better. While the de' Jenginald family rules with an iron fist, Ancefra is still made up of warring indigenous tribes. Who wants presents?"

Sammaria frowned at her father's dismissal of her question. King Enchardo pulled out two packages. The girls smiled at their father and sat next to him to see what he had brought home for them. He brought Sammaria a ruby necklace. It was beautiful. Rubies were one of Sammaria's favorite gems. Her father jerked them out of her hands and placed it around her neck.

When it settled, Jennica gasped. Sammaria looked in the mirror. It looked like blood was running from her neck, three bloody fingers of tiny red stones.

"A sign of greatness. A sign of what is to come," Enchardo said looking at the stones. The girls gave each other uneasy looks. If that was what was to come, Sammaria had a very grim future. The stones looked more like a warning than a gift.

Enchardo quickly moved on to Jennica's gift. He pulled out a velvet box. Inside sat a milky white oval. Rainbows swirled into the shell as Jennica shifted it. She tapped it, "What is it?"

He nodded at it. Jennica looked down at the parchment nestled below it.

"A dragon egg? Is it real?"

He said, "Only the best for my little girls."

Enchardo sat down at his desk. He examined papers that sat there. He glanced up at them with cool eyes.

Sammaria gathered her things and her sister. They shuffled out of the room. As soon as they were out of sight, Sammaria ripped the necklace from her neck, "This necklace scares me."

"You may have more to worry about than a necklace," snarled a voice.

The girls turned to find Pranshey standing there. Sammaria said, "What do you mean?"

Pranshey started to walk away. He said, "The perfect world of the Princesses is not so perfect. I expect you know that. I am simply saying you should watch your backs."

Jennica was back in her rooms examining her egg when her father rapped on her door. Jennica stood, placing the egg on her nightstand. As she had understood it, taking a dragon's egg was illegal, but for a King, nothing seemed to be.

Her father said without prompting or greeting, "There will not be a party tonight. We will celebrate when Prince Morlyn arrives on our Founding Day."

Jennica nodded. She did not care. She wanted nothing to do with any of it. King Enchardo continued ignoring his daughter's lack of enthusiasm. He said, "Now, at this time you must meet him."

"Who?" asked Jennica, confused.

"Lord Donichello. He's a knight, you know?"

Jennica frowned, "So you have said."

The King clapped his hands. Diana appeared at the door and opened the white box Jennica had tossed into her changing room. She looked at the dress, uninterested. From the way it was folded, she could see it had a conservative neckline. She pulled it out. It was deep purple. Flowers were embroidered on the bell skirt.

Diana waited for the King to leave before helping Jennica into the new dress. Jennica said, "Do you think this is crazy?"

Diana did not reply. Jennica said, her words cutting, "I wish Tyrina were here. She would tell me what she thought."

Diana ducked her head down. She said, "Countess Tyrina has the status, and your favor, to tell you her opinions without fear of retribution, my Lady."

Jennica said, "You know me, Diana."

Diana said, "I know your father."

Jennica sat down at her vanity and lightly applied rouge to her cheeks. She sighed, "The things we do to please people. It just makes me so mad."

Diana did not comment as she pulled Jennica's hair half up and began to weave flowers into it. When she finished, Jennica stepped into the hall to meet her father. His eyes did not leave her as he said, "You look ravishing."

Donichello was waiting for Jennica in the art gallery. As he waited, he wandered around the room, taking in the magnificent pieces basking in the blue light. On the ground was a large woven rug depicting Mestchina. She was wearing the traditional orange and yellow Dragonian warrior apparel. Mestchina was perched on of Tsnablia, her bonded dragon.

Near the bottom of the rug, Donichello saw two names delicately weaved into the depicted landscape. The rug had been made by the current princesses.

Donichello thought back to when he had first met Jennica. She had come with her father and sister to visit Likenton. She was laughing as she ran with the other children. He did not know then that anyone could be so happy. Her status did not matter to her. She judged people on their merit.

The doors at the front of the room were opened. Donichello looked up from the rug. He had to move from behind statues to see the royal family. Yellow light came pouring into the blue room. The King stepped aside, and Jennica strode into view. She had the same long, brown hair he remembered. With light pouring out behind her, she looked like a goddess.

He moved closer to her from behind the cases of ancient jewelry. She turned her deep, watery blue eyes on him. He stopped for a moment. Her eyes seemed to look right through him. He smiled at her.

Enchardo pushed Jennica forward. She stumbled, caught off guard. Donichello reached out to right her. She pushed away from him, frowning. Despite her covered face, he could see a small smile on the corner of her mouth. The King continued, "This is Princess Jennica Aeradal."

Jennica looked away as the door closed behind her. She glanced back at him subtly. Donichello bowed deeply. He did not move his eyes from her face. Jennica curtsied looking anywhere but directly at him. King Enchardo said, "Lord Donichello Laeranil."

Jennica said, "Just Jennica. Please."

She curtsied again.

The King left, leaving Diana to chaperone the two. Donichello and Jennica examined each other. Jennica did not know what to make of him, giving him a somewhat cold appraisal. He was tall with slightly tanned skin. His eyes were an alluring dark brown.

Jennica shivered. He was very attractive. She rubbed her arms. She could feel the touch of his hand. Though they were calloused, they were soft. He had charm, but that did not excuse her father's manipulations.

Jennica's revelation made her want to leave immediately. However, she was stuck. There was an awkward pause as they tried to find something to say to each other.

Finally, Donichello asked, "Jennica?"

She snapped her head around to look at him, "Yes?"

She could sense something brooding in his mind. He had many things he wanted to know and little time to ask. He could not seem to find the words. She watched him curiously. His eyes seemed to shadow as he fought to find the words. It seemed her gaze was too much. He shook his head, "Never mind."

Jennica asked, "What were you going to say?"

Donichello eyed the young woman in front of him. She was still very much the young girl he had known. Yet, he knew much had changed.

She was a different person. Her eyes bore into him with unspoken curiosity. She shifted her footing so she could utilize every inch of slender frame. Donichello reached out to it before he realized, catching himself. He coughed and asked, "Do you remember traveling to Likenton?"

Jennica thought back. She said, "I was nine. My younger years have grown foggy. I can barely remember anything from that time. I'm sorry."

Donichello's face fell. He hoped she would have remembered him. They had been friends. If she remembered that, then maybe she would not look at him as such an obligation.

Jennica asked to continue the conversation, "Have you ever been to Mestchester before?"

Donichello said, "I spent the summer here when I was sixteen. It is a nice city."

Jennica said, "It certainly is. There is so much beauty here if you just know where to look."

She ran a hand down the marble pillar next to her. She chewed on her lip. He was not saying what he wanted.

Jennica walked away from where they stood as color appeared on her cheeks. Donichello followed.

Jennica let her eyes roam the artifacts she had seen countless times. She gave Donichello a sidelong glance. He was studying a vase made over five thousand years ago.

Jennica said, "It was brought here from Degana. The Indigenous people there used them to bury their dead."

Donichello watched Jennica, "That's fascinating!"

The two continued around the room timidly talking about the art. Jennica stopped in front of a portrait. It was of Queen Milamare. It had been a wedding gift from Enchardo. Milamare was in a white dress with diminutive beading across the bodice.

Donichello could see the resemblance between Jennica and her mother. Jennica had her mother's heart-shaped face and large eyes.

Jennica said, "He really loved her, you know?"

"Who?" Donichello asked.

"My father," she said her face growing confused, "He loved my mother. That's why he married her. He is one of the few kings who married for love. I've always admired him for that."

"How do you know?" Donichello asked.

Jennica looked at him, her eyebrows raised. She was not happy that he was questioning her like that.

Jennica replied, "He used to talk about her when we were younger. It's one of the only things I remember about my childhood. Her death tore him up. It was always hard to talk about her, but he did for us."

She was silent for a long while before quietly saying, "I think that's why he has pushed who he has on us."

Donichello asked, "Princess?"

Jennica looked at him with her big, blue eyes. Her face was hard. She said, "We won't love them. And we won't have to feel the pain of losing them."

Donichello looked down at the ground. She knew what she was saying to him. Her words felt like lead on his heart. He did not get to say more. A servant came, announcing dinner. Their presence was needed in the dining hall.

Donichello held out his arm. He asked, "May I escort you?"

Jennica took his arm with a pit in her stomach. What was his game? Why did he bother being so nice to her? Jennica had not ever talked about that to anyone, not even Sammaria. She was stupid. Was she trying to hurt him?

His inviting eyes made her want to tell him everything. She had to watch herself.

Jennica and Donichello were seated at a long table. Most of the chairs had been removed except the ones in which the King and Sammaria sat. Two empty chairs sat to the King's left. Donichello pulled out Jennica's chair. Jennica forced a smile and sat.

Her irritation was starting to come back. Donichello sat down next to her. Food was brought in for the royal party. Jennica asked, "Where is the court, Father?"

Her father was tart, "Private dinner, Jennica."

Jennica looked down at her soup. She glared into it until it began to rock. She only looked up when she felt a swift kick to her shin. She looked across the table. Sammaria gave her a warning glance. Jennica snuck a peek at Donichello, but he was engaged in a conversation with her father about controlling the Resistance.

Jennica was happy she did not have to contribute much. A few spirited words were all it took to be silenced for the evening.

Sammaria projected her thoughts, "What do you think of him?"

"Excuse me," interrupted the boy, "Projected? What does that mean?"

The Storyteller said, "They were twins. Twins share more than the womb. Their minds are linked. They can essentially speak to each other in their minds."

The boy watched her, "It's more magic."

The Storyteller smiled, "Yes, it's more magic, and it could get a little annoying having someone inside your head at all times."

"How would you know?" snapped the boy.

The Storyteller replied, "Because I am a twin. There are blocks that one can place on their mind. I see some twins out in this little crowd. Is it the same for you?"

One little boy looked over at his twin sister. It appeared to the storyteller that they had never tried. She said, "All right. Try this."

She placed the little boy's hand on his sister's temple. "Now, try to say something to her."

The girl giggled and touched her brother. The storyteller said, "They are young still. After they grow up a bit, they will be able to connect even from great distances. Now, back to our story."

Jennica resisted the urge to shrug. She said back, "He makes me want to tell him things. I despise that. He seems to feed on Father's words. A true loyalist."

"So, you don't think he's dashing?"

"No."

"I think you do. You just cannot admit it!"

"Maybe a little," Jennica admitted.

Sammaria smiled, turning her attention back to the conversation. King Enchardo said, "The Resistance cannot survive. They are fueled by false hopes. Who is the leader? Didn't we kill him? I do believe we killed him."

He was drunk.

Donichello replied, "We did kill the man who headed the organization. However, it seems he had a son."

"A son? He wasn't married, was he?" asked Sammaria.

She would have known. She had made sure the Resistance leader's family was protected from the King's wrath. They did not deserve to suffer even if their father was a traitor.

Donichello said, "It was an adopted son. Rumor has it that he was a refugee from Gabvand. Someone by the name of Rekasi. The Resistance chose him to be their new leader."

"How old is the boy?" asked Enchardo.

Donichello replied, "Younger than I am. According to intelligence, he's around twenty years."

The King began to laugh, "A twenty-year-old running the Resistance? We have nothing to worry about girls. The Resistance will be crushed in less than a year."

Donichello was quiet. However, it was clear he wanted to say more. Jennica frowned as she watched his face struggle with the words he wanted to say and whether it was his place to say them.

Sammaria said in a low voice, "Father, I wouldn't underestimate them if I were you."

"Well, you are not me, thankfully. Go, Sammaria. Leave my presence."

Sammaria stood noisily, "You'll see in time. You will fall, and we will all come crashing down with you."

She spun on her heel and walked out.

Jennica sat there amazed at the way Sammaria always said what was on her mind. She never seemed to get in trouble for it, no matter to whom she was speaking. Jennica shifted in her seat as the silence in the room began to swallow her up.

It didn't take long, as she fidgeted in her seat before she was sent away as well. Her cheeks burned as she moved quickly from the room.

As Jennica opened the door to her chambers, she immediately knew something was amiss. Diana sat huddled behind the desk. Clothes and papers were strewn across the room. Diana said, "Don't enter, Your Highness. It will see you."

"What will?"

Diana choked, silent. She was too frightened of whatever it was. Jennica entered the room slowly. She picked up one of the books from the floor, ready to swing it.

Diana whimpered and hid her face. Jennica walked slowly into her sleeping chamber. She looked around. There did not appear to be anything wrong.

Her pillow twitched. Jennica slowly crept over to her bed. She reached out with a shaky hand and snatched the pillow away.

A dragon sat on her bed looking at her with large eyes. It yawned. Jennica reached out to touch it. She heard a warning cry from Diana.

The creature hunched back, hissing. It sniffed her hand before nuzzling up against it as if it were a cat. Jennica patted the small dragon's head. It curled around her wrist and sat on her arm. It was surprisingly light for a dragon.

Jennica said, "You are not going to hurt anyone are you?"

The dragon watched her with intelligent orange eyes.

Jennica said, "I bet she's hungry. Diana, go get her some meat."

"That thing is a girl?"

"Yes. Food, please."

Diana cast the dragon evil glances as she left the room.

Jennica set the dragon back on the bed. She said, "You need to have a name."

Before she could say anything more, she heard a slithery voice in her mind. It only said one word. Jennica watched as the dragon's eyes changed to green. As the voice receded, the eyes faded back to orange. Jennica asked, "That's your name, isn't it?"

The dragon thrummed a happy note. Jennica said, "Sniblea it is."

Later, Jennica and Sammaria stood before their father in his chambers. He said, "Behave these next few weeks. None of your tricks, or else you'll be sorry."

Jennica and Sammaria did not stick around to find out what the punishment would be. They retreated to the hall. Sammaria said, "No more tricks. So, no more banister slides. No late-night library visits. No messing around. We must act our age."

Jennica said, "You are such a bore."

Sammaria said, "I think we should listen this time."

Jennica said, "We'll see what you think after Prince

Morlyn arrives. I don't know about you, but I refuse to marry any stiff Father chose."

Sammaria replied, "Don't do anything rash, Jennica. Give Donichello a chance. He seems to like you."

Jennica rolled her eyes, "He likes my status. That's all."

Sammaria laughed, "Right. That's all he likes."

Jennica glared at her, "Good night!"

CHAPTER III

*T*he girls were idle for the two weeks leading up to
Prince Morlyn's arrival. Jennica was forced to
attend event after event to socialize with
Donichello. One day, she was forced to have tea with the
Duchess of Calprania."

Jennica sat in the waiting room outside the King's
chambers. Donichello sat across from her and was seated
next to the Duchess of Calprania. Jennica sipped her tea
politely. The duchess, Larissa, said, "Congratulations!
Marriage is such a wonderful gift and joy. I had an arranged
marriage to the Duke, and I am so very fond of him now."

Jennica forced a polite smile. Jennica said, "Oh
Larissa. You misunderstand…"

Donichello took a bite of his tea biscuit. Larissa
interrupted, "Oh, and the children. And the event to make
th-."

Donichello coughed on the bite of biscuit he had just
taken.

Jennica interrupted the duchess, "Excuse me, Madam
Duchess. Children? We are not -"

Donichello recovered from his coughing fit.

Duchess Larissa said, "Of course! You are royalty. It is
your responsibility as such to bring into being children for
the throne."

Jennica refused to look at Donichello. She could see
his face burning as he stared down at his cup of tea.

The duchess laughed, "I can see why you are a little
nervous. Love-making with a man you barely know. Don't
worry. When the time comes, he'll take control."

She winked at Donichello. He shifted uncomfortably.

Jennica did not reply. She clenched her fist around her cup. Her hands shook.

Donichello said, "My dear Duchess. You have grand ideas of how old friends should interact."

Larissa stood up, brushing small crumbs from her lap, and straightened her skirt. Her face was aghast. She eyed Donichello with hard eyes. She said, "Friends often make the best lovers."

She curtsied to the Jennica and said, "I must leave. Remember what I said, Highness."

Jennica mumbled, "How could I forget?"

She nodded to the Duchess. Larissa departed.

Jennica shook her head. Donichello said, "That was awkward."

Jennica burst out laughing. She looked at him. He started laughing too.

She said, "That is the understatement of the century."

Slowly, they calmed down. Jennica looked at Donichello, her eyebrows knitting together as if she were puzzled.

Donichello said delicately, "I suppose I should leave. There is no chaperone here."

Jennica said, "I suppose you should."

Donichello looked at her with his deep brown eyes, "Goodbye then."

Jennica met his eyes with a small smile. She found that she did not want him to go, "Good day."

"A few days had passed since the tea. Everyone was on edge. Jennica was fed up with trying to be perfect in front of every duchess who came through town. All of them were as disastrous as the first. The day the foreign prince,

Morlyn, arrived Jennica was ready to stab the next person who irked her. She just wanted to rest."

Sammaria heard the galloping horses as Jennica sat down before her next tea with Donichello. Sammaria looked out her window asking, "Are we expecting guests today?"

Jennica snapped, "I haven't any idea. If it is another well-wishing duchess from wherever… I'm ailing with the worst thing you can think of, okay?"

Sammaria said, "It's a man with guards." Suddenly it dawned on her, "Oh, Kiro! It's Prince Morlyn!"

Jennica sat up a little straighter. She asked, "Are you going to greet him?"

Sammaria said, "I must."

Jennica helped Sammaria into an orange dress. Her favorite plant, the Dragon Blood, was embroidered on the bottom in red. Diana plaited and twisted Sammaria's hair to a pin atop her head.

Sammaria stood stock straight. Jennica knew her calm façade was hiding the nerves she felt. Sammaria stood next to her father. She clutched Jennica's hand tightly. It was the only sign she was not calm and collected. The Prime Minister escorted the prince into the room.

Donichello walked with Morlyn down the hallway. Morlyn asked him, "Who am I marrying?"

His accent was thick and Donichello had a hard time understanding what he was saying.

Donichello replied, "You are going to meet her in just a few minutes, sir."

The prince waved his hand away impatiently, "Yes, but what is her name?"

Donichello looked at him in disbelief, "Did they tell you nothing of the marriage?"

Absently, Donichello mumbled, "How do they run that country of yours?"

A vein throbbed in Morlyn's neck. He pulled a sword so quickly Donichello was forced to take a step back. He yelled, "Why don't we find out, you filthy bloodmuck!"

Donichello nodded, "Bloodmuck? Original! I am a knight of the realm. Not some commoner off the street."

Morlyn glared at him, somewhat stayed, "Answer the question!"

Donichello replied absently, "Princess Sammaria Aeradal, heir to the throne of Dragonia is your future bride."

The doors were thrown open loudly. Both Donichello and Morlyn looked up. Light came pouring out from the bluely lit room. As the figures came into focus, the King roared, "Put that blade away!"

He moved out of the way to present his daughter, Sammaria, to the newly arrived prince.

As when he introduced Jennica to Donichello, he called Morlyn forward and pushed Sammaria toward the prince. Sammaria forced herself to stay put. She stood with her head erect as she was introduced to Morlyn. She glanced at Jennica. She and Donichello were examining each other again in uncomfortable silence. After he introduced Sammaria, Enchardo left Jennica and Donichello to supervise the couple.

Sammaria looked Morlyn up and down. He was a big man with broad shoulders and black hair that was sitting in tight curls just above his ears. His eyes were dark brown, but they had a tinge of red. They reminded her of the dirt covering the stones in the Kilhatea Mountains.

Morlyn reached his callused hands into his pocket, pulling out a handkerchief. He coughed awkwardly into it.

Sammaria looked at him. Their eyes touched for the briefest moment. It was long enough for her to see the memory hiding behind them.

"Sammaria had only had this happen once before. Seeing into someone's memory was rare. It only happened when the memory holder was forced to think of that moment. If their eyes lock with another's, the memory is viewable. Morlyn's was a memory of a man he had killed."

The image showed Morlyn, sword raised. His eyes were blood red. He showed no mercy as he cornered a man who looked remarkably like him. Morlyn hacked off his younger brother's head. She heard him say, "I'll take this. Just think this could have been Einar's head had you not been protecting the little wretch. You traitor!"

Morlyn sifted through his brother's clothes. He pulled out the handkerchief. "You won't be needing it. A little souvenir from Einar, eh? What's next? You running off with his little sister? Not anymore."

Sammaria pulled her eyes away. The handkerchief was the same into which he had just coughed. She watched as he pocketed it. Sammaria staggered back tripping on the rug Jennica and she had made the previous Erif. She slid herself back a couple of inches and hugged her knees to her chest.

In a raspy voice, Morlyn asked, "What's wrong with her?"

Sammaria kept staring at him, horrified.

Jennica ran to her sister's side. Donichello followed her to comfort the terrified princess. Jennica whispered in her ear. Slowly, Sammaria uncurled herself. Jennica asked, "What happened?"

"With their ability to communicate through their minds, they usually knew what was wrong," explained the storyteller.

The young boy said, "So, why did she have to ask? Jennica doesn't seem like the type to not use her magic."

The storyteller looked at the boy. She said, "You're right. At that age and at that time, Jennica really enjoyed using her magic. She felt she had a breathtaking secret, but, at that moment, Jennica had her mental blocks fully in place. She was too afraid of her own thoughts."

The boy silenced himself. The storyteller continued, "Sammaria raised a shaking hand. She pointed her finger at Morlyn gasping out, 'Him.'"

At dinner that evening, King Enchardo asked Jennica what she thought of Donichello. Jennica said, "I like him I suppose. I just do not see why it is my job to play nursemaid for him."

Enchardo said firmly, "Jennica, are you trying to shame me? You have a duty to me. He is an honored guest. You shall do as I tell you!"

Jennica replied bluntly, "And what if I refuse to listen? Will you throw me out in the streets? What will happen to you if you do?"

King Enchardo stood up, "Jennica, leave! Get out of this room before I send you to the dungeon."

Jennica narrowed her eyes at him. She shoved her plate toward the center of the table. She scraped her chair against the floor as she stood to leave. Sammaria cast a sympathetic look toward Jennica's retreating form.

After he had calmed himself, King Enchardo asked Sammaria about her meeting with Morlyn. Enchardo said, "I assume you have no complaints."

Sammaria grew uncomfortable, "Well..."

Enchardo roared, "What is wrong with my daughters? Do they not trust their father?"

Sammaria said, "Father, I heard something. Someone talking. They say he killed his brother for trying to help some man named Einar. He took his brother's life and then filched the man's handkerchief as a prize. He is a prince from a faraway country. I can hardly understand him! I don't think he'd make a good king. He is known for his love of death. Is that really someone you want as a king?"

Enchardo looked at her, "Who said all this?"

Sammaria said, "I don't know. I just heard people talking."

Enchardo ground his teeth for a second, "Morlyn is a world-renowned fighter. He will protect you and he will strengthen our ties with Ancefra. He will be a valuable assest in war."

Sammaria said, "What war?"

Enchardo said, "Good night, Sammaria."

Sammaria left, feeling more confused than ever. What was her father hiding?

CHAPTER IV

The morning was just beginning to shine through the great windows in the library as Jennica entered. She perused the shelves in search of a book on water creatures. She walked down to where she thought one would be hiding on the shelves. Instead, she found, lying on the table, an old, thick book. It was unfamiliar to her with its brown, leather covering. All of the books in the royal library had a blue, green, yellow, or black covering. Intrigued by the cover, she picked it up off the table. Opening it to the first page, she discovered it was called *The Time of Man and Myths*. She started to read:

ELVATETH –CALLED ELVES IN MYTHRAL– EXISTED OUTSIDE THE REALM OF ETHOTA. THEY TRAVELED BETWEEN REALMS AS THEY WISHED. IT WAS THEIR GIFT FROM THE GODS. OFTEN THE ELVATETH INTERBRED WITH MAN. THEY WERE CONSIDERED PEACEMAKERS AND THE FIERCEST FIGHTERS. NOW, THERE IS QUESTION AMONG HUMANS WHETHER "ELVES" EVER EXISTED. DRAGON...

"You may borrow that if you like."

She looked up surprised. Donichello gestured to the book. Jennica stood up and said smiling, "I'd like that."

Donichello watched as her smile abruptly vanished. She said impassively, "I'll return it to you shortly."

Jennica went to the last refuge of quiet tranquility that she had left. She went up the east tower. It smelled of an old pipe and burned wood. It calmed Jennica as she started to read.

Sammaria walked down the hallway, heading for the art room. A hand reached out from a supply closet and seized Sammaria's arm. It pulled her in and covered her mouth. The hand that held her mouth let go and she turned around. It was Antien. She smacked his arm, playfully, "What are you doing?"

Antien said, "I need to talk to you."

Sammaria looked around, "And this was the best way to do it? Did anyone see you? Like you said people will talk."

She pushed her hair from her face and fixed a stare on him with her amber eyes.

"Would that be the worst thing?" he asked, quietly staring at the floor.

Sammaria looked away from him. She waited for him to say more. He looked around the closet. His eyes stayed glued to the bucket in the corner.

"Well?" Sammaria asked, "What did you want to say?"

Antien coughed, "Oh – uh - Can't tell you here. Meet me tonight in the back garden."

Sammaria gave him a shrewd look, "Why there?"

He said, "Sammaria, please."

She nodded. She stood and exited the closet. She glanced around. No one seemed to notice her odd detour. She knew that did not mean no one had seen her. She straightened her dress and continued to the art room.

Jennica looked up as the door of the tower opened. Donichello said, "Sammaria told me you'd be up here."

Jennica said coolly, "Remind me to tell her never to do that again."

Donichello watched her as she closed her book and stood up, folding her arms across her chest. He wondered what had happened to the girl who had laughed with him at the crazy Duchess. Where had the hostility come from?

Donichello said, "I was hoping you could do me a favor."

"Really?"

"Yes, I wanted to know if you could give me a tour of the castle."

She looked out the window. She replied, "Can't Pranshey give you one?"

Donichello looked at the steps and back at her. He said, "Yes, but I want one from your perspective, Princess."

Jennica glowered at him, "Don't mock me!"

Donichello glanced down at the ground blinking. He looked up at her critical eyes, "I wouldn't dream of it."

Jennica gave him an irritated look and walked out of the tower. She called over her shoulder, "You better keep up."

Jennica led him down the winding stairs and said, "This is the east tower. I am up here most of the time."

She mentally kicked herself, "Why did you tell him that? Now he knows where you'll be."

She pointed to the offices of so and so. She turned toward the left and went into the east wing. There were parlors and tearooms. Jennica showed him the instrument room.

He said, "Play me something"

Jennica picked up a flute and played a sad ballad. Donichello clapped and praised her.

Jennica set down the flute and said, "Well, Sammaria's much better than me."

She gave him a probing look and left the room. He followed her and they headed to the west side of the castle.

They passed the library and Jennica said, "The library holds works from all over Ethota."

She leaned in conspiratorially. Her eyes glittered for just a moment. She said, "I have even found some that I think are from Mythral!"

Donichello asked, "How did you get books from the Human Realm?"

Jennica shushed him. She shook her head and hurried him along. She showed him the clock on the loft. It was a large dragon facing toward the east. The clock chimed and Donichello asked, "What was that tune?"

Jennica said, "Never Fear. It's a love ballad. Father told me it was Mother's favorite song. The bard who sang it wrote it for his love. It's quite tragic."

He asked, "Can you sing it?"

Jennica was going to refuse, but the look of interest on his face stopped her. He wanted to hear. She coughed and sang the chorus:

> While the gods look down on us
> We'll be safe. We'll stay loved.
> If ever we're together
> And all hope seems gone
> I just want you to remember
> Never fear

Donichello stood there for a minute, and then hugged Jennica. He said, "That was fantastic!"

It surprised her so much, Jennica could not help but smile. Remembering herself, she regained her slightly sulking appearance. She shrugged off his exclamations and continued to the art room.

He asked, "What here is yours?"

Jennica said, "Not much. Most of the stuff I created looked horrible. I never could bring myself to show anyone."

"Where are Einar's things?"

At the mention of his name, the image that Sammaria had seen reflected in the back of her mind. Jennica opened her mouth when Morlyn burst in, followed by King Enchardo. Donichello noticed that Jennica's face turned stony. Her eyes seemed to bore holes in her father. He, unaware, asked, "Jennica, darling, can you and Donichello please vacate this room?"

Jennica started to object, but Donichello led her away. Jennica thought of tearing her arm from his grip, but a strange sensation ran up her arm.

Jennica never got a chance to ask who Einar was. Antien came and took Donichello away. Jennica was slightly disappointed. His quiet disposition was nice. He made Jennica forget her anger for a little while.

Jennica went to find her sister, carrying the leather-bound book she had borrowed from Donichello.

Sammaria was holed up in her room. Jennica said, "What are you doing?"

Sammaria turned from her project, "Nothing."

Jennica shrugged, "I thought maybe we could play a trick on someone."

Sammaria said, "Aren't we a little old for that?"

Jennica picked up a small ball and tossed it around in her hands. She shrugged. Jennica put the ball down. She looked down at the people passing below. They seemed so hopeless.

Jennica said, "There was once a time when Dragonia was thriving. The most modern country in the world. Sammaria, do you know what caused the change?"

Sammaria looked up. She shook her head, "It must be some obscure historical occurrence, but you are going to tell me aren't you?"

"It was these portals. There is a place called a *glaret* or something … anyway. It's a place where the human realm crosses ours. If the portal is opened, well, then people can move about the two worlds."

"Where'd you learn this? I have a strange suspicion Father didn't want it taught."

Jennica shrugged and pointed to the book she had set down on Sammaria's nightstand, "It's in the book that Donichello lent me."

Sammaria said, "He's into obscure history as well. A match blessed by Kiro."

Jennica rolled her eyes, "But don't you think it's the tiniest bit interesting that they closed them when we had the most peaceful years in history just before then?"

Sammaria thought about it, "It was over two hundred years ago. I'm sure there was a good reason. Besides, who is to say that that is even true. People talk about the portals, but is there any proof that they even exist?"

Jennica shrugged as she opened up the book again. Sammaria went back to her work.

She sighed as she heard Jennica snap her book shut. Jennica said, "You can't seriously want to marry Morlyn."

Sammaria replied, "What do you think? What was Father thinking when he picked him out? He's going to be a horrible king."

Jennica smiled, "There is a way to get rid of him."

Sammaria said wearily, "What are you thinking about this time?"

Jennica set the book down and said, "Plenty."

❧

Morlyn stared out his window. He could just see Sammaria slinking off into the distance. He felt his brow pull into a furrow. He had followed her earlier that day. There was something about that girl he did not trust. That first day she had acted so strangely. She seemed so frightened of him. What had he done to her that she could have known about?

She had been pulled into a private meeting in a broom closest. Morlyn had tried to listen to the conversation within the closet. The noise did not carry well enough for even his highly trained ears to pick up. A giggle reached his ears making him hiss almost inaudibly.

Sammaria had flitted off. Every step seemed like she was gliding on air. A boy had emerged moments later looking smug. Morlyn had restrained himself then. He would not be made a fool by the princess and her lover.

Now, standing before his window he thought this again. Heat rose to his face. The Ancefran thought, "I will not be imported to be made a fool! Even if Father only agreed to this hoax so I could spy on them, I will not stand for this!"

Morlyn swept his curtains closed and marched to his bed. He did not want to watch his bride come home from her evening. He stared at his bed.

An image of Sammaria lying across it came to him. An uneasy feeling grew inside him. Shoving both the image and the feeling out, he retired to his bed.

Sammaria walked solemnly to meet Antien. She was going to have to refuse him. She wished Antien would not show. When she entered the rock cropping at the edge of the garden, she realized her wish had come true. She sat dejectedly on the bench beside the memorial placed in the center of the cropping. She wondered why she had come.

Antien walked out from behind the statue. He said, "Sammaria! You came!"

Sammaria said, "Of course I came. Why wouldn't I?"

Antien did not answer. He turned away from her. Sammaria stood placing a hand on his shoulder. Antien tensed under her hand. She asked, "What is it? What's wrong?"

Antien said, "I have to leave the city."

"I know."

Antien stared at her shocked, "What do you know?"

"You are being deployed. To fight the Resistance."

Antien shook his head. He held a hand up as if he were going to touch her face. He said, "No, Sammaria. I am not going with them."

"What? Why?" she asked.

Antien groaned and stamped his foot, "I can't tell you, Samma."

Sammaria cringed. She asked, "When are you leaving?"

Antien said, "I don't know yet. I am waiting on some others."

"No! You can't leave. Antien, what am I supposed to do without you?"

"Please don't make this harder. I just wanted to let you know I was leaving. And there is something else."

He kneeled on one knee.

"You know I can't."

Antien asked, "Can you at least listen to me?" Sammaria nodded. He said, "I know that you love me like a brother. I wish you didn't and I can't help myself. Sammaria, I am so in love with you. I pledge my life and heart to you."

Sammaria stared at him, dazed. He stood up and kissed her cheek. Her hand flew to her cheek and he left her there to make her way alone.

Jennica softly walked into Donichello's bed chamber to return his book. She did not want to face him. Jennica quietly cursed her cowardice. She loved the book, but she could not let him know that.

Jennica looked at his sleeping face. He looked younger. Her heart thumped in her chest. She chastised herself.

She walked over to a beautifully carved bookcase. For a moment, she stared at the intricate patterns of lilies, orchids, and salvias. Donichello rolled over in his sleep. Jennica froze, scarcely daring to breathe. He settled back into sleep. She released the breath, and then silently gasped. He rolled over again. He seemed to be asleep so she started to set the book flat on the shelf. He mumbled, "Jennica listen…"

He stopped.

She had pulled the book back to her chest when he had spoken so she started to set it down again. She drew back once again. There was a drawing of Donichello with a boy who looked familiar. She leaned closer. Who was that? She knew his face. It was so familiar.

Donichello mumbled, "Jennica, I want you to love me."

Jennica was so shocked she forgot to be quiet and dropped the book. The book was not large, but it thumped loudly against floor.

Jennica ran out the door. She tore a bit of her white nightdress on the desk by the door. She closed the door quietly. The piece of her dress had just fluttered to the floor as Donichello bolted up from his sleep yelling, "Kiro!"

Donichello threw the blankets off and got out of bed. His long, brown pants dragged on the floor as he walked over to the book. He picked it up with a sigh.

He looked at the brown, leather cover and set it on the shelf. He walked over to his bed and threw a tan shirt over his bare, muscular chest. Walking over to his open window, he stared out into the night. He prayed, "Kiro, please help me in my time of need. Please keep the royal family safe."

He walked back over to his bookcase and looked at the picture. He picked it up and put it back face down. He walked back to his bed and noticed a small piece of cloth glittering in the twin moons' light. He set it on his night table and crawled back in bed. He soon returned to sleep, having a dreamless night.

CHAPTER V

Sammaria sat on the stone bench next to the lake in the castle courtyard. She fiddled with the stem of the purple flower in her hand. Her mind kept returning to Einar and her father. Sammaria mumbled, "That makes no sense."

"I'm sorry. What was that?"

Sammaria looked up from her lap. She said, "I'm sorry. I was just thinking out loud."

Morlyn said, "No problem at all. You needn't apologize."

His eyes stayed cold even as he painted a smile on his face. She refused her intense desire to grimace and hid her uncertainty. She did not know what to expect of him. That smile had frightened her.

Morlyn asked, "May I sit down?"

Sammaria tossed the flower away as she nodded nonchalantly. She tried to act cheerful for the company. After a moment, she asked, "So, what do you think of Dragonia?"

Morlyn grimaced slightly. It was so barely perceptible that she thought she might have imagined it. He replied, "It's ... drier and colder in Ancefra."

Sammaria waited for him to say more, but he stopped there. There was an awkward silence following this statement. Neither knew what to say to each other. Sammaria, after a while, thought quickly of an excuse and left Morlyn on the bench. She clenched and unclenched her hands as she left, hoping Morlyn would not notice.

Jennica entered into the King's study. Her father faked a smile as he looked up. He said, "I'm glad you came."

Jennica smiled. He frowned. Jennica wondered if something was off in her face. She asked, "What is the matter?"

He said, "I was about to ask you the same. What's on your mind?"

He gestured for her to sit down.

She perched on the edge of her chair. She said, "I was wondering what you could tell me about the portals?"

His face had shown mild concern, but now it had become impossibly hard. Jennica braced herself for whatever came next. He asked, "Where did you hear of these portals?"

Jennica shrugged. She didn't want to include anyone else in his ire. He said, "I don't want to …"

He looked confused. He cocked his head for a moment. He seemed to make up his mind. He said, "They are not for you to worry about, child. They are just a story."

Jennica released her breath slightly. She said, "Father, please. I have been looking into them. And I do not-"

"Why?" he asked sharply.

His eyes flashed. They appeared almost black for a moment. Jennica drew back.

Enchardo said, "They are not your concern. Don't meddle in things you could not possibly understand."

Jennica snapped, "I thought you said they were just stories. What are they really?"

Enchardo's eyes narrowed at her. His face grew stony. He said, "Daughter. You are meddling-"

Jennica interrupted, "Father, please. I beseech you. Please, tell me."

Enchardo looked at her, "No!"

Jennica opened her mouth against her better judgment, "Why?"

Enchardo's face turned a deep shade of red. He turned the table over, flinging the teapot across the room. Tea soaked into the rug. Jennica shrank back in her chair. He said, "Never allow me to catch you mentioning that subject again!" He took a deep breath, "I forbid it." He stalked to the door, "I'm warning you, Jennica Animia. You will regret it."

Jennica walked along the edge of the stream that led to the lake in the center of the castle's courtyard. She pondered her father's reaction. Her heart still thudded with fear, but the stream calmed her. She always felt safer around water. Jennica sat down on the bank.

She did not know the extent of her Power. When her emotions got out of control, her Power reacted to it. She still had a hard time entering the Sight State on demand. She dipped her fingers into the cool water. The smooth surface parted slightly as they went in. Her troubled face became serene. She was not startled when Donichello appeared on the path.

Jennica looked up briefly. Urging her attention back to the pond, she said, "Good day, sir."

Donichello moved to stand next to her. "Good day, Princess."

Jennica pulled her hand from the water and flicked them dry. She said, "How many times do I have to tell you to just call me Jennica?"

Donichello frowned, "At least once again."

Jennica shrugged, "So… what are you doing here?"

Donichello replied, "I was just walking outside on this fine, Blessim day. What are you doing?"

Jennica smiled at his challenge. She retorted, "This is my garden. What do you think I was doing?"

Donichello laughed, "Okay. Okay, I get it!"

Jennica laughed along, "Do you really?"

Donichello watched as the smile faded suddenly from her eyes. She abruptly stiffened and said, "I should go, sir."

Donichello sighed inwardly, "Goodbye, Princess."

Jennica looked at him with an emotion he could not decipher before she left.

❧

"Sammaria? A word?"

The King called his daughter into his study. She entered somewhat reluctantly. Her father said, "Daughter…I hate to question you on this…"

Sammaria watched her father carefully, "Just say it."

King Enchardo said, "Your fidelity and virtue have been called into question."

Sammaria couldn't keep the shock from her voice, "What? By whom?"

The door swung open. He must have been listening through the door. Sammaria raised her eyebrows. She was beginning to question the drama of this man.

"By me," Morlyn stated.

Sammaria demanded, "And with whom am I supposed to have been unfaithful?"

Morlyn and Enchardo exchanged glances. The King replied, "With the squire, Antien. We have several witness accounts stating that three nights ago you were out with him."

Sammaria felt a burning fury rise within her chest. Her temperature rose. She said, "Did any of my ladies in waiting contact you? If I have been gone, their first responsibility is to contact you."

Her father stared at her with a mix of emotions

splashed across his face. He said, "No, but Morlyn would not tell me this had happened for no reason. From now on, a guard will be watching your room."

⁂

Brother Orlten and Pranshey were discussing something in harsh whispers in the hallway outside the palace library. When Sammaria entered, the whispering stopped. She was just able to catch the words, "Einar … Battle of Mersaya."

Now, the thoughts started clicking together in her head. That was the second time she had heard of the Battle of Mersaya. She wondered if she could find information in the palace library.

Sammaria wandered the library's shelves. She had hoped for it to be empty. It did not let her down. She did not want anyone reporting her reading choices to her father. He was very selective of the knowledge that could be learned. She searched through the books about battles, recent history, anything that she could think of that could contain information on Mersaya. However, she found nothing.

She slammed a book down in frustration. She jumped as the clock struck the half-hour. She looked at it. The dragon looked east toward the dragon homeland. The giant carved wings spread a fullsized wingspan.

Sitting in the claws of the dragon was a clock whose diameter reached an impressive eighteen feet. Surrounding the clock was an incredible amount of detail including even the minuscule scales on the dragon's long tail.

Suddenly, she remembered that cryptic note that she had received. *The information you seek is to the east.*

Sammaria pushed her chair back from the table. She hiked up the skirt of her plain, gold dress and climbed up the steps to the loft. She heard a creak and stopped. She listened. No one appeared.

She looked at the books and sighed. The maids never dusted up here. They hadn't since Milamare had died. She ran her finger along the dust-covered bindings and sneezed. Sammaria quickly moved toward the books the dragon was facing. She pulled out a red leather-bound book. She found it strange. Books in this library were not supposed to be this color. She opened the cover to see the book titled in gold writing:

RECENT WARS IN DRAGONIAN HISTORY

She pulled it out. It appeared to be blank. She almost placed it back when she saw a piece of parchment sticking out of the book.

Sammaria read: Many people associate the country of Ancefra with the skirmish in the year 1445.

"That was only fourteen years ago!" she thought. She continued:

At the time of the battle, King Malcolm de' Jenginald was on the throne. At this time, he was not the loosely bound ally that he is today. His men invaded our land on the request of the Pilleetain Army. They murdered and burned several Dragonian villages.

Malcolm believed he was in the right throughout the invasion. He thought it a betrayal when Dragonia decided to retaliate. However, the Ancefrans' anger came only because we could not supply enough precious gems to fulfill the Prince,

Morlyn's, wishes.

The Ancefrans learned that killing Dragonian peasants was providing them no advantage. Malcolm ordered his men to capture them instead. He crossed the Engen Bridge into Pilleetain.

He led his army into battle against the Dragonians. King Enchardo gathered his army and called on his allies. On Founder's Day, Enchardo met the opposing men.

Dragonia's army and cavalry are legendary, but the Ancefrans were ready. They had hired many Pilleetain mercenaries. Among their ranks was Memic Sina, son of the legendary Stath.

The Ancefrans appeared invincible. King Enchardo was relentless. He shed much blood and lost many men before he agreed to allow a truce. Duke Joromo rode out demanding a truce from King Malcolm. Dragonia offered to give up the Western quarter, which includes the Kilhatea Mountains and a small portion of the Draconle Woods, in return for the truce.

King Enchardo has never been known for his patience. While Joromo was negotiating with King Malcolm, Enchardo lost what little patience he had. Malcolm wanted more in exchange for the captured peasants. King Enchardo told Joromo to make an offer of his first-born daughter's hand in marriage for his third son, Prince Morlyn. This offer was more than generous. Not only would this marriage bring peace to the lands, but it would ensure a future and fortune for the child.

Unfortunately, Malcolm did not see it like this. He took his sword and locked himself in hand combat with Joromo. The Duke fought Malcolm till he could safely retreat back into the lines of Dragonians.

Malcolm called for hand combat. King Enchardo had no choice but to accept. The Ancefrans sent out Prince Matemat,

Malcolm's eldest son. Enchardo sent out his only son, Einar.

Sammaria gasped. The book faltered in her hands. It nearly tumbled to the ground. She knew he had looked familiar.

Einar was an amazing fighter. He was able to shoot a leaf several leagues away. It is said he had a second sight. He was head of the cavalry and engaged to be married to Lilliana Krulle. King Enchardo did not seem to have any regret in sending him to fight. Einar honored his mission without question. He knew he had to help the trapped citizens. It was his duty as heir to the throne.

Sammaria started as the clock sounded. The book slid out of her hands, crashing as it hit the floor. She listened for a sign that someone had heard the sound. All she heard was the crash of the book as it echoed through the hall. Sammaria waited, this was too loud to go unnoticed. Straining her ears, she heard the door click.

Quickly, she returned the book to its place. She scrambled down the stairs. Picking up the nearest book, she sat down in the chair off to the side.

Sammaria used her peripheral vision to watch for the newcomer. It was Pranshey. He turned the corner and sneered at Sammaria, "What is a princess doing snooping around the library? Do you wish to disappear like many before you? What are you reading?"

Pranshey pulled her up by her arm. He sneered in her face, "Well! We'll see what your father has to say about this."

She pulled away from him. She said coolly, "He'd say you're wasting his time telling him I was reading in the library again. Have a little faith! I'm a princess. I do know how to behave."

Pranshey said under his breath, "You know how to get out of trouble."

Sammaria smiled sweetly at him, "What was that? I'm sorry. I missed it."

Pranshey glared at her. With one last smile, she turned around. Her white golden hair whipped him in the face as she stalked angrily from the library. She thought fiercely, "I have to read the rest."

CHAPTER VI

Misseter sat at the head of the table. Bynakst'r sat at her right. Several O'rult sat in the chairs farther down. To her left sat the necromancer, Trydexzi. Misseter tapped her long painted fingernails on the black granite table. She said, "I'm becoming impatient, Trydexzi. You said we would have Mestchester by the princesses' birthday. My army has not even taken the border yet, and their birthday is in a few weeks. Am I going to have Mestchester in a few weeks, Trydexzi?"

Trydexzi said, "You are right, Highness. It has proved more difficult than we thought. The people of Dragonia trust Enchardo too much. I think it is more the memory of Milamare than anything. The princesses are starting to doubt their father more and more. This is good. My Queen, you shall have Dragonia soon."

A smile crossed Misseter's cruel face. She said, "Good. I will not be kept waiting much longer, Trydexzi. I will kill you if I have to. Your tricks are cute. They please me, but it's not like I cannot find another necromancer."

Trydexzi said, "More of a reason to hurry."

❧

Sammaria held out the clothes to Jennica. She said, "We really shouldn't be doing this."

"He questioned your virtue. That is unforgivable," replied Jennica as she took the clothes. She held up the green trousers and mused, "You'd think a prince wouldn't put up with this frou frou nonsense."

Sammaria leaned against the garden wall. She said,

"He probably enjoys it. We enjoy it. Most of the time. We do have more privilege than those around us… And I can't be mad at him for wondering, can I? I mean I did sneak out. It is understandable."

Jennica looked away from the pants, "Understandable? I mean sure you sneaked out, but the first logical explanation would not be to meet a beau."

Sammaria did not reply. She watched her sister rip stitching from the seat of Morlyn's pants. She thought it was amazing that Jennica could come up with these vengeful tricks. She was always so nice, but she had a mischievous streak.

All the pranks they played were in retaliation. Several courtiers had had buckets of soapy water dumped on them or bugs slipped into their underclothes among other things.

Sammaria said, "Give me those."

She took the pants from Jennica and scored the thread. If Morlyn moved wrong, the entire backside of the pants would rip out. Jennica handed Sammaria another pair of pants.

Sammaria asked, "What are these? We only need one."

Jennica said, "They're Donichello's."

Sammaria asked, "What did he ever do?"

Jennica didn't reply. Sammaria continued, "You know we don't take action unless someone has done something wrong."

Jennica asked sheepishly, "Can't we just do it on sheer principle? Just to get rid of him?"

Sammaria shook her head. Jennica dropped the pants into her lap with a sigh. She watched her sister mournfully as she stood up carrying Morlyn's outfit.

Sammaria said, "Wish me luck."

Jennica flicked her hand as if to throw the words back.

Sammaria knocked on Morlyn's door. She said, "Mistress Carlyn has asked me to return these to you. And His Royal Highness has asked that you wear them when you meet the court in the garden this afternoon."

"What have you done to them?" Morlyn asked suspiciously.

"Done to them?" asked Sammaria taken aback.

"Don't think I haven't heard about your little tricks on your guests. The crickets, the water, the black eye."

Sammaria said, "Sir, I don't know what you're talking about, but I believe your stories are incomplete. I'm sure whoever received those little tricks had it coming."

Sammaria smiled sweetly. Morlyn took the pants hesitantly from her hands. He closed the door, wary to her comment.

Sammaria returned to where Jennica was waiting for her. Jennica was holding a squirming bag. She said, "I got the snake from Brother Orlten. He said he found it crawling in the grasses around the stable."

Sammaria smiled, "How did you convince him to get you a snake?"

Jennica smiled, "Educational curiosity. Brother Orlten and I have an understanding."

Sammaria rolled her eyes. She said, "Will that understanding come to an end after today?"

Jennica stroked the wriggling bag. She shrugged, unconcerned.

Sammaria looked out the window of the sitting room to see how the King's private tea was progressing. They were both supposed to make an appearance at the party. Still, this trick had to play out.

Sammaria said, "Let's go down. I'll go to the party. You hide and wait for my signal. If they see me at the party, they won't suspect us."

"But what about me?" asked Jennica.

"You know the courtiers. If they've seen one of us, they think they've seen both. And if I start talking about your dress or something, they'll all admit to seeing you to everyone they meet. They can't be left out. Tyrina would notice, but she's not here.

Jennica sulked, "Yeah, she is off with her new husband. Bah! That man is a bore."

The girls traveled down to the garden. Before anyone truly spotted her, Jennica sneaked off into the bushes. From her spot among the dew blossoms, she could see everyone who arrived from the castle or approached the King at his table.

Jennica was surprised as Donichello walked into her line of sight. He was wearing a cream tunic with a maroon vest that accentuated his brown eyes. Jennica had realized he had dimples when he smiled, but now they were missing as he forced cheerfulness.

Jennica heard a hiss in her mind. She looked around. Morlyn was approaching from the castle. She had been gawking at Donichello. Not at all a good thing to do when she was supposed to despise him.

Sammaria said internally, "Wait until he is meeting with Father. Then release."

Jennica looked to see where her father was. The ivy was especially thick there. If she stayed low to the ground, she could creep closer to release the snake. This would ensure Morlyn seeing it.

She made her way around the dew blossoms and under the ivy. Jennica slowly pushed the snake forward. Morlyn was approaching.

Jennica untied the bag and wiggled the snake into the grass. With a stick, she pushed it toward Morlyn and her father. "Make us proud," she whispered.

The snake slithered in the right direction. Jennica watched as Sammaria entertained a baroness and her son. She kept glancing toward the grass. A girl screamed as the snake slithered across the hem of her skirt.

Morlyn turned toward the commotion. He caught sight of the serpant and followed the girl. He ran back, tripping over a server. He leapt over the table and down behind the King's chair.

Jennica buried her face in the grass to suppress her wild laughter. Yet, in all that, Morlyn's pants did not rip.

Sammaria broke away from a shocked crowd. She stepped down on the snake's head and picked it up by its neck. A woman swooned. Sammaria said, "It's just a little guy. He's not going to hurt anyone."

Morlyn yelped, "Get that death omen away from me!"

Sammaria handed the snake to a waiting servant. Morlyn picked himself up and came out from behind the chair.

Sammaria smiled to the crowd, "Now, that was exciting, wasn't it?"

Everyone laughed, relieved that the snake had been dealt with. She signaled to the musician who resumed playing a chipper tune. Sammaria asked, "Prince Morlyn, would you like to dance?"

Morlyn took her hand. They walked to the clearing. Sammaria curtsied, and Morlyn returned with a bow.

There was an audible rip. A small smile of satisfaction appeared on Sammaria's face.

Morlyn looked around as people began to murmur. He stood up and called for a serving boy. They ushered him away. Sammaria looked to her father. He did not look pleased.

Jennica bundled up the sack as she stood up. She had inched her way back through the ivy. Now she was standing among the dew blossoms looking for a place to hide the evidence.

"Jennica, there you are," called Donichello.

She whipped around hiding the bag behind her back.

He asked, "Where have you been? I looked for you at the party. I'm sure you'll hear about this one."

She replied quickly, "I was there. I saw what happened with Morlyn."

Donichello said, "Yeah, I suppose. It's strange how the snake got in here."

Jennica asked, "Oh? Why's that?"

He replied, "I always thought the King's garden was charmed."

Jennica snapped, "Well, it's not. No secret. We just have really good gardeners."

Donichello looked at her arms, "What do you have?"

Jennica shook her head, "Nothing."

Donichello reached for it. Jennica pulled it out. He looked at the sack, smiling slightly, "You released the snake?"

Jennica replied plainly, "Sammaria and I had a score to settle."

"With?"

Jennica did not reply. Her eyes drifted as she saw her sister approaching. Donichello handed her back the sack. He had heard, like so many others, about their pranks. It was something to keep them busy and make sure they were not taken advantage of. It gave everyone a laugh.

Jennica said, "Excuse me."

She left to join her sister and the two of them, along with the other young girls, walked back up to the castle.

Jennica glanced back briefly in Donichello's direction. He raised a hand in farewell. Jennica frowned and turned back around.

She whispered to Sammaria, "I'll meet up with you later. I need to clear my head."

The princess broke off from the group and hurried away. She walked along the backside of the castle and hustled into the stables. Jennica stroked the mane of her white and grey speckled mare, Twilight. She said to the stable boy, "Go and bring me back some fresh grain for my horse."

Quickly, the boy left the barn. Jennica waited until he was out of sight. She pushed her confused thoughts from her mind.

Climbing up into the loft, she uncovered a bow from under the hay. Jennica strung the bow. She nocked an arrow, stretched the bowstring back, and anchored it on her chin. Aiming down, she sought the post at the front of the stable. Jennica set for the release. She let the arrow loose.

A movement caught her eye. Donichello stepped into the stable. She cried out. He stepped to the side as the arrow was dropping. The head caught his pant leg before it embedded itself in the wood post. Jennica dropped the bow and scrambled down from the loft to see if he was all right.

He eyed her carefully, "You are quite a good shot."

She shook her head, "I don't know what to say, Lord Donichello. I did not know you were there. I am not supposed to be here. I am not supposed to…"

She glanced up at the loft. She blushed and looked down at the ground. Embarrassment burned across her face.

Donichello said, "I will not breathe a word."

Jennica still refused to look at him.

He lifted a hand to touch her. It hovered between them for a moment and then dropped. He said, "Please, do not fret. No harm done."

Jennica looked up skeptically. She looked at his pants. She said, "Your pants. I have gone and ruined them!"

Donichello covered the hole with his hand. He insisted, "You are quite a good shot. You should practice with a real bow sometime. I could help you."

Jennica replied, "This is quite out of the ordinary. I'm not supposed to… My father…"

Donichello said, "I could suggest it if you would like."

Jennica's face lit up. Donichello's smile rose to match hers. She asked, "Would you really? That would be astounding."

She stopped herself and frowned. "No," she said reluctantly, "I would not place you in that position."

Donichello said, "It is just something to think about."

She nodded curtly, still frowning.

He fiddled with the hole in his pants for a moment. He said, "Well, I should go change before you decide to impale me."

Jennica smiled slightly. He nodded at her as he turned to leave.

Morlyn seethed, "That little twit waltzes in there and grabs the snake. It is a sign. She is tainted. Poisoned blood. No person pure of soul would handle the messenger of the underworld. She is unfit for anything but death."

Morlyn's attendant said nothing. He scurried off, whisking away the tampered pants. Morlyn looked out and saw the Disan constellation glowing red. Morlyn narrowed his eyes. Disan had died from a venomous bite. A bite administered by a lover. Morlyn threw his drapes closed.

He would have his revenge.

❦

Jennica walked into the castle. A page met her. He relayed that the King was waiting for her in his office. Sammaria was already waiting there. Jennica walked cautiously to her father's study. He must have been angry. Jennica knocked three times.

The King commanded that she enter. Sammaria glanced back at her from where she stood. Jennica flicked her eyes to her sister and back to her father. She took her place in front of the King.

He asked, "So, do either of you know how a snake appeared in my private garden, a charmed garden at that?"

Neither girl replied. How did he always know when it was their fault? The King set down his reading glasses, "No, I don't suppose anyone does."

He leaned against his desk and bellowed at the girls, "Do you know how much money you cost us? How long it took to clean up the mess the screaming people made? To placate the terrified women? Yes, they seemed all right at the party, but soon requests came pouring in for accommodations. And you two ruined Morlyn's two thousand deve outfit! What were you thinking?"

Sammaria opened her mouth to answer. Her father held up his hand, "No! I do not want to hear your excuses. I'm locking down the castle. Brother Orlten is going to be watching your every move."

The girls hung their heads as they left. They begrudgingly accepted defeat.

Jennica said, "We will find a way around this. Never you fear."

Sammaria shook her head skeptically before walking

away. Jennica stopped and looked out the window longingly. It would be a long time before she would be allowed to wander as she wished.

"Hello, Princess!" said a voice.

Jennica jumped, a scream catching in her throat.

Donichello said, "I am sorry. I didn't mean to startle you, Your Highness."

Jennica looked at his face. There was true sincerity in it. He asked, "How much trouble are you in?"

Jennica asked, surprised, "You aren't mad?"

Donichello replied, "Mad? No! I thought it was immensely funny. The last trick I've seen like that was when my brother sewed my father's pants to his chair while he was sleeping. You should watch out, though. Morlyn is upset about his outfit."

Jennica grimaced, "Thanks for the warning."

Donichello smiled. "Well, I'll be seeing you, Highness," he said, turning.

Jennica placed a hand on his arm. He stopped, looking at her hand. She quickly removed it and hid it behind her back, "Your ... pants. Um, would you like me to fix them?"

Donichello said, "I appreciate the offer. I've already taken them to the palace tailor."

Jennica said, "They'll fix them nicely. I'm glad you aren't hurt. You aren't hurt, are you?"

Donichello replied coyly, "Alas, I do not know!" He patted his thighs, arms, and back. Donichello said, "I am fine, Highness."

Jennica smiled, "Good! I didn't mean for it to come so close to you. My intention is never to harm. Maybe to trick, but never to harm."

She smiled at him. She bit her lip for a moment, "Please don't call me Highness. It's worse than Princess. It's simply Jennica."

Donichello smiled, "I can do that, High … Jennica. And me too. About the tricking."

Jennica smiled mischievously, "Is that a threat?"

Donichello narrowed his eyes at her. He looked so serious Jennica was taken aback. Donichello smiled, "That's a promise."

Jennica laughed and stuck out her hand. Donichello wrapped his hand around hers. They shook hands and turned to go their ways.

Jennica walked down the hall. When she reached the end, she turned back around to take one last look at Donichello. He walked with a noble grace. Jennica took one last look and smiled. She turned the corner, heading toward her rooms.

At the last second, she changed her course and entered the office hall south of her room.

She smiled timidly, "I was wondering if I could talk to you."

Brother Orlten looked up from the scroll he had been examining. He said, "Yes, Jennica. Of course."

Jennica wrung her hands as she sat down. She said, "You mustn't repeat anything of what is said in here. I don't want my father finding out."

He stood up, "Sounds serious."

"It is. I need to know I can trust you."

He closed the door to his office. "What is your inquiry, Princess? I swear on my mother's grave to secrecy."

Jennica nodded, "I was wondering about the portals. I tried talking to Father about them … It didn't go over well."

Brother Orlten asked, "Is that the commotion I heard the other day?"

Jennica cringed. She picked at a thread on the chair in front of her. She said, "Sammaria doesn't think they exist."

He smiled, "The portals are mysterious things. They were open from before the time of the Draigar until about 1289. The reason for their closing has always been unclear. Some historians say the gods were punishing the Elvateth. Others say it was simply that we were losing our culture and nature due to the cross-breeding. It is agreed great Power was needed to close them. There is rumor that the Faven Crystal…"

He stopped and shook his head.

Jennica let his hesitation go. He looked as if he had said too much. She asked, "Why do *you* think they were closed?"

Jennica looked at him closely.

He said, "I believe the kings hungered for power. The realms were fighting. I think it was closed so the king was able to more easily control his subjects. The best way to solve the problem is to remove outside influences."

Jennica nodded, sad, "Seems how a lot of history goes. Power-hungry. Why is Father so cross about them? They aren't a deep dark secret, are they?"

Orlten said, "In a sense, yes. It's curious. His Highness used to speak of the portals often and about trying to reopen them. This was all in his youth, mind you. It's quite curious how he reacted. It's almost like he's a different man from the one I tutored when he was young." He paused reminiscing, "But then, all men change."

Jennica retorted, "I know what you mean."

The Brother asked, "Anything else, Your Highness?"

Jennica said, "Not today, sir. Maybe next time."

He said, "Any other questions, you know where to find me."

Jennica said, "I certainly do."

He smiled, "And as your jailer, we will be seeing more of each other."

Jennica grimaced, "I'd forgotten about my house arrest. We shall be."

He smiled and said, "Just as long as you don't try anything too daft, I won't do my job well."

Jennica said, "Thank you. I believe we agree."

Brother Orlten said, "Good night, Princess."

Jennica nodded, "Good night, Brother." He waved and sent her on her way.

CHAPTER VII

Sammaria was desperate to continue reading about Einar, but she felt Jennica should share in the information. She searched all the castle grounds to find her sister. Brother Orlten followed her, stalking her like a shadow. She looked in Jennica's room. She noticed her Seeing Stone was missing. She must attempting to enter Site State.

Sammaria walked out of the west hallway and down the steps to the large, silver doors. When Dragonia was allied with Gabvand, a southern country left devastated by war, King Lucian of Gabvand had the royal metalworker create the doors as a gift to the Dragonians.

Engraved into the doors were two gigantic eastern dragons, each holding a small sphere. Within the spheres were the images of Queen Ileana and King Stevor, then rulers of Gabvand.

Exiting the palace, Sammaria walked down the path that led to the garden. She walked past rows of carnations, roses, violets, hibiscus, lamb's ear, and dragon hearts. Sammaria passed the single Atlantsa plant Jennica had nurtured to life.

Frustrated, she sat down on a bench that had been carved by Mestchina's lover, Jonakil. She ran her hand along the pictures on the bench, which depicted Mestchina's many victories. Brother Orlten sat next to her.

She turned to him, "Sir? I know you are following your orders, but I am fine. I won't leave the garden. Can you please give me some time alone? You can sit in the next clearing over. It has an excellent view of this garden."

Brother Orlten left reluctantly.

Sammaria heard a sigh. She turned around and saw Jennica sitting still in the clearing by the lake. Jennica was wearing a white dress with a beaded flowering pattern. Sitting in the sunlight, she reminded Sammaria of their mother's wedding portrait.

Sammaria walked hesitantly over to Jennica. She looked down at her sister pleading, "Please come back!"

Jennica opened her eyes and fell back on Sammaria's shoulder. Jennica's voice was hoarse as she asked, "What happened?"

Sammaria said, "You were in Sight State. You did it! Did you see anything?"

Jennica nodded and asked, "How did I get there?"

Sammaria shrugged, "You need to answer that yourself. What did you see?"

Jennica said, "Morlyn's memory. The one you saw when you met him. I also saw … Mother. Who's Einar?"

Sammaria said, "I don't know what to believe. I was looking for you so we could find out."

She pulled Jennica up and took her to the library.

Jennica had caught up with Sammaria on the reading and was less shocked, surprisingly, than Sammaria had been. Jennica held the book so they both could read:

The fight between Einar and Matemat was fair. They were of equal skill; Matemat had a fair few injuries. Einar had a small cut on his forehead, fatigue was settling in, and he had a bad cut on his leg. Matemat had the upper hand, and he had found Einar's weak point. The Prince spat, "If you want the citizens so badly, then take them, but you are going to fight and die."

Einar raised his sword and brought it down on the prince's arm. Einar said, "Take me in place of the citizens. Let them go and leave my country in peace."

The Duchass Lilliana, Einar's future bride, watched in horror as they bound Einar's hands behind his back. Einar screamed out, "You shall not win."

Witnesses say Lilliana's hands strayed to her stomach as he said this. The Ancefrans pulled Einar into their camp, and the citizens were released. Lilliana burst into tears. With this selfless act, the male heir to the throne was lost.

Lilliana disappeared from Dragonia. No one knows what has happened to her, but we all hope that she is alive. She has to be. There are rumors that she fled to Ancefra to save her love. No one knows for sure.

At the same time, they asked, "Why didn't we know of him?"

A high pitched male voice said, "Now, that's a good question, isn't it?"

They turned to see Pranshey. "Obviously, you don't know much about your own brother though you spent the first three years of your life with him. Your memory was only developing. Very impressionable. Curious."

The girls exchanged looks and Sammaria replied for them, "We don't know what you are talking about."

Pranshey said, "What could dear Einar have done to make King Daddy so angry that he was erased away?"

Jennica searched his face. It was impossible to read. "No takers? Okay. I'll tell you. Einar was going to abdicate the throne. He was going to leave it to you. He was going to marry Lilliana and live within the woods."

Sammaria stumbled through her words, "What? He was captured by Ancefrans. That's what it says here."

Pranshey's eyes flicked over to Jennica.

Pranshey continued, "You can believe that if you'd like, but the King couldn't allow his son to abandon what he had worked so hard to create. Not even if the gods themselves told him it was needed. He hoped Einar would come to his senses, but he didn't. Then, the war came. King Enchardo hoped Einar would lead us. Einar's wish was for you, Sammaria, to take the throne. I guess he got that wish."

Sammaria yelled, "Go away, you liar!"

Jennica gasped.

Pranshey said, "Believe what you will, but the truth will reveal itself, and, when it does, I would appreciate an apology."

Jennica said quietly, "I think he's telling the truth."

Pranshey turned and left.

Sammaria looked expectantly at her. "Prove it!" she spat like venom.

Jennica quickly explained, "When I last went into Sight State."

She quickly looked around for eavesdroppers. She continued, "Mother came to me. She said memories would be coming back to me. She told me my mind had been altered. I remember a laugh. Then, something about you being queen. Everything went quiet and then someone yelled, someone cried, and a door slammed shut."

Sammaria shook her head, "Why wouldn't I see this?"

Jennica said, "I have a more sensitive mind. That is why I can go into Sight. My mind is reverting to what it once was."

Sammaria stepped down the first steps. She said, "Nothing is ever simple." She turned back, "Are you coming?"

Jennica shook her head, "No, I'm going to stay for a while longer."

Sammaria left the library. She was met by Narcissi, calling her to dinner. She met her father, Prince Morlyn, and Lord Donichello in the King's private chambers. Jennica was nowhere to be found. She had evaded her summons.

Sammaria talked quietly with the men as they ate. As dessert was served, Donichello asked her, "What languages have you been taught in your time here?"

The King interrupted, "The Princesses are both fluent in Common, Dragon, Pilleetain, and Old Elva."

Donichello looked at Sammaria with inquisitive eyes, "Really? You must have had a great tutor."

Sammaria said, "Yes. As a lady of the court, one never knows who you'll run into. Jennica and I believe it is for the best."

A short time later, Sammaria felt something being slipped to her under the table. She looked down at her lap. Jennica's name was written on a slip of paper. Donichello gave her a meaningful look. Sammaria nodded at him.

Sammaria tucked the note away into the confines of her skirt as The King announced that he would be retiring for the evening. He asked Morlyn to join him in his chambers for a moment. The two retreated.

Sammaria stood to leave. Donichello called her back. He asked, "What is wrong with your father?"

Sammaria frowned, "The doctor didn't say."

Donichello said, "No, that's not what I meant. Why isn't he doing anything about the Resistance?"

Sammaria replied, "I never understand anything my father does. He seems like he is an entirely different person from when we were young. I just wish he would do *something* about it."

Her voice cracked, "I just want the attacks to end. For the Resistance to fall. For everything to be the way it was. Maybe Father needs to be dethroned." She shook her head,

"That is treasonous." She shook her head again, "It would tear Jennica apart, but she has said the same. I couldn't do that to her, but what about the country? What about the Dragonians dying every day because of my father's decisions?"

Donichello nodded, "I'm sorry. I didn't mean to upset you."

Sammaria angrily set her jaw, "It's no fault of yours, Lord Donichello. I'm just hoping for a peaceful resolution, but I fear I won't get what I want."

Morlyn stood in front of the King's desk. The King sat down in his high-backed, red velvet chair and said, "Now, I know that you know why you are standing before me. I know that you weren't just sent here to marry Sammaria. I know about your assignment. I will give you whatever information you want if you will do the job."

Morlyn raised his eyebrows, "An interesting proposition. What would make you give up all of your secrets?"

"I know you have some idea of what I am talking about. Surely an ambitious prince like you has figured it out?"

"Surely not murder?"

The King looked at him slyly. "Murder? Now, that's something to consider. You, a prince of pirates and thieves, aren't having a bout of morals? A healthy man never has morals."

Morlyn faced the King, "Pirates and thieves? I am insulted. We are more than that. Our country was built on solid people. No morals? Every Ancefran man has morals. You know this well."

The King nodded, "Of course."

Morlyn asked, "So, who are the unlucky victims?"

The King paused for a second as if he were fighting some unseen threat, "Princesses Jennica and Sammaria and Lord Donichello. Be careful to make it look like Resistance thieves slaughtered them."

Morlyn stared, shocked. The King started to laugh and Morlyn followed more uncertainly.

"When do you want this done?" asked Morlyn.

"Soon. After the Meyeah moon."

Antien pulled away from the door. That was the princess' birthday, about a month away.

Morlyn asked, "What about the leader of the Resistance? That Rekasi?"

Enchardo replied sharply, "You blundering idiot! He is no match for the Royal Army. If he becomes a problem, I'll have someone take him out."

Footsteps sounded on the floor on the other side of the door. Antien ran swiftly down the hall toward the aviary. He had to tell someone. He had to keep Sammaria safe. The Resistance would know what to do.

Antien ripped the sash from his uniform and tied it to a pigeon. As he turned to leave, Morlyn stood before him with guards.

Morlyn grabbed Antien by the arm and lifted him off the ground. He said, "How dare you spy on your King."

Antien stammered, "I was sending a letter. I wrote it and came here after his Highness sent me away."

Morlyn's eyes flashed, "To whom?"

Antien replied, "To my sister."

Morlyn said, "You lie, boy!"

He shook Antien and threw him to the floor.

Antien said, "You will not get away with it. They will stop you."

The guards tied Antien's hands behind his back, "You do know what we do with traitors, don't you boy?"

※

"The day we feared has come," a young man said with a slight accent.

The room watched him with solemn eyes. The man continued, "The King has decided to end the succession. No doubt he will try to incite a war."

A few people gasped in the crowd. A man let out an angry shout. The man in the front held up his hand. He said, "We will have time for that later. We have friends in the castle. Now, I believe their lives are in danger."

A boy in the back piped up, "Rekasi, sir. Why would he want to kill the heirs?"

Rekasi looked around, "Who let you in?"

The children began to scatter. Rekasi shook his head, "No matter. We will need all the help we can get. Enchardo Aeradal has become corrupt with power. The death of his wife broke his last strain of compassion." Rekasi looked out at the crowd gravely, "This will be a difficult task. I need volunteers to infiltrate the capitol. One thing is certain, we have to get the princesses and Lord Donichello out of Mestchester."

Sammaria found Jennica in the West Tower watching the sunset. Sammaria saw she was not in Sight State and touched Jennica's shoulder. Jennica turned slowly until she was looking directly into Sammaria's eyes. Sammaria had never seen so much sorrow in Jennica's deep, blue eyes. Shocked, Sammaria dropped to her knees to comfort her sister.

Jennica tried to speak. She managed to say, "What Pranshey said. I know it's true. Why would these memories be plaguing me? Father has always been truthful, hasn't he?"

But then she dropped her head and said, "No. He hasn't."

Sammaria remembered the letter from Donichello. She handed it to Jennica and told her not to dwell on Pranshey. Jennica looked curiously at the letter, yet she was fearful of what it might contain.

Finally, she opened and read the note to herself: I need to talk to you. Please don't tell Sammaria. I will be waiting at your place tonight at sundown.

Sammaria asked, "What does it say?"

Jennica did not reply right away. She quickly thought of something to tell her and replied, "The Resistance is growing too strong. If anything, anything at all should happen, take your sister and leave."

She asked Sammaria, "Is something supposed to happen?"

Sammaria said, "I sensed Donichello knew more than he let on."

Jennica read the letter again. She could not help but smile. Sammaria looked at her and started at the crooked little smile that moved onto Jennica's face.

Jennica thought of what he might want to speak with her about. She both feared and anticipated the conversation. Sammaria said, "Come on. Let's get out of this dark tower.

Joromo, Duke of the Myhadry Peninsula and Donichello's father, entered the castle to dinner with the

King. He was dressed in his command outfit.

Joromo was surprised that he and the King were dining alone. The King served fish in a cheese sauce, salted asparagus, roasted pig, shrimp in a cream sauce, salad with fresh tomatoes, and wine.

The King said, "Let us propose a toast to your son and my daughter."

Joromo said, "To the future of the Kingdom."

The King nodded in agreement. Joromo gulped the wine. It was the strongest and had the most flavor of all the wines he had encountered.

The King stared at him and asked, "Good? It's my secret recipe. I'll tell you if you keep quiet. It's *gustanmado.*"

The Duke gasped, "Gustanmado is *poison.*"

He fell to the floor gasping, "You will not win."

The last thing he heard was, "I already have."

A guard came in and the King said, "Get rid of his body."

Jennica opened the door to the East Tower as the clock hit the last chime. Donichello turned from his place at the window. She asked, "What was so important that I had to come here?"

Donichello did not answer. His eyes were searching the room. She repeated her question.

Donichello shook his head. He adjusted his coat, "I need to tell you something."

"What?"

Donichello replied slowly, "There have been O'rult sightings in many areas along the border. They are silently taking over. King Enchardo hasn't done much to stop it. I..."

He stopped.

Jennica looked at him. "Donichello," she said, "The O'rult were destroyed. They aren't coming back."

Donichello grabbed her hands, "You must believe me. I saw them when I was traveling to Drannor. Likenton was almost taken over by those serpent beasts. The only reason it survived was because of the Resistance."

A look of sadness crossed Jennica's face, "The Resistance? I suppose you are joining them. If you are, I'm going to have to tell my father."

Donichello shook his head, her hands still in his grasp, "I'm not joining them. I just wanted to tell you that the threat of the O'rult is real. I fear I will have to leave. I fear you will be left unprotected."

Jennica said, "We've defeated them before. We'll do it again." She looked down at their interlocked hands, "Why?"

Donichello met her eyes and held them, "Because... I'm falling in love with you."

Jennica's heart jumped to her throat. She pulled her hands from his and ran to the door. A flicker of sadness crossed Donichello's face. Jennica's heart pounded as she hurried away.

CHAPTER VIII

*J*ennica was sitting next to Donichello during another *tea when news of his father's death arrived. Reports said that he was ambushed by the Resistance. Donichello was in shock. Jennica tried comforting him but did not know how. It was awkward between them since his confession. To make matters worse, King Enchardo had scheduled an execution for that day.*

Sammaria and Jennica stood next to the King on a platform a mere five feet from where Antien was to be killed. Jennica and Sammaria were dressed in long, blood-red dresses which they only wore to executions. Neither girl could believe that he had betrayed them.

Antien pounded on the door again, "Let me out. I'm innocent."

Morlyn yelled, "Shut your friggin mouth. You aren't leaving that cell except for the executioner."

Heavy footsteps thudded against the stone stairway. In his cell, Antien's heart jumped to his throat.

Someone fumbled with the keys as Antien had planned. The door squealed open. The executor stood in the doorway wearing all black with a black mask and his hands on his hips.

Antien gripped the top of the door frame and kicked the executioner backward. He collided with the guard. Both fell to the ground. The sound of metal clanged against the floor.

Antien scrambled to grab the sword from where it fell. He raised it to point threateningly at the guard. He let Antien come out of the cell. He threw down the keys and grinned.

Antien lowered his sword slightly. Someone ambushed him and tied his hands. They pushed him roughly up the stairs to the platform where he was pushed to his knees. His captors said, "You will show proper respect to the King."

Many around laughed. He heard a girl's voice hiss fiercely, "Stop it! You know he's innocent!"

He felt soft hands fumble with the ropes and a scream.

The King said, "Enough! This boy is a traitor. He was caught planning your death."

Another voice said in a façade of calm, "Why would he do that, Father?"

The King did not reply. Antien's heart swelled with Sammaria's defense. She did not believe the lie.

He turned slightly. Donichello's arms encircled Jennica as she sobbed. Sammaria was watching him. Their eyes met. She seemed to be peering into his soul.

Her face matched the mask her voice held, but her eyes were almost accusatory. Her eyes revealed the heartbreak within. It was too much for him. He broke the contact.

The King stood and said, "Citizens, we are gathered here to witness the death of this murderer and traitor."

Morlyn asked, "Your Royal Highness. With the upcoming nuptials, this man has not only insulted your country but mine as well. May I be granted the honor of answering this insult?"

King Enchardo nodded and extended the sword. Morlyn took hold of the golden hilt and raised the sword above his head. The crowd cheered. He repeated this motion twice more as was tradition. Jennica fidgeted. Donichello placed a hand on her side to calm her, but she pulled away.

Morlyn pulled the sword back one last time. His eyes grew hard. His muscles began to twitch, ready to ram the sword through Antien's heart. Sammaria held her breath. Morlyn yelled and ran forward with the sword.

Jennica ran to stop him, but Donichello caught her by the waist. He pulled her close to his body as she struggled. He kissed her hair. A few tears stained his cheeks. She screamed as she fought against his strong hold, "He can't die."

She turned in Donichello's arms and cried into his shirt.

Morlyn cried out in pain. The sword clattered to the ground at his feet. The crowd looked at Morlyn, an arrow sticking out of his hand.

Jennica stared up at the wall that surrounded the castle grounds. There, stood a man she recognized. He had run away from his training in Mestchester a year earlier. She pushed Donichello away from her.

The King traced the line of Jennica's eyes. He called for his guards. Everyone turned toward the walls as grappling hooks began to take hold. The citizens screamed and began to run for cover.

Rekasi, the leader of the Resistance, appeared on the wall next to the archer. He surveyed the scene taking in all the people frozen in place. He jumped down from the tall wall. He walked forward. Sammaria saw the muscles in his chest moving behind his open vest. In his commanding voice, he said, "Hand over Jennica and Sammaria and no harm shall come to your city."

King Enchardo said, "We shall do no such thing."

Rekasi laughed, "Bold words from a spineless man."

He pulled a torch from the ground and threw it at the platform in front of the King. The platform burned quickly.

Donichello grabbed Jennica's hand and pulled her to an area not yet consumed by flames. Together, they jumped off the platform. Jennica turned back to her sister.

Flames surrounded her. Sammaria took a deep breath and walked through them. Her Power saved her from burning. She breathed a sigh of relief. The train of her dress smoked.

Donichello grabbed Jennica and raced her to the stables. Jennica tried to pull from his grip. He would not let her go.

Donichello released her after he moved into the stalls. Jennica tried to run back, but she was not fast enough for Donichello. He turned her toward him, gripping her arms, "I need you to be safe. Please."

His eyes plead for her to listen. Something in them made her stop. She nodded, "I won't run."

Donichello searched her face for a moment. Jennica said, "I promise."

Donichello nodded. He saddled up Twilight. Jennica mounted the mare. Donichello slapped the horse on the rump, and she bolted out of the stable.

Jennica raced through town. She could see the destruction caused by the panicking crowd. The flames were spreading. Jennica pulled back on the reins. Twilight would not stop.

An ear-piercing scream echoed above the rest of the noise. Jennica wheeled her horse around and ran toward the sound. She knew the owner. She got there just as Rekasi did. He had his sword pulled and grabbed Sammaria by the shoulder. He put the sword to her neck.

Jennica leapt from Twilight's back. A man grabbed Jennica from behind. She screamed. Suddenly the man went slack and fell to the ground.

She turned around and saw Donichello pull his sword from the man's back. He said something to her she didn't understand. She whispered, "Sammaria."

Donichello looked past Jennica. His eyes were grim. He said, "Rekasi! Let her go."

Rekasi laughed, "What are you going to do about it?"

Donichello did not have a chance to reply. A horn called from a distance. Rekasi handed Sammaria up and over the wall.

"She is lost," Rekasi yelled.

Antien disappeared over the wall after them.

Jennica cried out. Her cry echoed through the town. The sky opened and rain fell from the sky, putting out all the fires that Rekasi's army had set. She quietly accepted the truth. Sammaria was lost.

"Jennica was devastated. Nothing could soothe her, and no one could reason with her. Jennica locked herself in her room, not taking food. Jennica did not even open her curtains. She stayed in the room, trying to contact Sammaria. No matter how she tried, Jennica could not access Sammaria's mind. That was even more terrifying than not knowing where Sammaria was."

Her father entered her room after a week of solitude. She asked, "Have you found her? Is she home? Can I see her?"

He replied, "No, Jennica. She's not home. There is no way to track her. The Resistance is too strong."

Jennica burst to her feet, indignant. She exclaimed, "We must do something. She is your daughter. We cannot leave her."

He shook his head and replied, "I'm sorry. We will search for her. We must gather strength. Tomorrow will bring answers."

CHAPTER IX

Jennica did not trust her father. Her suspicions turned out to be right. He did not send anyone after the Resistance the next day. Jennica decided to go after them herself. It took Jennica a fortnight to obtain the necessities for her journey. She had decided that she was Sammaria's only chance of being saved. The young princess filched a decent quiver of arrows from her father's supply. Jennica had only a few things more she would need. The next on her list was clothing for the journey."

Skirts were too restricting. Male clothing was necessary, but she didn't know how to get it just yet.

Jennica walked into the kitchen after breakfast. She was given six loaves of bread, ten apples, two handfuls of carrots, and two pounds of dried meat for her trip. The cook thought it was a riding trip for eight people. Jennica placed the food into her pack and stowed it in her room before walking out into the garden to gather some useful herbs.

She saw servants rushing around behind her as she moved further away. Jennica did not pretend to understand how the servants worked so quickly. She believed that her father had ordered them to not be seen. Jennica moved into the area Brother Orlten had cultivated with the princesses' help. Jennica quickly gathered some medicinal herbs. She looked nervously at a plant near the back of the garden that could be crushed into poison with no antidote. Jennica took a step toward it, but looked away. She knew she did not have the heart to use it. She wrapped the herbs into separate cloths and folded them away into her dress.

Jennica moved quickly back to the castle. She slipped inside without anyone noticing. There were servants on ladders hanging ribbons from the banisters. Tapestries had been beaten and hung. Flower bouquets were hanging from tall pillars and set on every available table.

She moved down the halls to the tailor's workroom. Her plan to steal clothing from Donichello's room had failed. His maid would not allow Jennica to go into the room with no explanation. Now she would just have to make do with clothing from the palace's mending room.

Jennica moved swiftly along the halls. She was no longer being followed since Sammaria had disappeared. Her strange placement would not alert any unwanted attention. She passed a questioning seamstress with the excuse of paying a call to Mistress Carlyn. Carlyn had worked in the palace for decades. No one was quite sure when she had arrived. She was the only one that the royal family would trust to create their ceremonial outfits. The other workers did not object.

Jennica entered the room, looking around to see if anyone occupied it. There was only an old cat. Jennica patted its wrinkled head. He stretched and snoozed.

Jennica dug through a stack of mended britches. She took two pairs, also grabbing three tunics from the top of the stack. She started up the steps but stopped as a pair of sturdy boots on top of a thick woolen blanket caught her eye. She grabbed them and hastily raced to her room. She hoped no one would look too closely at the bundle she was carrying.

Jennica climbed the steps to her room, her heart pounding in her chest. She relaxed as she approached her room. Her hand reached toward the doorknob.

"What are you doing with those boots?"

Jennica turned slowly, expecting Donichello. He always appeared at the worst of moments. Morlyn stood before her instead. Jennica smiled cordially, "Just helping out the lovely girls in the basement. They work so hard. Polishing you know? I just felt like it today. If you'll excuse me."

With that, she opened the door to her room and disappeared behind it. Jennica had just shoved the clothes under her bed when her door opened. She was flocked by servants. Diana led her to her bathing room. A warm bath had been drawn for her. She could see the fires below her room heating the water. She was confused as Diana started to strip her of her clothing. Jennica asked, "What is all of this? I already bathed today."

Diana looked around nervously but did not reply. She doused the princess with warm water. Jennica sat in the water as it rolled over her. She felt pain recede from her heart as strength filled her. Diana scrubbed soap into her hair. Jennica did not complain as she scoured her skin with a hard sponge.

Finally, the girl was done and Jennica was able to stand. Diana wrapped a towel around her and moved so she could step out of the tub. Immediately, her hair started drying. Jennica looked at Diana to see if she had noticed. Jennica had to restrain her use of the Power as it fed on the remaining water.

Diana and the other servants led Jennica to her changing room. Jennica was stripped of her towel and handed a loincloth and breast band. A young girl brought out a dress. It was golden orange. The petticoat was a deep navy. Its sheer sleeves flowed out slightly at the wrists, the neckline plunging. It was quite the opposite of the conservative dresses normally constructed for the princesses. The main bodice flared out as it moved down to her feet exposing the black under.

Sammaria would have had a dress similar to it with the black replaced with a yellow-orange petticoat. Jennica finally understood what all the secrecy was for as they dressed her quietly in her gown. They were trying to celebrate her seventeenth birthday. Jennica could see Sammaria's dress hanging on the hook in front of her. Jennica began to struggle. It was not right. She had demanded this canceled. They could not celebrate without Sammaria. It was her birthday as much as it was Jennica's.

Diana nodded as the other maids left the room for a moment. Jennica watched Diana finger something in the pocket of her apron. Jennica asked, "What do you have?"

Diana removed her hand from her pocket. She said, "It was your mother's."

Jennica could see a chain. Diana continued, "I suppose it should go to Sammaria. But considering …"

Jennica shook her head and pushed away Diana's outstretched hand. She said, "If my mother intended it for Sammaria, then give it to her when she comes home. I will not take her inheritance."

Diana said, "But Mistress! Sammaria is not coming back. No one captured by the Resistance ever does."

Jennica said, "Sammaria is alive. You just wait and see."

Diana sighed and pocketed the object. Jennica looked ahead as Diana piled the princess's gently curling hair onto her head. Small tendrils tickled her neck, giving her goosebumps. She knew Sammaria would return home. She had to.

A quarter of an hour later, there was a loud rap on the door. Diana left Jennica to answer it. Donichello stood at the door. Jennica came from her dressing room, and her breath caught in her throat. He looked stunning. His dark hair was tied back into a ponytail. He was wearing the formal clothing of a Dragonian knight. The red and orange tones of his uniform set his skin on a radiant display.

He smiled when he saw her, his face lighting up. He was completely unaware of how attractive he looked. Moreover, Jennica felt genuinely attracted to him. She pushed the feeling from her mind as she recalled everything she believed he stood for. What was he doing celebrating when Sammaria was lost in the hands of some murdering traitor?

He held out his arm to her. Jennica said, "I thank you for the gesture, but I'm not going."

Donichello frowned, "It's your birthday."

Jennica said, "No. It's Sammaria's and my birthday. If she can't be here to celebrate it, I won't."

Donichello said, "Princ- Jennica, please. Think of all the people who worked hard to put this together for you. I admire your resolve, but the staff and your father were simply trying to keep your life as normal as possible."

Jennica snapped, "Look at you! Scolding me like a rotten child! This is bigger than fighting against my wishes. This is about no one doing anything to find her. Donichello, do you know what the King told me? He said I should just forget about it. That we would never find her. What kind of father says that? Especially about his own daughter? Something isn't right."

Donichello said, "Come to the party. You can talk to the King there. He may be more agreeable if you comply with his wishes."

Jennica flicked her eyes up at him, "Don't be a voice of reason. I just want someone to agree with me for once."

Donichello replied, "I agree with you wholeheartedly.

I was simply suggesting a more effective method of achieving the desired result."

Jennica sighed, rolling her eyes, "All right. I will go. But only for a moment. Just long enough to talk to my father."

Donichello smiled, offering his arm again. This time, Jennica took it with a small smile in return. Donichello led her down to the main hall.

It had been completely transformed. The long tables had been moved to the front of the room, and food had been laid across them. People were eating at their leisure. A string quartet was playing. They were going through the standard and tired royal dance list. Jennica wished she could dance the country dances she had learned as a child. However, that was not how a princess should act. She would have to stick to the waltz and minuet.

Jennica looked for her father. He did not appear to be on the floor. She jumped slightly as a herald announced her and Donichello. Polite applause came from the dance floor. She was, after all, the guest of honor. Jennica looked down at the tight, cautious smiles of the cutthroat court. She was about to be fed to the sharks. Jennica's eyes sought out her one true friend in the room. Tyrina waved from where she was dancing. A dark haired man stood by her side. That must be the new husband. Jennica smiled to herself. She was happy things were going well for her at least.

Donichello led her down the stairs, stopping at the bottom. The entire time, Jennica searched for her father in the sea of faces. Jennica said, "I don't see him."

Donichello said, "He'll be here. He is the host."

Jennica said, "I know. I just want him to be here now."

Donichello said, "Well, while we wait, why don't we dance?"

"You want to dance?" she asked incredulously.

He smiled, "Why not?"

His eyes drew her in. Jennica nodded. She placed her hand in Donichello's. He spun her and pulled her into a waltz. Jennica's eyes searched the room. He had to be there somewhere. She faintly heard Donichello say something. She was not paying attention. Every part of her was focused on the search. Donichello said, "Jennica, look at me."

His voice was forceful. Jennica was shocked by the emotion in his voice. He seemed annoyed.

Her eyes met his eyes. They implored her to stop her search and just enjoy herself. Jennica did not notice as she continued the dance. It was not until he swept her into a dip that she realized what was happening.

Donichello asked her quietly, "What's your favorite dance?"

His brown eyes shone with mischief.

Jennica choked back the emotion she could in no way categorize as hate. She said, "It's a country dance. You would not know it. The court certainly wouldn't."

"Really?" he asked, "Which one?"

"You wouldn't know it!" she protested.

"Try me!" he challenged.

Jennica sighed as they moved along to the waltz. She finally said, "It's called the Dragon's Flight."

Donichello's smile grew wide. Jennica gave him a strange look.

"What?" she asked.

He replied, "You'll see." He led Jennica over to the musicians. He said, "Excuse me. Could you play Dragon's Flight?"

The lead violinist said in drone, "That song hasn't been approved by his Royal Highness."

Donichello winked at Jennica as he said, "The birthday girl has requested the dance."

Jennica looked at him as if he had gone insane. The wink irked her. He was acting like a completely different person. The musicians looked at her and stuttered, "Why of course! Your Majesty."

He started up the others after Donichello and Jennica had taken their places on the floor.

The song started as Donichello and Jennica started moving in strange patterns of twirls and leaps. There were only a few couples who knew the dance. Eventually, they stepped aside to watch the royal couple.

Donichello asked, "How did you come to know such a dance?"

Jennica placed her hands on his wrists as he lifted her into the air. He knew he had done something right by requesting the dance. Jennica was smiling.

She replied, "A boy taught me when I was just a child. I don't remember who. Just that he had soft hands."

Donichello's hands shifted in hers as he spun her. He did it in a strange way where he held her with one finger. Jennica frowned for just a moment. It reminded her of when she had first learned the dance. Donichello said, "I know who taught you."

Jennica looked up at him with her big eyes, "You do?"

He said, "I did. When you visited. You learned it at our welcome dance."

He spun her around and lifted her again. She let out a surprised laugh. The dance ended. Polite clapping came from the crowd. Donichello and Jennica exchanged glances as they moved off the dance floor. Quickly, they began sharing stories from when they were young.

They found themselves in a room, alone. Jennica was feeling something, no longer hatred. She watched Donichello as he moved. His muscles flexing under his loose shirt. Jennica laughed at something he said.

Donichello smiled, "You laughed."

Jennica's smile faded a little. Donichello cursed silently. He had ruined it. She smiled, "I guess I did."

Donichello said, moving closer to her, "I like your laugh."

Jennica said, "I like your –" she stopped.

Donichello was close. He took her hand. Jennica laced her fingers with his. He leaned down slowly as if seeing if she would let him. Jennica closed her eyes. His lips brushed against hers briefly.

"Jennica had never felt as giddy as this," said the storyteller.

"Excuse me!" interrupted the boy.

Margot smacked him, "Don't interrupt her! We want to hear the story."

The storyteller said, "It isn't nice to hit. It is fine Margot. What is it, Averyon?"

He said, "You're making this up. Who are you to know what the crown princess was feeling?"

"I'm a storyteller. I'm telling my story."

He replied, "And how did you gather this story?"

The parents looked at the storyteller suspiciously. She had just moved here less than a year ago. She was a complete mystery to them. The teen was making some good points. How did she know this?

"There are people everywhere. I have my ways."

"Really? What?"

"As soon as it began," the storyteller continued, "It was over."

Jennica let him lead her back to the dance floor. He moved her into another waltz. Halfway through,

Donichello mentioned her father being there. Jennica remembered herself and her purpose. She broke away from him and marched over to her father. She said, "I canceled this."

King Enchardo replied, "And yet you seem to be enjoying yourself."

Jennica looked back at Donichello. She turned back to her father and said, "Honestly, is this the best use of resources when you could be searching ..."

"That reminds me," he interrupted. Enchardo stood and cleared his throat. The instruments stopped and everyone turned to face their king. He said, "Kiro's blessing on this joyous occasion."

Jennica's jaw set. She tried to reign in her emotions. She could not lose control of her Power here. She could see Brother Orlten in the back. He was watching her with calm, collected eyes. She pulled back on her Power.

Enchardo continued, "We are all aware of the tragedy that took our other beloved princess away from us."

People grew silent. Jennica hoped her father was going to say he would begin the search. She never expected what he said instead, "We know the fate of those taken by the Resistance. Killed if they are lucky. Either way, they are never seen again."

Enchardo bowed his head as if accepting the fate of his first-born daughter. Jennica felt her hold on her Power beginning to break. She looked back at Brother Orlten. He had his eyes closed. She could feel the warmth of his magic wrapping around her. If her Power burst from her, it would not harm anyone. It would bounce harmlessly against Orlten's shield. The King said, "With that said, we still have reason to celebrate. Princess Jennica Aeradal is now seventeen. On this day I name her my heir."

A roar of cheering answered. Jennica looked horrified. Shocked, she screamed, "No! No! No!"

Her Power crashed forth like a tidal wave, smashing into Brother Orlten's barrier. Jennica felt it falter. Her magic leaked out. It began to rain. The guests looked surprised as raindrops fell from the cloudless sky.

The room fell silent. King Enchardo's face contorted with rage. Jennica said, "I am *not* the heir. I never have been, and I never will be."

She raised her voice as if addressing the crowd, but never moved her accusing eyes from her father's, "Sammaria is alive. The Resistance will not kill her."

She lowered her voice, "No." The rain became snow as she looked up at her father, eyes ice-cold, "They'll use her to overthrow you."

Jennica fled the room. Donichello followed quickly behind her, brushing her arm, "Jennica, wait."

She asked, "Wait for what? Look around. The party is ruined. Besides, I cannot stay here another minute."

Donichello said, "It's my fault. I didn't think you'd react like this."

Jennica backed away from him, "You knew?"

Her voice faltered.

He said, "Your father may have told me."

"You knew? And you let me walk around like a fool! While my father replaced my sister with me! You knew and still convinced me to come to this. Did you even think to mention it?"

"Let me explain."

"No. I don't want to hear your excuses. You know what? Don't talk to me – ever again!"

Jennica marched out of the room leaving a very stunned crowd behind her. Donichello was at a loss for words as he watched her go. There was nothing he could do to make her listen to him.

Jennica fumed, back in her room. She was still pacing the floor when her father burst in. "I should have you hanged for that. If you were anyone else, I'd have you strung up. As it is, I'll just have to settle with thirty lashes. Be prepared tomorrow."

"I wouldn't have had to embarrass you if you had a heart."

"That is a bold accusation, Princess."

"No, what's bold is allowing your daughter to be kidnapped! How much longer before the kingdom cries out? Sammaria is loved here!"

"I've already told you. There is nothing we can do. The Resistance is too strong. Too many people in the outlying villages support them."

"Whose fault is that?"

Enchardo slapped Jennica across the cheek.

Jennica spat, holding her cheek, "She's right. You hate her. And you hate me. All we are to you is competition."

Jennica lifted her head and looked him straight in the eye.

For a moment, the King shrank back. She said, "You've changed. Little quirks you've lost, but the compassion that everyone believes Mother left with you has finally died."

Enchardo said sternly, "You can stay here until you find the proper way to address your King."

Jennica glowered as he left, "Fine by me."

CHAPTER X

Jennica pulled the clothes she had gathered from under her bed and shoved them into a pack. She put a quiver of arrows into her pile along with a bow.

Jennica pulled the dagger from her bag and fingered her hair. It marked her status. Jennica reached up and let down the intricate patterns Diana had meticulously created. She concentrated on cutting a straight line and winced as the hair fell to the floor.

There was a click in the room adjacent to Jennica's. She quickly stowed the weapons and clothing beneath her bed. She could not hide her hair, but she lay on the bed covering it as much as possible. She pretended to be asleep. Diana came into the room and shook her gently awake and said, "I must change you from your clothes."

Jennica stood. Her short hair fell to her shoulders. Diana gasped, "Your hair!"

Jennica's hair had not been cut since she was young. Now, her hair fell just above her shoulders. Jennica pulled Diana close and covered her mouth. She said, "Listen, Diana. I'm leaving. I cannot stay here any longer."

Diana reached into her apron pocket. Jennica stopped her. She said, "No! It's Sammaria's. I will not take it."

Diana released it back into her pocket and looked around nervously. She said, "Let me help you out of that dress."

Jennica stood, waiting, wondering at the loyalty of her maid. Quickly, Diana stripped Jennica of her party dress. Jennica said, "Take the petticoats too."

She shimmied from the ruffles and stripped off her pantaloons. Jennica stood before the maid in a slip with a corset, breast band, and loincloth. Jennica turned and Diana unlaced the corset, leaving her breast band and loincloth in place. She pulled the slip over her head. Jennica said, "Thank you for all you've done."

Jennica pulled her pack out from under the bed. She removed the stolen clothes and boots. Diana gasped as Jennica pulled on the breeches. She secured them to her small waist with a rope. Jennica pulled the tunic and vest over her head. Everything fit snug enough to not be a problem, but loosely enough to disguise her figure. Diana glanced behind her nervously as Jennica began stowing money and weapons into the pack.

Jennica said, "I'm leaving now."

Diana asked, "How? His Majesty has the doors watched for the party. They aren't going to let you leave. Especially dressed as a boy."

Jennica went to her wardrobe and opened the bottom drawer. She pushed a knot in the drawer, and waited as a small compartment on the bottom of the drawer unhooked itself from the wood and flipped open. She pulled out a length of rope. Diana watched as Jennica uncoiled the long rope. Jennica said, "I suppose I'll have to use a different exit. I was just going to leave it, but can you pull it back up and put it back in that drawer. I would hate to lose this rope. I'll yank on it three times when I'm down."

Diana nodded, terrified. Jennica felt bad for involving her in this. She hoped her father would not catch her.

Jennica secured the rope to the bedpost. It would hold her.

Diana said, "Kiro guide you."

Jennica nodded as she swung herself down onto the rope. She was nervous of the height, but there was no other way. She repelled down the wall, letting the rope slide in her hands. She winced as a burning sensation rippled through them.

Diana looked down after her. She hissed, "Guards!"

Jennica had only moved ten feet down the wall. There was a tree covering her. The guards passed, stopping in front of a garden light to extinguish it. They continued to stand there for a while as they took nips from a hidden bottle.

Jennica's arms grew weary. She moved down. As she did, her boots clattered on the stone wall. Her hands burned. She slipped and tightened her grip. That just worsened the burning. She was going to fall.

The guards moved around the corner looking for the origin of the noise. Jennica breathed a sigh of relief, quickly moving down the rest of the wall.

At the bottom, she pulled on the rope as she said she would. There was fumbling at the top. Instead of it pulling up, the rope came cascading down.

Jennica swiftly coiled the rope back to its travel size and tossed it back into her pack. She raced to the stables, moving through the shadows.

Checking to be sure the stable hands were sleeping, she saddled Twilight. Jennica quietly attached her pack to the saddle and led her horse from the palace. She kicked Twilight into a swift gallop. They were soon outside the palace gates.

What waited for her outside the gates did not surprise her. Sammaria and Jennica had often mingled with the commoners of Mestchester. They knew their people. Without a hitch, Jennica moved down the deserted streets and passed through Mestchester's outer gates. Jennica looked up as the light from Dainia shone brightly and muttered, "Happy birthday, Sammaria."

"Jennica had wondered what had happened with the rope. She had told Diana to haul it back up. We shall return to Jennica soon, but, for now, I must explain what was happening on the third floor as Jennica was making her escape."

Donichello had been replaying Jennica's words in his head for hours. He now realized the full extent of his betrayal. He had lulled her into trusting him, done what he could to be amiable. He had known the King would name her the heir that night. It had been his task to convince her to attend the party.

That kiss.

Her blue eyes had closed, and his lips touched hers. She would hate him now. That kiss would be the deciding factor. Jennica would never look at him the same way again.

Without it, Jennica might have been able to forgive him. But with it, anything that they'd shared that night was instantly broken. All because he had not foreseen the loyalty of a sister, a twin.

Donichello had to talk to her. He had to make it right. But how could he explain how he had misjudged her character. That he did not know who she was. Maybe it would not have been so hard if she did not always avoid him. Yet, that was not fair. He should have known what her reaction would be. The fault was his. He was simply being selfish. He had wanted to dance with her and woo her in ways he did not get to before.

Donichello wandered the halls. Somehow, he had led himself to Jennica's room. He had no idea if she would see him. She had told him never to speak to her again. Yet, he knew he must.

He ran his fingers through his hair nervously and rapped his fingers on Jennica's door. It did not surprise him when she did not open the door.

He knocked again, harder. This time there was shuffling from behind the door. To his surprise, the door opened to a face that was not Jennica's. A girl with strawberry blonde hair stood before him. Her light eyes stared up at him meekly. She was frightened. Her small frame barred the entrance. She trained her eyes down.

Donichello looked past her trying to see her mistress. He asked, "May I speak to the princess?"

Diana wrung her hands together. She said, "Her Highness does not wish to speak to or see you, sir. She has specifically asked me to bar your entrance."

Donichello said, "Please, Diana … it is Diana, isn't it?"

She nodded.

"Diana," he implored, "I just need to apologize. I was selfish. I wanted to be with her. I did not think about the implications her father's announcement would hold."

Diana did not stand out of the way exactly, but Donichello saw a weakness in her eyes. He swept into the room. He expected to find Jennica there on the bed, in the antechamber, somewhere. He found her nowhere.

He turned to Diana, "Where is she? Why didn't you tell me she wasn't here?"

Diana looked up for just a moment, a hint of a smile behind her grimace, "You didn't ask, sir. Her Royal Highness left her quarters after His Majesty visited. Perhaps she visited the Tower. She loves it there so much. Or maybe the library. She didn't say when she left. She just told me not to allow you in here."

Donichello moved toward the window. Jennica's young dragon arched its back and curled its tail, hiccupping out into the darkness. Donichello stroked its spine. At least it did not share its owner's resentment toward him.

Diana moved over to reclaim Sniblea as he looked down. It was too dark to see as shadows shifted upon shadows. He took one last look at the hatchling as Diana placed it in its elaborate pen. The dragon's smoke curled as if a message to him. Diana seemed to notice too. Once again, it pointed to the window. Donichello took a step toward the dragon to get a closer look.

Before Donichello could sort it out, Diana ushered him back into the hall. He had no choice but to rejoin the party.

"The next morning commenced as normal. The guests from Jennica's birthday party began to leave. The princess did not come out to see them off. The King took Jennica's absence as unwillingness to apologize to him and the court for her rude display the night before. He knew she would come around eventually. It was not until Donichello came knocking that something seemed amiss."

Donichello hoped he would run into Jennica. She had gotten better at avoiding him now that she had yet another reason. Before, she would watch for him so she could leave immediately upon his arrival. Now, she was not anywhere he looked. She was not even in places he did not think she would go.

Donichello wondered if her father had confined her to her room. The King had been uncharacteristically angry with her after her outburst the night before.

Donichello abandoned his search of the grounds to knock on the princess's door. There was a muffled yelp and hustling around. Before long, the door opened to Diana's face. She tried to appear calm, but her eyes shifted nervously. He asked, "Is the princess in today?"

Diana glanced behind her. Donichello could not see what she was looking at, but he could see Sniblea in her cage. Her intelligent eyes were trained on him as if she were trying to communicate.

Diana said, "Yes. She still does not wish to see you, sir. Can you not understand that? She is frightfully upset. The princess is not one to hold a grudge. She must really be hurt."

The dragon rolled her head regally. She hiccupped and looked toward the window. Donichello frowned. The dragon seemed to motion toward it every time Jennica was mentioned.

Donichello asked, "Are you sure the princess is in her room?"

Diana glanced around nervously. That was all he needed. Jennica was gone. Donichello pushed into the room.

He asked, looking around for a sign, "Where has she gone, Diana? Let me go after her. I'll bring her back."

Diana said, "I know not where she planned to go. Only that she believed she had to."

"Why? Why would she have to leave here?" he asked.

Diana looked at him, "Can you think of no reason?"

Donichello cursed himself. Of course she had run after Sammaria. The girl was going to take on a man even the greatest of knights had failed to defeat. How could she possibly think to succeed?

Donichello rushed from Jennica's room. He had to speak with the King. He knew that, with Jennica missing, the King would be forced to mount a search. Not only for Jennica but Sammaria as well.

Donichello knocked twice on the door before entering the office. Morlyn stood there. He looked critically at Donichello. Morlyn looked angry for more than just Donichello's arrival.

The King demanded, "What gives you the right to interrupt a private meeting?"

Donichello bowed low in submission. He said, "Forgive me, my liege. I have urgent news."

King Enchardo waved his hand dismissively, "Yes, what is it?"

Donichello said, "Your Highness, Princess Jennica has run away. I have found proof she gathered supplies and ran late last night."

Prince Morlyn started to laugh. King Enchardo joined in. Morlyn asked, "Why would she run? What would make her do that?"

"She went to find Sammaria."

The King stopped smiling, "Do we know if she made it past the palace gates?"

Donichello said, "I checked the stables. Her horse is gone, but the guards from last night don't recall seeing anything."

The King rubbed his beard. He looked out the window of his office. Quietly, he said, "Leave me."

The King continued stroking his beard, deep in thought. This was just too perfect. Both girls had disappeared. He would not need to involve that oaf Morlyn after all. Of course, Enchardo needed assurance they were dead. Donichello would be a problem.

Enchardo moved away from the window and tapped the corner of his desk. He would need to send a special unit to do away with the runaway princess, and command Donichello to bring her home.

The wilderness was a dangerous place. Should the young Laeranil knight happen to catch a defending arrow, who would question the accident?

Enchardo smiled. Yes, everything was going according to plan. His mistress would be pleased.

Still, he hesitated. From the time he had spent with the girls, it was apparent there was a bond between them. If Jennica insisted Sammaria was alive, there was a good chance it was true. He needed to find someone to track Sammaria down.

Enchardo continued tapping his fingers on his desk. Before he could set this plan in motion, he needed to act the part of a worried father. Enchardo called his commander to his office.

"King Enchardo ordered five hundred of his finest troops out into the Dragonian wilderness to search for the princess. They were to search everywhere. They were to go through homes, stores, and barns.

Secretly, before leaving on the search himself, Enchardo dispatched three letters. One went to an assassin living in the mountains. The second went to a soldier only contacted when shifty business was afoot within the military. And the last was to a group of loyalists who were not afraid to take advantage of a frightened girl."

CHAPTER XI

Sammaria woke to a dim glow. Embers spit from a fire several feet in front of her. She flexed her wrists and ankles, checking for bonds. She was relieved to find none. She had been drugged. There was no need to restrain her when she wasn't even conscious.

Sammaria roved her foggy eyes around the camp, looking for signs of her captors. There was a lone man by the fire, the archer – Pennon. He poked at the coals before moving off into the grass to relieve himself. Sammaria could see no one else. Voices carried across the fire from further away.

"How long do the sedatives last?" asked a low voice nervously.

A calmer voice said, "A few hours. She should come to soon. We will have to watch her. No doubt she'll try to run."

"Is it necessary to drug her?" asked the first voice.

"Would you rather carry her kicking and screaming across the countryside?" snapped the third voice sarcastically.

The second man agreed, "This way at least we can transport her on a makeshift bed in the back of the cart."

The first voice still squirmed, "It doesn't seem right. How are we getting the cart into the mountains?"

The third voice said, "Shut up! Check the horses. Maybe *they* won't be annoyed by your prattle."

The second and third voices conferred for a while, deciding which path to take to the place where the Resistance was housed. The place did not have a name, but it was near what the men called Flyc-Antell Pass.

It was impassable nearly year-round, but the land above was green and fertile. The dragons had once used it as a breeding ground. Their magic still lingered, producing the perfect place to hide.

Sammaria slowly moved her arms a little at a time so she could escape without the men noticing. The voice behind her caused her to freeze as it said, "Is Antien sure of what he heard?"

It was the second voice talking. The calm voice – not nervous, just insistent. He wanted reassurance. Sammaria's mind raced. Antien *had* betrayed them. He sold information to the Resistance.

His companion replied, "Antien wouldn't tell us this if he did not believe it. Especially with how close he came to death. The…"

He hesitated. Sammaria felt his eyes rest upon her. She lay limp. He continued, "At least the heir is secure. The Event is to take place less than a fortnight's time past the Meyeah Moon."

Sammaria unwittingly looked up at the sky with them. Dainia glowed down upon the summer landscape. She thought internally, "Happy birthday, Jennica."

❧

Jennica reined in Twilight as morning broke over the gates of the first small town outside Mestchester. She supposed the palace square alone could have dwarfed the town. Jennica would have liked to ride around the town to avoid being seen, but she needed money. She would eventually need to replenish her supplies, and she had not been able to collect much gold before leaving Mestchester.

Jennica knew her jewels would be popular among the wealthy. She had gathered up the jewels she could bear to lose. Now, as she entered the town, she removed a few of the jewels from her pack.

The jeweler's shop was in a decent building with an apartment over it. A kind-looking girl with dark hair was tending to the various products in the shop. Behind her, a younger girl with lighter curls was polishing small stones with a dirty cloth. The older girl took the stones from the child and dipped them in some solution. The solution made the stone shine brightly. She then moved it into a pan of what Jennica could sense was water. The stone was then laid on a table for everyone to see.

Jennica watched a while longer before making her presence known with a small, polite cough. The young girl started. The older girl looked at Jennica, waiting.

Jennica said, "I have goods I would like to sell."

The older girl led Jennica over to a clear table covered with examining instruments. Jennica laid her jewels on the table. At once, the girl began exclaiming over their brilliant color and size.

In the end, Jennica was paid a large sum for her pieces. She left, following sun as it moved quickly across the horizon.

❧

The King and his army invaded Drannor. Before anyone could react, the military began bursting into homes and ransacking them, looking for Jennica.

They broke into the jeweler's house and grabbed the young girl working with the stones. The girl's father came running down the stairs from the house.

He demanded, "What is the meaning of this? Release Demetria, now!"

The man who was holding the girl let her go and drew his sword, "We are looking for Jennica Aeradal. By decree of the King, every home is to be searched. Get your family out."

The man was outraged and said, "How could we be hiding a princess in our small home?"

The soldier marched over to the man and stabbed him in the stomach. The soldier turned to the girl, "What did you see?"

She whimpered, lowering her eyes, "Nothing, sir."

He looked around the shop, his eyes lingering on a necklace of blood-red stones.

He demanded, pulling on Demetria's hair, "Where did you get that piece?"

Demetria winced, "A girl sold it to us yesterday morning."

The guard pointed the blood-covered sword at her neck and said, "That is the princess's necklace. Where did she go?"

Demetria gulped and said, "She went north, sir."

He took his sword and slid the tip across her collarbone, carving the letter T. Her chest bleeding, he said, "Something to remember me by. I'll be back for you."

He swung onto his horse and rode off, yelling, "North. She went north!"

He looked back at Demetria and winked.

She turned, running to her dead father's side. Her little sister, on the steps, said, "She didn't go north."

Demetria looked up and said weakly, "I know, but they can't catch her. Look at what they did to Father."

She glared out the door as King Enchardo and his guard passed. He rode out of town to the north, the sun setting to his left.

❧

That night, Sammaria dreamed that she had been locked in a chest. When it opened, it was not Rekasi there. It was her father. He stood there with Morlyn. They yanked her out by her arms. She stood in front of them, massaging her shoulders. Her father glared at her and said, "Mark her, Morlyn. Mark her so all will know she is a traitor to her country."

Morlyn smiled. He took his sword and slit the front of her dress. The dress fell away, and Sammaria stood there naked as she watched her father laugh. Morlyn moved the tip of his sword and carved the mark of a traitor on her cheek.

Her father came up behind her and hit the back of her knees so she had to kneel in front of Morlyn. Morlyn laughed and raised his sword. He brought it down. It whistled through the air as it flew down toward her neck.

Sammaria woke in a cold sweat. She shifted in her cramped position, shivering from the vividness of her dream. Faintly, she wondered if it were a sign. She thought she heard voices but quickly shook that off. She settled down again, but she could not get back to sleep.

❧

Jennica awoke suddenly. Something cold had touched her face. She jumped to her feet. No one was around. It was still dark, but she knew she would not be able to return to sleep. That hand was too real, too familiar. She rolled her blanket up and shoved it in her pack.

The hair on her arms began to stand on end. She stared into the darkness around her, hoping to find some sign of the intruders. A faint casting of a face appeared beside her. She blinked once, and it disappeared. The sound of scuffling on rocks found its way into the silence.

Shouldering the pack, she drew the dagger she had been carrying. She swallowed the fear, which swelled in her throat.

Suddenly, a rough hand grabbed her by the wrist. She swiped at him with her blade. He jumped back, trying to get out of range of her dagger. She pushed him back to the cliff's edge. He leaned on uneven footing, reaching for her wrist.

Unwittingly, she played into his trap. She hoped to make him slip and pushed forward. He looped his beefy hand around her wrist and twisted. She cried out in agony and released her weapon. He pulled her close and whispered, "You are more trouble than you are worth." The other men smiled. The man holding her said, "I think I understand now. She's a defiant little thing."

He turned, grabbing her by her neck and dangled her over the cliff's edge. Jennica looked down. She could only see shadows. She looked back at the man. A wide smile bloomed across his haggard face. Fear rushed through Jennica's body.

Jennica clawed his hand. The man simply tightened his hold around her throat. She coughed, struggling for air. Her arms and legs writhed.

The leader commanded, "Stop playing with her. It's going to be light soon. Just get it done, so we can get out of here. Remember, we still have to deliver the body to Mestchester."

The man turned to the leader then back to Jennica. He tilted his head, "It's such a shame to lose such a beautiful girl."

She felt the hand loosen. She pleaded, "No, please."
He let go.

A scream ripped from Jennica's throat as she plummeted. Debris kicked up into her face as she clawed the cliff face for a handhold.

A chill worked its way up her spine. A cool hand encircled her wrist, jerking her to a stop.

Pain jolted through her shoulder. Stinging radiated through her raw face and bloody hands. She reached up to grip the person's wrist.

It was comforting to find sinew and skin beneath her fingers. She looked up but saw nothing. Her hands were not even wrapped around anything.

Jennica twisted in surprise as a gossamer face appeared. Before her, she saw a shadow of an arm, a shoulder, a face. It pulled her onto the solid footing of the cliff ledge.

Jennica felt a mix of terror and giddiness building in her heart. She was looking at someone she had only seen in a rare photo. A face that until a few days ago she had forgotten. She was staring into the eyes of her brother, Einar.

Jennica looked through the translucent figure before her. The men who had assaulted her were gone. All that remained, apart from her and Einar, were bugs scuttling along the rocks. She asked, "Where did they go?"

Einar looked down at the cockroaches scurrying away from the light. He said, "No one can escape Kiro's great power. You have been blessed."

Jennica smiled faintly, then frowned, puzzled, "You. Why… How are you here? Why don't I remember you?"

Einar brushed her face and tucked a stray piece of hair behind her ear. He said, "So many things I wish I could tell you. I was sent to give you a message, but you were in trouble."

He smiled, "My little sisters, always getting in trouble."

Jennica looked at him with worried eyes, "Have you seen Sammaria? Do you know what has happened to her?"

Einar held up her hand, "It is not her you need to worry about. Kiro has given you a task."

Jennica drew back. She had not expected that. Tasks were supposed to be seen as gifts, but those gifted were most often never seen again. The tasks were difficult and deadly. Jennica asked, "What kind of task?"

"It involves the very questions you have been asking yourself about the portals. It's all connected. I cannot tell you much more than that."

"What am I to do?" Jennica moaned, "Can I refuse it?"

Einar replied, "No, sweet child. No one can escape…"

"Kiro's great power," Jennica finished.

Einar nodded. He said, "There is one who can help you. He lives deep in the Forbidden Katart Wood. A spirit almost as ancient as Ethota itself, existing in every realm."

"But Sammaria… I can't just leave her."

Einar said, "This task will lead you away from her."

Jennica said, "So, you do know where she is!"

Einar said looking pained, "I am forbidden to say."

He looked around, conflicted. He whispered urgently, "Look for the sleeping dragon by the elkmole tree. You will find her at the end of the trail."

Jennica said, "What?"

He squeezed Jennica's hand, "Go. Be careful. There are more who wish to harm you. Trust your heart. It won't lead you astray."

"What does that mean?"

Einar's whisper of a body disappeared with the wind.

"Einar!" Jennica raised a hand in farewell. He was gone.

She gathered her fallen pack and hefted it back on her shoulder. She turned and stared at the Kilhatea Mountains.

As she traveled, she heard rumors of search parties ransacking the country. Her father was a hypocrite. Jennica thought, "As soon as we both disappear, he decides he must find us. When did he make the change from adoring father to tyrant king?"

"The princesses had known of their Powers for many years. Their grandmother Nana Gentra had told them when they were two years old. She told them that the Power had run in the women of their family for centuries. Gentra had known at the moment of their birth that they had inherited the Elemental Power. She told them that she had control of the Earth and their mother, the fair Queen Milamare, had the Elemental Power of control over the Air.

She told them, "Sammaria, you have control over Fire. Jennica, you have control over Water. You must use these powers for good, never for revenge or hatred, or you will lose them."

Jennica and Sammaria supposed this was why their father always glared at them when he thought they weren't looking. That somehow he had learned their secret. Still, Jennica never truly believed that was the reason behind her father's hatred. Despite his anger, Enchardo had always held some compassion for his daugthers. Now, the raw hatred coursing behind his cold eyes consumed his every emotion."

Jennica was surprised as she stumbled into a grove of trees. She had arrived in the Katart Woods. It was not the direction she had intended to go. Jennica shook her head. The pull of Kiro's quest was strong. Fatigue clouded her mind. Not questioning why she was there, she climbed up a tree in which she found wide hammock-like branches. She stashed her pack under her head and finally let her body rest.

CHAPTER XII

King Enchardo barked another order, urging his men forward. The party had not seen a sign of Jennica for three days, not since they had found the jewels in Drannor. It was as if she had disappeared. Enchardo knew that Jennica was not experienced enough to hide her tracks. The jeweler's daughter had to have lied to them.

Jennica had never traveled in this direction. Yet, people kept whispering that she was here. The King grew ever more stubborn, marching them further into the Katart Woods. The depths of the woods was not for civilized life. The trees' canopy thickened, blocking the light of the sun. Still, the King demanded they push forward.

The trees became too thick for their mounts. The horses were left behind. They pulled at their tethers. Their protests could be heard as they passed deeper into the old forest. Several soldiers crossed themselves as the canopy blotted out the sun. They were in the Forbidden Katart Wood. This side of the forest was hallowed ground. Ancient spirits were said to walk there. They did not take kindly to intruders.

Donichello listened to the men, "Any person trying to hide would not stay on the path. Though she is a princess."

It was true that the group had been staying on a relatively straight path. It was almost as if the King were leading them to someplace specific. Someplace he knew Jennica would be.

Donichello sent another prayer to Kiro. A boy no older than fifteen turned to him, "My Lord, the King should not be pushing us forward. This is a dark place."

Donichello clamped a hand down on the boy's shoulder, "The King wouldn't place you in any danger. His Highness has a reason, I'm sure."

The boy shook his head, "You have too much faith."

A splintering noise ripped through Donichello's reverie. A tree toppled. Donichello watched disjointedly as it collapsed. The tree cut off the party's path at the head. The King stopped. The tree was too large for the men to simply step over.

Someone called, "Move it out of the way. It's just dead wood."

King Enchardo did not seem to care if it was cleared or not.

One of the soldiers, General Zike, approached the King, "Sire, the woods here are dangerous. The princess would not have come here. We should leave."

"Push forward," Enchardo called.

Donichello looked away, clenching his fists. If Enchardo was trying to prove something, this was not the way to do it. Innocent people were going to die.

A wave of cracking limbs came rushing through the trees. The crackling moved rapidly toward the group. King Enchardo ordered, "Keep going!"

The soldiers hesitated. The noise had stopped. The silence was deafening. King Enchardo took his whip and snapped it.

Donichello winced. He froze as he felt a tremor beneath his feet. The thing was coming back toward them. The trees began to protest once more. The noise seemed to come from all directions.

A shrill scream abruptly cut short. Donichello felt heavy breathing on the back of his neck. He turned in time to see a disembodied foot fall next to the king. Donichello met the young boy's eyes.

The men reacted with varying emotions as more cracking and creaking sounded within the forest. It was moving closer. Donichello tracked its movements. It would have to break into the clearing eventually. He watched as it pushed toward them from the north. The trees bent and swayed as the creature sprinted. Donichello yelled, "Get ready!"

The men prepared their weapons. Bows were drawn taut. Swords were raised. Donichello watched as he waited for the mysterious creature to breach the clearing. The creature abruptly vanished.

There was no noise at all. Not even the crows were calling out. Donichello told those around him not to let down their guard.

A garish roar reverberated through the air. Out of the cracking and twisting vegetation, an enormous griffin with wild eyes emerged. It was as tall as the surrounding trees with golden-brown feathers. Blood dripped from its beak. It stopped and stared at them for a moment. The archers cocked their arrows.

Detecting a threat, the griffin reared its massive head. Slowly, it lowered its enormous head and swept its eyes across the first line of archers. The griffin looked through the crowds and stared at the King.

Donichello took his eyes off the griffin just long enough to glance around. He wondered what was controlling the creature. Why was it not attacking?

The griffin stuck his head up in the air and roared. Leaves fluttered down from nearby trees from the force of the roar. One of the archers accidentally loosed an arrow.

The arrow breezed by the griffin's large ear. He roared again, swiping the front line of archers with a dagger-like talon. Charging forward, the griffin crushed several people beneath its talons and paws.

Donichello pushed the young boy out of the griffin's path before dodging the beast himself. The griffin was attentive, though. It caught Donichello by the belt with one of its large talons and swung him, tossing him into a small grove away from the other soldiers.

Donichello hit the ground hard. His arm snapped. Blood began to fill the inside of the armor covering his forearm. Pain surged through him with each breath.

The archers shot toward the giant beast. Most missed as the griffin swayed back and forth. One archer loosed her arrow. The royal army watched nervously as it headed straight for the griffin's heart. However, her efforts were in vain. When the arrow pierced the creature's skin, it merely roared in pain and continued to destroy everything.

"Jennica stopped. The roar shook the entire forest. The roar sounded like a lion but echoed with the screech of a crow. Jennica felt the vibrations of the roar in her bones. She began to run ."

Jennica ran quickly through the woods. Something was following her. A black flash ripped past her. Jennica scanned the trees as she continued to run. She raced by gnarled trees. Branches reached out like fingers to snatch her. Suddenly, the forest was quiet. Nothing was moving. There was no sound except her ragged breathing.

She stopped, dropping to her knees. Her chest heaved as she tried to catch her breath, scanning the surroundings. The black creature was not chasing her anymore. As she looked at the trees around her and listened to the silence, she realized that she was well into the Forbidden Wood. Something was pushing her inevitably toward this task. Nervous, she continued to walk deeper into the woods.

❧

Jennica raced toward the light. She needed to escape the horrible sound. Screaming men and the cacophony of clashing metal assailed her ears. Horrified, she watched the bloody rampage before her. She gasped as she recognized the Dragonian seal on the bright uniforms.

Looking around, she saw her father pull a young soldier from a yellow mare and mount it, galloping into the trees passed Donichello. The two men did not so much as glance at each other.

Bile rose in her throat as she watched her father ride away. Turning her attention to Donichello, Jennica noticed his arm was lying at a strange angle. He was still. So very still. Her heart pounded in her ears. He couldn't be dead.

As she jumped from the trees, the whole world seemed to have melted away. All that seemed real was Donichello. Just as it had been that night.

No! She must not think that way.

She knelt by his side looking for signs of life. The shallow rise and fall of his chest and a good pulse were obvious once she had calmed herself. She needed to move Donichello away from the battle and stop the rest of the men's fighting.

Jennica used her Power to search for underground streams. Finding several, she pulled at them, bringing them to the surface. Her body began to shake as she strained against the flow of the water. Blood trickled from her nose. Finally, she was able to pull enough water from the earth to flood the area until Donichello landed on the lowest limb of the nearest tree.

The griffin did not mind the water, but the rest of the King's party struggled to swim to the surface. The griffin stalked over to where Jennica was surrounded by a shield of water. The great creature snorted.

The soldiers nervously observed the griffin as it cornered Jennica. They quickly fled. They did not care if they lost the water witch. Magic users were feared, killed if necessary.

She used the water to push herself up into the tree before letting it sink back into the earth. The griffin stomped over to the tree ,put its beak beside Jennica's face, and opened its mouth. She flinched.

The griffin placed a claw on Donichello's chest and said, in Donichello's voice, "Jennica, your journey is long. Find me. Find me soon."

The griffin took flight, breaking more of the surrounding trees. Jennica found herself angry at the creature for destroying the forest. It grabbed the top of a tree and kept flying. The tree ripped from the ground and the griffin carried it away. Donichello moaned.

Jennica watched the griffin fly until it was a speck in the sky. Donichello moaned again. He was waking up.

She took his torn shirt and ripped it further into strips. Carefully taking his arm, she moved the bone back into place. She took the strips and wrapped his arm and a sturdy stick that she broke off the tree into a makeshift splint.

Donichello's arm throbbed. He looked around, but Jennica was nowhere to be found. Everything around him was black but a light that seemed to be moving away from him. An animal stood in the center of the beam. The creature turned and began to run down the path toward Donichello. The animal was upon him and knocked him to the ground. He closed his eyes and opened them again.

A cool tingling encircled his arm. The throbbing in his arm stopped. His eyes came into focus on a shape. Light burned his eyes, but he could see an angel's face.

Her face looked down at him, and she whispered his name. He lifted his arm to shield his eyes against the blinding light. Donichello caressed the angel's face, and she put her hand on his. She took his hand and lowered it from her face, her blue eyes shining. He asked, "Where am I?"

The angel said, "Donichello, please, I need you to focus."

The angel choked back tears. Donichello said, "Cry, Angel."

She looked down at him, "I'm not an angel, Donichello. It's just me."

Donichello let his eyes focus. Jennica's face was streaked with tears. He tried to sit up, but Jennica pushed him back down.

"Don't talk," she ordered.

He leaned back, his head spinning. He was still delirious from his encounter with the griffin, but he was stable. Slowly, he was coming out of his delusion. She knew that, if she were to leave him, he would survive. She could not involve him in her uncertain plan. He would just try to talk her out of it.

Jennica waited until Donichello fell asleep again before carefully trying to pull him down from the tree. Donichello was much larger than she was. It ended up being a rather rough landing. She dragged him away from the tree and laid him behind a bush near the soldiers' camp.

She cupped her hand behind Donichello's head and set it gently to the ground. It rolled down to rest against his shoulder, his hair falling across his face. Jennica reached down and brushed it away from his smooth cheek and tucked it behind his ear before she pulled back, realizing what she was doing.

She nodded and stood up. Donichello sighed. Jennica froze, afraid he was going to wake up. He seemed to fall back asleep as she backed away from the little place. She turned and ran into the forest, hoping to be rid of him. At least for the time it took her to find Sammaria.

CHAPTER XIII

Sammaria sat up in the back of the wagon. They had drugged her again. She pulled herself forward and looked out the back of the wagon. The breeze felt cool on her face, her body naturally heating under the strain of her panic.

They were following a path. She could not tell where it led, but three dragons circled over head. The cart hit a bump, and she made a small noise.

Pennon turned from where he was walking beside the wagon and tried to grab her. She held up her hands to protect herself, and a shower of flames fell onto the man. He writhed in pain. She stared at her hands in horror. She flicked her wrists, extinguishing the flames.

She looked down at the passing ground, then turned back toward the horizon. Toward home. She squeezed her eyes shut and leapt from the wagon.

She was running before she had even fully stood up from her fall.

Rekasi shouted something in a language she did not recognize, breaking off to chase after her. Sammaria yelped as she saw a shadow pass over her. One of the dragons had broken from the circle above.

There was a high-pitched squeal. Sammaria looked back to see Rekasi falling behind. The squeal came again. Sammaria looked up. The dragon dove, knocking Sammaria to the ground.

Rekasi, with a renewed burst of speed, was gaining on her. Sammaria jumped back up and started to run. Again, she heard Rekasi shout in that unfamiliar language. There was a short squeal, the dragon dove again and pulled Sammaria from the ground.

"She thought the dragon was going to kill her. It is an honor and a curse to be killed by a dragon. If they kill you, your soul is forced to wander for all time. She wasn't ready to die."

Sammaria looked up. The dragon's talons loosened around her body. She felt her heart swell as if someone were sending her their love. She closed her eyes and thought of her sister. An unusual calm came over her. She saw the ground growing nearer and squeezed her eyes shut, waiting for the impact. It never came.

A strange force had stopped her short. She tried to move, but her entire body was paralyzed. Just before she fainted, she saw a woman and a large man with a blue sextant tattooed just below his jawbone standing over her. Sammaria tried asking what was happening, but, at that moment, the blackness overtook her.

※

After losing so many men to the griffin, the King was forced to stop his search. He had to accept that, between the creatures and the nefarious outlaws, Jennica would not have been able to safely traverse the countryside. Enchardo had hoped to keep his men traveling until word of Jennica's body on the castle's steps spread across Dragonia. As it was, they were forced to assume they would never find her. Graver still, Lord Donichello had gone missing as well. Enchardo had not planned for this, but it could not have gone better for him.

Heartbroken, what remained of the regiment made their way back to Mestchester.

A council meeting was called. All of the King's advisors were present. He addressed them, "My youngest daughter is… dead."

Pranshey said, "Has this been confirmed?"

Enchardo snapped, "I am standing here before you telling you my child is dead and you have the gall to ask me if I am certain?"

Pranshey slid his fingers through his greasy hair saying, "I only wish the best for you. The people will not be happy about this. Jennica was very popular among the commoners. With Sammaria's kidnapping and Lord Donichello's *disappearance*, this news won't be taken with grace."

King Enchardo looked around his table of advisors, "Does anyone else share Pranshey's outrageous views?"

Everyone silently stared down at the table. Pranshey smirked, "They are too afraid to tell you what they think. But believe me. A riot will start as soon as you mention foul play in unison with Her Royal Highness's name."

Enchardo snapped his fingers, saying in a low tone, "I don't need your petulance, and you will be punished for your offense."

Guards came into the room, seizing the advisor. As they pulled him from the room, Pranshey said, "You are going to wish that you had listened to me."

Just as he was ripped through the doorway, as mockingly as possible, he looked at the King and said, "Your Majesty."

Later that day, the King walked out onto the castle's front balcony to address the commoners. The bright sun shone brightly in the sky. King Enchardo flinched away from the light, recognizing the irony of its brilliance. He made his eyes mist and haltingly pronounced the news he had come to bear.

"As you have all come to know, Lord Donichello has gone missing."

The crowd of people began muttering and exclaiming their anger. Donichello may not have been known well in Mestchester, but his name had been heard across the countryside for being a benefactor to the rural people.

The King paused for silence. Letting his voice crack, he said, "However, that is not what I am here to tell you today. There is so much that has happened in these past few weeks. So much pain has been caused. My daughter…"

A tear slid down the King's cheek. "My daughter, Jennica. It seems unfair that she had to go while I still live. She was killed. The Resistance sent us her last confession and confirmation of her death. She has been lost to us."

The crowd below grew livid. Unbeknownst to the King, many in the crowd had family members in the Resistance. They could not believe that anyone they knew would order the execution of that young girl. Someone cried out, "You lie!"

Another punched the man, and a fight broke out among the people.

The King tried to continue, unperturbed, "You all knew her. She was a kind soul. She was an imaginative girl with a great heart and dreams as wide as our vast world. A candle on the Macennar River can do little to ease my broken heart."

He murmured, "One daughter dead, one missing."

He turned to walk off the podium as the priests handed him a candle.

The crowd continued to fight. One of the King's advisors asked if they should send the guards to break it up. The King scoffed, "Let them fight. Let the fight be knocked out of them."

He ran his hand through his greying hair. The advisor stared at him as he walked away.

Brother Orlten watched the chaos from his window. He prayed to Kiro for some sign of hope. Their only hope had finally been destroyed with the death of the young princess. Brother Orlten lit a candle, deep in prayer to the high god that help would come soon.

A great light shone across the plaza, blinding Orlten and the crowd in the square below. A voice echoed from the radiance. The voice was calming and direct, causing everyone to stop and stare. Slowly, the light bent around the figure of a woman.

"Why are you fighting, my children? What harm has your neighbor caused you? A great falsehood has been told. Yet, you punish those most likely to expose it."

The crowd stared in wonder at the celestial being hovering above their heads. Those older in the crowd recognized the woman to be the deceased Queen of Dragonia, Milamare Deswayze Aeradal.

The Queen continued, "A lie can spread like wildfire, while the truth is just starting its journey. And how fragile hope can be, but its death is impossible. I am here to tell you your hope has not been killed. Jennica lives. Sammaria lives. Donichello lives."

Cheering broke from the crowd. Apologetic looks passed between those with bruised faces. Whether they were loyal to the Resistance or the King, they were all glad to hear of the girls' safety.

Milamare paused, "However, they *are* in danger. Many people are seeking to destroy them. If there is a shred of decency in any of you, please protect my daughters. Help them in whatever they choose to do. Keep them safe from whomever their enemies might be. Now, go."

CHAPTER XIV

Sammaria opened her eyes in a dark room. She sat up on the bed and could almost make out the looming shapes in the distance, but the room was too dark to see. She was not sure where she was or why her head was throbbing so intensely.

She stood up, her feet hitting something soft. Maybe a rug. She looked down, startled. Fire had come to her hand uncalled. She held the ball of light so it splashed across her feet. She could see the rug embossed with Kiro's ascension. She walked across the room to make out the looming shapes that called to her with fearful curiosity. Sammaria stumbled over a candlestick holding a small white candle. Putting Fire to the wick, the room was flooded with light. She let her Fire extinguish.

She could see now that the strange shapes in the distance had been statues. The one to which she was particularly drawn was a two-foot statue sitting on top of the dresser. Picking it up and examining it, she saw that it was of a green woman holding a torch high above her head. Sammaria did not know what it symbolized, but the statue was enticing. She set it back on the dresser and moved to stand before several life-sized statues.

She could see one was a statue of Mestchina. Her face was beautifully carved. She turned from the goddess and looked at the next one. It was a statue of a siren whose hair just barely covered her breasts. She had been exquisitely carved. Every scale seemed to protrude from her long tail. Her alluring eyes called to her lost lover. Sammaria could almost hear the siren's enchanting song.

She extended her hand to touch the scaly tail as she heard the door scrape open. She tried to call Fire back to her hands, but nothing came.

She felt a hot hand close around her wrist. Her arm jerked in its socket as she was pulled to a stop. Sammaria stifled a yelp. She felt pressure on her shoulder forcing her into a chair.

Her heart pounded as her captor turned from her to light another candle. She tensed, ready to run. A male voice said, "Don't even think about it."

Sammaria gasped as the candle ignited, and she could finally see her captor's face. He had short, brown hair. His eyes were liquid amber. They looked like a candle's flame smoldering with an underlying fury. He had smooth but somehow rugged features. His vest showed off a well-muscled chest. A complicated design on his chest resembled a person with a body made of flame. It denoted the man as a Flame Lord.

The man stood before her, emotionless. His face seemed almost thoughtful to her. She recognized him as the man who had kidnapped her. She asked, "What are -?"

Rekasi cut her off with a sharp movement of his hand.

She silenced herself, staring at the floor. He wrenched her into a chair. He leaned over her chair forcing her to look him in the eyes. She shrank back. She desperately considered using Fire to escape from this hopeless situation, but still it did not come.

He pulled back, "How is your sister? Jennica? Is she well?"

Sammaria looked at him, surprised. It took her a moment, but she finally found her voice, "Why are you treating this like a social visit? Just do what you want with me and leave."

He said, "Do you know why you are here?"

Sammaria rolled her eyes. Rekasi continued, "I can't…"

He stopped. He muttered in Pilleetain, passing his hand over his face.

"Just let me go," Sammaria pleaded.

"The Resistance is this country's last hope. I cannot free you."

Sammaria's eyebrows furrowed, "What? My father…"

She trailed off.

He stood up suddenly and moved toward the door, "I don't have time for this!"

"What do you want with me?"

Rekasi stopped at the door and looked back. He shook his head and left.

"Much time passed inside the walls before Sammaria had any interaction with the leader of the Resistance again. A rotating group of women came in to bring her meals three times a day and to escort her to the bathhouses. Otherwise, she was confined to the bedroom. It didn't feel much different from her life at home, she was just watched much more carefully.

The people around her talked to her, brought her things to read, sew, write. She was useful, just trapped. Once and a while, her captor would come in to ask her questions about her sister, father, once about her mother. She would look forward to his departure each time, but she wanted answers. Rekasi certainly wasn't offering any clarity, and her helpers weren't any more open."

One of the aides had told her that Rekasi would be coming that day. Sammaria sat there waiting for him. She had moved the courting chair and placed it so she could stare at the door. She waited until he came in before springing up.

Before he could say anything, before his interrogation could start, she said hastily, "I want answers. You are the only one who can give them to me. You are keeping me here, so you are going to give them to me. If you don't, I will find a way to end your so-called Resistance. So, I think you'll do what I say."

Rekasi stared at Sammaria, his eyes incredulous. She returned his stare with her large, amber eyes. He said, "We wouldn't want to hurt that well-bred body of yours. So, what do you need?"

Sammaria continued to stare, wondering if he was trying to trick her in some way. He gestured to the courting chair, inviting her to join him. She sat, trying to decide where to begin. She had so many questions. After a few awkward moments, she began with the question he would be most likely to answer. She said, "When I fell, before I passed out, there was a woman and a man with her. The man had a blue sextant tattooed onto his jaw. Who are those people?"

Rekasi frowned. He had not seen anyone there when she jumped from the wagon. She looked at him expectantly. He said, "I am sorry, Your Highness. There is no one here that I know of with that type of marking."

Sammaria's eyes flashed. She said, "You are trying to trick me. You don't want -"

Rekasi held up his hand to stop her. He said, "Please. There is no trick. We have refugees come to the headquarters all the time. It's possible they were arriving. I do not know everyone who lives here and I have not met the new arrivals. I will speak to Olo to see if he has seen them."

"Olo? Olo Hamwich? The Prime Minister is part of the Resistance? I thought he had been killed."

Rekasi shook his head, "They tried. He joined the Resistance very early when my mentor was still young. He asked to be in charge of the refugees."

"Can I see him?" Sammaria asked.

Rekasi was hesitant, "I will talk to Olo."

Sammaria could hear the "no" in his voice. Just as she had heard in so many voices before. She sighed in frustration.

Rekasi stood, "I have to go."

Sammaria shook her head, "No! I still have so many questions!"

Rekasi replied, "I'm afraid we'll have to shelve them until next time."

He turned and walked briskly to the door. He pulled it open.

Sammaria asked, "Why do you keep me here?"

Rekasi stopped. He turned slowly and looked at her. His eyes were sad. He said, "You do not have to stay in this room. The maids will no longer have to accompany you. But, Sammaria, please be back here by seven hours after the high sun."

"Thank you," Sammaria said, startled by her sudden freedom.

Rekasi nodded, "Oh, and, Sammaria, someone here wants to see you. I shall be back tomorrow to answer your questions."

Sammaria looked at him, surprised. So many unexpected kindnesses. He was rarely around. She was afraid to trust him. "He'll visit tomorrow before me." He left as Sammaria tried to understand why his voice had trembled so much with that last statement.

Sammaria pushed open the door and let out a breath of relief. It was unlocked. She could leave. He had not been lying. Sammaria stepped out of her room. She looked both ways as she closed the door behind her. The walls appeared to be cut from the same rock as the room she had been held in. The hallway was dark and narrow. A red rug stretched the length of the floor.

Sammaria tried to orient herself. She could not sense the direction. She could not sense the sun. She just felt nothing. She turned left and walked down the hall. She stumbled slightly, and as she moved she felt the air open up.

She stopped. She stood in a room with a big, open dome. Birds flew around the dome in flocks, a wire cage encircling them. Rows of walkways circled the large aviary. People walked briskly up and down the walkways about their purposes.

Sammaria stopped and gripped the railings. She felt her knees buckle beneath her. This place was much larger then she had originally thought. The people moved about their business as if they were not traitors to the throne. They acted as if it were perfectly normal for them to be here.

Sammaria stared at the birds. They fluttered about, looking for an exit. She took a deep breath, pulled herself straight, and fled back to her room.

The next day, the door opened, and Sammaria looked up at the visitor.

"Antien!" she cried as she threw her arms around him.

He hugged her back. She pulled away quickly and crossed her arms over her body. She looked at the ground.

Antien lifted her chin. She pulled away from him. He said, "Hey, where did you go? Rekasi said you were here and I wanted to see you."

Sammaria said, "I was so worried. I thought they had killed you. Oh, Antien, are you all right?"

Antien said, "I'm fine. I told you I would find a way out."

Sammaria said, "I've been so lonely. All I hear are those maids chatting about things I'm not allowed to know. No one will tell me anything. At least, in the palace, I could trick someone into talking to me. Now, I'm stuck in this room. Can you tell me anything that is going on out there? I am desperate. How is Jennica? And Dragonia? Do you know anything at all?"

Antien shook his head, "That's for Rekasi to tell you. Speaking of, Rekasi won't be in today. He wanted me to tell you that he is sorry for canceling."

Sammaria's face fell, "Not coming?"

Antien was rambling, "It's not like him to announce a cancellation like that. Hmm – I suppose because you are royalty. Oh, Sammaria, are you all right?"

Sammaria looked crestfallen. She said, "No. This was my one chance to get the answers to my questions, and now he isn't coming."

Antien nodded solemnly. He looked at her. She refused to make eye contact with him. He got up abruptly and said, "You are mad at me!"

Sammaria's jaw dropped, "I have every right to be. You may not have been plotting my death, but you did still betray the Crown. So, you betrayed me. Why? Why join the Resistance?"

Antien said, "I have to go."

"You have to answer me!" she protested, "I haven't even gotten to talk to you."

Antien replied, "I know, but I have things I must attend to."

He was hiding something. She could hear it in his voice. She knew, no matter how she pried, she would not get it out of him. She said, "Fine, but I expect answers."

She saw an uncertain promise as she stared into his brown eyes.

Antien went searching for Rekasi. He burst into Olo Hamwich's office and found Rekasi reviewing a plan for expansion of the network of buildings that made up the castle. He demanded, "What did you do to her?"

Rekasi stood up straight, his back rigid. Olo stood up from his chair. Rekasi demanded, "Explain yourself."

Antien said, "Sammaria. What have you done to her? She has lost herself. She has no idea what is going on. I thought you needed her so that she could take down her father."

"She is in good health. And, when she is ready, we shall tell her what she needs to know. How the Prime Minister and I have decided to handle the princess is no concern of yours."

"Like hell, it isn't! She is my gods' promised. I have every right to have a say in how she is treated!"

Rekasi started, taken aback. He took a moment to gather his thoughts. Olo simply shrugged. Intelligence had given no word of this. Still, their information about Sammaria had many gaps. She was a very private person outside of her public life.

Rekasi nodded, "Well, that changes things. I am sorry, Antien. We hadn't any idea that you were so closely bonded."

Antien nodded, "Now you do. I have done my part. I will do whatever it takes to keep her safe. Even if it means keeping her safe from you."

Rekasi slammed his hands down on the table. Olo held up his hand. He said, "Calm down, squire. She is perfectly safe here."

Antien said, "I have stayed away from her. I have not breathed a word to her about her sister. You must answer her questions. She will not be mollified for long. I cannot lie to her."

Rekasi raised an eyebrow toward Antien. The boy immediately dropped his gaze. Rekasi frowned and said, "I will listen to her questions and move forward from there. I will not make any promises. Satisfied?"

Antien nodded and left the office. Olo said, "He is one to watch."

Rekasi sighed, looking back down at the blueprints, "You don't think he's dangerous, do you?"

Olo said, "No, he's naïve. I think that he is just looking out for the girl. Answer her questions. All of them."

Sammaria slipped out of her room. She had not been out since she had discovered the aviary. She had been building up her nerve once more. She needed to be able to face the people.

The people met her with odd glances and sidelong looks. Everyone was working together to sustain the life they had built here. Sammaria's eyes followed the people leaving the building through a large double door. Her heart sped as she took a step toward the door.

Nobody noticed anything. She took another step. She kept taking steps toward the door. No one stopped her. No one even looked up. Sammaria made it across the room.

Taking a deep breath, she pushed the door open and stepped out.

The sunlight blinded her. Sammaria looked around and saw a fence running around the space. There were rows upon rows of crops that men and women were tending. She scanned the fence, and her eyes fell upon the gate.

At first, she thought she was mistaken. As her eyes backtracked, she saw it again. Quickly, she moved across the garden toward the gate. Her heart pounded as she thought someone would stop her at any moment. She reached her hand and rested it on the latch. She hesitated.

Her mind raced with the thought of betraying Rekasi's trust. Was this a test? Was he letting her wander to see what she would do? No. He was not that deceptive. The latch popped open under her hand, unhindered. The gate fell open.

Sammaria stared out at the mountains and took a step through the gate. No one said anything. Her mind conjured a picture of Rekasi's face.

He would not have such an innocently inquisitive look on his face if he saw her now. He would be angry. She pushed the thought from her mind. This was not about him. She had to make a decision. Did she want to leave? Sammaria took another step out from the gate and then another. Were they dangerous? What about her people? What about her country?

She grabbed the gate in a final decision. She pulled it back toward the fence. Quietly, she closed herself back inside her prison.

Rekasi let out a sigh of relief. The adrenaline that had been rushing through his system quieted. He looked out across the field from the shadow of his balcony. His heart had almost stopped when she had seen the gate. It was well hidden, but she had seen through his spell. Rekasi watched a while longer as Sammaria moved back toward the castle entrance. He could see tears glistening in her eyes. Remorse ripped through Rekasi's chest. Her stark defiance had been hiding her pain. He left his vantage point as she disappeared into the building.

Sammaria sat down on a windowsill and pulled her legs up to her chest. From where she was sitting, she could not see the gate. Everyone continued to go about their daily chores. She did not question her decision. She focused on nothing but the gate. A woman's voice startled her.

"Hello? Hello!"

Sammaria jumped, turning toward the woman.

The woman placed a gentle hand on Sammaria's shoulder, and in a calm voice said, "My name is Sundrie. Sundrie Clipar."

Sammaria smiled, "I'm Sammaria. Just Sammaria."

Sundrie smiled, "Well, Just Sammaria, you are in awful need of a bath. Did you know?"

Sammaria laughed, "I figured."

"Would you like to accompany me to the bath chambers?"

Sammaria looked down, "Yes, please."

Sammaria opened the door to her rooms to find Antien looking stricken. Sammaria asked, "What are you doing here?"

Antien stepped back. He said, "I was going to keep you company. What are you doing?"

Sammaria said, "I am free to wander as long as I'm back by the seventh hour past high noon."

Antien asked, "I was going to show you something."

"What?" Sammaria asked somewhat warily.

Antien said, "Well, I thought you would be excited. But if you would rather stay here…"

Sammaria said, "I'm sorry."

She rubbed her head, "I just don't know where my head is. I am very confused."

Antien said, "I have something that will help with that." He grabbed her arm, "Come with me."

Antien led her out of her room and up the hallway. Sammaria said, "Where are you taking me? Is this supposed to be an apology? You still have not answered my questions."

Antien ignored the jab. He said, "It is a surprise. You will love it."

He stopped as the room opened up. The birds fluttered around the different levels of the mountain castle. Antien dropped her hand and gestured toward it. Sammaria looked at it. She said, "I have seen this already."

Antien's face fell. He said defensively, "You do not seem very impressed."

Sammaria shrugged, gesturing at the birds, "I just feel like *them*."

Antien clung to the netting around the ledge. He tapped his foot for a second, "Follow me."

He started down a path that led through the netting. Sammaria watched him go. He turned, "Come on. You will like this, I promise."

She reluctantly followed him. They walked along the path and down a spiral staircase. He led her to a small door in the larger than life enclosure. Antien unlatched the door and held it open.

Sammaria stared at him. He said hesitantly, "Are you coming?"

Sammaria stepped into the aviary cage. Antien pulled the door closed behind her. Sammaria grabbed a handful of seeds from the supply near the door and spilled them on the ground. The white birds that flocked around the enclosure hopped around her feet and pecked at the scattered treats. She smiled.

Sammaria looked up at the levels of the castle that rose through the mountain. A ray of light shown up where the birds could enter and exit. Sitting in a tiny alcove was a medium-sized bird with black feathers. Its head was covered in a black helmet with yellow eyering and a barred stomach. Sammaria's breath caught.

She saw Antien smile. He held out something wrapped in a cloth. Sammaria said, "You knew it was here."

He nodded. She unwrapped the cloth to show a cooked piece of meat. She frowned. It was not as good as raw, but it would have to do.

She glanced at Antien. He stepped out of the gate and closed it. She waved the meat and clicked her tongue at the shadow in the corner. She said, "Come on beautiful. You have to be hungry."

The falcon preened its feathers but largely ignored her. Sammaria clicked her tongue and held out the food again. The bird let out one note of annoyed chatter.

One of the little white birds jumped onto her wrist and pecked at the meat. Sammaria dropped it surprised. She said, "Alright. Take it, you little devils."

She sucked on the wound left by the little bird. A group fought over the cube of meat. Sammaria shook her head and glared up at the stubborn bird.

"I could have told you not to bother with it."

Sammaria looked up at the level above her. She pulled her fingers from her mouth. Rekasi was looking down at her and Antien as he passed with Prime Minister Hamwich.

Olo bowed to her. She wiped her hands on her skirt, leaving a small trail of blood. She said, "My lord…"

Rekasi said, "He was here when we moved in. But no one has been able to bring him down. There is a reason he is called Asravi."

"Elusive…" Sammaria translated.

She saw Antien frowning at the man on the balcony. She said, looking at the bird, "Maybe he just does not know who he can trust."

Rekasi regarded her for a moment. He leaned against the railing, "Trust is a rare commodity."

Sammaria said looking back at the bird, "Let's hope we are worthy of it."

CHAPTER XV

Sammaria opened her door and found Antien stood there looking frustrated. He asked, "Where were you?" Sammaria said, "I was looking for the falcon." Antien sighed, "You and that bird. It is not Nyma. He will never be Nyma."

Sammaria looked down at her hands. She said, "I know. But Asravi does not have to be alone."

Antien sighed, "Come with me. You are just in time to go with me to training"

Sammaria smiled, "What type of training?"

Antien replied, "All kinds. Sword, fists, archery, and Rekasi has a select few whom he teaches something. I'm not sure what it is, though."

Sammaria nodded as he led her into a part of the castle she had not been yet.

The third floor contained a hall three times larger than the castle's main entrance hall. The ceiling was well over two hundred feet above them. Grunts and the clang of metal echoed off the walls. The smell of sweat burned in Sammaria's nose. Around her were padded floors where people practiced with blunt blades and wooden staves.

Antien led her across the room where he picked up a large knife. Sammaria asked, "What do you use that for?"

Antien looked at her and then threw it at a target. It hit dead center, "For throwing."

Sammaria asked, as she picked up one of the knives, "Isn't that what they use daggers for?"

Antien replied, "Yes, well these knives are usually used for hunting, but they are a lot easier to throw and deadly accurate."

Sammaria looked at the target. It was the outline of an O'rult. Antien's knife stuck in its stomach. Sammaria asked, "Could I try?"

Antien hesitated, "I'm not sure. It's not proper."

Sammaria looked at him, eyes flashing, "We are in a castle where I am being held captive, surrounded by hundreds of men and women training for war, and you are worried about what is proper?"

Antien rubbed his face, "Perhaps we should have you try archery."

She rolled her eyes. He handed her a longbow. Though unsure of her ability, she held the bow confidently. Carefully, Sammaria nocked an arrow. She pulled the bowstring back, using her chin as an anchor. With a twang, the bowstring snapped forward, and the arrow flew toward the target. The arrow struck just outside the center.

Antien clapped, "What? How did you do that? I thought you didn't know what you were doing?"

Sammaria shrugged, "I am good at hitting targets."

When she did not supply anymore, Antien said, "Here I thought I was the only person training you in weaponry."

Sammaria looked at him, "I had to find someone who wasn't so worried about propriety." Sammaria shot another arrow. It hit even closer to the center of the target than the first.

Antien asked, with a hint of sarcasm, "Can you fight as well?"

Sammaria retorted, "You know I can."

Antien laughed, "I am just trying to figure out what all you learned that I did not teach you."

Antien took her to a secluded corner of the hall and handed her a light sword. She hefted it in her hand a couple times. She crouched slightly. It was as if she were acting on instinct.

Antien said, "All right. Just block my blows. Don't attack."

Sammaria nodded, ready. Antien lunged toward her. She knocked his sword aside easily. He came at her from above. Sammaria was able to bring the sword up and grab Antien's wrist. He looked surprised as he prepared for his next blow.

Sammaria tensed, ready for him. She watched the muscles in his chest and arms twitch to predict his next move. Antien noticed her focus. Antien performed a complicated series of movements. She blocked them expertly.

Antien stopped, panting. Sammaria wiped the sweat from her brow. He said, "How in Kiro? Where'd you learn that then?"

Sammaria frowned, "You're angry? I watched the boys in the practice fields every day."

Antien said, "Well, I know *that*! I just thought my agreeing to train you stopped you from those foolish antics."

Sammaria eyed him, "You know I am a quick study. Plus, I found fencing diagrams. You'd be surprised how detailed they can be."

Antien shook his head, the anger draining him of his energy, "How much did you learn?"

Sammaria replied, "I don't know. Just whatever you taught me. Plus what I observed. I think the boys were intermediate level."

Antien laughed, "Right. Intermediate. I wonder…"

Sammaria was not paying attention. She was scanning the room, watching the other people train, some as young as eleven and others as old as eighty. Her eyes fell on a large Poccuottawan. His almond eyes tightened as he launched his next attack. Sammaria gasped as the man beat his opponent down. The man surrendered. The Poccuottawan looked around the room, his mouth set in a permanent scowl.

Sammaria looked back at Antien nervously. She asked, "Who is that?"

Antien said, "That's Simchu. He lives for each spar."

Simchu's eyes lighted on Sammaria. He looked down at the sword in her hand. He pointed at her, "You! Come fight me."

Sammaria shook her head. Antien pushed her forward, "Just try. It can't be that bad."

"You saw what he did to that other man."

He shrugged, "It was one fight."

She glared at him for a second before stepping into the fighting ring.

Her sword felt awkward in her hand. Antien said, "All normal sparring rules."

A few people came over to watch. Simchu jumped, loosening his muscles. Sammaria tensed, "And those are?"

Simchu laughed, winking at the girls surrounding the ring.

Antien replied, "No drawing blood, no killing, and no attacking an unarmed opponent."

Sammaria nodded nervously. She held the sword ready. Sweat formed on her upper lip. Simchu let out a cry as he lunged toward Sammaria. She barely parried the blow in time.

Simchu smiled and winked at her, "This is going to be easy."

Sammaria raised her eyebrows. Stubbornness set in her jaw, and a line of deep concentration appeared on her brow. Sammaria blocked Simchu's blows, taking them one at a time. She was able to adapt quicker than Antien thought possible.

She fought until she found an opening. She lunged at Simchu. He stumbled, blocking her blow.

Sammaria kept the blows and parries going. She had watched her father perform these exact moves against the training master in Mestchester. Simchu could not keep the surprise from his face. With a move that twisted the sword of the opponent's hand, Sammaria disarmed him.

She bowed to him, adrenaline coursing through her body and blood pounding in her ears. She turned to exit the ring. Someone reached for her sword. She smiled as she handed it to him, rejoicing in her small victory.

A collective gasp rang from the crowd. She whipped around, her skirts billowing around her.

Simchu lunged at her. She jumped out of the way. Tripping as she moved, she heard the whistling of the sword past her head. The sword crashed down where her head had been moments before.

Adrenaline continued to pump through her system, driving her. She slid to her feet as Simchu attacked her again. She jumped out of the way yelling, "Somebody stop this!"

Sammaria ducked, leaving the sword to whistle where her neck would have been. She demanded, "Antien!"

Antien said, "He is one of the best fighters here. I can't best him."

Sammaria jumped out of the sword's path. Heat rolled through her body. It seemed to fill every part of her. She gasped as she tried to hold it in.

Her face settled into a grim scowl. Sweat poured from her every pore, "Well, I can!"

Power coursed within her. She pushed back against it with every ounce of strength she had. It fought her, wanting to escape. Dodging out of the way she yelled, "Give me my sword!"

It was held out to her. She gripped its hilt and whipped it up to block Simchu's attack.

Simchu smiled maliciously, "Back for more? You are stronger than I thought."

Sammaria pulled her sword from his. They circled each other.

She smiled sweetly, "Funny! I was just about to say the same thing!"

Simchu grimaced and swept his sword at her legs. Her skirts blocked his attack. The sword ripped through the fabric, leaving Sammaria more room to move. Antien turned away for a moment, realizing the impropriety.

Sammaria prepped for Simchu's next move. He grunted as he lunged. Sammaria redirected the blow, tearing more fabric from her dress. Her pale thigh bled where the sword had scratched it.

As a trickle of blood ran down her leg, her Power leapt inside her. It fought against her limbs, threatening to break loose. Sammaria fought against it. She pushed all that strength against Simchu. She smacked his wrist with her sword, once again disarming him.

Panting, she said, "This time follow the rules."

She dropped her sword, letting it clatter to the floor. She turned from Simchu and started to exit the circle.

Simchu yelled. She whirled around. Simchu once more lunged for her.

Fire burst from her hands and swirled around him in the shape of a falcon.

Frightened, Simchu dropped to the ground before any harm could come to him. Sammaria called the flame back to her. She frantically looked around. People looked at her in fear. She pulled on it faster.

It soared one more time around the people's heads before vanishing into her hands.

When the last spark was beneath her skin, she collapsed. She tried to hold herself up, but her arms kept giving out.

Antien knelt beside her. He cradled her. She looked up with glassy eyes.

He said, "Sammaria! Stay with me!"

She looked at him, "What?"

The crowd parted silently. Sammaria did not notice. She was so tired. Her eyelids drooped. She popped them back open with a yawn.

Rekasi kneeled before her. He looked at her eyes. She blinked rapidly. "When'd you get here?" she asked, "I could have used you earlier."

Rekasi replied, "Sorry, I was detained. Antien! Help me pick her up."

Sammaria protested as they started to lift her. She barely heard the argument between Antien and Rekasi about who should carry her.

Rekasi's hand brushed her thigh as he lifted her. A jolt of energy raced up her leg, and she suddenly became alert to her surroundings. She fought him, "I can walk!"

Rekasi cradled her, "I'd rather not risk that."

She nodded, closing her eyes once more.

Rekasi shook her. He said, "Come on, Sammaria. You can't fall asleep on me."

Sammaria could hear a faint tinge of panic in Rekasi's voice. It did not register in her mind. She needed to sleep.

Rekasi insisted, "Don't sleep!"

She let her eyelids slide closed, "I'm just going to rest my eyes."

Rekasi shook her as he ran down the hallway. "Don't fall asleep, Sammaria. Come on. We're almost there."

Sammaria's head bounced against Rekasi's chest as they ran down the stairs. His breathing was loud in her ears. It meant nothing to her.

She could faintly hear the babbling of a stream. She wanted to ask what it was, but it did not seem important at the moment.

She clung to Rekasi. His body was so warm where it pressed against hers. It lulled her like a cradle. Rekasi looked down at her as her eyes slid closed once more. Rekasi shook her, "Wake up!"

Her eyes popped open for just a moment. He pinched her arm. She woke up, "Just let me sleep!"

Rekasi replied, "No! I can't! Come on, Sammaria. Stay awake. I know you can do this!"

She shook her head. Rekasi reached the edge of the walkway. The river ran slowly through the cavern. Sammaria's eyes slid shut again. Rekasi dropped her into the stream.

CHAPTER XVI

Sammaria splashed into the river. She floated on the surface for just a moment. Her ruined skirts dragged her to the bottom of the stream.

Her eyes snapped open. Her lungs burned. She planted her feet on the streambed and pushed to the surface. She coughed water from her lungs. Her entire body burned.

She wrapped her arms around herself. A chill set into her bones. Sammaria waded to the bank where a stern figure met her.

She looked up to Rekasi's stoic face and flinched. Rekasi glared at her, "That was incredibly stupid. I hope you know that! You could have killed yourself. You should never pull in your Flame."

Sammaria said defiantly, "I've done it a thousand times! I've never lost control like that before."

Her words echoed off the rocks surrounding her. She heard how childish they sounded.

Rekasi replied, "You almost killed yourself, Sammaria."

Sammaria looked up at him her eyes blazing, "Then why didn't you let me die?"

Rekasi flinched. Sammaria glared at him. He left.

Salty tears rolled down Sammaria's face. A hand gently touched her shoulder. Antien helped her from the pool. He asked, "Have you been hurt?"

New tears fell. Antien led her from the stream back to her rooms. He opened her door.

She stood in the doorway and felt like crying. She could not show such weakness in front of Antien. She turned to him and said, "I'm just going to go to bed."

Antien said, "Of course. Feel better."

Sammaria objected, painting a painful smile on her face, "I feel fine."

Antien gave her a knowing look.

Her false smile broke. "I'll try," she promised.

He nodded, "That's all I ask."

Hours later, a knock sounded at her door. Rekasi entered at her words of welcome. Her hands moved absently in complex patterns that Rekasi did not understand. "You are to start training."

He noted how, when he started speaking, her hands hesitated and shook for a moment before smoothly returning to the pattern. Sammaria looked up, her face like a ghost. She asked wearily, "For what?"

Rekasi replied, "To control your Power."

Sammaria shook her head, hands falling into her lap, "I don't have any Power."

She stood up and turned away from him. Rekasi said, "You do. I knew the moment I met you. You have the aura."

Sammaria watched his eyes. As they arrived at her waist, curving to her hips, a blush spread across his cheeks. He turned away, "You will meet me tomorrow in Ellington Hall at an hour past high noon."

Sammaria nodded and turned away from him. Rekasi looked at her and opened her door. He said quietly, "I am sorry for how I have acted. If you still have questions, I will answer them for you."

Sammaria looked after him mournfully as the door closed behind him.

Her chest ached. She whispered, "Kiro! When will this pain stop?"

Sammaria sighed as she lay back on her bed. She knew she would have to go to this training with Rekasi, but she was *not* looking forward to it.

The next day she slipped out of her room to find Ellington Hall. She moved down the hallways, hopelessly lost. When she saw Sundrie, she sighed with relief. Sammaria asked, "Sundrie, where's Ellington Hall?"

Sundrie smiled, her eyes crinkling at the corners. She pointed down the hall, "Take a left and go down the stairs."

Sammaria thanked Sundrie with a kiss. She shivered despite the warmth coming from the row of braziers lining the hallways. She pushed the door at the bottom of the stairs open, afraid of what she might find.

There were six people she did not recognize in the room. One watched her enter. He approached her, "Hello, Your Highness. I am Dakota Silentread. It is so grand to meet you."

Sammaria smiled. She hoped it did not look as false as it felt. Sammaria replied, "It is good to meet you as well, but please call me Sammaria."

Dakota replied, "If you don't mind me asking, which Power do you control?"

Sammaria frowned as she replied, "Fire."

Dakota smiled, "Very powerful. I'm sorry, Sammaria. Did I offend you?"

Sammaria shook her head mystified by this entire conversation, "No. I've just been hiding my Power for so long, it's … strange speaking so openly about it."

Dakota nodded, understanding. He told her, "I control Water."

Sammaria smiled, "Jennica has that ability as well."

Dakota jolted, "You and Jennica are *both* Elementals? That's unheard of. Usually, only one person every few generations has the ability."

Sammaria gave him a confused look, "What do you mean? There has been at least one female - Elemental you called them? – in every generation of my mother's bloodline for over two centuries."

Dakota's jaw dropped, "Very uncommon indeed."

Sammaria did not have time to say anything else, for Rekasi had entered the room.

Rekasi set the others to work before walking over to Sammaria. He said, "We'll start with breathing."

Sammaria stared at him. He lifted his hands over his head. Bringing them down, he breathed in. Shooting them forward from his chest, he released the breath. "Breathing is key."

He repeated the motions and gestured for Sammaria to begin. Sammaria watched his strong hands move. She slowed her breathing to match his and began to move her arms.

Sammaria's Power responded at once. Heat spread evenly through her body. She looked up at Rekasi, shocked.

His auburn eyes caught her amber ones. Something passed between them. The anger between them dissipated.

Rekasi blinked and averted his eyes from hers. He said, "Yes – um – good! Did you feel your Power level out?"

Sammaria moved her eyes to the wall behind him and nodded.

"Now we can work on control. When you lose control of your emotions, you lose control over your Power. When you are sad or angry, your ability to control the Power shrinks. When you feel good emotions, your ability increases. Power wants to break free, so you must constantly remain under control. So, let's try something. Think of a moment in your life where you have been hurt."

Sammaria looked back at him, "You want me to make myself sad?"

Rekasi hesitated but nodded.

Sammaria thought about Jennica. She missed her so much, but she had come to live with that pain. She glanced over at Rekasi.

Was his apparent concern for her genuine or just another opportunity for him to hurt Dragonia?

That thought made her sad. She wanted to believe that he was a good person, but she remembered how she had felt the previous night. Her face burned with the memory of the tears that had dried in her sleep, "I'm ready."

Rekasi replied, "Call Fire to your hand, and feel how it moves through you."

Sammaria flicked her hand slightly. She felt the heat slowly moving through her veins like tree sap in the winter. It pulled itself from her core and legs and slowly formed into a ball in her hand. Rekasi furrowed his brow. Sammaria said, "It feels sluggish."

Rekasi nodded, "Does it feel as if it is pulling from other parts of your body?"

Sammaria nodded, "Yes."

Rekasi placed his hand over the slowly rotating ball, extinguishing it.

His hand trembled as it touched hers. Something was troubling him, "Think of nothing at all and breathe."

Rekasi reached a hand up and rubbed his forehead. He said, "Now, try to think of something that makes you happy."

Sammaria searched her memory. When had she experienced extreme happiness? She frowned, confused.

Rekasi asked, "What's wrong?"

Sammaria replied, "I can't think of any times I've been just…happy."

Rekasi looked at her, surprised. He said, "What do you mean? You have everything."

Sammaria shook her head, "Not everything. I always felt trapped. I could never let myself trust anyone, except Jennica. I never knew who was pretending. I wanted freedom."

Rekasi touched her arm. It grew warm beneath his fingers. He said, "Maybe we should stop for today."

Sammaria shook her head, "I have one memory. It might work."

She let the feeling course through her. Rekasi waited, and she nodded when she was ready. He stepped behind her and whispered into her ear, "I want you to try pulling the Fire from your core directly to your hand."

He made a complex motion with his hands. "Once the Fire has reached your hands, move your hands like this to produce a guardian. Yours is a falcon, is it not?"

Sammaria nodded. He placed his hand on her waist, "Pull from here."

Her heart pounded as she pulled the amber strands of Power from her core. They coursed through her body and pressed against her hand. She let it build up as Rekasi had commanded.

"Release it," he instructed.

She moved her hands and released the Fire. The flames took the shape of a large falcon as they leapt forward from her hands. It smashed into the wall in front of her, and the flames exploded leaving the black outline of a falcon on the stones.

Sammaria looked up at Rekasi. He smiled. Her heart thudded, and her chest tightened, making it hard to breathe. She pulled her gaze away to stare at the scorched wall. Rekasi started to say something.

The door slammed open, and Antien stormed in. Rekasi moved away from Sammaria. She stared at the mud clinging to her old friend's shoes.

She could just barely hear Antien whisper angrily, "Our attempt failed. Jennica wasn't in Mestchester. She's run away. No one knows where she is."

Rekasi muttered a curse.

Sammaria gasped quietly. She turned from where the men talked quietly. Jennica was missing? She could be anywhere.

Sammaria had not been able to speak to Jennica through their mental connection since she had been kidnapped. She could be dead for all Sammaria knew.

She tried to control her breathing. She could not be hysterical here.

Rekasi touched her shoulder. She did not turn toward him. She did not want him to see the distress on her face. He said, "We're cutting class short today. There has been a problem."

Dakota was suddenly right next to her, "I'll take her around, sir."

Rekasi nodded, distracted, "Keep track of her."

Dakota nodded. Rekasi and Antien swept out of the room. Dakota said, "Let me introduce you to some people."

Sammaria followed him nervously. She asked, "Who am I meeting?"

He smiled, "My family."

They entered the great hall. Sunlight radiated through the dome ceiling. Dakota waved to a group of women by the fountain in the southwest corner of the room.

He introduced the youngest woman. She looked to be about thirteen, with a head full of black, bouncing curls.

Dakota said, "This is my daughter, Caliet." He took the hand of a lady whose scarred face was surrounded by long strawberry, blonde hair. He said, "This is my beautiful wife, Liza." She blushed while Caliet and an elderly woman giggled. He said, "And lastly this is my mother, Mila."

Sammaria curtsied to them. Mila waved her hand, "None of that, Miss …"

Dakota said, "Oh, my mistake. This is Sammaria. Just Sammaria."

Sammaria smiled, "It's wonderful to meet you all."

Liza smiled, "You are so pale." Sammaria rubbed her neck, embarrassed. "Spend some time with me in the garden tomorrow. It'll be good for you."

Sammaria replied, "That'll be nice. I'll be there."

Liza nodded, smiling. Sammaria looked up at the ceiling.

"What's wrong?" Sammaria looked down, meeting Caliet's dark eyes. Liza scolded her daughter.

Sammaria exclaimed, "No! It's fine. You are perceptive."

Caliet shrugged. Sammaria said, "I do have a question. What happened in Mestchester? Is Princess Jennica really missing?"

Dakota looked uncomfortable while Liza and Mila exchanged concerned looks.

Dakota replied slowly, "You heard?"

Sammaria nodded, "Please. I must know."

Dakota nodded, "Princess Jennica and Lord Donichello have gone missing. Our source says that Jennica ran away. Donichello went missing after an attack."

Sammaria said, "Please excuse me." She turned from the small family and rushed from the Great Hall.

She slipped into her room and stared at the statues. She hardly noticed when the door was shoved open. As she looked up, she noted Antien's angry face. She stood up, "What's wrong?"

Antien sat down, "It's nothing."

Sammaria retorted, "It doesn't sound like nothing."

Antien looked at her, "All right, fine. That man thinks he can do as he wishes because he is in charge, but he is bad news. He's going to hurt you."

Sammaria's ears perked up, "What are you talking about?"

"Rekasi. Do you have feelings for him?"

She wrinkled her brow, "I don't know, Antien. He's nice. I don't really know him."

Antien said, "Well, you sound like you might. You shouldn't. He has a reputation. He's using you."

"What do you mean?"

Antien replied, "He's bedded half the single women here. I think you are next. What better control over the Kingdom than bedding the crown princess."

Sammaria stood indignately, "I'm insulted that you think that I would let that happen! You have gone too far, Antien."

Antien shook his head quickly, "I'm sorry, Sammaria. I let my anger run away with me. I know you would never endanger the crown."

His words weighed on her. She nodded woodenly. Antien smiled weakly, "I'll see ya' later, okay? I have to go."

Sammaria nodded again. Antien looked back as he opened the door and tapped his fingers twice before leaving.

Rekasi slipped into Sammaria's room behind Antien. She moved to her seat in the courting chair. She would not meet his eyes. Her mind kept twisting itself into knots. Could Rekasi be what Antien said?

"So, your first lesson went well."

It had not been a question. She nodded anyway, not looking at him. Sammaria asked, staring at the door, "Where's my sister?"

Rekasi sighed and shifted in his seat, "Sammaria, I really can't discuss that."

Sammaria stood up and glared down at him, "You don't know, do you?"

He grimaced under her gaze. She said quietly, "You said you'd answer my questions."

Rekasi replied calmly, "We do not have her exact location."

Sammaria rolled her eyes, "I thought you were going to keep her safe. You told me she was in danger. You said Mestchester wasn't safe. The loyalists would do anything to frame the Resistance. And you lost her. She's gone!"

"We lost many good men in that raid. They are now rotting in your father's prisons."

Sammaria gave him a dirty look, "What am I supposed to do about it?"

Rekasi retorted, "Try being a little grateful. They risked their lives to save hers. To save you."

Sammaria looked up, shocked. She had not thought about the men who were captured when she was taken.

Rekasi said more gently, "The people of Dragonia are still loyal to you and your sister. They have been moving her safely across the countryside, deflecting your father's troops. We will receive word soon enough."

Sammaria shook her head, "I doubt that even *she* knows where she is."

※

Jennica looked up at the sky. The clouds just kept floating past. She stared ahead. A rock had fallen in the river, acting as a bridge. The forest across the river looked lighter than the one in which she stood. Thoughts rushed through her head, many of them making no sense. Finally, she decided that the other side could not be any worse than where she was. She took a step toward the bridge. She felt a presence in her mind that she had not heard in a long time. It shouted of sorrow stronger than Jennica had ever felt. She stepped on the bridge. Within her mind, she yelled, "Sammaria! Sammaria! Please, show me where you are!"

Jennica waited for the answer, listening hard for any sign. She did not hear the bridge cracking before it gave way beneath her feet. She fell, crashing into the water. A broken piece of the rock caught part of her tunic. She yanked against it. Opening her eyes, all she could see was the murky water surrounding her. She pulled harder on her tunic and felt it begin to tear. She pulled once more, ripping it free.

She pushed off the bottom of the river and kicked to the surface. As she crawled onto the bank, gasping, she felt something hit her. It surrounded her, knocking the wind from her. A weight sat on her chest. She opened her eyes, seeing nothing. The heat and thrill of Power suffocated her.

She stood, the Power receding to the flickering flame that was Sammaria's mind. Jennica jumped into the air. "Yes!"

Sammaria was alive. Jennica had a trail to follow.

Someone shouted her name. Jennica stopped. She looked around, but she saw no one. Still, she had distinctly heard her name. She shrunk back into the cover of the trees.

A boy wandered past, calling her name. She did not move. She relaxed, but her heart still pounded with fading fear.

The child stopped. He turned in a circle. He cocked his head to where she crouched. He smiled, "I have food and shelter for you, Princess. Please, stop hiding."

Jennica thought of sleeping next to a warm fire. It had been days since she had had any comfort. She had been on the run, hiding from her father's troops, for three weeks now. Her stomach growled – traitorous as it was – as she thought of a home-cooked meal.

The boy said, "Please. We mean you no harm."

Jennica crawled out from the shadows. The boy's face lit up. He ran toward her saying, "My name is Alejo."

The boy grabbed her hand and began leading her away from the trees. He kept up a continuous stream of chatter, "I live in Drannor. Well, not anymore. My family and I left because my father's friend was killed. My brothers, Anaranjo and Lunen, are apprenticing with masters so they had to stay."

Alejo led her out of the trees to a small group of cottages. He opened the door to one that had a quilt hanging in the window.

Jennica stared at the quilt. The symbols sewn onto it were entirely random but seemed to make a pattern. There was a sleeping dragon at the base of an elkmole tree.

She stopped the boy, "Alejo. What is that quilt? What does it mean?"

He looked around nervously and hurried her inside. "You'll have to ask Mother. I'm not supposed to talk about it."

He whispered, "Mother? I found her."

The house was small. There was a common room just inside the door, a small kitchen that stood adjacent divided by an arching doorway, and a bedroom divided by a curtain. A short woman came from the kitchen. In a calm and motherly voice, she greeted Jennica, "Welcome. We have been expecting you."

"You have?" Jennica asked in disbelief.

"Of course," the woman said, "Rekasi passed through here weeks ago. We heard you had run away. We figured you were following her. It was only a matter of time before you stumbled across our path. I sent Alejo out every day to watch."

Jennica swayed. The woman exclaimed, "How rude of me! Please, sit down! You must be exhausted."

Alejo pulled up a stool next to the fire. Jennica collapsed gratefully onto it. The woman said, "My name is Penelupe. Here, have some bread and stew."

Jennica took the food gratefully and began to eat.

Penelupe said, "You asked about my quilt?"

Jennica swallowed, "Yes. The design. I think I've seen it before… but I don't know where."

She said, "Your Highness, can you keep a secret?"

Jennica nodded. Penelupe said, "The quilt is a message for the Resistance, and to you, and for all seeking protection from the King. It says 'this house is safe.' We will provide food and shelter. It gives directions to the next safe house. All one must do is find the next quilt like mine to find shelter."

Jennica stared at Penelupe, surprised. The woman showed her what each symbol meant: the sleeping dragon, the constellations, the Elkmole tree, the wreath of berries. Jennica had seen several quilts like this hanging in windows across the countryside as well as one laid out in the palace.

When she had walked into the room where the maids were sewing it, they stopped talking and stowed their work. It had seemed odd at the time, but now it made sense.

Penelupe said, "I will let you sleep now."

She took the bowl from Jennica and laid a pallet down for her in front of the fire. Jennica thanked the woman and her son for their kindness and quickly fell asleep.

CHAPTER XVII

The rain caught Sammaria by surprise. She let out a laugh. Sundrie tutted. She grabbed her rake and ran inside. Mila ran inside the mountain palace flanked by the other garden workers.

Sammaria took a bit longer to gather her tools. She let the rain fall against her hot skin. It left little trails of steam as it hit her.

She glanced up. There was a small secluded cavity in the rock. She frowned. It looked like the balcony would be located right outside the library. If she looked, she was certain she could find it. She smiled. It would be a nice spot to watch the storm.

Sundrie called, "Sammaria! Hurry up. You will melt with the soil."

Sammaria looked down. The garden plot had already turned to a thick sludge sucking at her feet. She pulled free and ran toward the entrance. Mila handed her a towel. Sammaria thanked her and dried her hair. She sat, wiping the mud from her legs.

Mila said, "Sundrie? Sammaria? Would you like to come over for a cup of tea?"

Sundrie shook out her hair. She said, "That sounds lovely."

Sammaria hesitated for a moment. The two looked at her expectantly. She said, "You ladies go ahead. I want to spend some time in the library this afternoon."

Sundrie said, "Just make sure you take care to warm yourself. I do not want to see you in the infirmary tomorrow with a cold."

Sammaria promised she would read by the fireside. This pleased Sundrie and Mila. They left, already discussing other topics.

Sammaria took the path opposite of them, keeping her eyes peeled for signs of the hidden ledge. She pushed open the door to the library. The vanilla smell of old pages greeted her. She quietly closed the door behind her. The walls of books silently stared back at her watchful gaze.

Sammaria tried to orient herself to the garden. She crossed the room to the large window. She looked out. Rain pattered against the glass. The garden plot was at the far end of the field. When Sammaria had looked up, the ledge had been to the right of the window. Sammaria looked to her left.

A staircase led to a second story of books. There were only a couple of shelves. A large tapestry covered the wall at the top of the stairs. Sammaria eyed it. It showed a dark-eyed woman holding a flower in both her hands. A man in the background seemed to be stepping through a door. He looked back at her.

Sammaria was unfamiliar with the story, but something about it drew her eye. She climbed the staircase to look at it closer. Sammaria reached up to touch the white flower. The tapestry wavered behind her touch.

Sammaria smiled her, pulse quickening. She quickly pushed the wall hanging aside. An alcove, ending with a door, sat behind it. Sammaria walked forward, letting the tapestry fall behind her. She pushed open the door, anticipation bubbling.

The sound of rain hitting stone caught her attention immediately. She let the noise sink in for a moment. Her heart ached. She missed her sister so much. It all came crashing in on her at that moment. If she could just reach her. Sammaria reached out with her link. There was nothing. Not even a hint of her.

Movement caught her eye. She jumped back from the door startled. The balcony was occupied. Rekasi turned from the tall backed chair he was sitting in. It had completely hidden him until he had moved. Their eyes met. Sammaria looked away, "Um…sorry..uh – sir."

Rekasi raised his eyebrows at her. She continued, "I did not know anyone would be up here. I will leave you alone."

She moved to close the door. Rekasi stood, "Please, Your Highness."

His eyes shone in a slightly mocking manner, "Join me." They turned sincere, "If you want."

He gestured for her to take a seat in the chair next to his. She sat and looked away from him. She rubbed her chilled arms. A crack of thunder rolled across the sky. Sammaria jumped and let out a startled gasp.

Rekasi chuckled, "I suppose the storms are a bit more intense here then what you are used to."

Sammaria leaned back in her chair. She nodded, "I always thought people were too worried when Jennica wanted to go out in the storms. Now I see why."

She shivered again.

Rekasi said, "Here."

He pulled a low brazier between them. He leaned over it and blew on the coals. Heat flared up, warming Sammaria's legs. She sighed as it warmed her. She smiled at him, "Thank you."

They both looked out at the field below and watched the rainfall.

Rekasi said, "Storms were thought to bring blessings where I grew up."

Sammaria held her hands out to the heat. She said, "Hmm? Where was that?"

Rekasi looked out as the lightning flashed, "Gabvand."

Sammaria dropped her hands and stared at him. The following thunder caused her to jump slightly.

Rekasi said, still looking out at the gardens, "I came here as a child with the refugees who made it through."

Sammaria said, "Before…"

The words unsaid hung in the air. Rekasi said, "I have seen what poor leadership has done to a country. Done to a people."

Sammaria watched his face, scarcely daring to breathe. He looked at her, his auburn eyes fierce, "I won't let it happen again."

He turned his gaze back out to the field. He set his hand on the chair arm. Sammaria turned her eyes back to the field as well. The same fire burned within her.

Dragonia was her country. It was hers to protect. Rekasi was not what it needed protection from.

The lightning flashed again. A loud burst of thunder followed. Sammaria jumped and grabbed at the chair arms. Her hand clutched hot flesh.

She looked down. Her hand was clasped around Rekasi's. He looked at her, surprised.

She let go, equally surprised, and stood up.

Rekasi said, mirroring her, "Your Highness?"

Sammaria said, "I should go. I told Mila I would help her with the mending."

She spun to leave, her cheeks coloring. Rekasi caught her hand. He held it respectfully. He bowed, pressing his lips to the back of her hand. He looked up at her, "Your Highness."

Color rose in Sammaria's cheeks. She turned and rushed from the balcony.

She ran to the first level and entered into the aviary. Asravi had been starting to show interest in her. He would eat food that she brought him. He was starting to let her get close.

Sammaria sat down on the steps. Her mind whirled. She could feel the ghost of his lips on her hand. Sammaria shook her head. Rekasi was the enemy. He was trying to seduce her.

But if that were true, why did he tell her about his childhood? He was trying to gain her sympathy. It wasn't going to work. Still, he had seemed so sincere. No hint of deceit. No hidden agenda.

Sammaria looked up, watching the white birds flock around the aviary chittering. She saw Asravi in his normal nook. He cawed at her. She smiled. He was waiting for her.

Sammaria pulled a handkerchief from her pocket. She pushed all thoughts from her head. There was no need to confuse the falcon with her turmoil. She held out the raw meat. The falcon let out another note. It fluttered down to the ledge that Sammaria typically set the meat on. She stayed very still. This was the closest Asravi had come to her.

He cawed at her. She set the handkerchief down where she was. It was a short distance from him. He ruffled his feathers and hopped away as she moved. He did not fly away. She backed up two steps. Asravi hopped forward and pecked at the meat.

A smile spread across her face. The bird ripped the meat from the handkerchief and flew to a safe distance to eat it. Sammaria grinned at the beautiful creature. She said, "I will see you tomorrow."

Alejo led Jennica through the forest. He told her about his brother and their friend Demetria. Jennica was surprised that the Resistance had caused so much damage. She was surprised that these people still trusted them.

Alejo and his mother had been sent to the countryside for protection. They had moved in with Alejo's aunt. Alejo said, "When we moved out here, Mama joined the Resistance with her sister."

Jennica stopped and stared, "Why would they do that? After everything? What about Demetria's father?"

Alejo frowned at her, "They joined the Resistance because of that."

Jennica said, "But they killed him."

Alejo said confused, "No…The royal troops did. They came through looking for you."

His face and his voice held no accusation, but Jennica felt it all the same.

Alejo continued, "The Resistance has done nothing but protect us. Even before. They have always protected us."

Jennica stopped him, "What do you mean?"

Alejo skipped along. He looked sidelong at her. He said, "Mama is a magic user."

Jennica stared. He said, "The Resistance helped train her. They helped her stay safe from magic hunters."

Jennica looked at her hands. She had heard rumor that the Resistance was hiding magic users. Her father had always said that magic users were gathering against him. Jennica felt the danger of holding the same Power. Still, she felt secure in her privilege. She never truly thought her life would be in danger if her secret were to be discovered.

Alejo looked back at her. He said, "Come on. It isn't much further."

⚘

Sammaria tucked a bit of meat into her napkin. Antien frowned at her, but he said nothing. Sammaria finished her food quickly. She washed her dishes and returned them to the storage area.

Sammaria took her bundled meal and hustled down the corridor. She looked into her napkin, taking stock. She had a pink piece of meat and a fatty edge. Nyma had loved the fatty edges. Hopefully, Asravi had the same taste for it.

Sammaria glanced up. Rekasi closed the door to the aviary behind him. He said, "Your Highness."

He bowed. He was still continuing his formal act outside of training.

Sammaria frowned, "I wish you would stop that."

Rekasi frowned, "I thought your title would make you feel more comfortable."

Sammaria said, "No one else goes by a title here."

Rekasi said, "No one else has a title here."

Sammaria said, "Neither do I. I'm just Sammaria."

Rekasi smiled at her. He asked, gesturing to her hands, "What do you have there?"

Sammaria looked down at the handkerchief. Grease had begun to seep through. She gestured to the aviary, "It's for Asravi. I have been bringing him scraps the past few weeks."

Rekasi asked, "Is it working? I haven't seen him any more than normal."

Sammaria said, "I think so. He seems to be warming up to me."

Rekasi smiled, "Well, don't let me get in the way."

Sammaria said, "Come with me. He should get used to more people." She transferred the food into his hands and opened the door. She clicked her tongue. The falcon cawed from his perch. Sammaria said, "Seems like he doesn't know what to make of you."

Rekasi said, "Should I leave?"

Sammaria shook her head, "He should recognize you because you handle the other birds. He is just uncertain."

Sammaria unfolded the cloth in Rekasi's hand, "Here. Put the food on that ledge, and come sit over here."

He set the food where she had indicated. She patted the step for him to sit next to her. He asked, "Now what?"

She pressed a finger to her lips. She whispered, "Now we wait. Asravi will see you are not a threat to his food. And he will come for it."

The falcon squawked. He preened himself from the upper ledge. Rekasi asked, "How long does it take?"

Sammaria said, "Depends on the animal. Depends on the people."

Rekasi asked, "Does he come quickly for you?"

Sammaria looked at him, "He is starting to. He does not know what to make of your presence."

Rekasi said, "I don't want to ruin your progress."

Sammaria shook her head, "Just wait. Watch."

She turned back to watch the bird. She could feel Rekasi sitting so close to her on the step at the entrance of the aviary. The little white birds pecked the ground around their feet. Heat rolled off his skin onto her. She tried to breathe normally.

Asravi fluffed his feathers. He bounced down onto a lower ledge. She heard Rekasi catch his breath. The bird watched the two of them with his large eyes. He crowed again.

Asravi took flight. He soared around the chamber and landed on the handkerchief. Asravi grabbed at the fatty meat, tossing it up and swallowed it.

Sammaria said quietly, "Animals sense more than we do."

Rekasi looked over at her. He said, "I always believed that."

Sammaria said, "Nyma was always my loyal guardian. She would know who I trusted. Who I didn't. And even then who I should trust."

Asravi pecked at the next piece. They were quiet for a moment. Rekasi said, "When I was a kid, my mother told me that animals could see into your soul."

Sammaria said, "Brother Orlten said that the Draigar believed something similar. Not just that they saw your soul. They believed each person had an animal – a guardian – who *was* their soul."

Asravi chortled happily. He pulled at the handkerchief, shredding the fabric. Rekasi stood to protest. The falcon took flight, cawing.

Sammaria said, "It is fine. He does that every so often when he wants more."

Rekasi pulled one from his pocket. He pressed it to her hand, "Take mine. Maybe you can get the ungrateful creature to come to you."

Sammaria smiled. She felt the heat of his hand beneath the handkerchief pressed between them. He dropped his hand and nodded at her as he left.

Jennica looked up to the sky. She stretched her back. Alejo had left her at the edge of the forest a couple of hours before. He had told her to keep the sun on her back. The clouds were out, but she could see the light faintly. Alejo had told her to keep an eye out for the quilts. Not all would be as prominently displayed as theirs.

Jennica took a sip of the water from the canteen Penelupe had sent with her. She capped the bottle and continued down the path. Drizzle fell around her. Jennica sighed and closed her eyes. She reached out curiously with her Power. She did not expect to find anything.

There was a sharp tugging in her body. It pulled her off the path. Jennica fell into the ditch. She clutched her stomach. She grabbed at the ground trying to steady herself. Nothing helped. Soon, the vision overtook her.

A blonde girl stabbed a tree covered in lotus flowers. Power flowed from her. People around her fell. She looked toward Jennica and her skin turned dark.

Sammaria called a falcon to her hand. The animal cawed and flapped its wings. The shadow on the wall morphed into a giant fiery animal.

Jennica was chained to a wall. She whispered weakly.

That man, Rekasi, faced a girl with raven hair. She bowed to him.

Donichello stood before a man with eyes that stared back at him.

Jennica curled into a ball, breathing heavily. She clutched her head. Her Power pulled at her in two different directions.

One pulled strongly toward the east, back toward Mestchester. The other pulled at her faintly toward the Kilhatea Mountains. Jennica reached out. She whispered her sister's name. The thread leading her to the mountains faded. The pain faded with it.

Jennica sat up and looked down the path in which the Power flowed. It led her back into the woods in a different direction than she had come. She stood. Sammaria was that way. She could feel it. Jennica grabbed the tether and walked toward it.

⚜

Sammaria held out a piece of meat in a handkerchief. Rekasi's family crest was visible on the edge. Sammaria looked up. Asravi was looking down at her. He made clicking noises with his beak.

Sammaria clicked her tongue at him. She spread seed across the ground. The white birds began fighting over the treats. Sammaria clicked her tongue again, holding the food up to the falcon.

Asravi chirped. He took flight and circled the chamber. Sammaria stayed still. Asravi fluttered down onto Sammaria's wrist. Talons dug into her skin. She winced. She had always used leather gloves when training Nyma. That was until Nyma learned to control her strength. Sammaria did not have those here. Blood welled up under the handkerchief. Asravi snapped at the meat in her hand. He gobbled it down.

Sammaria brought him closer. She hesitantly stroked the feathers on his back. He stopped for a moment then continued devouring his food.

Sammaria smiled. She held out her other hand and clicked her tongue. Asravi looked at her with one black eye. He reluctantly walked over to her other hand. He swallowed the meat.

Sammaria clutched the greasy handkerchief around her hand. She lifted her hand and pushed. Asravi took flight. He flew around the aviary, startling the little white birds still pecking at seeds on the ground.

Sammaria wrapped the handkerchief tighter around the talon marks. Small pricks of blood appeared on the white cloth. She held out her hand again and clicked her tongue.

Asravi was slower this time. He landed on her hand and nuzzled her fingers, looking for a treat. Sammaria stroked the bird's stomach and looked into its eyes. He stared back at her, knowingly.

CHAPTER XVIII

Sammaria looked up as Rekasi entered her room. She sat on one side of the courting chair, her knees tucked up against her chest. Her eyes flickered toward him and back to the wall. "Sammaria, I have good news for you."

She shifted to look at him, frowning, "Yes?"

"News has come from one of our safe houses. Jennica has been found. She is safe and well."

A smile spread across her face, but it retreated quickly. Rekasi moved over to her with a confused look painting his face. He brushed her hand, "She is heading this direction, Sammaria. She is looking for you."

Sammaria regarded him with fire in her eyes, "But she won't find me, will she? You're going to keep me hidden. You're going to take her too."

Rekasi pulled his hand away from hers, "Where is this coming from?"

Sammaria shook her head back and forth and looked at him mournfully as tears began to flow from her eyes. "You say you're protecting me – protecting us – but from what? You sit here day after day just … toying with my emotions. Are you sure that you aren't just protecting your interests?"

He replied calmly, "Please, you have to know that I do not want to harm you or your family. Just trust me."

Sammaria scoffed, throwing her head back, "Trust? How can I trust you when you cannot even be honest with me?"

Rekasi stared at her incredulously, "I have never deceived you."

Sammaria whipped her head around so fast it made her head spin. She glared at him with a terrible intensity.

He quietly said, "I would never lie to you."

She said steely, "Please just go."

Rekasi stood, "I'm sorry, Sammaria."

She turned her head to the side as he closed the door.

"The storyteller pulled up short. She took a deep breath. The children continued to look at her, enamored. The young man looked at her frowning. He said, "Are you all right?"

The storyteller looked up at him, eyeing him shrewdly. She said, "As I have grown older, it has become harder and harder for me to tell it."

She looked out the window at the stars glittering. She said quietly, "Perhaps we should stop for the evening."

The children began complaining. The young man spoke up, "No!"

She looked up at him with her deep blue eyes. He said, "If that is alright. I would like to hear the ending. Ma'am."

The storyteller smiled. She straightened, "A short time later, there was a knock on her door."

Sammaria stood to answer. Her eyes were swollen from crying. As she opened the door, Antien exclaimed, "What happened?"

Sammaria glared at him as she turned and curled up in a chair in the corner of the room. She stared at the courting chair. The chair that forced the two occupants to look at each other, smile at each other. Laugh, discuss, and enjoy each other's company. It was all a sham.

Antien kneeled in front of her, resting a hand on her foot. She turned toward him. Gently, he pleaded, "Sammaria, please tell me what's wrong. You know you can tell me anything."

She turned back to the chair. "You wouldn't understand."

RISE OF THE DRAGON QUEEN

She could not see him, but she could tell he was wounded by her words. She whispered, "I scarcely understand it myself."

Antien frowned, "It's about Rekasi, isn't it? You have begun to care for him."

She was shocked. She should have given him more credit.

Sammaria asked, "Is it wrong? Am I stupid to have these feelings?"

Antien took Sammaria's hand, "No, you are not. You have a good heart. Rekasi's intentions are pure and he -"

"But you said-"

Antien cringed, "I know what I said. I lied."

"Why would you lie to me?" Sammaria asked.

"The same reason I told Rekasi we were secretly betrothed."

"You did what?" Sammaria interrupted.

Antien ducked his head, "I thought if I destroyed your relationship with him, you would be safe. And you could love me."

Sammaria stroked his face, "You have always been my closest friend."

He looked down glumly, "That does *not* make me feel better."

Sammaria said, "In a different time…"

Antien shook his head, "You love the warrior. I understand."

Sammaria laughed darkly, "If it is love, then why does it hurt so much?"

CHAPTER XIX

Jennica heard footsteps ahead of her. She stopped, confused. A small village was up ahead. A sign further back had designated it as the town of Athers. Still, she had not expected to hear movement.

Athers was home to the small tribe of Fraychavae, Night Dancers in Draigar. Legend said the Fraychavae developed from the final remnants of the ancient Draigar. After the Elvateth began to exterminate the Draigar, a group of shaman performed the first ritual. They turned to their gods which were embodied in the Havae trees. It was said they danced in the darkness of the new moons and feasted upon dreka, a drink made from the water of a deep well and root of a sacred Havae tree. It granted them powers of speed and strength, but it also cursed them with a fear of the light.

Jennica took a step. Something slammed against her. She screamed. A hand clamped down on her mouth. She struggled as the person dragged her into the ditch. She twisted and caught a glimpse of a face she recognized. Donichello was fixated on the horizon as the sun slowly sank below it. An earthen cave suddenly surrounded them, a curtain of vines covering its entrance. Dumbstruck, she said, "You have Power!"

Donichello nodded, hushing her. He continued to stare toward the mouth of the cave. Jennica hissed, "What are you doing here?"

Donichello hushed her again. Jennica jumped as she heard gravel crunching under feet on the road. She peeked through the rubble covering them.

Two men with dark skin were walking down the road. Donichello moved slightly, barely making a sound. He silently cursed as the two men stopped.

Jennica shifted to get a better look. She saw that the men were scantily clad, dressed only in knee-length tattered pants. They surveyed the area. Jennica let her breath out slowly, trying not to bring attention to where they were hiding. One of the men shouted something and pointed toward the ditch.

A face dropped down in front of her. Surprised, Jennica screamed. The boy peered in at her with golden-green cat-like eyes. He pulled at the rocks covering her and grabbed Jennica by the wrist.

Donichello pulled her back. The ground shuddered for a moment. It stopped when he locked eyes with the boy.

Before she knew it, Jennica was standing on the road between men with dark skin. She shivered as they smiled greedily at her. The light-skinned boy stood behind her. She glanced past him hoping to see Donichello. Instead, she caught the young man's cat-like eyes. One of the dark-skinned men jerked his head toward the surrounding forest. He ordered something Jennica did not understand. He shoved her forward.

Donichello shook his head, trying to clear it. Fog swirled in his head, clouding his memory of the past few moments. He remembered someone was supposed to be with him. A girl. He was supposed to protect a girl. Jennica!

He let the cave collapse into a pile of rubble. He hurried to the road and headed toward the village. He stopped when he heard a falcon cry above him. That was a Dragonian Cavalry signal.

"What are they doing here?" he asked himself.

He searched the shadows, looking for a sign. In the shadows of the trees, he saw a lurking figure. It was far larger than any elf.

His mind tried to place the strange shape. The figure noticed him. It rushed him. The strange gray body pinned him and bound him. He reached for the magic that was spitting inside of him.

A gruff voice above him spoke something unintelligible. It spoke as a strange combination of guttural and serpentine. Donichello felt a sharp sting behind his ear.

The pull of his Power was blocked. A cloth was shoved in his mouth. Donichello yelled through his gag as he was dragged into the forest.

The dark-skinned man threw Jennica into a small hut. She looked around. A small pallet covered with a fur blanket was laid on the dirt against the wall. Nothing else was kept there. Pictures of historical events were carved into the wooden walls. She examined them carefully, and they appeared to depict ritual sacrifices. A sacrifice in the absence of the twin moons. A new member would emerge.

Jennica sat down on the edge of the pallet, the fur coarse under her legs. She took a shaky breath. A lump welled in her throat. As a child, the Fraychavae were only a story she had been told to scare her. Brother Orlten had not even done anything to assuage distrust. He was from the land across the water. He did not know what to make of the rumors. They scared him. That scared Jennica. She calmly braided a small strand of her hair, accepting her death.

The lock on the wooden door jostled, and Jennica leapt from the pallet. She pressed herself against the wall opposite the door, hiding in the shadows. Her heart thumped against her chest. Her time had come.

The door opened, revealing the pale boy's face, which had been adorned with intricate designs in blue paint. He closed the door and locked it. Jennica saw he was only dressed in a loincloth. She averted her eyes. He said, "You know why you are here?"

Jennica replied, shaking, "To die."

"How much do you know of our ways? Do you know *why* you are to die?"

Jennica could feel him getting very close to her. His breath surrounded her, the scent making her unsteady. It was a mix of mint and raw meat.

She shook her head. He replied, "They gave you to me for my enjoyment. They gave you to me to become Fraychavae. I shall have your blood."

Jennica shuddered. He looked at her blankly. He sighed before lighting a small candle and set it beside the pallet. Jennica could feel her resistance melting as she watched the flame glitter in his nut-brown eyes.

"Wait!" she said pushing him back "That's not right!"

He peered into her, lulling her into a trance. Her hand slipped down his chest. His lips found hers, and he pushed her down onto the pallet. Her legs scraped against the coarse fur as he tore at her tunic.

He kissed her harder. She felt her stomach drop and shoved his hands away. Wedging her hands between them, she pushed him to the floor.

She scrambled out of his reach, knocking the candle over. The flame extinguished and melted wax spilled in the dirt.

The air suddenly became frigid. She heard him breathing. He had somehow sneaked behind her. She spun out of his way. He reached out a hand and held it against her heart. She jerked, trying to move away.

He said, "You have passed."

Jennica froze, "What?"

He grabbed her wrist and pulled her toward the door. "You have resisted. You are worthy of my transformation."

⁂

Trydexzi smiled as he surveyed his prison. The heads of rebellious prisoners were mounted on pikes around the yard, a warning to those remaining. The O'rult were marching through the gates with the most recent throng of prisoners. He moved down from his tower to where the prisoners had been lined up. Trydexzi carefully analyzed each prisoner's face. Emotionless, looking at a blonde man in the line, he ordered, "Kill him."

His assistant, Pridan had followed him down from the tower after he had been specifically ordered to remain. "On what charge, sir?"

Trydexzi brought his hand up, "I do not like his face. It is more beautiful than mine."

A man at the end of the line smirked. Trydexzi marched over to him and shoved his sword into his gut, "You think I'm funny?"

He ripped the sword out, letting the man fall. One of the O'rult removed the blonde's head from his shoulders. Trydexzi slid his finger along the trail of blood on his sword. He smelled it, pacing along the line of prisoners. He rubbed the blood between his fingers and randomly flicked it into the other prisoners' faces.

He stopped in front of another Elf. He stared at him with glowing hatred. "Well," he said, "This is rare indeed."

He pushed his already smooth, oiled hair back over his ears as if preparing himself, "It's not every day one is in the presence of a Lord. How wonderful it is for you to visit our pleasant abode."

Trydexzi bowed mockingly.

Donichello muttered, "I hadn't much of a choice."

Trydexzi said, "Tsk, tsk. Is that any way to treat your host?"

Trydexzi killed the woman standing next to Donichello, but never took his eyes from the Elf. He signaled for his guards, "Take Lord Donichello to the *special* dungeon."

He clapped excitedly. Donichello felt fear, but he knew better than to let it show. He let them lead him away. Trydexzi looked down the line, "Kill the rest."

He walked away, grinning as innocent men and women fell to the ground.

Rough hands shoved Donichello into a dark room. Slowly, his vision returned. He saw the walls of the room were stained the blackened red of dried blood. He was shackled to a chair in the center of the room. He struggled, but it was useless against the strength of the O'rult who guarded him. Their serpentine eyes were impassive as they kept watch over him.

The door opened with an alarming clang. From the shadows, stepped the necromancer. His eyes glowed dangerously in the dim light. A long, pointed nose extended over full lips that were bent into a permanent scowl.

"The mighty Lord Donichello has at last been captured. How wonderful!"

His lips pulled up at the corners into a tight smile that did not touch his eyes. The man's teeth were pale white. Trydexzi examined his nails as the O'rult returned to their posts. He held the flame of a candle close to his prisoner's face. Donichello could feel the heat but not the lick of the flame. Trydexzi asked, "So, how are you?"

Donichello replied, "Well. Thank you."

Trydexzi nodded, blowing out the candle. "Where is that little blonde friend of yours, Sammaria?"

Donichello stared past Trydexzi, saying nothing. Trydexzi said, "Oh, so you are protecting her. Well, I have ways of changing that. Now, what would hurt you the most?"

Donichello remained silent. Trydexzi placed one of his skinny fingers to Donichello's temple. Pain shot through Donichello's head. It was as if something had crawled inside his brain.

Donichello felt himself succumbing to the pain, but at the last moment he threw up blocks in his mind. Trydexzi plowed through them. Black spots appeared in front of Donichello's eyes as the pain continued.

Trydexzi pulled his overgrown fingernail from his temple. Donichello grunted in relief. The necromancer had left him weak, his head hanging.

Trydexzi laughed giddily. He said, "So, the King's pretty daughter has led you to weakness. Tut tut! I expected more from the son of Joromo. To be brought down by a woman. What would your mother say?"

Donichello said, "She hasn't led me anywhere."

Trydexzi looked at him incredulously, then turned his back to Donichello as he struggled at his bonds. Donichello felt his wrists becoming raw where the metal chaffed against them.

Trydexzi turned back to face him, and, with a sinister smirk, he flicked his fingers. Donichello gasped out in pain as he felt a burning sensation surge throughout his body. The Power within Donichello surged. He felt the walls shake as they responded to his call.

Trydexzi ceased the spell. "Ah, I see that just *excites* our prisoner. Shall we see what is happening to this man's weakness?"

He swiped his hand through the air as if grasping for something and a bubble-like image appeared, floating above the ground. As it expanded, they were able to see her. A man pushed Jennica down in front of a bonfire. She looked up. Donichello could see how afraid she was. Trydexzi said, "Just like a picture, only better. You can feel the pain in these."

Trydexzi laughed, receiving great pleasure from the pain he was creating. He looked to Donichello, but the Lord's face was stern, his eyes flaring with Power. Trydexzi frowned, "Is that hope? No, no, no. You are not paying attention!"

The dark men grabbed Jennica and began to chant. The pale man held up his hand. Jennica pleaded with him, whispering, "Please!"

Trydexzi trilled with excitement, "Lovely! The Princess will soon be sacrificed to the Havae tree. There is no way she can escape her death this time."

Donichello frowned. Trydexzi said, "She is a wiley one. Luck has saved her thus far. No longer."

Donichello turned his attention back to the image. The pale man accepted a curved, jeweled saber from one of the dark men surrounding him.

Jennica bit back a scream. Terror mounted inside her. Donichello struggled against his bonds.

The man ran his finger along the blade, testing it, and smiled, "The blood of the worthy must be spilled."

Turning back toward the terrified girl, he thrust the sword up into the air. Jennica flinched as a roar erupted from the crowd. The pale man turned toward Jennica. She held up her hand as if it could protect her from that wicked blade. Donichello jerked forward as the man seized her wrist. Trydexzi hissed with pleasure.

The pale man said, "It is time."

He placed the blade against Jennica's palm and curled her fingers around it.

Donichello gritted his teeth to stop himself from looking away. The pale man gripped the hilt, looking into Jennica's eyes. His cat-like eyes enticed her more than ever. She did not flinch as the blade bit the skin of her palm. She winced when she looked down at the blood spilling from the cut.

Donichello watched, scarcely daring to hope, as the man forced Jennica's hand into the mud at the base of the Havae tree. She winced as it touched the soil.

As soon as he released her hand, she drew it back. Tears pricked at her eyes. Someone yelled, "Kill her! The blood of the worthy must be spilled!"

The white man said, "The blood of the worthy *has* been spilled! Do you not see the blood rolling from her hand? This satisfies the tree. This satisfies me."

He scooped up mud from where her blood had mingled with the dirt. He brought his hands to his lips and licked them clean.

Jennica stared at the pale man, horrified. Black patches began to splotch his pale skin. He slammed both hands into the mud and brought more to his mouth. His face turned completely dark, then his chest, and then his feet.

Donichello mirrored Jennica's surprise. The man stood, his skin blending into the darkness. His brothers and sisters hissed at him, "Kill her! Kill her!"

The new Fraychavae man looked down at Jennica. She turned her fearful eyes on him. "The girl lives. Our customs require that the blood of the worthy be spilled. Must we spill *all* blood? No. This will suffice."

Trydexzi roared, "What?"

Donichello breathed a sigh of relief.

The necromancer swiped his hand, obliterating the image of Jennica. He said, "I will break you, son of Joromo. You shall join me."

Donichello laughed softly and slowly shook his head, "That will never happen."

Trydexzi screamed and slammed his fist into Donichello's face. Donichello jerked back into the chair but said nothing. The necromancer ordered Donichello to be taken away.

CHAPTER XX

The elder cried, "Se! This cannot be! You break tradition!"

The new Fraychavae - Se - said, "Do you not see? I am fully Fraychavae. Just like you! Yet, she still lives."

Jennica shrunk back against the tree as more and more people called for her death. She whispered, "Kiro, protect me."

Se said, "Stop! All of you."

The crowd silenced. Their anger radiated toward Jennica. She stood up, reached forward, and gripped Se's arm. She said, "You don't have to defend me."

He turned his cat eyes onto her. They flashed between their strange green and gold. He said, "I'm afraid I do. You are my charge. I am bound to you now. They will listen to me. They must."

He addressed his people, "Family. Can you not see the sacrifice that we've been making? A mother, a daughter, a family member who will never be seen again. That is why we are hated and feared. I can see the distaste for their lives in your eyes. Blood is necessary, but not the loss of life."

Someone cried out, "We cannot let them live. They will send their armies to kill us!"

Jennica whispered in Se's ear, "Let me speak to them."

Se said, "I do not think that is a good idea."

Jennica said, "Please?"

He nodded. Jennica said, "People of Athers. My name is Jennica Aeradal."

There was some murmuring in the crowd.

She said, "Yes, I am the crown Princess of Dragonia. Letting me go will not be the end of your civilization. I will do everything in my power to preserve your way of life. I do not think you are monsters. Please. I will keep your secret and provide you with goods to survive. You have my word."

The elder who had addressed Se seemed to consider her words. He said, "Your word is good. Still, if this satisfied the Havae tree, our ancestors would have realized it sooner. She must die."

Se pushed Jennica behind him. She stumbled back into the Havae tree. Her injured hand hit something hard wedged between the roots of the sacred tree. She shifted so she could look down into the burrow. There was something rectangular tied in a cloth. Jennica reached her hand between the knurly branches and pulled on the package. A rectangular book with gold edging sat in her hands

She heard a collective gasp from the elders. Se turned to look at her as she asked, "What is this?"

The man demanding her blood proclaimed, "It is nothing more than a trinket from a worthy one."

Jennica opened the book.

The man yelled, "No!"

She saw page after page of names. All young girls and the male or female name that corresponded with it. She said, "It's a list of the sacrifices your people have made throughout their history."

Jennica flipped through the book's many pages, stopping on the second to last page as she saw a name that couldn't possibly be written there. It was dated before the Pilleetain Raids. Jennica said, "This cannot be possible. I am a worthy one. My word can be trusted?"

Se nodded.

The elder nodded, "Worthy ones cannot lie to us."

She said, "Then, explain this to me. If your ancestors

have always killed everyone, never let anyone free, never learned what Se has now shown you, how did my mother become a sacrifice before I was born?"

The elder cried out in pain. He said, "Impossible! Impossible! What is this?"

Jennica said, "Listen closely to my words. My mother's name was Milamare Aeradal, formerly Milamare Deswayze. She lived in the furthest borders of Dragonia. She was one of the citizens captured by the Pilleetain bandits. Her name is listed here in this book six months before she was captured. She transformed a man by the name of Lunak."

Everyone turned and looked at Se. The elder said dumbfounded, "Give us the book."

Jennica held out the book. Se held up a hand. He said, "Give me your word that you shall not destroy it."

The elder said, "Yes, we would never destroy the records."

Jennica glanced at Se. He nodded. She handed the book to the elder. He looked at the entry she noted. He said, "Lunak's transformation was always a mystery." He looked up at Jennica, "She can go."

Jennica smiled. She looked up at the twinkling sky and whispered, "Thank you, Kiro."

Se led Jennica to a hut separate from the rest. As he swept back the flap, Jennica ducked her head and entered. He gestured for her to sit on the pallet as he lit the candle inside a small lantern. Jennica could not tell what it was he was using, but it did not look like fire.

She said, "I don't understand. How did the elders not know about Lunak's transformation? How did they not know he had spared my mother?"

Se set down the lantern. He said, "Lunak was a chieftain of the Fraychavae people. Fraychavae chieftains follow a different set of rituals than the rest of us. The inductee performs the ritual by himself after a test of survival. Your mother must have made an impression on him. He kept her survival a secret, but there is no telling what the elders knew or hid."

Jennica sighed. Why was this so controversial? Should these people not be happy they did not have to slaughter people?

Se took Jennica by the hand, "Thank you for helping me show my people the truth. They are so rigid in their traditions. The elders won't let us change, but this will force change upon them."

She replied, "I don't understand. Have they seen the truth?"

She remembered the stares she received as she walked with Se. He had placed an arm around her shoulder and hissed at the glares.

He said, "They may not listen today, or realize what has changed, but in years to come they will look back at this and they will praise the Maker."

Jennica replied, "You must have great influence over your people."

Se's dark face clouded over. Jennica frowned. She was still frightened somewhat by this strange man. Se replied, "No."

Jennica was uncertain whether she should question him further. He said, "It is not a hidden fact. I have embraced it."

Jennica looked at him, confused, "What happened?"

Se said, "My father left the Fraychavae. He was a Chieftain. He led our tribe bravely, but he left one day and didn't come back. He just left us."

Jennica touched his arm gently with her good hand. She said, "I am sorry."

Se said, "I want to do something in return for all you've done for me."

"I haven't done anything," she replied.

Se replied, "I have a debt to you. That means something around here."

Jennica said, "Well, there may be one thing. My friend. I need to find the man I was traveling with when you took me."

"This man is special to you?" he asked.

Jennica sighed, "He is a ... friend."

"You do not seem happy about this."

Jennica said, "It is complicated. Still, I cannot leave him lost. It...just wouldn't be right."

Fear gripped her heart as she moved through the shadows to where Se had said Donichello was being held. She found it hard to believe her life had changed so much in just a short amount of time. It had been what? Two months? Two months could change everything. She listened to her muffled footsteps shuffle along in the dirt. She flinched at every sound.

Suddenly, a great, stone prison rose out of the darkness. As quietly as possible, she climbed the railing that surrounded it and carefully moved inside. The conversation with Se was still prominent in her mind. He had said, "He is on the sixth floor. You'll have exactly seventeen and a half minutes to get him out."

Jennica nodded. Se had sensed that something was still bothering her. He asked, annoyed, "What?"

Jennica had replied, "What about the others?"

Se snapped, "What others? Donichello was the only one captured. He's the one we are worried about!"

Jennica shook her head, "There have to be others. More people who were captured before Donichello."

Se sighed, "The Fraychavae will handle them. You just worry about Donichello."

Jennica protested, but Se simply stared at her with those mysterious cat eyes. Jennica felt her heart start to pound as she stared, transfixed.

Jennica's eyes narrowed as she remembered this encounter with Se. She was still not happy about leaving behind so many innocent and terrified people.

So many things were dependent on her success and so many things could go wrong. She needed to stay calm. An audible crash came from behind her. She whipped around. A searchlight scanned the area. She slipped into the shadows as the Fraychavae unleashed upon the guards.

Each step rang out and echoed against the prison's cold, stone walls as she began climbing up the stairs. After she reached the sixth level, she rushed down the hallway. She heard echoing footsteps from ahead. Frantically, she whispered Donichello's name as she passed each door. She heard people responding, but it was not him. Jennica passed a door halfway down the hall. A wave of familiarity rushed over her. She knocked softly, "Donichello?"

His voice returned, "Who's there?"

"It's Jennica. I'm getting you out."

Jennica silently inserted the foaming liquid that Se had given her. The foaming liquid hardened into the shape of the lock. She gave it a turn, and the lock popped open. She pulled on the door, releasing Donichello. He looked at her questioningly with his brown eyes, but soon after, he had enveloped Jennica in his arms. She let him squeeze her to his chest. It was good to see him.

Jennica gently broke from him, feeling a little awkward. She said, "We do not have much time. We must go."

Donichello stopped, "I need to get someone out first."

Jennica shook her head, "The Fraychavae will get him out. They owe me."

Donichello shook his head, "The Fraychavae won't bring her. They would not know to."

Jennica was powerless to stop him as he went back into his cell and brought out a woman with blonde hair. Her legs were bent at awkward angles. Jennica asked horrified, "What happened?"

Donichello replied, "I'll explain later."

Jennica led Donichello and the girl back the way she had come. As they came to the steps, they could hear footsteps on them. Jennica slid along the wall. She looked over the edge of the balcony. Trydexzi's face looked up. She jerked back. The climbing footsteps grew closer. She hissed, "Do something!"

Donichello asked, "What?"

Jennica replied, "Use your Power!"

Donichello conjured something that Jennica could not see. The footsteps ceased.

Jennica led them down the stairs. She gasped when she saw the rock-covered Trydexzi.

Fraychavae moved in the shadows, watching for any dangers. Jennica led them back to the entrance that Se had led her through. Jennica looked uncertainly at the woman cradled in Donichello's arms.

Donichello set the woman on one the horses that the Fraychavae had left them. He handled the woman as if she were made of glass. She looked back at Jennica. Thanks filled her face. Jennica stared back, guilt catching in her throat. The woman looked familiar. Did she know her?

He mounted the horse. Jennica mounted the other. Guilt settled in her stomach. She banished it and set the horse running. Before long, they had come to the Fraychavae encampment.

Lifting the woman down, Donichello laid her on the soft mat Se had brought out. She whipped her head around, looking at the people surrounding her. Jennica recognized her. She was the woman she had seen stabbing a tree. Jennica looked up at the Havae tree. It was not the same. She frowned.

Donichello spoke to the healers. They said, "We shall do our best."

Se came to stand next to Jennica.

Donichello said, "Thank you."

Se nodded, "We had heard that Trydexzi had taken up use of that old prison, but we had yet to believe the rumors. It's so strange."

Se walked off, leaving Jennica to question Donichello. He grasped Jennica's wrist, surprising her. He led her to the boundaries of the small village. He pulled her into his arms. She did not hug him back. Relief flooded her. He said, "How did you do this?"

Jennica asked, "Do what?"

Donichello replied, "Rescue me. Ally the Fraychavae. Jennica, people have been trying to do that for centuries."

Jennica said, "It was Se. I just stumbled upon it. Please, tell me about the girl."

Donichello sighed, "They tortured her. They thought she knew of Power. I can hardly imagine the horrors she went through." He shuddered.

Jennica shook her head, horrified, "That's so horrible! That man must be stopped."

Jennica rubbed her arms, feeling suddenly cold. She looked behind her. Se was walking swiftly toward her. He said, "Donichello, the girl isn't responding to our treatments. The only way to heal her is if …"

Se's eyes flicked toward Jennica.

Donichello said, "What?"

Se looked back at Donichello, "You must understand it is normally their choice, but there is no other way."

Donichello growled, "Do what?"

Se said uncomfortably, "She must be transformed. She must become Fraychavae. That is the only way to heal her."

Donichello bowed his head, "I understand. Just save her."

Se nodded, "Jennica, will you please assist. We need your blood."

Jennica nodded gravely. Donichello's head snapped up and stared at her. She said, "I have to save her."

Donichello looked as if he would protest, but nodded.

The woman sat in the mud before the Havae tree. She looked frightened. Jennica smiled gently at her. She scooted back and looked toward Donichello.

Se asked, "What is your name?"

She said shaking her head, "I can't tell you that. I can't. More torture. More pain."

Se looked at the girl's disfigured feet. He said, "We're trying to help you. We won't hurt you."

He gently touched her ankle. She jerked her head up, her blonde hair whipping around her face.

She looked at him and both their faces seemed to melt. Se whispered, "Tell me. It's all I ask."

She said, "Anahi. My name is Anahi."

Se gasped and looked back toward Jennica as if it should mean something to her.

Jennica looked toward Donichello. He whispered in her ear, "Her name means the Immortal. She is over three thousand years old. The story goes she shall only begin to age upon finding someone to love with her whole heart. She is destined to be the greatest saint that ever walked this earth."

Jennica asked, "How did Trydexzi get her?"

Donichello looked at her, "Jennica, Trydexzi doesn't want someone that innately good walking the planet. She opposes him too strongly. He must have found out where she was and had her captured."

Anahi stared at Se. Her eyes seemed to glow in the firelight. Se gestured for Jennica to unwrap her hand. She did so and teased blood from her wound. She pressed it into the soil.

Anahi looked uncertain. Se reassured her as she gathered the mud into her hands. The woman brought the mud to her mouth and consumed it. Her eyes were on Se as her pale skin turned dark. She waited until it covered her skin, turning a rich brown like the soil around her.

Se helped her stand. She looked down in surprise, "My feet! They're healed!" She jumped and threw her arms around Se, "They're healed!"

Jennica said, "I don't think she'll have to wait much longer."

Donichello looked down at Jennica. He asked, "What?"

She gestured to the two new Fraychavae. She said, "They are falling in love. Can't you see it?"

Donichello shook his head. Jennica shrugged. She watched as Anahi skipped around with Se, testing her new legs. Ripples of laughter came from her. Her blonde hair streamed around her dark face. She was beautiful.

CHAPTER XXI

Sammaria looked up as a shadow fell over the piece she was sewing. Sundrie asked her, "Have you ever been to the library?"

"A few times," Sammaria replied.

Sundrie said, "I was thinking about heading over there for an afternoon read. Do you think you could accompany me? I would love to have your sunny smile with me."

Sammaria nodded, "I would love to go with you, Sundrie."

Sundrie led the young Princess down a hallway carpeted in red. She stopped in front of large, plain oak doors.

Sammaria stared at Sundrie. Sundrie smiled, "People adorn their rooms too much. Makes a place much easier to navigate and thieve."

She pushed the doors open. Sammaria looked around at the shelves upon shelves filled with books. She commented absently, "Jennica would love this place. If only-"

Sundrie said, "Yes, if only, but we mustn't dwell on the if onlys."

Sammaria browsed the large selection. Sammaria pulled a book off the shelf. It contained hundreds of tales of lore. She felt an instant ache in her heart, missing her sister. She walked down the stack of books and found her friend.

"Have you ever wondered if anything we consider legend is true?" Sammaria asked.

Sundrie looked up from what she was reading and replied, "Like what, dear?"

Sammaria cocked her head, "I don't know. The portals. All the stuff with the Draigar. Things like that?"

Sundrie said, "No. At this point, the way it is talked about, it is all folklore."

Sammaria looked down, "Oh…"

She asked, "Why?"

Sammaria wrinkled her nose, trying to decide how much to tell her, "Oh, it's just my sister would get hooked on a topic and would scour the library, friends, scholars, random people she met on the street about it till she found the answer. I was just curious."

Sundrie said, "The only one I've ever believed in is the Dragon Queen."

Sammaria's ears perked up, "Really?"

The older woman nodded seriously. Sammaria said, "Tell me the story, please."

"At the end of the War against the O'rult, the Ultimate Protector Kiro told of a vision he had. He saw the demise of our world. He saw the great creatures fighting each other to extinction. Kiro hoped to protect our races. It is said that he stole the power of one Grumpice, one Hawkatie, and one Elemental. He placed them into lockets that he had forged in the mines of Deadilly. The lockets were hidden in the furthest reaches of the earth. He buried the powers to preserve our races until it was time for us to be tested. Our test shall be great. Many races will come from afar to see this. One queen – a great and terrible queen most likely – will bring the creatures together once more. She will be crowned the Dragon Queen."

Sammaria said, "That sounds right. Why is this the only folklore you believe to be true?"

Sundrie tapped her book, "My grandfather said he had found one of the lockets once."

Sammaria looked at Sundrie, surprised. She laughed, "I never saw it. Heard the stories. He gave it away. Some girl he met before my grandma. Thought maybe he could win her over. But the lockets seem to be more than a myth to me. But then, don't all myths have some basis in truth?"

Sammaria smiled, "You may be right."

⁂

Jennica hugged Se goodbye. He smiled, "Thank you for all you've done."

Jennica smiled, "You are most welcome."

He replied, "If ever you need us Fraychavae, just blow on this whistle. We'll come to you no matter the distance."

Jennica took the whistle from him. It was wood from the Havae tree carved into the two moons.

"Thank you, Se."

He smiled, "You're welcome, Princess."

Jennica looked up. He winked, his cat eyes flashing. Jennica placed the whistle in her pack.

She embraced Anahi who said, "I shall come to your aid as well. I swear it. I've been on this earth long enough to pick up a few tricks. If it weren't for you and Donichello, I might never have escaped that man!"

Jennica smiled, "Thank you, Anahi."

Donichello shouldered his pack and handed Jennica hers. She took it from him with a smile. Donichello clasped arms with Se with a firm nod. Anahi gave him a small kiss on the cheek. He and Jennica turned and headed out of the village.

They walked in comfortable silence for a long while, following the path down which Sammaria's magic was pulling them. About three and a half hours after leaving Athers, Jennica said, "What happens if we can't find her?"

He said, "Don't worry about it."

Jennica said, "She's my sister. She shouldn't be hidden from me like this."

Donichello said, "This is true. You are also a princess. You are the targets of many political disputes."

Jennica said, "Is this even a political dispute anymore? It seems to have grown larger than that."

Donichello slowly nodded, "That it has."

Jennica said, "What is it then?"

Donichello replied, "I think it has more to do with your power-hungry father than anything."

She sighed, "You *might* be right."

He looked at her and noticeably rolled his eyes. Jennica glared at him as he continued on his way. Donichello watched the ground as he began walking more quickly, knowing he had irritated her. Jennica almost missed his thoughtful questions.

She felt as though something had snapped inside her. She had come so far, but it all seemed so hopeless. She held in the tears that burned in her eyes. Her Power raged, trying to burst free.

Jennica snapped herself out of it. She heard a surprised oath. She glanced up at Donichello. He had a look of utter surprise on his face. "What is wrong?" she asked.

He said, "You have Water Power."

Jennica looked down. Her shirt was soaking. She looked up at him, afraid. No one was to know of her Power. Stones dropped in her stomach. She knew he had Earth Power, but this was different. She was in the royal family. Her father had exterminated many Elementals.

She looked at him like she was going to say something. He held out a hand to her. Jennica's small trust in him snapped. She was moving forward before she was up from her crouch.

Jennica felt the wind in her ears. She let herself glance at Donichello walking just behind her. All he had to do was extend his arm and she would be his. He yanked back on her shoulder, "What's wrong?"

He struggled to look in her eye as she twisted in his grip, "You know my secret! We are the same."

Jennica broke from his grasp. Donichello ordered, "Stop!"

Jennica shook her head violently as she continued to run. Her legs burned. The pull of Sammaria's magic kept her going.

She yelled, "You don't understand."

Jennica pitched herself into the forest. She slowed her speed and weaved through the trees, trying to confuse Donichello. She glanced behind her. He never seemed to miss a beat.

Jennica went too far to the west and crashed through the underbrush, stumbling onto a path behind a large caravan. Disoriented for a moment, she stared at the people before her. They gave her a strange look but said nothing. Jennica took a step forward and disappeared between two wagons.

Jennica looked ahead of her. The wagons were headed for a narrow pass in the mountain. She almost did not see it at first. The path was situated so the rocks towered above it like spires on a castle. Farther up the mountain, the spires disappeared and the path became a sheer drop off the side of the mountain.

Jennica glanced to either side of her. The travelers looked worn and wary. There were wagons bearing everything from children to food to furniture. It seemed as if they had packed up their entire lives. Jennica looked toward the pass again. She could see a faint line of magic twisting up the mountain. Her knees suddenly went weak at the impossibility of the task ahead of her. She had been hoping that Sammaria had been left behind somewhere that she could easily be found, but her sister's magic was leading her deep into the Kilhatea Mountains.

Shouts passed through the caravan, causing everyone to stop. They would rest here for the night and continue into the pass in the morning.

Jennica tried to stay out of people's way as the tired travelers settled down for an evening meal. She wondered what had caused their displacement. She knew there could only be one place they were heading. They had to be searching for the Resistance.

The refugees set up their campsite, and Jennica could tell this was not the first time. The caravan of several hundred people and dozens of wagons had cook fires lit and tents pitched in under ten minutes. Jennica inched closer to the spires looming above the path.

Her tie to Sammaria burned stronger. She examined the path, looking deep into the darkness. The spires loomed ominously like the fingers of some tortured soul reaching for the mercy of the stars.

Jennica reminded herself to breathe as she took a step forward into the shadow of the mountains.

"I thought you'd come here. Nothing will stop you, will it?"

Jennica turned slowly, looking Donichello square in the eyes. She said bluntly, "Please, stop following me. Stop trying to bring me home. I'm not going. I don't expect you to understand."

She crossed her arms across her chest.

Donichello said, exasperated, "Take you home? Jennica, I'm trying to help you!"

Jennica dropped her angry stance, surprised, "You are?"

He nodded, "I want to bring her back." He took a step toward her, "I know how important she is to you." He tucked a strand of hair behind her ear.

Jennica felt her anger flare. She pulled away, backing up, "What if I don't want your help? I didn't ask for it."

Donichello said, "I know you don't trust me. You have every reason not to. But you can't do this alone."

Jennica frowned at him and shook her head, "You betrayed me. You helped an entire country begin to forget her. All it took was the carelessness of not speaking up. If you were me, what would you do?" Her eyes implored him. She scoffed, "Please, don't answer that. You are wrong. I don't need your help. I suppose since you discovered my secret, I don't have to explain it to you. I can take care of myself."

She turned and continued up the path. Donichello said, "Rekasi has Fire Power."

Jennica stopped, closing her eyes. She turned to look at him, "Why should I believe you?"

The man replied simply, "Can you afford not to?"

She glared at him as he moved to join her on the path. Jennica shoved him a small distance from her. "This changes nothing."

"Of course not, Your Highness."

Jennica stopped and stared at him as he passed. This was going to be a long trip.

When the moon was high in the sky, Donichello stopped and said, "You should get some rest."

Jennica walked past him. She looked over her shoulder, "What about you?"

He said, "I'll keep watch."

She shook her head, "If one of us is going to be up, we both are. We might as well keep walking."

She lightly tripped at an uneven part of the path. Donichello sighed inwardly. He said, "You will do no good for Sammaria or yourself if you drop dead of exhaustion."

She looked back at him with a wry tilt of her head, "And you will? Come on."

Donichello had no choice but to follow her down the path. He said, "Is there any way I can convince you to rest?"

"Are you getting tired already?" Jennica taunted.

Donichello said, "No. I'm worried about you, Your Royal Highness. How much longer can you keep up this pace? Aren't you tired? Can't you feel the exhaustion in your limbs? Your eyelids are already getting heavier."

Jennica looked at him with sleepy eyes. His words pointing out what she had so stubbornly hidden. A voice, rich and convincing. Donichello said liltingly, "Sleep. Sleep."

Jennica's eyes slid shut. Donichello caught her as she fell. He cradled her in his arms and laid her down gently on the hard earth. He covered her with the blanket from his pack. Sighing, he looked back toward their trail. She shifted as she slept, but she did not wake. For that, Donichello was grateful.

Jennica woke with a start. She frowned. The blanket was warm, but it was not hers. She kicked it away and looked around the camp for her companion. She had a few choice words for him this morning. Her stomach growled, and she smelled meat cooking. She stood and looked for Donichello. He was sitting at the crest of the ridge they had been climbing the night before, stoking a fire. She tramped up the rocks to his side.

He said, "Good. You are up."

"How dare you?" she demanded.

"Excuse me?" Donichello asked, looking confused.

"How dare you use magic on me? I told you I was fine, and you went and cast a spell to make me sleep!"

"Your Highness-"

"And stop calling me that! I already told you it is just Jennica!"

Donichello said, "I didn't cast a spell on you, Jennica. I cannot do that any more than you can. I just pointed out your fatigue."

Jennica deflated. She harrumphed, "Well, all right, but still."

Donichello said, "I promise I won't do it again if you won't push yourself to the point of exhaustion."

He handed her a bowl full of rabbit stew. She breathed in and hummed with pleasure. Donichello smiled. She ignored him and began to eat.

After they finished, they packed up camp and continued into the mountains.

They had not gotten far when Donichello stopped her. Jennica demanded, "What are you doing?"

Donichello held a finger to his lips, listening. The faint crackle of shifting rocks boomed in the otherwise silent canyon.

Jennica hissed, "Are we being followed?"

Donichello shook his head, uncertain of the source. The caravan was too far off. Besides, the noise was too quiet. They would be able to hear the chatter of the caravan from a great distance.

Donichello stepped away from her, looking into the sparse brush coating the canyon edges. He thought he saw the shifting shape of a body.

A muffled yelp brought him back. He twisted, unsheathing his sword.

A woman dressed in grey held Jennica. A gag was tied around her mouth. Jennica struggled to break the woman's grip, but she held her fast to her sturdy frame.

Donichello surveyed his surroundings once more. More grey-clad people emerged, moving out of the trees like ghosts. They were well-armed with their weapons trained on him.

He felt two people restrain him. One knocked his sword to the ground. A tall blond – older than the rest – stepped forward.

Donichello gasped, "Olo... Olo. Please, release me. Friend, please."

The Prime Minister looked at Donichello, appraising him. He took the fallen sword and knocked Donichello unconscious.

Jennica screamed through her gag, calling his name. She pulled against the woman restraining her. She kept fighting as they dragged them both away.

Olo said, "Blindfold her. We can't let her know the way."

Jennica was powerless as they led her away, bound and blind. She prayed her death would be quick.

CHAPTER XXII

Rekasi hesitated at Sammaria's door. She had not spoken to him since their argument. In training, she was cold and distant. Rekasi did not know how to tell her. She would not take it well.

He pushed his hair back. Why did it matter? She was making him soft. Emotions were for those without responsibility. He needed to stay focused. She was only a distraction. Besides, there was no chance she would ever return his feelings. Not being who they were.

He pushed the door open. Sammaria looked up, excited. Her eyes faded into malcontent when she realized it was him.

She asked quietly, turning away, "What do you need?"

Rekasi crossed the room. He grabbed her wrist and spun her around, "Look at me."

Sammaria pulled her hand out of his grip. "What?"

Her amber eyes bore into his. He was taken aback by the intensity in them. It was not hatred. It was pain.

Rekasi asked, "How long are you going to ignore me? How long are you going to try to avoid me?"

Sammaria said, "I…"

Rekasi dropped her wrist and turned away from her. He said, "Why do you make me do this? You make me feel so unarmed."

"I what?" Sammaria asked, confused.

"Never mind. I have news."

Sammaria looked at him, hope in her eyes. He said, "We have found someone who claims to be a friend of your sister. He is a knight."

Sammaria dropped her eyes. She stared at the floor, "Oh. Is he all right? Can I see him?"

Rekasi nodded, "You will be able to see him soon."

"And what of Jennica? Has she been found?"

Rekasi nodded, "They are together. They are being brought here now."

Rekasi tensed waiting for her outburst.

Sammaria asked, "She is here?"

Rekasi said, "Yes. Well, she will be soon. Sammaria, I am sorry. I know you did not want this, but you have to trust me."

"Trust you?" Sammaria asked, surprised.

Rekasi said, "I understand your distrust and your disgust, but you don't have to make it known."

He stalked angrily toward the door. Sammaria caught his arm and pulled him back.

He turned back toward her. Rekasi pulled her into an embrace and kissed her. His fingers intertwined with her hair. He felt her respond to his kiss. Her hands held tightly to his arms and hesitantly encircled his waist.

He released the princess. All the walls he had so carefully built around his heart had fallen. He brushed a stray eyelash from her cheek. She blinked twice.

Rekasi said, "I'm sorry. That was a mistake. I shouldn't have …"

Sammaria felt like she someone pierced her heart, "It was a mistake to kiss me? What am I to you?"

Sammaria trailed off.

Rekasi said, "No! You are promised! You and Antien. I was out of line. I can't… I'm sorry."

Sammaria looked down at the ground. She did not say anything for a moment. She whispered, "It's all right. Let's just forget about it."

Rekasi looked at her with doleful eyes. He did not want to forget, but he nodded.

"My sister?"

Rekasi said, "In time. There is more news. Things I think you should know."

He perched on the end of his side of the courting chair. "Sammaria, you may not think as much, but you are so much safer here among outlaws and traitors."

Sammaria said quietly, "I don't think you're a traitor."

He looked at her hands folded in her lap. He thought about taking them, but she would probably push him away. Sammaria said, "Just tell me."

Rekasi said, "Your father was trying to have you killed."

"What?" she asked, horrified.

Rekasi said, "Morlyn was paid to kill you and your sister shortly after your seventeenth birthday. Antien risked his life to…"

Sammaria said, "Antien?"

Rekasi said, "Yes, he sent word to us as soon as he found out. He had to keep you safe."

Sammaria shook her head, "No."

She looked at him. Everything made sense. Antien would not have joined the Resistance for anything less.

Rekasi sighed, "It is the truth. You know it is."

Sammaria said bitterly, "The truth has never been a friend of mine."

❧

Jennica pulled against her restraints. They had been moving up a hill for nearly an hour. She could not see. She had to carefully place her feet to keep from stumbling. She thought they must be moving toward a large building at the top of the hill. She could feel it bearing down on her and her small band of captors.

Someone said, "This way. No need to cause a commotion."

Jennica twisted. It was a small attempt to free her bound hands. The woman holding her elbow moved her grip to Jennica's writhing hands. She hissed, "You aren't going to escape. We aren't going to hurt you."

The woman forced Jennica's head down. They continued forward. Earth pressed in around her.

They continued to march her through the dark, down tunnels and hallways. Jennica was surprised when the blindfold was removed. She was standing in a clean, sparsely furnished room.

She turned back to her captors. They were already retreating behind the closing door. Jennica flew at the door. She pounded on the wood until her hands were numb.

Jennica slowly turned back into the room. There was a simple bed with a nightstand. She counted the doors in the room: three including the one through which she had entered.

She crossed the room to investigate the others. The door directly parallel to her bed was a closet filled with simple clothes. The other door was wedged between the corner of the room and the single chair.

She gripped the handle. It was jammed, but, after a moment, the knob turned without a sound. Jennica leaned against the door, forcing it open. Jennica found herself in another room identical to her own.

Donichello had been deposited on the bed. He was still unconscious. Jennica hurried to his side. She touched the bruises and cuts on his face gently. She asked whispering, "What did they do to you?"

Jennica's body writhed violently. A vision flashed in front of her eyes. She stumbled back away from the bed. She leaned against a wall as the vision overtook her.

She was in Mestchester, but everything was different. She could see herself beside Sammaria. They both looked younger. They were dressed for the party their father had arranged for the announcement that Sammaria was of marrying age. This had not been that long ago. She glanced at her and Sammaria's specters. They played their part as it had happened. She closed her eyes and let her Power lead her through the vision.

When she opened her eyes, she was standing outside of her father's study. She passed through the door.

A man stood there. His black hair and shrewd features were foreign to Jennica, but the shape of his face was familiar. Trydexzi glanced up and said, "I'm not alone, am I?"

Jennica looked around, surprised. Could he sense her? He said, "I am in the presence of royalty, am I not? Don't worry, Princess I won't give your little secret away." He laughed, "Come now. We wouldn't want anything to happen to you."

His hand shot out and seized her around the throat. He squeezed and pulled her close to his face. He said, "You do not know the extent of my Power. You would do well to disappear, or I will *make* you disappear."

Jennica's vision grew dark. How could he affect her in the Sight State?

She wriggled in his grasp. He laughed. Suddenly, she felt his grip loosen, and she fell to the floor.

A noise at the door caused her to look up. Her father walked into the room. Jennica reached for him, crying out. The necromancer turned to face her father. He said a strange word, and King Enchardo crumpled.

Jennica screamed. Her spirit pulled her back to her body. As she left, the man raised her father's dead body. The body's eyes opened and slowly faded to black.

Jennica sat panting against the wall by Donichello's bed. The necromancer's aquiline features and intelligent voice were etched into her mind. She sat there, drenched in sweat. Her body felt weak. She couldn't stand.

She exhaled heavily. These visions did not always show things exactly as they had happened. She pushed it out of her mind. What she had seen could not be true. It was her fears playing tricks on her.

She pushed herself up. Donichello still had not woken up, so she opened the door to her room and walked to her bed. She heard voices outside moving closer to her room. One voice was deep. It sounded like an argument. The deep-voiced man whispered angrily, "It is not time. I need longer to observe."

The other voice belonged to a woman, and it was ice-cold. It sounded far away and reedy as if the woman was speaking from somewhere else. She commanded, "Get me the information on Sammaria, Tosin. Do that, and you will be rewarded when I am queen. If you do not, so help me-"

Jennica gasped. Who was this woman? Why would anyone in the Resistance help her?

Tosin interrupted, "Yes, thank you, Your Majesty. I shall not fail."

The woman replied, "You would do well not to."

Jennica wondered if this man had black hair. She looked through the keyhole, trying to see him as he passed.

He had blonde hair. The man turned his head. Just below his jawline was a blue tattoo of a sextant. He continued down the hall and disappeared around the corner. Jennica sighed as she slid into her chair. Even in a group of traitors, there were traitors. But, she supposed that was to be expected. Nothing was ever as it seemed.

Sammaria raked the ground in the garden. Caliet stood and pushed her dark curls off her neck. The sun was shining bright that morning. She cocked her head at Sammaria and asked, "What is bothering you? You seem very troubled today."

Sammaria dug her rake back through the weeds. She said, "What would you do if you found something out about someone that completely changes everything that you have ever known about them? And it is so horrendous that you just can't make sense of it?"

Caliet looked at her friend with wise eyes. She appeared much older than her thirteen years. Caliet asked, "Are you talking about Rekasi?"

Sammaria frowned, dropping her rake. She said, "No. Why?"

The girl's curls bounced as she shook her head. She said, "I don't know. I thought you might have heard something. Then what is it?"

Sammaria said, "I suppose I should have seen it. He seemed to hate us for so long."

Caliet closed her eyes and breathed in. She asked, "Your father?"

Sammaria winced. She leaned down to pick up the rake. She glanced up, and something caught her eye. There was a blistering scar on the outside of Caliet's leg just above her ankle. The scar was two different markings that Sammaria did not recognize at first.

After a moment, she realized it meant Caliet had been marked a witch and a traitor. The first was a curved 'L', and the second looked like a shepherd's hook.

Sammaria said, "My dream."

Caliet looked at Sammaria as she stood up, "What?"

Sammaria said, "My dream. I had a dream that my father and Morlyn marked me. I have known all along that I was in danger. And still, I am angry at Rekasi and Olo for keeping me here."

Caliet said, "Let go of the anger?"

Sammaria smiled, "Easier said than done."

Caliet said grimly, "Believe me, I know."

Sammaria glanced at Caliet's ankle again, "How did you receive those marks?"

Caliet looked down at her feet. She said, "Oh, well, you know my Power is ... unusual to say the least. No one wants to feel like their emotions are being spied on. The people of my village turned on me. They ambushed me on my way home from the fields and dragged me down to the river. The priest of our town carved those marks into my ankle so that when they found my body everyone would know, but my father arrived in time to stop them. He used his Power to force them away. Of course, we had to flee. He brought us here, and we've been here ever since."

Caliet pushed the dirt around with her toe. She said, "You should go to Rekasi."

"Go to him?"

"Yes. Tell him what you now understand. I know you want to."

Sammaria smiled, "Thank you, Caliet." The girl smiled, her dark eyes still troubled from the memory. Sammaria touched her arm before hurrying away.

She found Rekasi in the training room. He was sitting on the floor surrounded by a circle of papers. Rekasi looked up, confused, from the papers he was examining.

Sammaria said, "Um, sorry. Mila said I would find you in here. Is this a bad time?"

"Mila?" Rekasi asked.

"Dakota's mother," Sammaria replied, twisting her hair around her finger nervously.

Rekasi said, "Oh, of course. Nice woman. No, this isn't a bad time. Please, take a seat."

Sammaria sat cross-legged in front of him. She watched as he set down one paper and picked up another. He examined each one carefully. She watched his face. It was creased with worry. He sighed, setting the paper down. He looked at Sammaria and smiled, letting out a little chuckle. He said, "I never thought it would be like this."

"Like what?"

"When Huor recruited me... he adopted me really. I thought that the Resistance was this perfect vision of the world. I thought that fighting the Kingdom would be almost romantic. Huor made me believe it was romantic. But this...it's nothing but bloodshed and sadness."

Sammaria reached across the papers and gripped his hand, "I'm sorry."

Rekasi looked down at her hand on his. She continued to watch him. He said, "No, I'm the one who is sorry. You must think I'm a monster."

Sammaria edged closer to him across the papers. She said, "No."

Rekasi touched Sammaria's shoulder. She peered into his eyes. Her fingers touched his face. Rekasi caught her hand and pulled it away. He said, "Sammaria-"

She said, "You said you couldn't. That I was promised."

"Yes. I cannot compromise you. I will not do it."

"Rekasi," Sammaria said, speaking slowly. She knew what it meant saying these words, "Antien lied. I am not promised to him. I am free to do as I please."

Rekasi did not reply. He stood, pulling Sammaria to her feet. His fingers caressed her face, "I had hoped like a jealous fool that this was true."

She smiled. Rekasi said, "Sammaria, I will spend my life trying to amend all the pain I've caused you. I will do everything in my power to make things right."

Sammaria ducked her head. She leaned against his chest. After a moment, she said, "Don't you understand? You've already made amends. How could I find fault in you now?"

He lifted her chin and kissed her for the second time. This time, however, it was not a desperate surprise to them both. It was gentle and delicate. Sammaria's mind went blank as she fell into the warmth of his touch.

CHAPTER XXIII

Jennica sat curled in the chair next to Donichello's bed. She had washed and was wearing a simple, tan frock. Two women had come in, bathed her, and had taken the clothes she had stolen from Donichello.

Jennica rested her head against her knees, watching his breathing. He looked peaceful.

She supposed that she was the one who had caused him so much undue stress. She sighed. She *could* stand to be a bit nicer to him. He just frustrated her so much. Then again, if she stopped fighting him… she groaned and buried her head in her knees.

Donichello opened his eyes. He was confused. The room was unfamiliar. He could feel that his Power was stunted. He tipped his head up to look around, and the room began to spin. He grunted as he laid back down. Jennica looked up and said, "You are awake. Thank the gods!"

Donichello touched his head, "I don't feel well. What happened?"

Jennica said, "Olo – that spy – he hit you with your sword. You've been asleep since they brought us here."

He slowly propped himself up onto his elbows. He examined the room around them, then looked back at Jennica, "Do you know where we are?"

Jennica hesitated, "We are somewhere deep in the mountains. They blindfolded me. I don't know where exactly. I think we are with the Resistance."

Donichello cursed, "If I get my hands on that man, I'm going to-"

"What? Kill him? Do to him what he has done to your friends? What does that prove?"

Donichello stared at Jennica in disbelief. Jennica's pale face colored. She looked away, "It's just … I mean… Revenge…"

Donichello said, swinging himself into an unsteady sitting position, "You don't know him, Jennica. You don't know what he's done to people. Both as the leader of the Resistance and before."

Jennica stopped forming an argument in her head. She placed a hand on his shoulder, "You know him, don't you?"

"I'm surprised you don't know his name. Rekasi Tathrina. *Sir* Rekasi Tathrina. His adoptive father trained knights in the Myhadry Peninsula. Rekasi and I trained together. He was always uncontrollable, had his own idea about things. We never liked each other. We were dueling one day, and he lost control. He used his Power." He rubbed his calf on his left leg. "I will never forget how it felt to have those Flames touching me."

Jennica said, "I'm sorry."

Donichello pushed his hair from his face. Jennica wondered if he was feeling the strain from the beating he had taken. He said, "We have to escape."

Jennica said brusquely, "What is your brilliant plan? I've already tried the doors. Locked tight. They're not going to let us out. It's too dangerous."

Donichello said, "Yes, but there are more ways out than the door."

Jennica rolled her eyes and crossed her arms across her chest. Donichello gripped her shoulder and peered at her with strained eyes. He said, "Please stop fighting me. I know you are upset with me. I know that isn't likely to change, but, if you even want to think about saving Sammaria, we are going to have to work together."

Donichello shook his head and slumped against Jennica. He said weakly, "Do you feel it too? Do you just feel... *drained*?"

Jennica shook her head, "All right. What is your plan?"

Donichello asked, "Can you reach the vent above the fireplace? I'm not sure if I can stand."

Jennica looked around the room. She spotted it above the closet door. She said, "If I get a chair I can, but there isn't a hope for either of us to fit in there."

Donichello said, "I know. But she can."

Donichello reached into his jacket and pulled out a small ball of scales. Jennica looked at the creature, surprised. She asked, "Is that Sniblea?"

The small bundle uncurled as if it had been in a deep slumber. She blinked at Jennica with her wise eyes. The small dragon tipped her head to the side. Jennica glared at Donichello, "Why did you bring her?"

Donichello said, "I had no choice. She was tracking you. She had nearly caught up to you before you reached Athers. She was the reason I found you there. At the first sign of trouble, she curled up into a ball and has been asleep ever since. She must have used some kind of magic that hid her from Trydexzi and the O'rult."

The dragon watched Jennica. She said, "Fine, but what now? You are going to send her into the vent to do what, exactly?"

"Find Sammaria," Donichello said, "She can aid in our escape."

"What can she do? She's a prisoner herself."

"Jennica, she's been here for months. I think she's probably more than a prisoner at this point."

She shook her head, "How can you say that? Sammaria would never-"

"If you say so," Donichello said uncertainly.

Walking over to the door, Jennica said, "Well, she's not. She wouldn't join these people. Not after what they've done. Donichello, they killed your father!"

He stared at her. She turned away from his gaze and touched the door. It was solid. She tried the handle again. It was still locked. She pushed up against it with her shoulder. It did not budge. She slammed her body into it. Still, nothing.

Donichello said, "Stop it, Jennica."

Jennica threw herself into the wood once more. She cringed as she hit. Donichello seized her arm. She had not even noticed that he had stood. He said, "Don't hurt yourself. It isn't worth it."

Jennica stomped, frustrated. She said, "I cannot touch her mind. Why can I not find her myself? She never hides from me. Not like this."

She crossed her arms, barely holding her emotions in check.

She allowed Donichello to hug her for just a moment before pushing him away gently and saying, "This doesn't help our situation any."

Donichello said, "Well, suppose Sniblea is able to find Sammaria. She could give her a message."

Jennica sighed, "I suppose that isn't a *completely* terrible idea."

Donichello swayed. Jennica gripped him. He leaned his weight onto her unintentionally. "But you are going to have to sit. You are going to hurt yourself."

She lowered him onto the bed. He looked at her, his eyes unfocused, "Thank you."

Jennica tucked a strand of hair behind her ear, flustered. She replied, not looking at him, "You're welcome."

She quickly crossed the room, placing the chair in front of the fireplace.

A knock echoed loudly from the main door. Jennica froze. She looked at Donichello. He shook his head. They heard the jingling of keys in the lock. Jennica slid the chair away from the wall as the door was slowly pulled open.

Jennica gasped as she saw her sister's familiar face. She was holding the keys in her left hand.

Jennica covered her mouth with her hand. She felt a churning in her gut. Speaking slowly, she asked, "What is going on?"

Sammaria threw her arms around Jennica's neck. The keys thumped heavily against her back, deepening the pit in Jennica's stomach. Burying her head in Jennica's shoulder, Sammaria said, "Thank Kiro! I've been so worried."

Jennica pushed her away, "*You've* been worried?"

Sammaria stared at her sister, confused. She asked, "What's wrong?"

"I could ask you the same thing. Why are you *here*? And for all the gods, why do you have the keys?" Jennica demanded.

Sammaria looked at her hand. She dropped the keys as if they had burned her. Sammaria touched Jennica's arm, "There is much we must discuss."

Jennica twisted out of her grip, "Yes, there is. Like how you decided to join these traitors! And how you have betrayed everyone you've ever known. I don't even want to talk to you."

Donichello exclaimed, standing up, "Jennica! Stop!"

Sammaria shook her head, tears on her cheek. She said, "You aren't being fair. You don't know them. They are good people."

Jennica snapped, "Was it good of them to burn Mestchester? To leave all those people homeless? Murdering Duke Joromo? How about kidnapping you? How is that fair? And is it fair that for the past month I have been traveling the countryside looking for you? And now you've joined them? I thought you were dead. Is that fair, Sammaria? Do you think they care what happens to you? As long as you are useful to them, sure, but once you get them what they want… They. Don't. Care."

Donichello grabbed her arm, "Stop it, Jennica."

She pulled away from him, "You stop. This doesn't concern you."

Sammaria retaliated, "You don't know what you are talking about! These people are protecting me. And you. And Donichello. All of us. They aren't the enemy. Our *father* is the enemy, or are you still blinded by his lies?"

"You are the one who's blinded. What did they promise you? Did they seduce you with power?"

Sammaria reached out to slap her. Donichello grabbed her wrist. She yelled, wrenching her wrist out of his grip, "Power has nothing to do with it!" She looked down, "You know I don't care about that."

"Then what? What is so important?"

Sammaria flicked her eyes toward Donichello and back at her sister. She did not reply.

Jennica stared at her sister in realization, suddenly deflated, "Oh my gods. Tell me it isn't true."

Sammaria picked up the keys from the ground. She said, "I have nothing more to say. I had hoped you wouldn't hate me."

Jennica said weakly, "Sammaria …"

She walked out of the room, closing the door behind her. Jennica collapsed to the ground, exhausted.

Donichello turned to look at her, "What was that about?"

Jennica wrapped herself into a protective ball. She said, "Please don't start."

He said, "How can I not? You have been searching for her for weeks. For what? To kill her yourself?"

Jennica stood up to face him, "I'm not killing her! She's killing me! She joined him. She betrayed me. How could she do that? How could she forget me? And for what? That awful man Rekasi?"

"You don't know it's him," Donichello said.

Jennica said, "Yes I do. She really, honestly loves him."

Donichello asked, "Is that what's bothering you? You think she chose him over you?"

Jennica frowned and snapped, "Since when are you the expert on how I'm feeling?"

Donichello ignored her snide comment and sat down on the floor beside her. He said, "Did you consider that she is choosing both of you?"

"How can she? He has done nothing but harm us. Why are you defending him? You said you hated him."

Donichello said, "I do hate him, and, if I get a chance, I'll fight him. But Sammaria is your sister and your closest friend. I'm saying maybe you don't have all the facts yet. You should listen to her, or you are going to lose her."

"So, you fought?" Rekasi asked. It was more of a statement. He already knew the answer.

Sammaria tried to hide her face as it reddened. He was already at her side pushing her hands away from her face. He said, "You never have to hide from me."

She said, "Jennica thinks I've betrayed her. She thinks I chose you over her."

Rekasi asked, "Did you?"

Sammaria shook her head, "No! Rekasi, why does there have to be a choice? Why can't I show her that we're on the same side? I knew it would be difficult for her to accept, but I never expected *this*."

Rekasi lifted her face and gave her a questioning look. Sammaria reddened further and looked away, "Well, perhaps I did wonder. She is fiercely loyal. Especially to Father. I think she sensed there was something wrong, but she just hasn't let herself believe it yet."

"You just need to talk to her. I know that she means the world to you. Don't let this break you. Not now."

Sammaria wrapped her arms around Rekasi and just held him for a moment. His head rested on hers. It felt so reassuring to be enclosed in his strong arms. She squeezed him once and let go. He smiled and said, "I'll be here if you need me."

CHAPTER XXIV

S purred by the fear incurred by the deceased queen's spirit, King Enchardo assembled a team to once again search for the missing lord and princesses beginning in the Draconle Wood. Talk spread to the furthest reaches of the kingdom that Sammaria was alive and leading the Resistance against her father. Others said that she had abandoned politics altogether and had married a farm boy.

The King was beginning to wonder if searching for them was futile. Still, the spirit had been clear. While they were alive, there could be no peace in his mind.

As you already know, the Elvateth are wonderful trackers. However, when searching for one of their own, it becomes difficult. Along with being excellent trackers comes the ability to hide one's tracks. And – as I'm sure all of you have begun your training – this skill is learned early, which can cause quite a scare for your dear parents, am I right?"

As they entered the Draconle Wood, the air became cold. Enchardo's mind flashed back. He saw the face of a young man. It looked eerily like his own. Enchardo clasped the boy's hand.

The King shook his head. The memory was cloudy and made his head hurt as he strained to remember. Suddenly, a mist descended upon them, bringing his mind back to the present.

A screech caused the party to look up. A dark spot in the sky dove, growing ever larger as it neared the ground.

"Dragon!" someone cried out.

A knight pulled the King from his horse and flattened him against the ground, using his body to protect

Enchardo. The dragon breathed flames into the air and landed among the trees in front of them. The trees groaned under its weight as it screeched again. The King watched the creature with grim amusement. The beast did not frighten him. Instead, he mulled over possible methods of harnessing its wild power.

The King threw the knight away from him, stood, and moved toward the dragon. He made noise to get its attention. Several of his men tried to restrain him, but the King fought them off easily. The dragon whipped its head toward the noise. It glowered at him with an intense, unconstrained fury. Enchardo inched forward, trying to touch it. Just one touch and he could steal some of the beast's magic.

The dragon howled and attacked. It snatched Enchardo up in its claws. He cried out as one of the claws impaled his gut. The beast's bright red scales were sprayed with the King's dark blood.

Enchardo twisted, pulling the claw deeper. He winced and pulled a dagger from his belt. Enchardo plunged the blade between the scales of the dragon's breast.

The creature howled again, twisting in the air. It released its hold on the King who fell to the rocks below.

General Ebiyo released a volley of arrows, driving the creature away. He rushed to the King's side. Ebiyo jolted back as the King's eyes flashed from black to a startling green.

Enchardo said, "Please. Please find my daughters. Tell them...Tell them I'm sorry."

There was a hiss of steam. Ebiyo was pulled back by the other men as red smoke rose from the King's body. It slowly changed from red to purple to dark blue to black to white. By the time the smoke was gone, the body had disappeared. Ebiyo looked up as a wispy figure rose toward the heavens.

He cursed and warded himself against evil. To his colonel, he said, "A golem. Someone must have trapped the King's spirit inside that creature. Someone else has been controlling the Kingdom."

The colonel asked, "Should we inform someone? The Prime Minister?"

General Ebiyo spat, "We should find those girls."

"The news of King Enchardo's death sent Dragonia into chaos as the Loyalists and Resistance grappled for power. Sammaria was still missing, not seen since her kidnapping. Jennica had fled the kingdom. The Laeranils were the only family besides the Aeradals that could take over. However, the Duke had recently died, and the rest of his family had been found dead in their beds as well.

To make matters worse, rumors were starting to reach the central region that O'rult were weakening the border. Fear and anger infiltrated the lower classes of Dragonia, which led the nobles of the land to make rash decisions that they would soon regret."

CHAPTER XXV

Sammaria sat on the rug in the center of her room. The moonlight shone through her window, illuminating the tear that rolled down her cheek. She sighed deeply and opened her link to Jennica. Quietly, she whispered her name.

A flood of emotion washed over her as Jennica finally opened her mind. She felt Jennica start and rise from her bed. She had been asleep.

Jennica felt guilty, and that guilt pulled on all the pain in Sammaria's heart. Sammaria said, "I know you feel betrayed. And I am probably the…"

Jennica's thoughts interrupted hers, "No. *I* was wrong. I don't know these people. I have no right to judge them. More importantly, I trust you, and I should act like it."

Sammaria smiled, "If you just talk with them, I'm sure you'll see what I have seen. They are just looking to live their lives and make their own choices."

Sammaria asked, almost fearful, "Am I forgiven?"

Jennica hesitated. She said, "Yes. Always."

Sammaria left her room and ran to her sister, throwing her arms around Jennica when she opened the door. There were tears on both of their faces.

Jennica said, "I'm sorry."

Sammaria shook her head. She asked cautiously, "Would you like to meet him?" She was careful and slow. She was not sure how Jennica would react. She did not want her to be angry again.

Jennica said, "Let me get Donichello."

Sammaria shook her head. She said, "I can't let you. Donichello is dangerous. His Power could bring this mountain toppling down. I've been asked to have him stay in his room until we know he means us no harm."

"He wouldn't do that, Sammaria," Jennica protested. "You asked me to have faith in you. In Rekasi. Now, please have faith in Donichello. He is a lot of things, pushy and a bit condescending, but he is kind. He would never hurt the civilians."

Sammaria smiled as she led Jennica down the hall. She said, "You see him very well. You must love him."

Jennica hesitated, "No! We're just-"

Sammaria took her arm and led on, patting her hand. She opened the door to the library. Rows of books covered the small space. A man Jennica recognized from so many weeks before stood hunched over a map. She stopped as the memory of a knife pressed to Sammaria's throat flashed in front of her eyes. Pulling Sammaria back, she shook her head, "I don't think I can do this. Please-"

Sammaria said, "It will be good for you to talk to him. I will be here the whole time."

Jennica nodded, uncertain. She did not say much as they approached the nook where Rekasi stood. He looked up and smiled brightly at the two girls. Jennica frowned, trying to assess if his smile was genuine. It seemed to be. The smile cleared his eyes, but she could not shake that chilling voice out of her head. He turned to her and bowed. As he rose, he said, "Ah, Princess Jennica. Your Highness."

Jennica's brows knitted together. She blurted, "Do you know a man with a blue sextant on his jaw?"

It was Rekasi's turn to frown. Jennica wondered if perhaps she had shown her hand too soon.

"That is the same thing Sammaria asked me upon her arrival. I am beginning to think I've missed something. Pray tell me, Princess. Is it code?"

Jennica clamped her lips shut and shook her head viciously. Sammaria stared at her sister, puzzled.

Rekasi sighed, "No. Well, I don't suppose you would tell me if it was. If not, I'm going to have to find this man with a blue tattoo that so intrigues the royal family. Maybe we can ask him what he knows. What do you think, Mari? Could he solve our mysteries?"

Sammaria blushed just a little. Jennica turned to look at her sister. No one shortened her name. She hated it. Jennica caught Sammaria's glance and raised her eyebrows. Her sister gave a small shrug.

Rekasi said, "Your Highness, I am pleased that you agreed to meet with me."

"Don't mock me, sir," Jennica said wearily.

Sammaria scolded, "Jennica!"

Rekasi put up a hand, "It's fine. Sammaria, could you give us a moment?"

Sammaria gave both Jennica and Rekasi equally hard looks before she moved far enough away so they could speak privately.

Rekasi waited until she was out of earshot, "Mock you?"

Jennica did not back down, "You regard me as Your Highness, Princess. After capturing me and locking me in your Power-draining rooms, you address my sister – the rightful heir – in such a familiar way. Not even I do that! She may have forgotten that you kidnapped her, but I haven't. The image is burned in my memory. So, just...do not mock me."

Rekasi spread his hands in submission. She stared down at them. He said, "That is the last thing I wished to do. I simply wished to show you proper respect."

Jennica stared down at the floor, feeling foolish. She had not meant to insult him. She nodded in acknowledgment of his apology. Rekasi looked over to where Sammaria was hovering on the other side of the room. He said, "There is something Sammaria and I need to tell you."

"What? That you are in love?" she scoffed, "I already know that."

Rekasi started to interrupt. Jennica talked over him, "Rekasi, I'm not going to lie to you. I'm not sure I like you. There's just... with… I'm going to give you one chance. So, you had better not mess it up."

Rekasi examined her closely. She seemed about as threatening as a child, but her steely tone told him there was indeed some iron to her threat.

He said, "I appreciate the opportunity. I will do my best not to let either of you down. I promise you my intentions are pure, but that is not what I wished to discuss with you."

Jennica mentally kicked herself again. This man was very hard to read. His voice was very grave. He said, "I have news from Mestchester. It's about your...father."

Jennica felt her stomach drop, "He's dead, isn't he?"

Rekasi nodded. Jennica felt weak. She asked, "Does Sammaria know?"

Rekasi nodded, "She was with me this morning when the news came. That's not all."

Jennica stared at the young man, her face had paled. Rekasi seemed tired, worn out. Whatever was on his mind weighed upon him heavily.

"It appears your father has been gone for a while."

"I don't understand."

"The man – the thing – that was killed yesterday was not your father. It was a golem. Dark forces are entering this war. To be completely honest, I'm not sure I'm ready for them."

Jennica had frozen on the word golem. Those black eyes. Jennica felt faint. She said, "Excuse me."

Before she had received a reply, she ran from the room. Hot tears streamed down her face. She collapsed against a stone pillar.

"Your Highness?"

A face she had known but had not seen in what felt like ages appeared as she looked up from her hands. Antien held out a hand to her. She gripped it, and he pulled her upright. He wrapped her in a tight hug. The tenderness of the hug caused her to cry harder. Antien said, "Let me take you to Sammaria."

Jennica surprised herself when she said, "No, take me to Donichello."

Antien led her back to the room where Donichello was being held. Jennica thanked him and entered the room.

Donichello sat up when she entered. He stood when he saw her face. She ran to him, throwing her arms around his solid torso. He enfolded her in the safety of his arms. She sobbed into his chest. Carefully, he picked her up and set her down on his lap. He cradled her there against his chest until she calmed. Jennica looked up at him, her face red. She said, "He's gone. Murdered."

"Who is, Jennica?" Donichello asked quietly.

"My father. I saw it. Some man killed him and used his body to create a golem."

She hid her face in his shirt. Donichello kissed her hair. Jennica looked up at him. Her peered into his eyes. She said, "You are a good man."

She leaned toward him. Donichello kissed her, and she sank deeper into his arms. He pulled away softly and shifted so she could lie down. He stood, but she grabbed his hand and said, "Stay. Please."

He laid down next to her and wrapped her in his arms again. She buried her face in his chest and fell asleep. Donichello sighed and whispered to her, "I love you."

Jennica awoke to warm breath on her face. She opened her eyes to Donichello's full form. She tried to move but was tangled in his strong arms. She laid there, listening to the whistling of his breath. She cursed herself for being so vulnerable. She never should have sought comfort from him. She quietly touched her lips. She could still feel the pressure of his there. Jennica shook the memory from her head.

The movement woke Donichello. He looked down at her with sleepy eyes, "Hey. Good morning." He stroked her hair.

Jennica smiled faintly, "Can I get up?"

Donichello looked down as if he had just noticed he was holding her. He gave her a half-smile like he might refuse. His arms loosened, and she scooted off the bed.

Jennica tucked a lock of her hair behind her pointed ear. She held onto the hair, tugging nervously at it. Finally, she mumbled, "Thank you."

She hastily retreated through the door connecting their rooms.

She turned around at the rapping on her door. Jennica turned and frowned at Donichello when she saw him leaning against the frame watching her. She said, "You know that didn't mean anything, right?"

Donichello pushed himself off the frame and walked toward her, "Right."

"I was upset," she said indifferently. Donichello was standing right in front of her. Jennica's breath caught.

"Of course."

His face was close to hers. His eyes flicked between her eyes and her lips. She said with difficulty, "So, nothing has to change."

Donichello kissed her. She slipped into his grasp. He held her tightly to him and cradled her head, mussing her hair. He slowly let her go.

"Oh!" Jennica gasped, surprised.

With a smile in his voice, he said, "Nothing has to change."

He walked into the adjoining room. Jennica sat down on her bed staring after him.

"Oh," she said again.

※

Misseter said curtly, "This had better be good."

Her spy replied, "Sammaria has become involved with Rekasi. He plans to take her to Mestchester and establish her as queen."

Misseter tapped her nails against the arm of her chair. She said, "That won't do. That won't do at all."

She stared at the map on the wall. She controlled much of the southern half of the Drehean continent.

No one had expected her - a lowly noblewoman from Arctos - to take control of what she had. It was the march into Gabvand that had alerted the world to her power. There, neither side could claim victory, but Gabvand, in their eternal arrogance, claimed the victory anyway. Still, the rulers answered to her.

At one time, Dragonian and Pilleetain controlled the entire Drehean continent. Their influence was still felt across the world. Controlling Dragonia was essential to taking the rest of the continent.

Misseter said, "Kill her."

The spy said hesitantly, "Ma'am, there is something else. Sammaria is an elemental. She controls Fire."

Misseter slammed her fist down. She screeched, "I don't care if she's a *dragon*. Kill her, or I will kill you! Don't think that you are so important to me that I can't replace you."

The man stammered, "Yes. Of course. And what of Jennica?"

"What about her?" spat Misseter.

The spy said, "She is here. Under lock and key."

Misseter tapped her fingers, "Interesting. We'll have to think of a special fate for that little slut."

She looked back into her spy's eyes. She said, "Carry out your duties. Report back soon."

Misseter mounted her horse and smiled slyly. The princesses would never know her plans. The Resistance would disband, and she would rule Dragonia. She whipped her horse, and it jolted forward. The wind blew through her long hair as she let out a laugh of pure joy. She kept her eyes on the horizon, set with determination.

※

Rekasi and Sammaria opened the door to Jennica's room. Antien had gone to find Sammaria after returning Jennica to her room. He was concerned for her. Sammaria was worried that the news of their father's death was weighing more heavily upon Jennica than she had anticipated.

Donichello was in the room with her sister. Jennica looked like she was trying to find words for something. She glanced up at the intruders. She looked panicked at her sister. Donichello stood to face them and stared at Rekasi. There was mistrust in his eyes. He asked steely, "What is *he* doing here?"

Sammaria took Rekasi's arm, "He just wants to talk. We were concerned about Jennica."

Donichello said, "As you can see, she is fine. So, you can take that filth away from here."

Jennica said, "Donichello, leave him be. What do you need, Rekasi?"

Rekasi bowed to them, "Are you all right? You ran away so suddenly. I didn't mean to upset you."

"It wasn't you," she replied.

"It wasn't?" Sammaria probed, "What was it?"

Jennica said, "It was something I… saw."

Donichello's glare faded as he raised his eyebrows, "Saw?"

Jennica cringed. It was supposed to have been inconspicuous language. However, Donichello was quick. He knew what she was saying. Rekasi stared between them.

She said, "Yes. In Sight State, while you were unconscious."

Rekasi glanced at Sammaria. She shrugged.

Jennica said, "Father was murdered…" She hesitated, looking at Donichello. He watched her with a frown. She said, "By a necromancer. He reanimated him. Turned him into a dark creature."

"Is it possible that you were just projecting your fears into your vision?" asked Rekasi.

Jennica looked at him, annoyed, "You don't think I thought of that? This happened before you told me, and in the vision, the man could sense my presence. That never happens. He … tried to strangle me."

Jennica touched her neck, remembering it.

Donichello said, "It's Trydexzi."

Jennica asked, turning toward him, "I know. Do you think that was why he captured you?"

Rekasi held up a hand, "Trydexzi captured you?"

Donichello glared at the man, "Yes. When I was looking for Jennica. Who ran away, by the way, because you *kidnapped* her sister. Where was your Resistance then?"

Rekasi said, "Cleaning up the mess you knights made."

Donichello took a step toward Rekasi, "Oh really? All we've done is try to right the chaos your so-called help has caused this land."

The two men stood nose to nose. The tension in the air was palpable. Jennica held her breath, waiting for it to break.

Donichello said, "You have always been a reckless coward."

Rekasi spat, "Better than an arrogant fool."

Donichello punched Rekasi in the nose. Rekasi butted him in the stomach, knocking him to the ground. Jennica cried out. Sammaria pulled on Rekasi's arm. He shrugged her off. The two men fought, beating each other with the fury of forgotten years.

Jennica could not take it, letting out a shrill scream. That stopped the fight. Sammaria pulled Rekasi off Donichello. Jennica pulled Donichello off the ground.

She said, "You two are acting like children!"

Donichello pulled from Jennica's grip saying, "Still up to your old tricks? Taking the virtue of innocent women?"

Rekasi said, "You just know you are no match for me. You always *were* weak."

Donichello said, "While you hid out in this god-forsaken place, I trained with the masters. Let's see who isn't a match for whom, shall we?"

Rekasi lunged at Donichello.

Sammaria grabbed his arm, "No!"

Rekasi spun out of her grip and punched Donichello. He laughed, "Didn't see that coming, did you? That is a fatal flaw. Not everyone sticks to the rulebooks, least of all me. Be ready for me ,sir!"

Donichello tackled his old rival. His hands went to the man's throat. Jennica pulled on his arm. Donichello shrugged her off.

Rekasi laughed, "Do it, dear Donichello. Kill me! See if you ever escape."

Sammaria pushed on Donichello's chest, forcing him off the other man.

She said, "If you want to kill him, you'll have to kill me too."

Rekasi whispered to her, "Don't do this."

Jennica took Donichello's hand. She said, "Please. It will be all right."

He was rigid under her touch.

Donichello said to her frantically, "I thought you wanted the attacks to end! I thought you wanted your country to be safe! I thought you wanted the Resistance to fall!"

Jennica said, almost yelling, "No, Donichello! Not anymore."

Donichello asked harshly, "Then what? What do you want? That man is taking it from you."

Jennica mumbled, turning away, "No he's not."

"What?" he demanded.

She turned, yelling at him, "I want you, you idiot! I'm in love with you. As much as I fight it."

Donichello's fists unclenched. He wiped the tears from her face. The tension in the room broke.

Sammaria helped Rekasi to his feet. He held out a hand to Donichello, "Can we let old hate die?"

Donichello shielded Jennica with his body. He said, "Hate dies hard. I am not ready to forgive you for what you've done."

Jennica peeked up at him from under his arm. He looked down at her, "I guess you're a better person than I am."

Rekasi said, "All this aside, I can't do this alone. Now that the King is dead, Sammaria can take her rightful place on the throne."

Sammaria looked at him, "Is that what you want?"

Rekasi said, "Yes. When the Resistance started, they wanted the entire royal family gone. Now that we have seen the woman you've grown into, they are confident we can place our trust in you. Dragonia already follows you. You are the true queen."

Sammaria put her head on his chest. She did not say it, but they could both feel what she was thinking. They would be parted.

Donichello said, "I shall help you, Sammaria. Dragonia cannot survive without you."

CHAPTER XXVI

Jennica held a bow to her chest. Blocking out the noise of the training room, she nocked an arrow. She pulled back on the string, aimed, and released the bowstring with a snap. She did not look as she nocked the next arrow. She released the string again. The second arrow hit next to the first, each in the center of the target. Unlike Sammaria, she enjoyed archery. She lacked Sammaria's grace with a blade, but archery was where she excelled.

Donichello came to stand behind her. He said, "You are good at that."

Jennica smiled at the compliment. Pushing against him with her shoulder, she said, "I'm sure a knight like you has seen better."

He put his arms around her waist for just a moment, "I'm sure I haven't."

Donichello was leaning down to kiss her when a loud noise pulled their eyes up away from each other.

Sammaria cried out. Jennica grabbed Donichello's hand and pulled him toward the commotion.

Sammaria held a gash on her arm and stared down at a man lying dead at her feet. Antien held a bloody sword. Rekasi jumped down from a platform above them. He held Sammaria's face asking, "Are you all right?"

She did not reply. He beckoned for a healer to look at her. He shook her shoulders, "Mari! Are you all right?"

Sammaria tore her eyes away from the dead man. She replied, "I'm fine. He tried to kill me."

Rekasi said, "But he didn't. You are safe."

He rolled the body over with his foot. Clear on his jaw, was a blue sextant. Jennica gasped. Rekasi cursed. He waited until Sammaria was bandaged before gathering her, Donichello, Jennica, Antien, and Olo in a secure room.

He said, "The Loyalists have forced our hand. We must move more quickly than I had planned. I believed placing Sammaria on the throne would please both sides."

Jennica said, "I'm not so sure it won't."

Rekasi said, "That man tried to kill her!"

Jennica gritted her teeth and continued, "Yes, but he was gathering information on you and Sammaria. Just you and Sammaria."

"How do you know that?" Rekasi demanded.

Jennica shrank back, "When I first arrived here, I heard him talking to a woman. It had to have been over a scrying dish. His name was Tosin, I believe. He was calling her Your Majesty. That doesn't sound like a Loyalist to me."

Olo said, "If I may, My Lord. Our intelligence has spoken of unrest in the south. They say that a woman controls the minds of many kings."

"And you believe that woman to be the one I heard speaking with this Tosin?" Jennica asked the prime minister, "I thought the southern unrest was just talk."

Olo shook his head, "We don't think it is. Especially now. This woman is said to have allied with a necromancer."

Jennica unconsciously rubbed her throat. Donichello said darkly, "Trydexzi."

Olo nodded gravely.

Rekasi, Antien, and Olo plotted the route the princesses would take back to Mestchester. They had to return soon. If Trydexzi had been manipulating the court already, there was no telling what danger the country was in. Dragonia's position was strategic not only in location but for its magic. Returning Sammaria to the throne was vital. Without someone stable at Dragonia's helm, the instability would be felt throughout the continent.

Rekasi left Olo in charge of the Resistance in his absence. He was to lead the princesses back home. A smaller party would be less conspicuous than a mounted guard. They were to leave in secret. If word of Sammaria's return were to spread, it would only lead to more danger.

Rekasi said, "Antien, have Liza, Mila, and Sundrie create some disguises to ensure the citizens believe the Princesses are here. Follow behind us when I give you the signal."

Antien nodded, "I'll tell the general right away." They moved into the hall toward the door.

Having donned their disguises, Rekasi, Donichello, and the princesses left the immense mansion. When they were in the cover of the trees, Donichello asked, "Now what?"

"Jennica?" a small voice hissed in Jennica's mind. Jennica looked up. Sniblea flew down and landed on her shoulder. There was a sudden gust of wind, and a moss green dragon landed near them. Sniblea said, "Dratasha will take you as far as the Ssnalanbar."

Dratasha knelt to allow the four to mount her.

They had been flying above the countryside for several hours when Jennica heard a roar from behind them. A large dark creature rose through the clouds.

Dratasha growled low in her throat. Her spine went rigid.

The dark shape released a spray of fire. The riders cried out. Dratasha banked hard. Jennica barely kept her grip on the spikes.

The black dragon shot fire at them again. Sniblea's voice touched Jennica's mind. She wailed about the abomination.

Dratasha rolled, escaping the black creature. Rekasi seized Sammaria, holding her tightly to the dragon's back. Donichello reached for Jennica. She let go for just a moment to reach for him. Their hands grasped for a second. Jennica's hand slipped. She closed her eyes as she fell into the darkness below.

CHAPTER XXVII

The remainder of that night's journey passed in a blur. Sammaria remembered Rekasi using Fire to rid some bats fluttering around their heads, but then just tears. Dratasha took them to the Katart Wood. It was still too dark to do anything but sleep. So, they made camp, and the dragons stayed to protect them.

The morning came with Jennica still missing. Rekasi woke to an empty stomach. Their packs were lacking greatly in staple supplies. As the other two awoke, he told them, "I'm going for some food."

Donichello eyed him with hostility, "I will not have you bring me my food. I shall accompany you."

Rekasi nodded in acceptance.

The terrain was rough. After a long silence, Rekasi slowed and held up a hand to Donichello. The deer they were tracking had stopped to graze. Rekasi pulled the bow from his back and nocked an arrow. Concentrating, he pulled the bowstring taut.

An arrow, not his arrow, bedded itself in the deer's side, and she fell to the ground. Rekasi looked behind him. Donichello relaxed his stance and walked toward the doe. Kneeling, he mouthed a small prayer to it. Rekasi muttered under his breath, "Oh Mokana, help me. It will be a wonder if we survive this."

Rekasi moved over to where Donichello was tying up the doe. He asked, "Do you need any help?"

Donichello retorted, "Not from you."

Rekasi took a step back, "Point taken. I am still hated."

Donichello nodded, "You're still hated."

"Isn't this all a bit juvenile?"

Donichello froze, sitting rigidly, "You are exactly why we are in this position. You pretend you are all righteous, but all you want is power. Am I supposed to love you for that?"

Rekasi replied indignantly, "You do not know me."

Donichello glared at him with steely eyes.

While arguing, the two men missed the faint sound of hooves trampling through the forest. Donichello drew his sword. They had been surrounded, but by what? Moments later, several men riding huge horses galloped into the clearing. These men, however, had tough, gray skin and cavernous mouths filled with needle-like teeth. Three large horns curved from their heads. Skulls decorated their armor. Rhiloxes.

A rhilox to their right barked, his voice like a mill's grinding wheel, "Drop your weapons, Elva!"

Rekasi dropped his bow and slid the quiver off his back. He had left his sword at their camp. Donichello clenched his sword in his fist. Rekasi could see him calculating the risk. Finally, the sword fell to the ground beside Rekasi's bow, Donichello slipped his bow off his back, adding it to the pile.

A female rhilox moved forward from the trees. Her blonde hair was swept up out of her face, tied up behind her horns. Her leather jerkin barely covered her chest. Blue patterns were painted on her flat stomach. She looked critically at Donichello and Rekasi with eyes the color of the night sky and pupils white like the moon. She picked up their weapons. Her deft fingers ran along the bow, and for a moment, Rekasi saw longing shining in her odd eyes. She turned around, her skin rippling in the moonlight, and faded back into the trees. The first rhilox snapped his fingers.

Two others moved out of the shadows. They bound Rekasi and Donichello's hands with ropes. The fallen deer was tied to a pole carried by the other two. Donichello and Rekasi were led away.

It was a relatively short journey to the rhilox village. Donichello didn't look at Rekasi. Two guards stood on either side of them. Rekasi muttered, "We can get out of this."

"How?"

Under his breath, Rekasi replied, "Well, rhiloxes usually challenge their prisoners in duels. We can escape when they aren't expecting it."

Donichello nodded, "I see. So, when they free us we fight our way out of the arena and into the woods."

"Exactly."

Rekasi felt something jab him in the back. He hissed something unintelligible as the locks were opened. The two were taken to a large patch of grass that was to act as the arena. Rhiloxes surrounded them on three sides. The open forest was directly behind them, and a handful of guards were positioned there.

Rekasi looked to Donichello whose mouth was twisted in grim determination. They were thrown into the dirt before a platform. A rhilox, whom Rekasi assumed to be the chief, stood on it surrounded by servants and slaves of other races.

He glared, "Elva trespassing in my land. I challenge the trespassers. Hascor, arm the prisoners. There are archers trained on you. If you attempt to kill Hascor, you will die before you have completed your stroke."

Rekasi gave an involuntary shudder.

The female rhilox from the hunting party emerged from the crowd bearing their weapons. Her blonde hair had been braided along her face and pulled back at the nape of her neck. A gold circlet shone from her upper arm. Her horns had been tipped in the same blue paint that was painted on her stomach. This marked her as royalty in the clan. She turned her black eyes on them as she handed over their weapons.

Donichello thanked her for his sword as he drew it from its sheath. She gave them a strange, strained smile. Rekasi drew his sword andwatched as she whispered in the ear of the Chief. His black hair shook as he looked at her in surprise. His narrow face seemed to realize something, and he nodded. Moving away from Hascor, he banged his staff on the ground.

Two warriors split the crowds and sent them into fits of cheering. Both rhiloxes were strongly built. Their hair hung loosely around their shoulders, and they had woven burrs into the strands. Donichello tightened his grip on his sword. Rekasi held up a hand, "Relax."

Donichello readjusted his grip but didn't loosen any. He thought this was going to be easy. Rekasi wasn't so sure. The rhiloxes exchanged looks and laughed. They weren't expecting more than a simple fight either.

The rhilox on Rekasi's right pulled a curved sword from the belt tied around his waist. The one on his left hefted a long spear. They looked to their leader, who nodded. They slowly walked forward and tried to surround the two men. Rekasi hissed, "Don't let them get behind us. They'll cut us off."

Donichello contacted the curved sword with his own as the rhilox attempted to move behind him. The rhilox didn't expect the move. Donichello followed up with a swinging hit as Rekasi knocked the other rhilox's spear aside.

Rekasi lost track of Donichello's fight as he focused on the speartip. He moved carefully, eyeing his opponent's movements. This rhilox fought with brute force. Still, his strength was no match for Rekasi's skill. Rekasi was able to land a hit on the spear's wooden shaft. A notch remained as Rekasi removed his sword. The rhilox fought more cautiously from then, realizing Rekasi was not some dimwitted woodsmen.

Rekasi disarmed the rhilox and held out his sword threateningly. Donichello twisted the curved sword from the other rhilox's grip. The chief commanded them to stop. Rekasi lowered his sword. The chief said, "Elvateth. You have defeated our best fighters. You are free to go."

A voice said, "Let me fight them."

The chief shook his head, "No, Hascor! I will not allow it."

She pawed the earth, "Is it because you believe I cannot match their skill or because I am a woman?"

The chief didn't answer for the longest time. He said, "Neither. You are my charge. I will not have you fighting mere prisoners."

Hascor seemed to mull this over. She said, "I have a suggestion then. Send in Maeoka."

One of the servants attending the chief looked up at the sound of the name. The chief stared at the servant for a moment, then nodded, "All right, She-Elva. Fight your comrades."

The servant looked toward Rekasi and Donichello, confused. The woman walked forward from the platform. Her strawberry blonde hair was tied up in knots. Her green eyes flashed.

She traded her tunic for a short, leather jerkin. She replaced her billowing skirts with hose and leather shorts. She pulled a sword from the sheath that Hascor held.

She muttered something to Hascor in a language Rekasi did not know, but he assumed it was the dialect normally used in the area. She turned back to them, ready.

The woman leapt toward Rekasi. Readily, he moved out of the way and struck from behind. She blocked his attack clumsily, but the blade did not touch her skin. She whipped around and sliced the air. Donichello moved behind her as if to grab her. She fought fiercely as Rekasi began to gain ground. Her eyes held much fear and dislike.

He waited for her to turn on Donichello. She whipped around and launched her attack. As she brought her sword back, Rekasi hit her wrist with the flat of his blade shattering it. She howled and writhed in agony. Donichello grabbed her un-shattered wrist and placed her in an arm lock.

Rekasi asked, "Why would you fight as you have, Lioness?"

She spat out, "I'll never answer you, scum!"

Rekasi didn't respond to the insult. He said, "Scum we may be, but answer, my Lady."

She stared at Rekasi with more hate than he had ever seen. "Elva," she spat, "You are what sent my love to Deildly! You caused the death of my child. Kiro has forsaken me."

Donichello said cautiously, "Lilliana, we have not forsaken you."

She looked up in surprise and glared at him, "If it weren't for Dragonia, Einar wouldn't be dead! He wouldn't have felt the need, as a prince, to fight."

Donichello said, "Einar was a friend. A brother in arms. He would have fought just the same. It was part of his spirit. The one who has caused you all this pain is now dead. King Enchardo is *dead*."

She hissed at him, stepped back, and launched Donichello over her shoulder. Lilliana turned and leapt into the trees surrounding them.

The rhiloxes surrounded Donichello first. Rekasi sighed. This escape was going to be more difficult than he had assumed. He jumped onto the back of one of the rhiloxes. The rhilox bucked him until he was able to knock the rhilox unconscious with the hilt of his sword. Donichello did the same.

The Chief gestured to the archers. Donichello was fighting three warriors at once and missed the signal. A bolt flew toward him. Rekasi tackled Donichello to the ground as he knocked out his last opponent. The bolt whistled past his ear and hit the foliage behind. Rekasi hopped to his feet and pulled Donichello with him.

The Chief was irate. He ordered that Lilliana be found and that someone recapture his prisoners. Rekasi pushed Donichello toward the unprotected trees. Just as they had reached the grove, the head of an arrow embedded into Rekasi's upper leg, causing him to fall. He yelled out in pain. He broke the arrow's shaft so it would not catch as he stumbled to his feet. Rekasi yelled to Donichello for help. Donichello, hair plastered to his face with sweat, stared back at the man he had hated for his entire life. He looked back at the open trees, then back at Rekasi.

Rekasi knew he would leave. Donichello had never forgiven him. A heavy arm pulled him up. Donichello mumbled, "Don't let me regret this."

When they reached their camp, Donichello removed the arrow from Rekasi's leg and tied up the wound. "For a while there, I thought you'd leave me behind."

Donichello didn't say anything right away, "For a while, so did I."

Rekasi nodded, "I'm sorry for everything."

Donichello said, "Yeah, well, me too. You saved my life. Debt paid."

Sammaria stared as she came back into the campsite to see Rekasi bleeding through a hastily made bandage. She rushed to his side and placed her hand on the edge of the festering wound.

"What happened?" she demanded.

Rekasi didn't reply. She looked up at Donichello. He turned from her. He said, "Don't wander far into the forest. It's dangerous."

Sammaria felt her fury rising, "It's dangerous? Jennica is out there. What about her?"

Donichello's shoulders sagged, "Jennica isn't with us. She's gone, Sammaria. Just accept it."

Sammaria shook her head, "She is my sister. I can still sense her. I don't know where she is, but she is alive."

Donichello sat down next to the dying fire. "What happened, Rekasi?" Sammaria said again.

"We were attacked. That's all you need to know."

Sammaria's amber eyes flashed as she set her jaw. Rekasi seemed to have noticed as well. He said, "Love, don't be angry."

She retorted, "You have a *hole* in your leg, and you refuse to tell me how it has come to be there. I'm supposed to be fine with this?"

Rekasi replied, "Sammaria, we would tell you, but…"

Sammaria took in his pleading face. His auburn eyes begged as they held off the pain from his leg. She sighed, rolling her eyes, "All right."

Rekasi stood up, wincing, and helped pack up the camp. Sammaria noted something different between the two men. She didn't know what had happened while they were away, but aside from Rekasi's wound, it might have been for the better.

CHAPTER XXVIII

Morlyn opened the door to Enchardo's office. It was empty. Everything looked the same as it had on the day he had been hired to murder the princesses. He looked behind him. Seeing no one, he entered the room and locked the door.

He moved to the bookshelves and pulled a book down. Behind the book, he found a bottle of rum. Smiling, he took a sip as he sat down with the book and put his feet up on the King's desk. He read absently through the text. It was something about foreign accounts. He shoved the book off his lap, annoyed.

A piece of paper flew from the book. He read through it, a smile spreading across his face. This is what he needed. Something to incriminate Dragonia, giving Ancefra reason to invade. Quickly, he inked a pen and wrote:

Most High,
I am sending you the incriminating evidence for which you have asked. It is worse than we had suspected. I am sending this letter in an unmarked envelope. From what I gather, King Enchardo has been dealing with the menace Trydexzi. To add to this, Enchardo has paid me to kill the heirs to the throne. If this is not enough proof, then I have failed you. I will send more news as soon as I can,
Morlyn

Morlyn sealed the letter in an envelope and walked toward the aviary. He picked an inconspicuous bird and tied the letter and evidence to its foot. In the corner of his eye, he thought he saw a shadow move. He blamed it on his paranoia and began to leave. Something stopped him.

In the darkness, he could make out a pale face. Full of distrust, the man said, "Did you think you could get away with that, Morlyn? Sending secrets from the castle without being punished?"

Morlyn shook, afraid. He pled, "Sir, what are you going to do?"

The man in the darkness said, "I will show the world your true face."

He lifted his long fingers. He stared at the trembling prince, "Eserpte."

He snapped his fingers. Morlyn screeched as his arms shrunk and he transformed into a snake. The man walked from the shadows and picked up the writhing sidewinder.

"Now, learn to fear the power of a necromancer."

He tossed the snake from the aviary window.

🐾

Jennica laid on the bank of Caspar Lake. She had used her Power to pull water up from the lake, breaking her fall. She stood, pulled the water from her clothes, and started walking.

Her connection to Sammaria had always been strong, but now she could barely sense her. How far had they gone after she fell? She was terrified, but Sammaria's faint pull kept her traveling through the night.

Jennica was hurrying through the bushes when an arrow soared past her shoulder. Looking back, she saw the arrow lying in the pink light of the sunrise. Its shaft was juniper, and it had owl feathers for fletching. The tip was a sharpened dragon tooth. These were the same arrows that Donichello used.

She shouted as she ran forward, yelling out Sammaria's name. She broke through the trees and stumbled into their camp. Donichello walked toward her, dumbfounded, but Jennica ran past him and hugged her sister.

She slowly took in Rekasi's injury.

"Don't even ask," Sammaria said. "They won't tell me what happened."

Jennica smirked, "Really? Donichello, what happened?"

Donichello sighed. He glanced at Rekasi. The other man looked away. Jennica raised her eyebrows. Donichello said, "Rekasi and I came to an understanding."

"An understanding?" Jennica crossed her arms over her chest, "Did someone help you along with that?"

Donichello grimaced and nodded. Sammaria covered the smile spreading across her face. Jennica shook her head, "See that it sticks. We don't need any more injuries."

Rekasi and Donichello avoided looking at each other. Jennica pushed her hair behind her ears. She asked, "Do you know what attacked us? Sniblea called it an abomination."

Rekasi spoke up, "I do not know. I can only assume they were trying to prevent Sammaria from getting back."

Donichello said, "It is a priority to get to Mestchester. We need to stabilize the throne."

Jennica looked down. She scratched her foot in the dirt. Sammaria glanced over at her. She asked, "Jennica, what is the matter?"

"I can't go with you to Mestchester. I haven't figured out how to tell you all this."

"What do you mean?" Sammaria asked.

Jennica frowned and looked, "I was visited by Einar."

"Your brother?" Donichello asked.

Jennica nodded slowly, and she felt her stomach twist in knots, "He said the gods have chosen me for a task."

Sammaria's hands flew to her mouth. Jennica kept her eyes down. She said, "I have been avoiding it. I had to keep you safe."

Sammaria asked, "What are you supposed to do?"

Jennica looked up, avoiding Donichello's eyes, "I keep feeling pulled deep into the Katart Wood. I can't help but feel that black dragon was meant to pull me back toward my quest. I need to go. I need to find the griffin."

Donichello shouted, "That is ridiculous! That griffin almost killed me. It massacred your father's troops."

Jennica stubbornly looked to Rekasi.

Rekasi slowly shook his head. He knew what she was asking. He said, "Sammaria must return to Mestchester. The Resistance is only delaying their attack until Sammaria can get into the castle."

Jennica said, "This is where I leave you then."

Donichello said, "I will not let you go alone."

Sammaria said, "Nor will I."

Rekasi said, "Sammaria, no."

She said, "No, Rekasi. She is my sister. If I abandon her in her quest, how can I focus on leading my people? You heard her. She fought their wishes for me. I can do this for her."

Jennica called for Dratasha and asked if she could fly them to the griffin.

Dratasha said, "I cannot. If I were to even take a breath in his territory, it would be far worse for all of us, *Kiata.*"

Jennica looked at her, "What does that mean?"

Dratasha said, "It is a name for chosen Elvateth. It means friend of Wygair, friend of dragons. I bond my fury to you."

Dratasha touched her green muzzle to Jennica's forehead. Warmth flooded her body. She felt strength well up in her muscles. Jennica took a step back, feeling lightheaded.

Dratasha said, "Call on us in your time of need, and we shall come. My fury shall support you as long as you live."

Jennica bowed to the dragon, "You don't know what this means to me, Dratasha. Thank you." She watched as Dratasha and Sniblea flew away from the clearing and out of sight.

Most of the day was gone by this point, and the sun had just fallen behind the tops of the trees. Donichello said, "Rekasi, Sammaria, would you mind making us some torches?"

Soon, all four of them were holding a flickering flame. The firelight showed just how ragged the four of them looked. Donichello looked at the others and said, "We must take a bath at the first river we find. We reek of Dratasha. The griffin will probably not like that much."

Several hours later, Sammaria was walking with Rekasi when she stumbled and fell down a slope. After a few moments, there was a loud splash. Rekasi scrambled to find Sammari and found her just as she was pulling herself onto the bank of a wide river. She shook out her hair and said, dripping with sarcasm, "Found it!"

Jennica and Sammaria stayed, and the men went upriver to bathe. They stripped off their mud-caked clothes, laying them next to Jennica's pack, and jumped into the tranquil river. With the torches burning on the bank, the girls splashed around and cleaned themselves.

Jennica said, "I wonder how our friends are faring back in Mestchester."

Sammaria shrugged, "I couldn't even begin to guess."

Jennica asked, "How much time has passed since we left?"

Sammaria said, "I was kidnapped during the Blessim days. If I'm not mistaken, we have entered the Erif days. We've been gone for at least half a year. The Frez days will start soon."

Jennica sighed as she pushed her long hair back from her face. She said, "Kiro, save them. I hope that Dragonia will survive."

CHAPTER XXIX

Demetria heard marching. Not the slow and steady sound of the King's army; these footfalls were erratic and heavy. She looked up from the bushes where she was picking berries and saw a black mass just on the horizon. She squinted, but she couldn't make it out.

As it moved closer, the mass became clear, and Demetria's heart skipped a beat. It couldn't be. She had heard stories throughout her life. There weren't supposed to be any of these monstrosities remaining. The stories were just told to scare children now. But there was no question in her mind. The advancing mass was the O'rult.

Demetria raced toward town. As she reached the first house, she yelled, "O'rult! Heading this way!"

Anaranjo said, "O'rult? Hah! They aren't real."

Demetria said, "The rumors were true! They are coming!"

A shepherd ran in from the fields. He was yelling the same message. Quickly, mothers grabbed their children and families and hid them within their homes. Anaranjo said, "You're both full of it."

Demetria ran home to warn her family. They were already locking the place up. She had just slipped inside and locked the door when the O'rult were reaching the crest of the hill and entering town.

They marched into town down the main street. Anaranjo was playing in the street, trying to prove that there was no reason to be scared. He said, "Demetria! Come out. There is nothing to worry about."

His eyes grew wide as he saw the first O'rult. Anaranjo tried to dart into a house, finding all the doors to be locked. The O'rult were on top of him. At first, Anaranjo was able to weave through the O'rult. Then, Demetria heard a scratching of metal. Someone drew a sword, and then there was a scream. The O'rult finally cleared, and Demetria flinched as she opened her door.

Anaranjo was laying on her step, bleeding badly from his left shoulder, his face badly bruised. Demetria thought his skull must have been shattered. He picked his head up slightly, "You were right."

Demetria called her mother to come and help her. Demetria's mother appeared beside her. She gasped when she saw the state of the boy. She went back into the house, returning with her eldest son. They carefully picked him up, took him into the house, and laid him on the closest bed.

Demetria's mother looked at the wound in Anaranjo's shoulder, gently prodding it with her finger. Luckily, he had passed out. She said aloud to no one in particular, "It's amazing it missed his heart. Quickly, bandages, he is losing too much blood."

Demetria retrieved a bowl of water and some bandages and started to soak up the blood. While she placed pressure on the wound, she prayed to Jonakil that he would live.

Anaranjo's hand snapped up and gripped Demetria's. A small scream escaped both of their mouths. Anaranjo said, "Demetria!"

She leaned in and said, "I'm here."

He gasped, and Demetria put pressure on the wound once again.

He spoke and his voice was of someone much older, "Earth and Fire and Sky and Water. Lightning will boom. Thunder will crash. She will come, and they will fall."

Demetria stopped what she was doing. Her mother stared at him. Her mother pulled her back. Anaranjo reached up and touched the T scar on Demetria's chest. His eyes closed, and his head fell limply against his shoulder. Anaranjo was dead.

❧

Sammaria climbed out of the water, followed by Jennica. They put on their underclothes. Jennica was putting on a grey dress when she saw something slink into the water from across the bank. Sammaria must have seen it as well because she was already screaming before Jennica realized what it was.

She finished dressing in a hurry when she heard Rekasi and Donichello running over. A melody seemed to float up from the rippling water.

Sammaria picked up the one torch that had survived their bath and shined the light across the water. A woman's head, with thick, reddish-blue hair and nearly translucent skin, was bobbing in the water. She moved closer and placed her hands on the bank.

Jennica clutched Sammaria's arm tightly when she saw the woman's hands. Each of her fingers was connected by translucent skin.

The siren pulled herself out of the water, revealing a naked torso and a tail as clear as glass. The sirens hummed melody shifted, and she began to sing in a clear and intoxicating soprano.

All alone I stay, day after day.
Since he had gone away, hoping for a man to stay.

Then the siren's voice became piercingly high. She was screeching. Sammaria and Jennica had to cover their ears.

When he left, he broke my heart.
Now, I want revenge.
No one can have the man I lost.

Jennica urgently slapped Sammaria's shoulder. Sammaria turned to see Rekasi and Donichello's eyes in a haze. They hadn't even noticed the shrieking. They simply continued to stare at the foul creature as they both walked into the water.

Sammaria grabbed Rekasi's arm, and he turned slowly to look at her. His eyes clouded, full of rage. He shook her off, shoving her into Jennica's arms. Sammaria said, "They are going to die."

Sammaria waved the torch along the ground and picked up a rock she found on the bank. Jennica picked up another. Sammaria shifted the rock in her grip and hurled it at the siren. The rock hit the siren's face. She screeched, her melody faltering.

Donichello shook his head. His memory of the past few minutes was hazy. He looked over to his left where Jennica was staring at the creature at the water's edge. He pulled his sword and ran toward her. The siren recovered from the hit and chanted again. The sword fell from Donichello's hand to the dirt. Jennica thought furiously. She threw another rock at the vile woman.

The siren, outraged, hooked her long, twisted nails around the roots on the river bank and pulled herself from the water completely. She used her webbed hands to pull herself across the ground toward the girls.

In the full firelight, the creature screeched again revealing two rows of sharp, pointed teeth. The siren pulled herself forward, her face twisted into a hideous mask. So shocked by the sudden transformation, Jennica stood still, unable to move.

Sammaria picked up a piece of wood and hollered, "Jennica, duck!"

Jennica did as she was told. Sammaria swung the branch and hit the siren in the stomach. The siren faltered in her melody. Then, along with Rekasi and Donichello, the creature crumpled.

Jennica dug through her bag looking for anything to cover their ears. She pulled out a pack of herbs. Inside was a spool of lamb's wool, an herb used to stop bleeding. She pulled it apart and ran over to Donichello. She seized his hands and tried to pull him up. Her feet were sliding in the mud. She grunted as she pulled free of the mud onto solid ground. She looked at his face with concern and shoved lamb's wool into both of his ears.

She pulled on Rekasi. He moved a little, but then he was jerked back into the water. A brunette siren held onto his leg. She picked up another stone and threw it. The siren screamed, dropping Rekasi into the water. The water was filled with them. She dragged Rekasi up the bank and shoved the herb in his ears.

Sammaria was struggling to keep back the first one. More emerged from the water. Jennica ran to help her. She took the branch from Sammaria and started to beat the sirens. Sammaria shot Fire at them and four fell back into the depths.

More sirens advanced. They seemed more powerful. Jennica said, "Fire makes them stronger. Sammaria, stop."

In the flurry, the girls hadn't noticed two sirens slink away toward Rekasi and Donichello. The brunette took Rekasi, and a greenish-blonde creature took Donichello. The green-blonde leaned over Donichello, her hair dripping on his face. She lowered herself and kissed him.

A siren's kiss was death for every man. They lure men into the water with promises of kisses, and they never return. Donichello woke and returned the kiss. He wrapped his arms around her back. More sirens came up from the water and stroked his body. They took hold of him and pulled him back toward the water.

The sirens engaging the girls started to retreat. Sammaria looked up and saw Donichello being dragged toward the water. Rekasi was standing, brandishing Donichello's sword. A siren advanced on him. Sammaria ran out into the river and yanked the siren by the hair. It shrieked but didn't return. Outraged, Jennica shot ice toward her adversary. The siren shrieked and retreated.

Sammaria rushed into the water. She grabbed Donichello by the shoulders and shot Fire at the sirens that were latched onto him. They retreated, and she pulled Donichello back to shore. Jennica rushed to help, and they laid him down. Rekasi, released from his trance, fell to the ground beside Donichello.

Jennica didn't know how to wake them. Sammaria lit some more torches, hoping their light might rise the men from their stupor. As she and Sammaria sat beside the men in a circle of torches, Jennica said, "I'm going to kill Donichello when he wakes up."

Sammaria laughed and said, "He was attacked by a siren."

Jennica snapped, "And he enjoyed it too."

As she finished saying this, Donichello began to cough, water spraying from his mouth. Jennica hugged Donichello's chest. He put his arm on her back and raised his head a bit, "Jennica, what's wrong?"

She didn't answer.

Sammaria said, "She's mad at you for kissing a siren."

Donichello looked like he had seen a ghost. He was horrified. He sat up and kissed Jennica. She pushed him away, frowning slightly. Donichello shook his head.

CHAPTER XXX

The O'rult had just reached the Mestchester city gates when Bynakst'r called them to a stop. The O'rult stood still and straight.

A young farm boy looked out on the brown, unclean bodies of the O'rult. The descriptions he had heard said they looked almost human and were strong as dragons. They were supposedly fierce, merciless, and defiantly heartless. The creatures that stood in front of his house now did not match this description.

A woman joined them. The O'rult threw their hands in the air and roared, "Long live Misseter! Long live Misseter!"

They continued on their way, marching through the city gates. The first few who tried to enter fell back as a volley of bolts from crossbows buried in their necks.

However, the O'rult overwhelmed the Dragonian defenders. Misseter led a bloody path to the palace. She took her place on an empty throne.

ॐ

Jennica, Sammaria, Rekasi, and Donichello stood at the mouth of a cave. Jennica said, "I go in. Alone."

Donichello and Rekasi looked at her, ready to protest. Jennica said, "I'm going alone. You can't talk me out of it."

With that said, she turned on her heel and entered the cave. Torch in hand, Jennica realized that the cave was rather shallow. However, there was a complex system of tunnels. The darkness within the cave was beyond normal. The torchlight could barely penetrate it. She could not see more than a foot in front of her nor below her waist. She felt as if she were floating through the cave, detached from her lower body. Jennica pinched her leg. The pain was very real.

Jennica waved the torch around carefully, looking for the griffin's nest. As she moved the light, a small green item caught her eye. She moved the light back over it. It was the tip of a tail. She moved the light over more. Before her, lying on the floor, was a large snake. Its nostrils flared out slightly. The eyelids flickered, and its gigantic, yellow eyes flipped open and stared at her.

The snake spoke, "You have to answer a question to pass to the next tunnel."

Jennica shifted nervously as the snake reared up to ask her the question. Jennica flipped the hood of her cloak down off her head.

She asked, "What's your question?"

The snake glared at her with one eye. It then said, "Your question is a riddle. You must answer correctly to pass.

Only one color, but not one size,
Stuck at the bottom, yet easily flies
Present in sun, but not in rain,
Doing no harm and feeling no pains.

She had never heard a riddle such as this before. She stared at the wall as she thought. Her shadow was cast upon it. It swayed uncertainly in the wavering lights. That was the answer, there cast upon the wall. Grey all the time and feeling no pain. She looked up at the giant snake and said, "It's a shadow."

The snake hissed angrily but allowed her to pass. She watched for any signs of a trap. She stepped on a pebble, sinking it into the ground. A rumble followed. Jennica looked up to see a boulder rolling toward her.

She jumped and shot Water down with her hands, propelling herself off the cave floor. She landed upon one of the rolling boulders and jumped to the next, one after another as they crashed into the wall.

Once the boulders finally stopped, she let herself fall to the ground. She moved on to another chamber. Looking up, she saw it was filled with bats. The smoke from several lanterns rose, making them restless. She quickly hurried through to the connecting tunnel.

Within the next chamber, she finally found a young griffin. It said, "If you don't answer this question correctly, I will be forced to kill you."

Jennica nodded. He asked, "Why did Einar send you here?" Jennica was stumped. He had not given her a reason. She guessed, "He sent me because he knew that the griffins would have a way to save Dragonia."

The young griffin squawked. He said, "I'm sorry, Jennica, you are wrong."

Jennica said, "No!"

The griffin reared, its claws raking across her face as it came down. She fell to the ground, blood dripping from the scratches. She watched the griffin as it moved toward her. She waited to die.

Donichello was pacing back and forth at the entrance to the cave. Sammaria was getting annoyed, "Donichello, stop pacing. She's fine. I can feel it."

Donichello said, "But you don't know that for sure. She could be hurt."

Sammaria said, "But she's not."

Donichello sat down, but he kept fiddling with his hands, "She's been gone for a while. I should go after her."

With that, he entered the cave despite Rekasi and Sammaria's protests. He slowly called Jennica's name. No answer came but the echo of his voice. He reached the end of the cave, seeing nothing at first. He moved his torch, and the light fell upon a hand. He moved the light farther. Jennica lay as if she had fainted. Her face, with four parallel lines of blood streaked across it, looked troubled. Donichello took her hand. It was cold. Her eyelids fluttered.

Donichello called for Sammaria, "Quick! Build a fire. We must keep her warm. Whatever she is doing, we have to keep her safe."

Donichello looked up as creaking in the forest caught his attention. He stood still as the trees continued to moan. In his mind, he replayed the struggle with the griffin. Sammaria asked, "What is going on?"

She moved to the edge of the cave. An eerie light lit within the forest. The trees continued to creak and sway. Donichello felt Sammaria move closer to Rekasi and watched as the trees parted, making a path. Donichello said, "We should follow it."

Jennica woke to darkness. She felt the ghost of someone's hands on hers. She barely lifted her head. The young griffin was still at its post. She stayed close to the ground. Keeping her back to the griffin so he couldn't see her movements, she touched her face and felt the bleeding scratches. She approached the griffin. It said, "Why did Einar send you?"

This time, Jennica repeated her answer but in Old Elva. The griffin bowed and allowed her to pass. Jennica entered the next cavern carefully, unsure of what to expect. She came face to face with another griffin. This creature was at least four times larger than the young griffin that had injured her, and it was staring at her with intense, golden eyes.

Jennica had been staring back at the griffin for several minutes before he said, "Well, now that's something. I'm in the company of a princess. Your spirit seems injured. Look at those scratches. That griffin can never kill anything properly."

Jennica looked at the griffin wearily. It stood saying, "Jennica, did you know that the only way to arrive in my lair is to pass into the spirit realm? After you are done talking with me, I will return you to your body. Considering you behave and it hasn't been moved."

She said hurriedly, "Yes, yes, of course."

He said, "Only speak when you are spoken to." He waited, "Do you understand?"

Jennica snapped her head toward him and said, "Yes, sir."

The griffin said, "My name is Dyumkl."

Jennica nodded again. He said, "You will address me as so." Jennica nodded yet again, trying not to be rude. Dyumkl told her, "Einar sent you here, did he not?"

Jennica nodded, "Yes, he did."

Dyumkl said, "Yes, of course."

He eyed her critically, "He puts too much faith in you and your companions. However, the gods seem to think he is right. Otherwise, he never would have been allowed to talk with you. You have a quest, do you understand?"

She nodded.

"You are probably going to save Dragonia, so I'd pay attention. If you want to save your home, find the Island of the Hawkaties. Do you understand?"

Jennica said, "The Hawkaties are extinct, aren't they? No one has seen them for a hundred years."

Agitated, the griffin said, "It is true that they have not been seen in nearly a century, but they are not extinct. They reside on a hidden island. Understand, the O'rult cannot be defeated without the Hawkaties. They hold the power to return order to your civilization. If you can call it *civil*."

He looked at Jennica; he was testing her to see if she'd keep her cool. He asked, "Do you agree?"

Jennica looked down, and in a solemn voice said, "Yes, I agree with you."

He asked, "Why?"

She replied, "I agree. My father was cruel. He committed crimes that I would never have believed possible. It was as if he enjoyed the suffering of others."

Dyumkl said, "Perhaps Einar has placed his faith rightly. This task won't be easy, however. You will likely die."

Jennica looked down at her hands.

Was dying worse than what had happened with her father? He was gone, but it wouldn't be long before someone seized the throne.

Countries that didn't have a king were always fragile. She could always send Sammaria back to Mestchester to take the throne so she could return the country to normal while she left to find this island. She asked in a stronger voice, "How do I find it?"

Dyumkl laughed, "Complete this and our real intentions may be known."

"Our?" she asked.

The room went black.

Jennica struggled to open her eyes. She lifted her hand to her face. There was blood on her fingers. The scratches she had received in the Spirit Realm seemed to have affected her in the real world. She was surprised to find that, while there were four lines of blood that ran from her right eyebrow to the left corner of her lips, there weren't any cuts below them. Pushing herself to a sitting position, she looked around her. That unusual darkness surrounded her again.

She pulled herself to her feet, smoothing the dress that wrapped around her legs. She felt along the walls for the entrance of the cave. She found it strange that she couldn't see light ahead of her. She hadn't gone far into the tunnels. Her hand never found the opening she searched for, only more and more rock.

She slammed her hand against the wall. The sound of her strangled sobs vibrated throughout the small cave. Dejected, she sank to the floor. The uneasy darkness surrounded her. She closed her eyes. It didn't matter if they were open or not, the darkness was the same. She felt her hair fall around her face, but she didn't have enough energy to brush it from her eyes. Jennica sat there, listening to the silence of the cave.

Rekasi thought he heard noises coming from within the cave. This forest made him uneasy. Rumors of spirits and dangerous beings made him wary. They had already encountered beasts that were normally only whispered about over the fires of Dragonia. He shifted from his post. Sammaria and Donichello had gone to discover the meaning of the ghostly light. He prayed to the gods that they would remain safe.

Rekasi looked back into the cave. This time he was sure he heard a noise. It sounded like wailing. He created a torch and entered slowly, sword raised. The noise stopped. Rekasi followed the tunnels back.

He shouted, "Hello? Who is there?"

It was some time before he heard the noise again. This time it sounded like a voice. The voice sounded like it was pleading with the gods. He said, "Jennica?"

A faint reply called his name. He heard feet slapping against stone, the sound growing louder as it moved closer. Soon, a body slammed into his. Jennica's small frame embraced his. She said, "I do not know how, but I got so very lost. Please, get me out of here."

Rekasi pulled her from the cave. When they came into the light, Rekasi noticed blood on her face. However, she didn't look injured. He asked her, "Whose blood is that?"

She touched the blood on her face. The griffin scratches must have healed. Jennica took a long time to respond feeling the trails of blood, "I do not know."

Rekasi said, "We should go find your sister. We need to return to Mestchester. Sammaria must establish her claim before it is too late."

Jennica shook her head, "I cannot return to Mestchester now."

Rekasi objected, "We don't have time for this, Jennica."

Jennica replied, "I will go alone if I have to. I have to find the Island of the Hawkaties."

Rekasi scoffed, "Did you hit your head in the cave? The Hawkaties are gone. If they ever even existed. We cannot detour for nothing but a fool's errand."

"Please, Rekasi. I have to do this. It will save Dragonia."

"Taking Sammaria to Mestchester will save Dragonia. The country cannot survive without her leadership."

"What if whatever is threatening Dragonia is something Sammaria cannot fight? I don't believe that all of this would have happened for a fool's errand."

Rekasi sighed, "Let us not decide anything now. We should find Sammaria and Donichello."

Sammaria looked up. The lights twinkled in the trees above her.

Donichello sighed, "I don't believe this is going anywhere. We should go back."

Sammaria said, "No. Don't you believe in divine intervention?"

Donichello sighed again, "You and Jennica are very much alike."

Sammaria grinned as she forged ahead.

A mist covered them. Donichello gripped Sammaria and pulled her down as a dark figure approached them. The man was dressed in rags, and his hair was ratty. The light seemed to be emanating from him. His eyes glossed over as he called, "My Queen. The one true queen. Take my hand. There is much you should see."

Sammaria tried to rise. She felt no fear of the man. There seemed to be no malice in his presence. Donichello pulled her back, "It isn't safe. I cannot allow you to go."

Sammaria shed Donichello's clutch. He pulled on her. She said, "I can do this."

She took the raggedy man's hand. As soon as their hands touched, Sammaria gasped, and a vision overtook her.

She was surrounded by grey smoke. On the streets, lay bodies of many men. She looked up and saw the old man standing in the middle of the street. He pointed at her, then held his hand open for her to take.

Her eyes swept past women lying dead to children standing in the streets crying. Her eyes lighted on O'rult weapons lying beside an open door. The stench of burnt flesh and decaying bodies hung in the air. She hesitantly took hold of the man's hand again.

She was standing in front of the palace. The front entrance had been destroyed. The silver door was crumpled, lying slightly out of the water in the moat. She flinched at the destruction.

The man released her hand. He waited for her to enter. Sammaria took a deep breath before she entered her former home. She knew no one could see her as she walked through to the throne room, but she still moved slowly, avoiding their eyes. Everything was streaked with blood. She stepped over a body. She looked down. Pranshey's empty eyes stared back at her.

Sammaria screamed. Pranshey was someone she could never imagine dying. She never thought of him having any other life than being her father's sneaky advisor.

Sammaria ran from Pranshey's body, leaving the hall long behind her. She passed the entrance to the wing which held her bedroom. It was blocked off by piles of crumbled stone and splintered wood, but she simply passed through them.

She saw the bodies of starved nobles lying on the steps. She moved along the stairs, seeing the families of her friends and the people she had simply ignored while she was princess. She whispered, "How could this have happened?"

A hand shot out of the pile of dead. It reached out. Someone called, "Kiro! Oh, Kiro! Why abandon us to this fate?"

Sammaria pushed the bodies from where the hand had raised. She looked upon the face of Duchess Larissa.

Sammaria gasped. Larissa said, "I am truly sorry for my sins!"

Larissa bowed her head and slept. Sammaria turned away from the gruesome sight and fled the East Wing. She moved toward the throne room again. Something about it called to her. As she walked, she noticed broken rum barrels and glasses along the walls. She stepped on old meat bones and rotten fruits and vegetables. She heard a crack as she stepped on the back of a picture. She picked it up, flipping it over. In the picture, King Enchardo was holding Sammaria. Jennica was standing before a tall boy who she thought must have been Einar. Brushing a tear from her eye, Sammaria dropped the picture to the floor and moved over to the throne.

A woman was sitting upon the throne, and an O'rult stood at her right. They were laughing hysterically with another O'rult. The O'rult was pulling in a woman by her hair. They made her dance while whipping her to make her move faster. Sammaria whispered, "No!"

The old man appeared before her again. He grabbed her hand. She was returned to her physical self.

She opened her eyes and fell to her knees. Her throat caught, but she stopped the emotion that was threatening to overtake her. She looked up. There was no sign of the man or the strange light. Donichello knelt beside her. He asked, "Are you all right? What happened?"

She said, "I saw death. So much death."

Donichello asked, "What do you mean?"

Sammaria looked up at him, seeing fear in his eyes, "The O'rult have taken Mestchester."

CHAPTER XXXI

*I*t took some time, but Jennica finally convinced her companions that the Hawkaties were real and alive. The problem remained that Jennica did not know where the Island of the Hawkaties was. According to legend, the Island had disappeared from the world many centuries earlier. Hawkaties were sighted throughout the land after that, but then they simply disappeared.

Stories about the strange creatures that had lived on the Island had disappeared into myth. So far removed, the Hawkaties were revered as gods. Jennica retraced the legends. Based on the last sightings, the Island might have been east in the Mystic Sea, which bordered Mysticus and Griffinia. Or it could lie in the west in the Sea of Mytositsa. They would have to split up. Donichello and Jennica said goodbye to Sammaria and Rekasi and headed east toward the Mystic Sea. Rekasi and Sammaria departed toward the southwest border of Pilleetain."

Sammaria walked in silence beside Rekasi. By the day's end, they had reached the border of Dragonia. They finally understood that the rumors were true. They saw whole villages burned, the inhabitants nowhere to be found. Occasionally, someone would appear, begging for food. Rekasi and Sammaria gave them what they could spare, but there wasn't much to go around.

Sammaria felt an aching in her heart as she watched the people split up the meager food they received. The beggars told them of the attacks, which all seemed to have occurred after sundown. The villagers had had no warning. Sammaria watched Rekasi as the people's stories unfolded.

His brow knitted together as he listened. When they departed from the beggars, she asked, "What is the matter?"

Rekasi said, "The O'rult must be receiving help from some other force. O'rult have to be controlled. It is how they are created."

Sammaria said, "Who could control them? And to what purpose?"

Rekasi sighed, "O'rult have to be created by necromancers. Dangerous ones. It is a terrible thing distorting souls as they do. To what end, I can only guess. Perhaps he seeks power."

Donichello stumbled forward in the lead. He checked behind him. Jennica was fairing much worse. He knew that Water gave Jennica her strength, just as the Earth gave him his, but they were landlocked. She kept trudging along without complaint, but he knew she wouldn't last much longer. She was drawing her last strength from the groundwater, but that used up more energy than it gave.

This was the unfortunate disadvantage for those who could wield the Elemental Powers. The elements were strong and provided great strength and bursts of power. However, when still learning to use them, the overwhelming power was entirely draining to the body. Donichello had been trained at an early age by a secret tutor. The tutor had learned of their Power and taught both Rekasi and Donichello everything he knew. Jennica and Sammaria's Power had been discovered relatively late in their lives, and Jennica had used a great deal of Power in the griffin's cave.

On they went, and he hoped that Jennica would call for a rest. He knew they must reach the looming landform ahead of them before it would be safe for them to make camp. He could barely make out the cliff called Trydid Rock in the distance as it was starting to get dark. He looked behind him. Jennica was just coming over the last point in the mountains that looked over the Meadow of Gamerana. A few more miles past Trydid Rock and they would be in the allied country of Mysticus. They still had a two day journey to reach the Mystic Sea.

Donichello looked back at Jennica once more. He saw the determination on her face but also saw the weariness taking over. She stumbled. She would never admit that she wasn't going to make it much farther. Donichello said, "We just have a few more feet. Just let us get to Trydid Rock, and then we can make camp."

Jennica nodded and continued. They stumbled on to the plateau. Donichello helped her up to the ledge. He emptied his flagon of water into a pan and did the same with Jennica's. He sat the pan next to her. She looked up at him and smiled weakly. She placed her hand in the pan and instantly Donichello saw the weariness ebb away from her face. She said, "Let's make supper."

They made a meal of cooked vegetable stew. Donichello added wood to the fire to keep it going.

Jennica asked suddenly, "Could I ask you a personal question?"

He nodded, "You can ask me anything."

She looked down, gathering her nerve, "Why, in Mestchester, did you like me? You didn't know me. And I was so mean to you."

Donichello sighed. Jennica looked down. "Sorry," she mumbled.

He shook his head, "I like it when you ask questions. It proves to me that you are who I think you are."

Jennica looked at him, confused. He looked at her before looking back at the fire. He asked, "Do you remember when you were about seven or eight? When your father would take you riding to meet the people of the kingdom so they wouldn't fear you anymore?"

Jennica nodded. Donichello said, "Well, you came to Likenton during that time. We met then. I was about fourteen. Your father introduced us. I could see an untamed spirit in you that I hadn't seen in anyone else. It reminded me of how the snow looks when the sun rises. It turns the whole world orange and pink. It's something you know you can never capture no matter what."

Jennica ducked her head. She wasn't sure that she liked being loved because he thought her to be beautiful.

Donichello continued, "And then I saw you in the courtyard of my house. You were playing with the servants like you had known them your whole life. I know that you hadn't told them you were a princess. You could see in their eyes that they admired you, but they didn't hold the suspicious look their parents' eyes held when they saw you. You never seemed to be bothered that people feared you. You just seemed to win them over. That's why I was so infatuated with you before I really knew you."

Jennica blushed, "I never knew that they feared me. I just saw that they were happy or sad. I never saw fear. And I always tried to make them happy."

Donichello nodded, "That's what I thought. It's making me love you more."

Jennica looked at the fire. Donichello moved over to where she was sitting. He wrapped his arm around her, and she leaned her head on his shoulder. They sat there for a long while before going to sleep.

Jennica smiled as she pulled the blankets up to her chin. Falling asleep under the shining stars, she didn't notice the startled birds flying from the forest.

Sammaria woke with a start in a cold sweat. She placed her hand on her temple. It pounded underneath her fingers. Her dream faded in her mind. She had seen Jennica dying. Her sister's screams echoed in her ears. She absently looked around her. A rare flower caught her eye. It was delicate and light. There were three heart-shaped petals around a bright red spiked center. She looked at the Lalysd as she recalled its properties. It allowed one to look into the future and to see real dreams. She looked over at Rekasi. He said, "You have been moaning for about an hour."

He held up a small golden platter. Sammaria recognized it to be a scrying dish.

"Why didn't you wake me?"

"It is better to let dreams play out than to wake up in the middle. If you weren't meant to see it, you wouldn't."

Rekasi stared into his scrying dish through the entire exchange. Sammaria took a blanket and draped it across his shoulders. He muttered a thanks.

"What do you see?" she asked.

Rekasi tossed his dish aside, "Nothing! The Hawkaties must have this place guarded with a power stronger than mine."

CHAPTER XXXII

Jennica awoke and looked over at Donichello who was still sound asleep. She crawled over and shook his shoulder. He mumbled and turned over, still asleep. She said, "You leave me no choice."

She placed her hand on Donichello's forehead and let droplets of water trickle through the lines of her hand. His eyes popped open, saying threateningly, "Jennica?"

She hissed, "Wake up."

He yawned, "I am awake."

Jennica said, "Sammaria and Rekasi can't find the Island. It is cloaked with some powerful magic they can't trace. They want to know what you plan on doing."

Donichello asked, "Well, I plan on going to the Mystic Sea and imploring the help of the monks."

Jennica said, "Sammaria said they will continue on. They might still be out of range."

Donichello nodded, "That very well could be. Tell her to continue as planned."

Jennica nodded. She closed her eyes to concentrate on Sammaria's mind.

A howl echoed throughout the meadow. Jennica's eyes snapped open, "What was that?"

Donichello said, "I'm not sure I want to wait to find out."

Jennica heard crashing sounds heading their way. She scowled at Donichello as he silently made a barrier of rock.

The creature stopped for a second. Jennica sucked in a breath and held it. She said, "It must be trying to get our scent."

It started to crash through the trees and into the meadow. Donichello said uncertainly, "It looks like a wolf."

Jennica said, "Wolves? Like from human stories?"

She crawled to the side of the cliff. The creature certainly looked like a wolf, but it was far too large, and it was completely black.

The creature clamored up the steep cliff. It fell on the gravelly side, but it wouldn't give up so easily. There was a shuffle of rocks as they slid under Jennica from her side. She saw a crack in the side of the cliff.

The wolf continued up. Jennica looked over at Donichello. He was still watching the wolf make its way up to the ledge. Jennica moaned as she watched it gain on them.

To her left, a blur of green and red passed. She whipped her head around. There was nothing there. She heard a sword being pulled from its sheath and turned to see the wolf creature was upon them. It prepared to leap.

Rocks clattered. The creature jumped. It never made it to the ledge. The wolf slammed into an invisible barrier and slid halfway down the slope. It stared at them, and slobber dripped from its mouth.

Still, the wolf wasn't deterred. It began crawling back toward them. Jennica looked around at the rocks scattered on the ground. A swirl of colors flew into the crack. She jumped up. Donichello grabbed her arm and pulled her back to her knees, "Don't move."

"Trust me," she said.

Jennica crawled beside a large crack in the cliff face. She kneeled before it, feeling Donichello's eyes on her back. She slowly reached inside and felt around. Her hand clasped a round object. She pulled it out.

She was surprised to hear it chattering angrily at her. She opened her hand, and it jumped, catching the edge of her hand with its little fingers. It scrambled, stood on her palm, and yelped at her. Its voice was deep but high pitched. It said, "What do you think you're doing? You should be thanking me! Not grabbing me with your large hands and squeezing the breath out of me."

Donichello gaped at the creature swinging from Jennica's palm. He asked, "Thanking you for what, exactly?"

The little creature voiced, "For stopping that wolf phantom!"

Donichello closed his mouth. Jennica looked at the creature. It was shaped like a round pot. It had yellow, tulip-shaped eyes and green arms that looked like vines. It swung around her palm with its rose arms and short legs. Its clothing looked like it was made of wild grasses.

Jennica asked, "If you don't mind me asking, what *are* you?"

The little flower man huffed. His words were clipped. Words that started with w's came out like a y. He said, "What am I? I'm a Mountain-Valley Grumpice, of course. What else would I be?"

Jennica said, "I'm not sure."

She glanced over her shoulder nervously at the wolf. It paced back and forth, snapping at the shield of the Grumpice's light.

Jennica looked back at the Grumpice. It gave her an inquiring look and then scurried up her arm, stopping on her shoulder before jumping. From its back, two little wings spread. It flew up until it was level with Jennica's eyes. It flew closer and peered at Jennica. He exclaimed, "Kiro!"

Jennica gave him a quick, puzzled look. He said, "You are a princess."

Jennica said, "Yeah, so?"

He continued as if she hadn't spoken, "You are the twin from the writing," the Grumpice said. He stared at her as if she should know what he was talking about.

Donichello asked, "Huh?"

The annoyed Grumpice said, "Stupid Elva. I'll just show you."

Donichello reached for the creature. Jennica held her arm out and said, "Leave him. He'll show us."

The Grumpice said, "Stupid Elva should listen to the she-Elva."

Jennica stifled a snicker. Donichello gave her a look.

The Grumpice said, "Move back. I must create an entrance for your large bodies."

Jennica stood back. She was careful not to slip off the ledge.

He blew on his small rooty hands and threw his arms to the sides. The crack in the rocks split to form a large, solid arch. The little Grumpice landed and walked in. Jennica followed. Donichello protested, "Jennica! It might not be safe."

Jennica said, "He saved us from – whatever that is." She gestured to the wolf still prowling the perimeter. After this, we can continue to the Mystic Sea."

He said, "We need to find the Island, and I have a bad feeling about this."

Jennica said, "I have a feeling I need to see this."

Donichello relented. He followed her into the cave. There were more Grumpices than Jennica could count. They had created a honeycomb of tunnels in which numerous tasks were being completed. There were Grumpice tailors and chefs, and Jennica even saw one Grumpice writing on what looked like paper. Rocks fell as new tunnels were mined.

A thin Grumpice with a head full of thick, leafy hair approached them. She glared at the Grumpice hovering near Jennica's head, "Truckle, Mossk is requesting you. He wants to know about the wolf phantom and the Elvateth."

Truckle said, "Vineyeedle, show them the writing and then turn them out. Answer any questions they might have."

He whispered something in her ear that Jennica couldn't detect. Vineyeedle's eyes flashed at them and she said, "Follow me."

Donichello said to Jennica, "They aren't very friendly, are they?"

Vineyeedle said, "We don't like strangers in our midst. That is why we prefer people to think this place is cursed. Not many make it as close to the Rock as you did. No one, besides you, knows that Grumpices still exist."

Donichello said, "Why must you keep your clan a secret? Aren't Grumpices peaceful creatures?"

Vineyeedle said scornfully, "Yes, we are. Until the Elvateth come and ask us to vanquish their enemies. Enemies they cannot handle on their own. The poor Elva, they say. So, if that is why you are here, you just turn that Elva arse of yours around and exit the colony!"

With that said, she turned and headed into one of the tunnels, leaving Donichello and Jennica dumbstruck. Agitated, Donichello asked, "What now?"

Jennica said, raising her voice, "What? You think that this is my fault? How was I supposed to know that the legendary Grumpices were going to abandon us? Don't you get all mad at me! I only came here to see the stupid writings on the stupid wall. And that accursed Vineyeedle just left us here."

Jennica huffed.

Donichello yelled, "Jennica! I tried to tell you that we shouldn't come here. But did you listen to me? No, you wanted to see the stupid writings because the stupid Grumpice complimented you."

Jennica turned around and crossed her arms on her chest. She ignored Donichello. She heard the buzz of wings around them stop and looked around. Everyone was staring at her. She gave a couple of them harsh looks and work resumed. Jennica wouldn't look at Donichello. She could feel his angry stare stabbing her in the back like daggers

A young, female Grumpice stood just before Jennica's feet. She had layered, rose petal hair and river-rock eyes. She said, "Vineyeedle meant no harm. She is just testy. 'Specially when it comes to the Grumpices' secrets. She thinks if the world knows that Grumpices live, that the world will come after us. After all, we are the only ones that know how to defeat the O'rult."

"The O'rult?" Jennica asked, surprised.

The girl nodded enthusiastically, "We figured it out. We are excellent creators."

"What about the Hawkaties?" asked Donichello.

The girl looked at him, "The Hawkaties *think* they know about the O'rult. The Grumpices *do* know about the O'rult. We figured it out. We need their Power, but we have the knowledge."

Jennica looked at Donichello. He rolled his eyes. The girl said, "My name is Grumrose. I'll show you the writing. It is pretty cool. No one knows when it was written."

She led them into a dark chamber. The writing was carved into the walls. Jennica ran her fingers over the words. They were in the original Dragon Script:

As two halves of a whole become united, the evil will be divided. The regal Hawk persons of the sky, the noble burrowing clans of the earth, and the burnished gold of Elva glory. Power trapped and scattered, land left in tatters. Release the power. Healed forever.

Grumrose said, "No one really remembers when it was written. It has been here as long as I can remember. I think it is about the Dragon Queen."

Jennica looked at Donichello who was looking at the wall. He seemed to be in pain. Jennica frowned at the first line. She read, "Two halves united."

Donichello scowled, "The evil divided is the O'rult reverting into two again."

Jennica asked, "What are you going on about?"

Donichello tossed a sour look in her direction. Jennica mumbled, "I don't want to fight with you."

Donichello ignored her, "An O'rult isn't just a creature. It is two, bound together by the black magic of a necromancer. Trydexzi. They are murdered humans possessed by the soul of a dragon. If we separate them, the dragons will rest in the afterlife, and the humans will be able to rest in peace."

Grumrose said, "That makes sense. What else could it be?"

Jennica said to vex Donichello, "It could be plenty of other things."

Rocks shifted from somewhere in the cavern. The rumbles echoed. Jennica looked over at Donichello accusingly. He glared at her.

The rocks slid from their place above Grumrose. Jennica dove, pushing Grumrose out of the way. She looked up in time to see an avalanche of rock sliding on top of her.

CHAPTER XXXIII

Rekasi scried Donichello and Jennica. The dish shimmered as a snarling wolf appeared. A burst of light scared the animal away. Out of the light appeared the shape of a woman. She had the palest eyes, dark blonde hair, and a tall slender body. Sammaria looked at the woman with disbelief.

She questioned, "Mother?"

Rekasi said, "What?"

"That is my mother!"

"Sammaria, that can't possibly be your mother."

"Why not?"

Rekasi said, rubbing his neck, "Well, for one thing, she's dead!"

Sammaria said, "Yes, but if Einar came back, why not my mother?"

Rekasi eyed Sammaria warily as she looked back down to watch Milamare's movements.

Milamare looked up into the scrying pool. Only a powerful magic user could see a scrying patch. She said, "Sammaria, I know it is you watching me. Follow your path. What you need from the Hawkaties is this."

She held up a locket. A sapphire was mounted in the center. She said, "You already have one.

Rekasi asked, "What does that mean?"

"The gods are leading you to them. The lockets must be found. You must find them. You must unite them."

"I will try."

Milamare gave her a sharp look, "Do more than try."

She raised her hand and disappeared with a flash of light.

Sammaria laid back. She stared at the spot where her mother had been standing. Was *she* to be the Dragon Queen?

Rekasi just took her hand and placed his over it. Sammaria smiled. Then a look of fear passed over her face. She whispered, "Jennica is in trouble."

Donichello watched as Jennica jumped to save the little Grumpice. She tossed Grumrose into the next cavern and looked up to see the rocks falling upon her. The fear on her face made him forget his anger. This was his fault. He had let his emotions take control over his Power. Yet, he hadn't felt the familiar warmth of Power flowing through him.

Donichello launched himself into the path of the avalanche, landing next to Jennica. He threw himself over her as she curled up, bracing for the impact. She moved her arms from her eyes and relaxed. Donichello pulled his Power to hold the rocks above them. He made enough room for them to stand up. Silently, he picked himself up and clutched Jennica's hand, pulling her up. She looked up at Donichello as he asked, concerned, "Are you all right?"

Jennica opened her mouth and closed it again. Finally, she stammered, "I'm sorry. I was being stubborn."

Donichello interrupted her, "No, this is my fault. I let my control down. I'm so sorry. It was my mistake."

He wrapped his arms around her waist and kissed her. When he released her, he said, "Marry me, Jennica. Be my wife. I cannot lose you again."

Jennica smiled. She nodded, "Yes."

His lips pressed against hers.

He released the shield and Grumrose frowned at a new honeycomb-shaped hole in the ceiling. She said, "That was not very nice of Vineyeedle."

She glanced back at them, "But I am glad you are no longer arguing. Otherwise, our journey together would be most unenjoyable."

Donichello looked at Jennica. She shrugged. He said, "What do you mean *our journey?*"

She giggled and said, "I have to go with you now. You can't leave me out of this adventure. Besides, I can help you find the Hawkaties. Who better than a Grumpice?"

Jennica said, "I suppose you can't argue with that."

Grumrose retreated to her room and gathered her things. As she shouldered her small pack, made from the vines growing in the trees just outside of the cave network, loud chattering brought her attention to visitors. Vineyeedle marched into the room, looking around disdainfully as if she were mentally calculating her superiority. Following Vineyeedle were two others. Mossk nodded to her.

The elderly Grumpice said nothing. He stroked his long beard. Grumrose bowed deeply to the Grumpice. She murmured, "It is an honor, Treescet."

Treescet nodded to her. With a frail voice that seemed to echo, he said, "I've heard a Grumpling is leaving our home."

Grumrose narrowed her eyes, "I am hardly a Grumpling anymore!"

Treescet nodded, "True, very true. Still, it is concerning that you will be exiting the colony."

Grumrose asked, "Why, sir?"

Treescet said, "You are breaking customs with this rash decision of leaving. With Elvateth no less."

Jennica exchanged looks with Donichello. Grumrose said, "Customs? Isn't it a custom to *sacrifice* what is the norm for what will benefit the posterity of the colony?"

Vineyeedle hissed, "She is abandoning the colony, sir! She is trying to sabotage everything we've worked for! She is going to expose that Grumpices have survived."

Grumrose asked, "What's so wrong with that? That could help us as much as it could hurt us!"

Treescet was silent. He pulled gently on his wispy beard. Then, he nodded twice.

Vineyeedle squealed, "You cannot actually be thinking of allowing this! She mustn't leave the colony!"

Treescet said, "Silence, Vineyeedle! Grumrose must understand the full weight of this responsibility. If she leaves this colony today... I hate to say this, but she might not be welcomed back as she should be. Many would consider this a betrayal to Grumpice kind. And, in this state, I cannot give Her Highness the backing she is desperately seeking."

His stone eyes turned to Jennica.

Grumrose said, "I understand, Treescet. Jennica needs me. She can't do this without us. Please, reconsider."

Vineyeedle said, "Don't bother! We would never..."

"That is enough, Vineyeedle!"

Treescet nodded to Grumrose, "I can see that nothing that we might say will change the state of your mind. For that, I can only say..." he paused.

Vineyeedle smiled. For a moment, Grumrose thought a berating would be thrown at her. He said, "That I can see you are no longer a Grumpling. You have been raised well, young Grumrose. I offer you a blessing."

Grumrose smiled faintly. Treescet reached into his beard and pulled out a medallion. He handed it to Grumrose. She held it, looking at the inscription. She silently read it as Treescet chanted.

Jennica knew better than to ask what the chanting meant. She smiled as Grumrose returned the medallion to

Treescet. Vineyeedle hissed between her thorn teeth. She looked menacing as she stormed from the room. Treescet handed Grumrose a package wrapped in cloth. He said, "Do not open this until you have left the colony. I fear many would not wish for this to leave our colony walls."

Grumrose nodded. She hugged Treescet. He gently pushed her away, "Now, go Grumrose. Maybe when we meet next the Grumpices will have changed their mind. I can only hope for a better outlook. Watch your back for Vineyeedle as you leave."

Grumrose promised she would. Treescet nodded once before he too left the young Grumpice's room.

Grumrose led them to the entrance. As they exited the cave, Grumrose unfolded the cloth. A silver locket lay inside. It held a large green gem.

Grumrose exclaimed, "The Gem of Gamarana!" She caressed the green jewel, then looked up at Jennica. She said, "We were told it had been lost to us!"

Grumrose looked back at the closed entrance to her home. She tucked the locket into Jennica's pack and said, "Let's go."

Sammaria stepped onto the jungle's moss carpeting and immediately felt a change. Something in the air was different. Everything felt ancient. She looked at Rekasi. Did he feel it too? She stopped, and he looked back at her. She asked, "Did you feel that?"

He asked, "Feel what?"

Sammaria looked around. The canopy of trees revealed nothing. She said, "Something has changed. I'm not sure what, though. It's almost as if there is a presence here. Like we awoke something. I don't know. How can you not feel this?"

He said, "Do you think it's dangerous?"

Sammaria said, "It's an ancient power. I don't know, Rekasi. It's very old and wise."

Rekasi said, "Give me the scry dish. Quickly, before it's too late."

Sammaria swung the bag from her back and pulled the gold dish from it. Rekasi filled it with water and spoke the required words. Clutching Sammaria's hand, he said, "The Island of the Hawkaties."

The water clouded. In the center, it showed a port bearing a statue of Mestchina. Rekasi said, "Dayterral?"

The dish showed the water as it zoomed across it. The body of water was distinct, marked by coral reefs and atolls. Rekasi mused, "It is showing us the Gavenalla Pass. It's a route!"

The movement continued past the reef and moved quickly over the water until it showed water lapping on a beach of golden sand. There was a jungle just behind it. A strange creature walked out of the trees. It looked directly at them before the dish cleared up.

Rekasi said, "Do you realize what just happened?" Sammaria looked up at him. He smiled, "We just found the Island of the Hawkaties!"

CHAPTER XXXIV

Jennica looked up at the stars. The night glimmered with thousands of twinkling lights. Mist rolled over the meadow.

Grumrose had directed them back across the Meadow of Gamerana, and they had bedded down in the fields for the night. Grumrose was sleeping inside Jennica's pack, and Donichello was asleep on the other side of the dead fire. She couldn't sleep.

Jennica quietly stood and moved away from Donichello, careful not to disturb him. She could feel Power calling to her in the mist. It called her into Sight State. She could feel the danger.

Jennica had heard of the people Donichello had thought to seek out. The Mystics were highly respected and highly feared. They often went into Sight State and couldn't return for decades. People would live with them and record their mumblings.

Mystics attained apprentices, more and more every year. Many of them couldn't even enter Sight State. They were used to record the Mystic's visions. To be sent to Mystic training was a condemning sentence. One was subject to the magic and ultimate power of the Mystic Sea.

Jennica shook off the feeling. She was far from the Mystic Sea. They were not calling to her. Still, she could feel something trying to take over. She used all her strength to resist. She had a mission. She had to find the Hawkaties.

She smiled when, out of the corner of her eye, she saw Donichello sit down next to her. She leaned her head on his shoulder. He asked, "What is keeping you up?"

Jennica shrugged, "Tonight, it's the stars. They are so beautiful. I can't help but stare at them."

Donichello said, "I know what you mean."

Jennica looked at him. He was watching her, not the stars. Jennica ducked her head.

He said, "What is it that you want?" Jennica didn't reply but instead kissed him.

All the restraint she had been using to push back the strange feeling fell away. The strange magic slammed into her, Power taking over. Jennica needed Donichello. Her kisses grew hungry as the Power pulled her into Sight State. Donichello was pulled under as well.

The darkness swirled around them until they could see a field. Donichello could see himself standing next to a priest. The other Donichello was smiling like an imp as a woman in white moved toward him. He saw the woman behind the veil was Jennica. This was their wedding.

The real Jennica took his hand and said, "We must move."

He followed her behind the trees. He could see a small smile on her face. They stopped in front of a cottage. Jennica walked through the wall then poked her head back out to see Donichello standing dumbfounded. She said, "We don't exist in this world. We are like ghosts."

She went back into the house, Donichello following her. He asked, "Who lived here?"

Jennica moved toward the back.

The other Jennica sat on the bed cradling a baby girl. She looked up at her husband. He said, "She's beautiful."

The two kissed, and they looked down at their child.

The real Jennica leaned back into Donichello's embrace. He asked, "Are we seeing the future?"

Jennica frowned, "The future?"

Donichello nodded.

Jennica looked afraid, "No! It can't be!"

She moved from the cottage, fearful. She said, "How could I be so stupid? This isn't a dream!"

Donichello grabbed her by the shoulders. He said, "Everything is fine. We will come out of this."

Jennica nodded, calming. She said, "You are right. I'm sorry."

He kissed her forehead. She led him to the next scene. They had two children now: a three-year-old girl and a one-year-old boy.

The two played together happily. A small dragon played along with them.

The real Donichello kissed Jennica. He said, "I knew our life was going to be happy."

Jennica looked out at her projected family. She said faintly, "I never had any doubt." He kissed her neck. She shrugged out of his grip, "We need to keep moving."

They moved deeper into the forest. The little boy was now five. He seemed to be alone. Jennica wondered where her apparition was. She wondered why he was unsupervised. The boy cried. He was lost. Jennica waited. Where was she?

A stick cracked, and Jennica relaxed. The boy tensed up. He said, "Momma?"

A figure stepped out from the trees. It wasn't anyone Jennica recognized. The man moved toward the boy. The boy backed away in fear. Jennica reached out for the boy.

The man seized Jennica's son, encircled the boy's neck with his hands, and squeezed. The boy struggled for a while before he went limp. The man laid the body down. He lit the ground with a message that read, "Revenge is sweet."

The real Jennica ran to the boy's side, weeping. Donichello pulled her, "We must go."

Jennica refused. He picked her up. She struggled against him. He said, "There is nothing we can do."

The scene changed. It showed Donichello and Jennica with their daughter, staring off to nowhere in particular. A casket was being lowered into the ground. Donichello put an arm around his wife. She shrugged off his touch. Donichello's face grew sadder.

A sob escaped the real Jennica's lips. She buried her face in Donichello's chest. He moved her away from the tragic scene. Before he knew it, they were in another.

It showed Jennica. She said, "I can't do this. It is my fault he died. We couldn't fix it. I knew we couldn't. Sammaria asked. I should have said no."

She didn't seem to be talking to anyone. She was by the river. There was a man blending into the shadows. He looked remarkably like the one who had killed her son. Jennica pulled out a dagger, "I don't deserve to live."

She plunged the dagger into her stomach. She fell by the river, her blood mixing with the already wet soil.

The real Jennica cried out. Donichello wrapped her into an embrace. She couldn't look anymore. He continued to watch.

Donichello ran to his dying wife. He asked, "Who did this to you?"

Jennica whispered with her red lips, "I did this to myself. I killed our son." Her eyes slid shut.

Donichello carried her back to their house and laid her on the table. He said, "You are my love."

He took their daughter from the house and burned it down.

He and the girl began to walk. To where, they didn't know. The scene seemed to follow them for weeks. They were plagued with despair and starvation.

Donichello laid down next to the girl one night. In the morning, the girl couldn't wake him. He had died. She sat down next to him and cried.

The real Jennica grabbed the real, alive Donichello's hand, "Take us back!"

She willed it. She willed it with all her heart. She opened her eyes. They were still in the Sight State. She cursed, tears in her eyes.

Donichello said, "Everything is going to be fine, Jennica. Everything is going to be fine."

Jennica shook her head, "I let myself be weak. Someone has trapped us. Something felt off with that mist."

Donichello said, "Mist?"

Jennica felt the familiar tug. She gripped Donichello as they returned to their bodies.

She looked around. Grumrose whispered, "You've been crying for almost two hours."

Jennica turned to Donichello and said, "I will not let that happen. That won't happen to us. I swear it."

Jennica asked, "How did you free us?"

Grumrose scoffed, "A Grumpice's power has always been stronger than a necromancer's."

Jennica twisted, looking around the empty meadow. The mist was gone. There was no sign of anyone else.

Jennica jumped when Sammaria spoke in her mind. She said, "Meet us in Dayterral. We found it."

Donichello said, "We will leave as soon as it is light." He squeezed Jennica's hand. Try to get some rest."

Jennica rubbed her arms and nodded.

In her dreams, Jennica saw a tall, dark man. He was the kind of man one would run from if they saw him in the woods at night. Jennica frowned. He looked familiar.

He turned his sights on Jennica. The man said, "Haunting you already? You don't know the pain we'll cause you."

Jennica asked, "We?"

More men stepped from the trees. They all looked alike. The same sneering smile, the general sense of fear, and the dark aura of magic. Though their hair was a variety of colors, she could tell they were related.

One stood out to her. It was the man who was to kill her future son. Jennica leaped at him with intense fury, scratching at his face.

Before she knew it, she was awake. Donichello was watching her. He said, "I really wanted to wake you. You kept slipping into Sight. I couldn't do anything."

He looked so sad. Jennica wondered what she had said. She pleaded, "Please make it go away. That vision of the boy dying."

Donichello opened his arms and asked, "You dreamt of it?"

She nodded. He held her. Jennica said, "Don't leave me tonight."

He kissed her forehead. They fell asleep together.

❧

Sammaria walked along the shore, looking for Jennica. She had said that they would be there soon, but Sammaria kept worrying. It must have been from her mother's appearance in the scrying dish. Rekasi watched her, his eyes flicking back and forth solemnly. He knew something worse than nervousness was weighing upon Sammaria's mind.

They heard an owl hoot and a twig snap, adding to Sammaria's nervous attitude. Rekasi said, "You know she's fine. So, why are you still flitting around like a chickadee?"

Sammaria asked, "A what?"

Rekasi said, "A chickadee. It's a bird in the human realm."

Sammaria said, "It's just something Jennica saw a few months ago. She saw that her time was up, and now she's doing all these dangerous things. I don't want her to die, but I can't tell her because… She's too headstrong."

As she said this, Jennica came running through the brush followed by Donichello. She ran in front of Rekasi. She jumped to the side, laughing as Donichello lunged at her. She plopped down by Sammaria and said, "I win!"

Donichello said, "Oh really? I think someone cheated."

Jennica said, "Only because you cheated first."

Sammaria asked, "What in heavens and earth happened?"

Donichello said, "She sprayed me with water."

He shook his wet hair for emphasis.

Rekasi said, "I keep forgetting you are only seventeen. This mission determines the future of Dragonia, and you are playing games. We have to cross the blasted Gavenalla Pass, which is infested with pirates."

Grumrose popped out of Jennica's pocket and said, "And not to mention the ill-tempered Hawkaties."

"What's that?" Sammaria exclaimed.

Jennica pulled Grumrose from her pocket, "This is Grumrose the Grumpice. She decided to go on a little adventure with us."

Sammaria poked Grumrose in awe.

Grumrose said, "Hey! I still have feelings. I don't like being prodded."

Sammaria muttered an apology.

Jennica said, "So, she's all we have. The rest of her people refused to help. I don't believe they like us very much."

Grumrose said, "That is an understatement. Treescet, our leader, doesn't share those feelings, thankfully."

Rekasi said gently, "We really should be going. We're glad to have you along, Grumrose."

CHAPTER XXXV

The beach was warm beneath their sandals as they walked across it. Jennica walked with water lapping around her feet and her hand lost in Donichello's. Rekasi and Sammaria walked far from the water.

Jennica glanced at Donichello mischievously and smiled with the crooked grin she seemed to possess only when she was around him. She twisted her free arm in circles, winding the water around it. She moved her hand like it was pulling something toward her. The water followed the motion and hit Donichello in the face. He looked surprised, and his smile was sly. Jennica slipped her hand out of his and ran ahead. Jennica was swift, but Donichello was quicker. He caught and wrapped his strong arms around her. He picked her up from the ground, and she screamed gleefully.

Jennica gasped. Donichello sat her down when he saw it too. The cumulous clouds cleared and, above them, was the statue of Mestchina straddling the Riaf Canal where it met the natural harbor with a Grumpice sitting on her enormous shoulder. They had arrived in Dayterral. Grumrose peeked out of Jennica's pocket to look at the statue. She gasped in awe. There was a white dragon painted on Mestchina's gold shield, and her sword was raised above her head. The rest of the statue was silver, except her eyes. They were the largest jade pieces any of them had seen.

The jade had been brought to Dayterral through a portal located in Keyinture.

"But the portals are closed!" interrupted a boy.

The storyteller looked up at the young man. The child on his lap said, "Don't interrupt! It's not nice."

The storyteller said, "True. During King Socorro's reign, the portals closed. At this time, however, many places had natural portals. These portals were called glarets. They are places where Mythral and Ethota intersect.

Strange things happen at these portals. In Mythral, people attribute the mysterious happenings around the glarets to metaphysical reckonings. In other words, they call the places "haunted."

At certain points, a person, if they know how can move between the two realms. Not many people knew how to do this or ever will again. But here in Ethota, the city grew around the glaret. People gathered the strange items that appeared near it and sold them."

The boy pursed his lips, but pressed the storyteller to continue.

A roughly dressed man pushed passed Sammaria. She pressed ahead. He winked at her as she turned away.

A man with skin pale as parchment came up to them. He was dressed richly and holding a small red book. He was wearing black knee-length pants and a cream shirt, which washed out his already pale skin even more. On top of the cream shirt was a maroon vest with gold buttons and a gold pocket watch. He wore a darker maroon coat over the vest.

His sea-green eyes flashed mysteriously behind thin, wire-rimmed glasses. His thin lips pressed into a slightly forced smile. His white hair was threatening to fly out of the pins holding it to his mostly bald scalp. He spoke with an odd version of a Poccuottawan accent, "Messers and Misses. Welcome to the lovely Port of Dayterral. I'd be needing your names and homeland. If it ain't... sorry... *isn't* too much trouble."

Rekasi took the man aside. He told the man fake names for the group. He asked, "We are looking for passage. Is there anything heading to the Gavenalla Pass?"

The man, Phronty, said, "Kiro, almighty, are you insane? It is infested with pirates," He tipped his eyes up, smiled, and continued, "No one...Well, there may be one ship. No. You are much too respectable for them."

Rekasi said, "We'll manage. What ship?"

Phronty took Rekasi away. Jennica glanced around nervously. She met eyes with a girl wearing a scarf tied over her hair. The girl gave her a hard look. Jennica looked away. Sammaria asked, "Are you alright?"

Jennica shivered, "I wish Rekasi would hurry up. I am getting a strange feeling from this dock."

Donichello said, "Look. There they are."

Phronty and Rekasi came walking back up. Rekasi's face was drawn and tight.

Phronty said, "Well, Messer, happy sailing. Kiro save your soul."

He walked away.

Jennica frowned at her sister. Something was not right. She looked back at the man. An unusual look passed between them. He turned uneasily and walked down the dock.

When he had disappeared into the crowd, Rekasi led them into a nook of barrels. He said, "The ship is called the Death Arrow. The man seemed to think the crew was rather unscrupulous. But they will take us to where we want to go. Just keep on your guard."

Rekasi led them to a single-masted sloop. Jennica hesitated before she followed them up the gangway. Donichello squeezed her hand. She gave him a small smile.

A handsome boy greeted them on the deck. He looked fairly young, much younger then the other deckhands milling about. His eyes looked past them as if he was looking at a point above their heads. He said, "Your cabins are being prepared below. Do you have any items that need to be brought up?"

Rekasi shook his head. He asked, "When will the captain return?"

The boy frowned for a moment. He seemed to process the information. He blinked once then said, "Captain Ornae will be here soon." He turned abruptly and said, "The women's cabin is this way."

The boy continued walking without looking to see if they followed. The man led Jennica and Sammaria down below deck. He opened the door to a small cabin. The room was cramped. Two wooden bunks were built into the wall on the right. A trunk was shoved into the corner to the left.

Sammaria turned to the boy. He continued to stare at the point right above their heads. She said, "Thank you, sir. We greatly appreciate your kindness."

A trumpet sounded from above their heads. The boy turned and walked back up the stairs. Sammaria looked at her sister. Jennica shook her head. Sammaria sat down on the bottom bunk and sighed. Jennica dropped her pack on the bunk. The ship shuddered beneath them as it pushed away from the dock. She asked, "Are you staying down here? I want to watch us leave."

Sammaria waved her hand. She pulled Jennica's pack under her head. She said, "I will just rest here for a while. Wake me when we are out to sea."

Jennica nodded. Grumrose popped up out of her pack and said in her lilting accent, "I would like to come."

Jennica hesitated, "You should probably stay hidden. I am not sure if we should trust these men."

Grumrose frowned but nodded. Sammaria said, "You are free to join me here."

Grumrose sighed, "I guess that would be all right." Jennica smiled sympathetically at the Grumpice and headed away from the cabin.

The deck was alive with motion. The crew raced around, tying some ropes and untying others. Jennica looked around in wonder. Rekasi seemed to be locked in conversation with Donichello. They were in a secluded corner out of the way of the deckhands' path. Jennica allowed herself a small smile. She was happy they were getting along.

She moved along the rail and watched as the shoreline became a distant line along the horizon. She cocked her head to the side. A lump swelled in her throat. The land grew more distant. The lump changed to an ache. Jennica dug her nails into the wood of the railing until her knuckles turned white.

"I get that feeling every time we leave," said a voice beside her.

Jennica turned, surprised. A woman stood there leaning against the railing. She had wavy, dirty blonde hair and rough features. She was wearing a red scarf pulled low over her forehead. Hanging from her belt was a sword with a gold-plated hilt set with rubies and sapphires and a gun. Jennica jerked back in shock.

The woman looked down at it hanging against her gray pants. She said, in an accent Jennica couldn't place, "It is mostly just to deter ruffians at the port."

Jennica looked back at the horizon. The strip of land was no longer visible. She asked, "*What* do you always feel?"

The woman said, "Homesick. It is hard being out at sea."

Jennica stared at the woman for a moment, "I saw you. On the dock."

The woman smiled, her emerald eyes sparkled. She said, "You did. I'm Jessie. I may or may not have paid Phronty to send you our way."

Jennica frowned, "Why would you do that?"

Jessie shrugged, "You seemed like you were looking for something. Something specific. That is what I specialize in."

Jennica cocked her head. She surveyed the strange woman. She asked, "Are you Captain Ornae?"

Jessie shook her head, "No. The captain is downstairs. You will meet him soon enough."

Jessie pushed off the railing, "Make yourself comfortable."

Jennica watched the other woman walk off. She met up with the boy that had led her to her cabin. Jessie pulled something from her belt and handed it to him. He gave her a small smile. Jennica heard her call him Luke.

She looked around the deck. Donichello and Rekasi were no longer standing in their corner. She figured they had also gone to their cabin to rest. Jennica shook out her arms.

Energy kept her muscles tight. She wandered into the corner that Rekasi and Donichello had been in. She sat down on the barrel, watching the wavering horizon.

Jennica reached her Power out to the water surrounding the ship. Strength flowed into her limbs. She felt herself relax. Soon, her eyelids were heavy. They drooped, and she fell into a slumber.

Jennica jerked awake. Someone was shaking her. She bolted upright, unconsciously pulling on her Power. The light was fading. She blinked her eyes quickly, centering her vision.

Sammaria held up her hands, "It is just me. Did you have a nice nap?"

Jennica gave her a snide look, "I suppose I did. Why are you waking me?"

Sammaria said, "We have been summoned. We will finally be meeting the captain."

Jennica stood and straightened her dress. She asked, "Grumrose?"

Sammaria said, "She is hidden."

Jennica looked out at the sea. There was no sign of the shore. Ocean surrounded them. Sammaria said, "We have been sailing for several hours. I believe we are a good distance from Dayterral."

Sammaria looped her arm through Jennica's. Jennica stood next to Donichello. He quickly squeezed her hand, and then let it go.

Jennica bit her lip. The four of them stood nervously together in a semicircle of the Death Arrow's crew. Jennica looked around, her energy pulling her muscles tight. She noticed the boy Luke sitting in the fore section of the deck. He fiddled with a small ring puzzle.

Sammaria squeezed Jennica's arm. Jennica frowned at her. Sammaria gave her a familiar look, demanding she pay attention. Jennica sighed inwardly.

A red scarf blew in the breeze just over Sammaria's shoulder. Jennica and Jessie met eyes. Jessie winked at her. Jennica's eyebrows furrowed. She turned back toward the stairs leading to the captain's cabin.

Someone said, "Attention! Entering the deck, Captain Reness Ornae."

CHAPTER XXXVI

Captain Reness Ornae climbed the steps from below deck. He was a tall man with short, black hair and dark eyes. His jaw was square and held firmly. It was an imposing face but also one in which a person could place their trust. His skin was tanned like sailors normally were. He was dressed no differently from his crew, except for his hat.

He strode up to the group and bowed low to them. He said, "We are so honored to have you aboard."

He looked up at Sammaria. He took her hand and kissed it. She blushed, "You honor me, sir. I have never been on a ship so fine. I am not sure why you would be…"

"Now…Now, Your Highness," Reness said.

Sammaria pulled her hand away. Donichello and Rekasi moved to draw their weapons. Jennica pulled back on her sister's arm. The crew moved in on the four of them. Jessie pulled a gun and aimed it at Rekasi's head. Jennica gaped at her. Jessie smiled apologetically.

Reness just smiled and held up his hand. The crew settled back. Rekasi and Donichello did not release their grip on their weapons. Jessie continued to hold the gun trained on Rekasi.

Sammaria stepped forward, "How did you know who we were?"

Reness laughed, "Two beautiful young women accompanied by two men armed to the teeth. One with a sword bearing the seal of Dragonia."

Sammaria looked back at Donichello. He looked down at his sword, surprised. On the scabbard, two dragons curled around a crown. Donichello swore and slammed his sword back down into the scabbard. Jennica closed her eyes.

Sammaria said, "What do you want?"

Reness said, "That is an interesting question, Your Highness. I want a great many things. But that is not the question you are asking me, is it?"

Sammaria did not say anything. She stared straight ahead. Reness said, "I think what you want to know – now let me know if I am correct – is what do I want with you?"

Sammaria clenched her teeth. She did not respond. Jennica reached out for her. Donichello pulled her back. Sammaria looked back and smiled. She nodded, hoping it looked reassuring.

Reness smiled, "I seem to have hit a nerve."

Sammaria clenched her fists and nodded her head slightly, "Well then, Captain Ornae."

She stopped and swallowed. She clenched her fists once more., "What do you want with me? With us?"

No one moved. No one breathed. Reness smiled, "Was that so hard?"

Sammaria glared at him.

He said, "Now, now. There is a price on your pretty little head. Try not to anger me."

Sammaria snapped her head to look at Rekasi. Reness continued, "Your father. He offered a reward for your return."

Sammaria said, "That is no longer valid. King Enchardo is dead."

Jessie said, "No matter. A queen will fetch a fair price."

Jennica took a step toward the other girl. Jessie turned the gun on her. Donichello pulled her back and shielded her with his body.

Reness said, "Jess, enough."

Jessie flicked her eyes to him. He nodded at her. She put the gun back into her belt and folded her arms across her chest.

Someone spoke up in the back, "Her country wants her back."

Jessie said, "Luke!"

Reness shot Jessie a look and asked, "What was that, Luke?"

The boy didn't look up. He didn't come forward. He said, "There is a price on all of their heads. New queen wants her dead. Returned for execution."

Jessie glared at the boy. He did not seem to notice. Captain Ornae glared at Jessie. She pointedly ignored it. Reness rubbed his face, "This has given me much to consider."

Sammaria held Jennica's arm as her sister clutched hers. Jessie led them back to their cabin. She said, leaning in the door, "Luke panicked. He wasn't supposed to say anything."

Jennica sat down on her bunk and refused to look at Jessie. Sammaria gave the girl a tight smile. Jessie nodded once and left. They heard the clicking of the lock behind her.

Grumrose popped up from her hiding spot beneath the blankets. She asked, "Is everything alright?"

Sammaria sat down next to Jennica. Jennica sprang up and began pacing back and forth in the small cabin. She asked, "What have we done? How could we have been so stupid!"

Grumrose asked, "What has happened?"

Sammaria said, "Isn't it obvious? They are smugglers. Pirates."

Jennica stared at her. Sammaria continued, "Even if we were more careful, there is the chance we would be in this same situation. Whoever this is. This necromancer does not want to leave loose ends."

Jennica collapsed on the bunk next to Sammaria. Grumrose climbed up onto Sammaria's shoulder. Jennica laid her head on Sammaria's lap and muttered, "This is all my fault!"

Sammaria pushed her upright. Grumrose said, "Excuse me?"

Jennica scrubbed her hand across her forehead. She said, "I have sent us on a wild goose chase. And now we will be sold to our deaths."

Sammaria smiled and smoothed her sister's hair. She said, "You sent us nowhere. We are here to get the locket and find the Hawkaties. Then, we will be able to defeat the O'rult and regain Dragonia."

Grumrose said, "The Hawkaties will listen to us. They will help us. And you will have the Grumpices' support."

Jennica leaned against her sister's shoulder. Sammaria put her arms around her. Jennica said, "We are still missing the Elvateth locket."

Sammaria said, "We will find it."

Jennica fell silent. Sammaria smoothed her hair, calming her like she had when they were little. She bit her lip. She wondered if Jennica could sense her worry. The confidence in her words did not match the fear she felt rising in her stomach. She had lost her country. Sammaria gritted her teeth. She would get it back.

A knock rapped on the door. Jennica jumped, letting out a small yelp. Grumrose skittered back into her hiding spot.

The door opened. Jessie stood there with two crew members behind her. She said, "Come. The Captain has reached his decision."

Jessie led them back to the top deck. The crewmen escorted the girls from behind. The rest of the crew gathered in the same halfmoon as before. Captain Ornae already stood at the forefront awaiting their presence.

Jennica tightened her grip on Sammaria's arm. She asked, "Where are the boys?"

Sammaria glanced around. No one had brought Rekasi and Donichello back up from their room. Sammaria squeezed Jennica's arm. Everything was going to be alright.

Reness bowed to them. Sammaria could not decide if he was mocking her or not. Jennica frowned deeply at him. She was struggling with the same question. Sammaria said, "My captain. I hear you have come to a decision…"

Reness smiled wryly, "A decision…There are many here who think I should keep you here as the ship whore. Pretty thing like you."

A few men chuckled behind them. Jennica shuddered. Sammaria swallowed, her mouth suddenly feeling dry. She forced her face to remain neutral.

Reness continued, "Others think I should allow the sailors to have their fun… And then turn you over to the new leader of Dragonia. I'm sure we would get a hefty reward."

Jennica's grip loosened. Sammaria frowned. She stayed silent and continued to stare straight ahead, watching the horizon rise and fall with the waves.

Reness said, "So, my decision - "

A rush of waves crashed across the deck, knocking Captain Ornae from his feet. Several crew members also fell to the deck under its force.

Sammaria turned. Jennica's arms were raised above her head. The water continued to writhe around them. The crewmen still standing lunged to grab Jennica. She flicked her wrist, sending salt spray into their faces. They halted for a moment, blinded. Jennica seized Sammaria's arm and pulled her toward the starboard rail.

Sammaria said, "Rekasi!"

Jennica pulled herself up on the rail, "They can take care of themselves! We will find them later."

Sammaria pushed herself up onto the ledge next to Jennica.

Jessie yelled somewhere behind them, "You are making a mistake! No!"

Something hard slammed into Sammaria's back. She lost her footing and fell toward the sea.

CHAPTER XXXVII

Sammaria's limp form hit the lurching waves. She did not move as the water tossed her about. Jennica turned back to the deck. Luke stood with an oar in his hand. Jennica bared her teeth at him. She lifted her hand to sweep him away. Jessie leapt in front of him, "Just go!"

Jennica glared once more before leaping off the ship's rail after her sister. The cool, salty water engulfed her. She spread out her Power, trying to find Sammaria. She made contact with Sammaria's fading Power. Jennica took a deep breath and dove into the depths. She let her magic be her eyes. She kicked down past a coral reef and into the black abyss. She swam after Sammaria's sinking form. Jennica looped her arm around Sammaria's torso.

She kicked toward the surface, her lungs burning. Their clothing pulled them back down. Jennica pulled on her Power. She kicked, sending a pulse that propelled them to the surface. Jennica broke the surface, gasping for air.

The pirate ship was nowhere to be found. Jennica tread to keep their heads above the surface. She could not see anything but the ocean all around them. She leaned Sammaria's limp form on her shoulder and felt out with her Power.

Faintly in the distance, she felt a stop in her Power. Land.

Jennica shook Sammaria gently. She groaned. Jennica said, "Hold on."

Jennica kicked with her Power once again. They hurtled to the blank space. Jennica once again let her Power be her guide. It was not long before land rose out in the distance. Jennica's muscles burned. Her arms shook as she held onto her sister. Her breath ached in her lungs. Her Power faltered.

Sammaria and Jennica crashed down into the water. A sharp, stinging pain tore through Jennica's shoulder. The water around her tinted red. Jennica tried to touch the injured spot. She could barely lift her arm. She cried out in pain. She scooped Sammaria up again, "We are almost there."

Jennica pulled both of them over to the rocky surface of the atoll. She laid Sammaria on the rock and collapsed next to her. She said, "We are safe."

⁂

Donichello stood as the lock turned. Rekasi looked toward the door. It opened to Jessie. She nodded to the man behind her. He closed the door and relocked it.

Donichello said, "Where are Sammaria and Jennica? What have you done with them?"

Jessie said, "That is what I am here about."

Rekasi said, "Cut to the chase. We heard a commotion. What is going on?"

Jessie looked around uncomfortably. She said, "It seems they decided to disembark."

"Disembark?" Rekasi asked skeptically.

"Disembark!" Donichello demanded, "Where are they?"

Jessie didn't as much as flinch. Donichello looked her up and down. She said, "Reness was telling them his decision. He was going to help them. The Princess completely freaked out." She trailed off slightly, "Albeit, he was teasing them rather harshly. He didn't actually get to that part."

Donichello clenched his teeth. Jessie said hurriedly, "They jumped ship."

Donichello yelled, "What?"

He rushed at the girl. Rekasi tried to restrain him. Donichello twisted out of his grip. He slammed Jessie up against the wall of the cabin. The scarf she kept tied around her head came off in his hand. Donichello noticed a long puckered scar above her left eyebrow. Her face registered momentary surprise, pulling tight against the welt before she resumed her usual calm. Donichello said, "Let me tell you what is going to happen now."

Jessie said, "You are going to release me."

Her eyes flicked down to her waist. She smiled at him with a challenging glare. It reminded him just for a second of Jennica. Donichello frowned and looked down. She held a dagger to his ribs. Donichello bared his teeth at her. He pushed off her and took a step back.

Jessie straightened herself. She held out her hand with a pointed look. Donichello scowled at her. He flung the scarf back at her. She snatched it out of the air and said, "Thank you."

She tucked her hair behind her rounded ear and started turning the scarf around in her hands. She said, "Now -"

Rekasi gasped. Donichello said, "You are a human!"

Everything made sense now. The gun, the rough voice, her rugged features. She was human.

Jessie stopped for a moment, looking back and forth between the two of them. She touched her exposed ear. She blushed, "Oh…yeah. I am."

Donichello said, "Who are you?"

Jessie said, "My name is Jessica Conrad. I'm the navigator for the *Death Arrow*."

Rekasi said, "How did you get here Jessica? How did you become a navigator for a pirate ship?"

Jessie bit her lip, "I haven't thought about that in a long time." She rubbed a hand faintly over the scar on her forehead. She seemed to notice and pulled the scarf onto her head.

The two men waited for her to continue. She said, "We fell."

"Fell?" Donichello asked.

Jessie glanced over at him, annoyed. Donichello fell silent. The look she gave him again reminded him of Jennica. He crossed his arms. Rekasi said, "Please, Jessica. Sit."

She sat down on the bunk. Rekasi said, "Please start at the beginning."

Jessie frowned, "I don't really remember all of it. But I am from a country called America. For as long as I can remember, weird things happened in my town. People would go missing a lot."

She shuddered. Rekasi looked over at Donichello. He shook his head.

Jessie said, "One day, Luke and I -"

"Luke?" Rekasi asked.

Jessie said, "Yeah, Luke. He's my brother."

Rekasi nodded and gestured for her to proceed. She said, "Luke and I were wandering in the woods. And we saw these little goblin creatures and these large serpent men. They saw us and chased us. We ran. One of the serpent men grabbed me and cut my forehead. But Luke threw a rock at him. We ran. Fog surrounded us. We were lost. And then we were on a beach. Here in your world."

She fell silent, reluctant to go on. Donichello pressed, "How did you join the *Death Arrow?*"

Jessie glanced at him, "I married the captain."

CHAPTER XXXVIII

Jennica dozed, her head slipping down under the water. She awoke with a start. Above her, a sea hawk called to his mate. Jennica, excited by the sight, stood up on the thin atoll and watched the bird intently. Seahawks did not travel more than ten miles from solid land.

Jennica looked at Sammaria, her cheer fading. Sammaria couldn't swim that distance. Jennica pulled on her Power. It moved sluggishly. She had strained herself too much earlier. She would not be able to take them.

A shadow passed near their perch. Jennica fell to her knees, searching the water. The creature had a large dorsal fin and a notch taken out of its tail. The nose was elongated and surrounded by two large tusks.

A second shadow covered her overhead. She snapped her head up. This creature had the head of a hawk and the wings and ears of a bat. The creature also had four wolf-like legs and sharp talons on its feet.

Jennica wasn't sure which creature would be worse. Both creatures seemed like they would be able to harm the girls in their weakened state. Jennica frantically scanned the water. The elephish was leaving. The creature flying overhead seemed to be following.

A faint breeze caught Jennica's hair. The creature overhead turned. It caught sight of the girls stranded on the spit of land. The animal dove and let out a screech.

Jennica cowered, covering her ears. The creature raked its talons over her hair. Jennica laid protectively over Sammaria. The creature soared back up over the atoll. It let out another screech.

Sammaria groaned and whispered Jennica's name. Jennica hushed her and pointed up. Above them, five more of the creatures had emerged from the clouds. They circled them slowly, making tighter circles. The first creature screeched and dove once more. It landed on the rocks, looming over Jennica and Sammaria. It bent its huge hawk head and sniffed Jennica's hair. It looked toward the sky and made a series of squawks, clicks, barks, and then howled.

Sammaria clutched Jennica's arms. Jennica held up her hand, "Stay back! I am warning you!"

The creature looked at her intently. A guttural voice asked, "What are you going to do?"

Jennica shook her head. Sammaria said, "This cannot be happening."

The creature standing over her said, "And yet it is."

Sammaria grew very pale. The circling animals laughed. One swooped down and said, "Oh, little Elva. This should be fun. Looks like your kind is still brutal and uncivilized. Unless I am mistaken from those bruises"

The one looming over the girls said, "Well, yes. Why do you think we hid?"

Jennica said, "You are the Hawkaties?"

The Hawkatie closest to Jennica said, "Oh, so they recognize us. This is less fun now."

The large one in the air clicked and howled. The two Hawkaties took off. The smallest of the three in the air dove and plucked Jennica from the rock with his talon. Another scooped Sammaria up.

Jennica asked, "Where are you taking us? Are you taking us to the Island?"

The Hawkaties laughed in unison, and the female said, "Maybe or maybe not."

Jennica was not sure if they were supposed to be scared. Jennica weakly watched the ocean roll by. She immediately felt tired as they glided into a thick fog. Her eyes grew heavy.

A dark shape loomed ahead. She forced herself awake and watched as it grew closer. The lead Hawkatie let out a series of beautiful clicks that sounded like a flute. The fog broke for just a moment.

Sammaria gasped. Trees full of fruit covered the island. Flowers grew everywhere. Jennica smiled when she saw a meadow carpeted in Atlantsa. It was an island. Not just any island, it was the island they had been searching for: The Island of the Hawkaties.

The fog returned. The fatigue quickly overtook Jennica. Her eyelids slipped closed.

Sammaria woke to the sun's light shining through a patio door. She laid there for a moment, thinking of the dream from which she had woken. Hawkaties had plucked her and Jennica out of the Sea of Mytositsa. Sammaria rolled over. She reached out as she fell to the dirt floor. She cried out.

Sammaria looked down. She was wearing a green dress. She was not sure where it had come from. Jennica rushed into the room, "Are you alright?"

Sammaria rubbed her neck, "Sore."

Jennica eased herself into a chair. She winced as she bumped her bandaged shoulder against the back of the chair.

Sammaria scanned the room. She saw sturdy walls of bamboo and straw. The doors let in streams of light, even with the white sheer curtains drawn. A mirror was set up in the corner.

Sammaria had stopped. She stubbornly set her jaw. A single tear rolled down her face. She angrily brushed it away.

Jennica said, "Sammaria, I am positive he is fine."

Sammaria took her sister's hand, "Kiro's will."

They sat in silence. Neither felt like talking. Jennica idly scanned and flipped through the books while Sammaria paced the room.

Sammaria came to a stop in front of the patio doors. Frustrated, she flung them open. The sight made her take a step back. The scene was beautiful. The blue sea lapped at the golden beach. The trees of the jungle were deep green. There was a field of nothing but dragon blood plants. She stared out. The sight was breathtaking.

Someone cleared their throat. Sammaria turned and saw a silvery figure standing in the doorway. The figure said in a deep voice, "Follow me."

The figure led them to another door. She knocked in a strange pattern of alternating long and short knocks. There was a short pause. There was some shuffling around, and the door opened.

The figure drifted into the door and gestured for the girls to enter. Sammaria entered, cautiously looking around. The figure behind her dissipated.

A voice came from the brown, high-backed chair, "Welcome to the House of Mokana."

The chair moved a little. They could see a man. His face appeared tan but changed the more they looked at it. It went from pale to tan to black to yellowish. His eyes were shaped like almonds. His shoulder-length hair was a golden gray. His beard changed lengths. It went from long enough to tuck into his belt, to nothing, then to just enough to cover his chin, then it was even with his breast.

Jennica's jaws dropped. Sammaria's heart leapt in her chest. She was having a hard time looking at him.

Mokana said, "Your Royal Highness."

He bowed to Sammaria. He reached out with his shifting hand and brought hers to his lips. The changing hair felt strange against her skin. He said, "Does this form cause you discomfort?"

Sammaria noticed Jennica nod out of the corner of her eye. Sammaria bowed her head, "It is an honor to be in the presence of a god. No matter the form you take."

Mokana said, "I had heard you were diplomatic. Still, I would like your honest opinion, Your Highness. Do you find my shifting form discomforting? Your sister has made her opinion known."

Sammaria glanced over at Jennica. She looked down at her shoes and blushed deeply. Mokana gave her a kind smile.

Sammaria said, "It is a bit unsettling, Most Honored."

Mokana nodded. He closed his eyes and took a deep breath. His features settled on young, olive skin, and the beard disappeared.

He said, "Where are your companions?"

Jennica whispered, "Grumrose!"

Sammaria said, "We were separated. Do you know if they are alright?"

Mokana flicked his hand. The silvery figure appeared once more. It opened its hands. Sitting on the metallic palm was a small plantlike creature.

Jennica said excitedly, "Grumrose!"

Mokana said, "Yes, this little Grumpice was the one that told us where you were."

Sammaria nodded her head, "We are once again in your debt."

Grumrose pulled at something around her neck. She pulled up a circular locket, "I brought this. I did not think you would want those scoundrels to find it."

Jennica said, "You clever thing."

Grumrose beamed, her thorny smile flashing.

CHAPTER XXXIX

"Yes," Jessie said, annoyed, "I am married to Captain Ornae."

Donichello frowned. It was improper. Humans and Elvateth were not supposed to mix. It was biology. A human was simply too different. Bad things happened when their blood mixed.

Rekasi said, "Yes, so you said."

He shot a look at Donichello. Donichello folded his arms across his chest and fell silent. Rekasi said, "How long have you and your brother been in Ethota?"

Jessie said, "Several years. Thought I feel like I have known this land all my life. Almost like I knew it before I got here."

Donichello broke from his closed stance. He exchanged looks with Rekasi. He asked, "Jessica, have you heard of the Keepers of Knowledge?"

Jessie frowned, "I have heard of it. Just old stories while in port on the Dragonian coast. What does that have to do with anything?"

Donichello mused, "I thought it was a story. Something people talked about after the Good Queen's death. Something to bring hope."

Jessie looked back and forth between the two of them. She said, "I do not understand."

Rekasi said, "Let me explain. There is a story in Dragonia. No one was ever able to confirm it."

Donichello nodded in agreement. Rekasi said, "Before the princesses were born, the Good Queen Milamare sent out her falcons. They were gone for months – which was most unusual. One never saw the queen without one of her birds."

Jessie said, "All right. So, the lady sent her pets away. I don't understand why we are talking about it."

Donichello said, "Exactly. You do not understand. She had sent them to Mythral."

Jessie gave them a confused look, "Okay? How do you know? And why would- Just why?"

Donichello looked at Rekasi. His face did not change. He frowned. He did not know how to answer her. Rekasi said, "The falcons did not return until after Queen Milamare's death. Each one brought back a token from their journey."

Jessie said, "I never heard that part of the story."

Donichello said, "Nor have I."

Jessie looked at him, surprised. She turned her gaze to Rekasi, suspicious. Rekasi said, "The flock was gifted to her daughters. Sammaria was given the items that were brought back."

Jessie said, "That is all well and good, but what were the falcons doing? And what does it have to do with me?"

Donichello said, "You said you had heard the story before. Milamare was blessed with a task from the..."

He trailed off. The story was so similar to Jennica's journey. He had dismissed her quest from the gods. He had thought it too fanciful. If this story was true, Milamare died before she completed whatever it was they wanted. Now, the gods had turned their eyes to her children to finish what Milamare could not. Donichello's heart leapt in his chest.

Jessie said, "From who?"

Donichello said slowly, taking in the new information, "The gods. It is said she sent the falcons with the wisdom of Ethota."

Rekasi said, "Sammaria said the items seemed to belong to children. She said she and Jennica played with them when they were younger."

Jessie didn't say anything. She just stared at the two of them. She asked, "Do you think I am one of these? What did you call them – Keepers?"

Donichello said, "It would explain a lot. The O'rult – your serpent man – do not travel into Mythral without order. Traveling deliberately between the realms is hard. And they seemingly sought you out."

Jessie started to laugh. It started slow, but soon her whole body shook with mirth. She wiped a tear from her eye. Rekasi and Donichello exchanged looks.

Jessie said, "You really had me for a moment. Good job, boys. Quite the storytellers. Both of you."

Donichello said, "This is not a jest!"

She nodded turning, "Sure it isn't."

She knocked on the door. Donichello heard the click of the lock. The door popped open.

Rekasi said, "Do you have an ability you cannot explain? Knowledge of a place you have never been or a story you never heard?"

Jessie stopped and looked at him suspiciously. She narrowed her eyes at him.

Rekasi said, "Perhaps there is more to the gift than meets the eye, Jessica Conrad."

※

Jennica, Sammaria, and Grumrose were led down a long hallway. They had been led away from the House of Mokana. The silvery figure from before took them across the island to a cave. When they had entered, it was as if they had gone into an underground palace.

The figure had only said they were being summoned to the Hawkatie Council. Sammaria's heart was in her throat. She could sense everyone was on edge. Their guide led them down an empty hall to an old dark door. The door, as they grew closer, revealed an intricate lock. There were three circles engraved into the lock. One that symbolized Fire, another that symbolized Earth, and the third which symbolized Air.

A Hawkatie greeted them at the door. It made a low, strangled noise. Jennica and Sammaria exchanged looks. Grumrose soared into the air and did a flip before sending a shower of rocks soaring at the symbol of Earth. Sammaria looked horrified, thinking that Grumrose was destroying such an old and beautiful object.

She was about to voice her protest when the rocks hit the door with a dull thud. The symbol for Earth pressed into the door, the rocks creating a circle around it. There was a grinding sound as the rocks and the symbol started to spin faster and faster. Then the Hawkatie threw her head back, turned, and flapped her giant bat wings. A whirlwind of air flew toward the Air symbol pressing it into the door. A low blowing like a horn sounded as the lock spun ever faster. Grumrose watched Sammaria.

She flew up to Sammaria's face and said, "Do something quickly!"

Sammaria thought quickly and furiously. She didn't want to scorch the door. Closing her eyes, she accessed her Power. She spun in a circle and punched toward the door, sending a continuous flame toward it. The Fire pressed in the proper symbol, and it began to spin with the sound of a crackling fire. Her flame snaked through the crevasses in the door and lit a ring around the other spinning symbols. Sammaria let the fire die, and the Hawkatie nudged Jennica.

Jennica looked at her and said, "There is no Water symbol."

The Hawkatie said, "Look closer."

Jennica scanned every inch of the door. She stepped back and suddenly saw it. The door *was* the Water symbol. It was circular with a cloud carved lightly into it. The Fire snaked into the cloud, illuminating it.

Jennica drew a half-circle with each hand. The water sprayed out of her hands and circled the door. It caused the Fire and the spinning to stop, and there was the sound of lightning hitting the ground as the door opened slowly.

The Hawkatie gave Jennica an approving look and walked inside. She made a low, strangled growl, and more Hawkaties arrived from the shadows. Sammaria, Jennica, and Grumrose filed silently in behind the Hawkaties.

A great foreboding weighed heavily on Sammaria's mind. The Hawkatie in the middle stood. He wore a silver locket with a large sapphire set in the center. Sammaria gasped. She squeezed Jennica's hand. The Patriarch said, "Friends, we are gathered here to hear Sammaria Aeradal speak. Your Highness?"

He gestured to Sammaria. She stood up and said, "Thank you, Council. Hear well what I have to say. O'rult forces have invaded my country. My sister and I plead that we - the Resistance, the Evfiah Dragon Fury, the Grumpices, and the Hawkaties - might band together to ward off this enemy that will only grow stronger unless we act quickly."

Murmuring rippled through the crowd. One of the Hawkaties on the panel asked, "And what would you have us do? Surely you don't expect us to bow to the Wygair. It is their fault that you have O'rults in the first place."

Sammaria implored, "The dragons have lent us their aid. They wish to be rid of the O'rult. Their very existence is destroying the Dragon furies. As a magical race, I plead that you show them sympathy."

The Hawkatie scoffed, "All the sympathy that they showered us with when Delfan needed us."

Jennica said, "Delfan was cruel. He controlled the dragons. He took over their minds and slaughtered their brethren."

Sammaria stopped and took a breath, "Please, this is not what I came to discuss."

One of the Hawkaties on the panel extended her wing to allow her to continue. Sammaria said, "My mother has spoken to me. She told me that there was a way to defeat the O'rult threat once and for all. A way to rid our land of the evil that *will* threaten all of us. I need your locket."

The hall fell quiet.

Sammaria said, "Will not one of you come forward? After they have taken over Dragonia, they will not rest. They will continue up to the beaches of the Sea of Mytositsa. Who's to say they won't find this place? Who is to say they won't kill or enslave every single one of you in this room?"

The Council conversed with each other. Sammaria's stomach was in knots. They needed the Hawkaties. The Patriarch stood again and said, "Sammaria, we will not be joining you."

He gestured to the locket around his neck, "The locket is too precious to the safety of this Island. The Sapphire of Mytositsa protects us all." Sammaria's heart sank. He continued, "We can take on the O'rult. We have done it before and triumphed."

Sammaria said, "Sir, no disrespect, but these O'rult are not those you faced before. In the past, they were conjured by mere mages. These O'rult have been created by a necromancer, Trydexzi. This breed can think for themselves."

The female Hawkatie said, "Oh posh. O'rult will never be capable..."

The door burst open, interrupting her. A creature walked in.

The creature looked like a Hawkatie. However, his lower body appeared to be deformed. He marched up to the panel and said, "Permission to speak to the Council."

The Patriarch said, "Permission granted, Criketchen."

He said, "I have been following the closest threats to our island, and I have found a new one."

The Patriarch said, "Well, spit it out. We're listening."

Criketchen said, "There was a small clan of O'rult swimming toward the island. We searched their minds to see who had sent them, but their leader was nowhere to be found. They were acting of their own accord. After we searched them, they drowned themselves."

Sammaria looked over at the female Hawkatie who had contradicted her. She open and closed her mouth like a fish.

The Patriarch said, "Criketchen, thank you. Please take a seat."

Sammaria said, "Did you change your mind?"

The Patriarch said, "We'll put it to a vote."

He addressed the Hawkaties in the room, "Who here believes that we should join this alliance that the princess has proposed?"

A few let out a hollow noise made by snapping their beaks together. Among the creatures voting yes were Criketchen and the female who had initially challenged them.

"Who's against this?"

The room became a symphony of the previously made chomping sound. The Patriarch turned to face Sammaria,

"The Hawkaties have spoken. We shall not help you. I'm sorry."

Sammaria nodded, "I understand."

Criketchen said, "Well, I don't. After the news you've heard, why won't you help? These O'rult are as much a threat to us as they are to the Elvateth."

The Patriarch bellowed, "You dare have the courage to challenge me? Not just me, but the whole population?"

Criketchen said, "I'm going with them. They need us. You disappoint me."

CHAPTER XL

The lock clicked, and the door flung open wide. Jessie stood there by herself. Her hands sat firmly on her hips. Rekasi sat up and rubbed his eyes. Donichello pulled a fork from the tray next to the bed. Jessie gave him a withering look. He set it back down.

Jessie walked into the room, leaving the door open. She said, "Say I believe you. What does it matter? You don't know why the 'Good Queen' as you call her cursed me with this."

"Cursed you?" Donichello said with a mixture of disgust and surprise.

Jessie gave them a tight smile, "That's what I thought. You don't have any more answers than I do." She stared at Rekasi, imploring him.

He looked away, "You are right. No one knows why Milamare did what she did."

Jessie dropped to sit on the footlocker. "Damn," she said, "I was hoping you could help me understand why I constantly feel like I should be doing more. That I am running out of time."

Rekasi shook his head, "I am sorry, Jessica."

"God! Jessie. Please!" she said, exasperated.

"Sorry, Jessie. I wish we knew more."

"Yeah, me too." She slapped her knees and stood up, "Oh well. No use crying over spilled milk."

Rekasi frowned. She certainly had mercurial emotions. He wondered if because humans felt their lives moved so quickly, they had to feel things that way as well.

She stood and walked out of the cabin. Rekasi looked at Donichello, bewildered. After a moment, she peeked back in the door, "Are you coming?"

Rekasi and Donichello scrambled to follow her up onto the deck.

Jessie said, "I have decided to help you." She stopped and cocked her head, "When I say it like that, it makes it seem like I was never going to. I was. But I just feel guilty that Reness frightened the girls."

Donichello said, "You are going to take us to them?"

Jessie frowned as if she were thinking, "No. We can't do that."

Donichello's face grew stormy. He opened his mouth to protest. Rekasi interrupted, "I do not understand."

Jessie sighed, "You were right when you said I have abilities I can't explain."

She walked over to the railing and looked out at the sea. It was black under the moon. She said, "That has led me to find some things that do not want to be found."

Donichello said, "You found the Hawkaties? Take us to them!"

Jessie looked at him, annoyed, "I cannot. The *Death Arrow* is forbidden to enter their waters. We got too close. Now we sail at their pleasure. I will not endanger my crew."

Donichello stepped forward. Jessie held up her hands. She pointed off the port side. Purple and green lights danced across the water. Rekasi and Donichello turned to look at the lights. They seemed to emanate from a city far on the horizon.

Jessie said, "The creatures monitor the water miles around their home. Their location is a jealously guarded secret. If the girls strayed near them, the flock will have taken them in."

Rekasi grasped the edge of the rail. He looked at the lights once more. He asked, "What am I looking at?"

Jessie said, "Those lights are Lavinrac. We sail there, then we will return to Dragonia by way of the gulf. You can join us if you wish."

The door opened, waking Jennica. Rubbing the sleep from her eyes, she looked to who was intruding. A looming figure pulled back the drapes around the bed. A Hawkatie greeted her and said, "Young one, get dressed. You are to begin your training."

Jennica stared. The Hawkatie continued, "For control over the Water."

Jennica sat up a little straighter. She rushed out of bed and started to pull on one of the dresses from the closet. The Hawkatie said, "If I may say something. Training is difficult. It would be better if you wore breeches."

Nodding, Jennica slid into the required clothes. The Hawkatie led her into the hallway. She said. "Sammaria should already be there. This is a very special thing. We don't usually train anyone outside of our own race, but the High One demanded it!"

Jennica smiled as they reached the room.

Sammaria was indeed there. She smiled as Jennica entered. Jennica went to stand next to her. The Hawkatie that had escorted Jennica said, "My name is Cheo. I will be assisting your teacher."

A man with salt and pepper hair walked into the room. He announced, "My name is Cypol. If you fail, you shall leave. If you don't want this training, you are finished. I won't teach you if you don't want to learn. Let's begin."

He pointed to Sammaria, "You!" He circled her slowly, "You have had semi-formal training. Fire Power. Very strong. Rekasi trained you if I am not mistaken?"

Sammaria's heart ached as her mind unwillingly assaulted her with memories. She nodded.

Cypol turned to Jennica. She trembled slightly. Cypol asked, "Are you afraid?"

Jennica hesitated. "Yes," she admitted.

Cypol replied, "You have Water Power. You are very powerful, but only have basic control. You will have to train harder than your sister. Are you up for the challenge?"

Jennica nodded, "I'll take what you give me."

Cypol nodded. The queer glint in his eye gave Jennica shivers, but she had a firm resolve to finish what she would soon start.

Cypol nodded again, "All right. Let's see your breathing patterns."

Jennica looked toward her sister. She had started performing the patterns Rekasi had taught her. Jennica felt alone. She stared into the corner of the room, holding back her frustration. Cypol touched her arm. He lifted his arms to his chest, breathing in. Breathing out, he sent his arms straight out. He brought them back in and then shot them straight up. He pulled them down again, breathing in. Then, shot them forward, breathing out. He then started the whole thing over again. He started the routine a third time before he said, "Copy."

Nervously, Jennica mimicked Cypol's breathing. After a while, he left Jennica to her breathing and adjusted Sammaria's. He tweaked her posture, but he mostly just listened to them breathe.

At the end of the lesson, he said, "Good practice. Meet me here again tomorrow, bright and early, and we'll start with something new."

CHAPTER XLI

The ship docked at the Port of Lavinrac. Rain fell onto the deck. Jessie smiled and tilted back her head. Rain rolled down her cheeks. Donichello pulled his hat down low over his ears. Jessie looked up and shook out her hair. She tied it back with a bright purple ribbon. She laughed at Donichello and Rekasi as they hunkered down against the rain. She said, "The city comes alive in the rain."

Donichello cocked his head. He looked down at the docks, feeling a buzz of excitement. Brightly colored lanterns were hanging from the eaves of every building. People wore brightly colored scarves and matching clothing. They appeared to be chatting happily. The rain did not bother them.

Jessie picked up a pole leaning against the rail. She extended it into the air. Attached to the pole was a circular band of cloth. The cloth bounced the raindrops off the multicolored fabric with a faint thump. Donichello looked back at the streets again. Several people held objects similar to Jessie's.

Reness took her arm. He winked at the boys, "Have fun!"

They began to disembark. Jessie turned back, "Remember we will leave tomorrow at high sun."

Donichello nodded. He followed the two off the ship. Jessie and Reness were quickly swallowed by the crowd.

Rekasi and Donichello walked away from the dock and down the market row. Donichello noted the terse looks as they passed. He ignored them and kept his eyes on the shops. They would have to do something about their attire soon.

Someone moved into Rekasi's path and crashed into his shoulder. Rekasi protested. The man glared at him before moving on. He tossed his vibrant yellow scarf over his shoulder.

Rekasi said, "What was that?"

Donichello replied, "Do you really not know about Keyinture's rain festivals?"

Rekasi said, "I do not. I have been a little more focused on what has been happening in Dragonia."

Donichello pressed his lips together. He noted a shop up ahead with bright attire in the window. He gestured to their dull, dirty clothes, "The festival occurs every rain during Blessim. We are offending their gods by not celebrating."

Rekasi glanced around them. He was greeted with several more hostile looks. Donichello said, "Come."

He led them to the shop. The tailor turned with a large smile on his face. It faltered when he saw their drab apparel. Donichello held up a hand in greeting. He bowed his head, "Kind sir. Forgive us. We mean not to offend. We are travelers and were caught unaware by the rain festival today."

He sniffed, "You need to learn to read the skies." He looked out at the rain falling against the cobblestone streets, "Besides, it is not me you offend. It is Mother Teara of the Bounty."

Donichello bowed again, lower this time. He said, "We beg forgiveness. We have come here with humble hearts to right this offense. We wish to rightfully praise Mother Teara as was intended."

The tailor smiled. He ushered them further into his shop. He said, "This festival is predicted to be one of the last of the season. You will need a spectacular outfit to end the festivals. Luckily, you came to me. I have just the thing!"

Rekasi gave Donichello a skeptical look. Donichello gave him a sympathetic smile. The tailor said, "You are lucky I still have items left. I have been absolutely swamped with business this festival season. Teara bless!"

Rekasi said, "Why is that?"

The tailor rummaged through a stack of orange and red fabric. He said, "Hm? Oh, the refugees of course. From Dragonia. And of course, they cannot offend Mother Teara. So they come to me - Master Rowle – for penance and dress. Much like yourselves."

He looked at Rekasi with a spark in his eye, "Ah! Here!"

He pulled a blue shirt from one stack and orange pants from a different pile. He held them up to Rekasi, "Yes! Yes, this will be perfect." He handed the clothes to Rekasi and ushed him into a changing stall.

Donichello said, "What do you know about these refugees? My friend and I have been away for some time."

Rowle moved to a different stack of clothing. He rifled through and pulled out a deep purple shirt. He held it up to Donichello, shook his head, and tossed it away. He dug back into his piles.

Rowle said, "They all came very quickly. Though not all of them figured out how very offensive they were."

Rekasi called from his stall, "What were they running from?"

Rowle said, "Now you just take care to put those on." He pulled a yellow pair of pants out and examined them. He cocked his head, "It sounds like the invasion happened very suddenly. The refugees were able to escape before the O'rult set up their occupation."

"Kiro!" Donichello breathed, "Where was the Royal Army? Or the Resistance that I have heard so much about?"

Rowle set down the yellow pants and laid an orange belt across them. He said, "You really have been away for a time. The King is dead. The heir missing. The chain of command disintegrated. The country has been crippled."

The tailor tossed the pants at Donichello. He plucked a maroon shirt from his stack, "Ah, perfect!" He tossed it at Donichello as well.

Rekasi pulled the curtain on his changing stall. Rowle said, "Ah! Beautiful!"

He gestured for Donichello, "Come come. Let us think of happier things. Mother Teara has blessed us with this fine season. You must change."

Donichello changed. He paid the man for their elaborate clothing. They stepped out into the street. With their vibrant apparel, no one gave them a second glance.

Rekasi said, "Things are worse then we thought."

Donichello said, "We need to get back to Mestchester. We need to get Sammaria home."

Rekasi glanced over his shoulder and whispered, "Not here."

Donichello ducked under an awning. Several people sat on benches enjoying warm drinks and talking. The brightly colored lanterns gave the teashop an eerie glow. Rekasi continued to glance around the room as Donichello led them to the back corner. Rekasi sat facing the street.

The soft ticking of a clock droned from somewhere nearby. He closed his eyes for a moment. When he opened them, steam rose from his clothing. Donichello glanced around. No one seemed to notice.

Rekasi held out his hand, "Do you want me..."

Donichello shook his head, "I will be fine."

Rekasi shrugged and scanned the room again. He said, "With the refugees coming in, Keyinture has an influx of people. That has to have put a strain on the citizens in the area."

Donichello looked around. A strange device that looked like cups on a wheel spun as the wind picked up. People on the terrace cheered. He said, "I do not think they have realized it yet. They are still praising Teara for the increased business."

Rekasi glanced around the room. He frowned for a moment and gestured for the waitress. He ordered two ciders for the table.

Donichello said, "I am more concerned about getting back to Dragonia."

"If that is your goal, you are going to need some help," someone said.

Rekasi stood, his hand falling to his sword. Donichello mirrored his movements. A familiar face approached the table.

Donichello said, "Brother Orlten!"

Rekasi remained tense. The man inclined his head. Orlten said, "I have heard much about you, Lord Tathrina."

Rekasi said tersely, "I am not a lord."

Brother Orlten smiled, "My mistake."

Donichello interrupted, "How are you here? Are you all right?"

Orlten replied, "You can thank your friend, Lord Calen. He was able to get a good many people away from the capitol. I figured with so many people fleeing here, it was only a matter of time before Sammaria came for her people."

He looked at the two thoughtfully, "If she were still alive?"

Rekasi said defensively, "She is."

Donichello said, "We were separated."

Orlten inclined his head. Donichello said, "We plan to meet up with her at the Resistance base."

Orlten raised an eyebrow, "A most ambitious plan."

Rekasi frowned, "Brother? Will you excuse us for a moment?" Orlten nodded.

Donichello said, "He is of no danger to us. He was Sammaria's tutor."

Rekasi eyed him suspiciously. Orlten said, "I see you are uncomfortable, Lord Tathrina. My name is Pegor Orlten. I am a sage from Iohonus."

Donichello quietly gasped. Rekasi looked between the two men, "You…"

Orlten said, "Yes, I come from the far west."

He lifted his sleeve showing the brand of a two-pronged symbol branching from an open circle. It was the mark of the Order of Inquisition.

Donichello recoiled. Rekasi asked, "How did you become tutor to the Dragonian heir?"

Orlten said, "A story for another time. My purpose is to teach. I have."

Donichello said, "Enchardo would have killed you if he had known."

"A great many people would die if all secrets were known," Orlten replied cryptically.

The serving maid brought the two cups of cider. She looked at their tense postures. She asked, "Shall I bring one more?"

Donichello nodded. He gestured for them to sit. Brother Orlten said, "Please. We have much to discuss."

CHAPTER XLII

Lady Jessie," Brother Orlten said.

Donichello and Jessie turned from the map they were examining. Jessie flashed Donichello an annoyed look. She smiled tightly, "Brother? What can I do for you?"

Orlten glanced at the map. Jessie maneuvered to block his view. Donichello crossed his arms over his chest and frowned her. Orlten said, "Your brother said you had questions for me."

Jessie looked annoyed again. She muttered, "He needs to leave well enough alone."

Orlten bowed to her, "I mean no disrespect."

She said, "Stop that fool groveling! I am no more a lady than a codfish!"

Brother Orlten suppressed a smile. Donichello gave him a steadying look. Jessie shot a glare at him. She gestured Orlten over to the table, "This cove is where we usually set in." She pointed to a spot in the Gulf of Trisanth. Orlten shook his head. Jessie folded her arms, "What?"

Orlten said, "This whole coast is crawling with O'rults."

Jessie pressed her lips into a thin line. Orlten continued, "When the citizens began to flee, the O'rult took over the gulf to prevent flight."

Donichello asked, "Why would they care if the Dragonians stayed or not?"

Orlten shook his head, "I was not able to figure that out. It was under the order of the woman with them. Someone that I heard called Lady Misseter."

Wood crashed against wood. The group turned to look at the noise. Rekasi stood there. A crate sat at his feet. He asked, "Misseter? Of house Veron?"

Orlten said, "I do not know. It is possible. Do you know her?"

Rekasi frowned and shook his head, "I know of her. She was hailed as some kind of hero when the O'rult invaded Gabvand. She took responsibility for Oliswood."

Orlten looked thoughtful, "Are you sure?"

Rekasi frowned, "Yes. Oliswood is where my parents died."

Orlten said, "I am sorry." He tapped the map, "This is interesting. This Misseter veiled herself behind many others. No one was certain who was responsible for Oliswood."

Rekasi said, "How did she end up involved with the O'rult? When I fled, she had vowed to oust them."

Jessie murmured, "Absolute power corrupts absolutely."

Brother Orlten nodded slowly. He examined the map. He jabbed a small point in the Keyintian Channel, "You should set in here."

Jessie shook her head, "Those cliffs are suicide!"

Orlten said, "The O'rult believe so as well."

Jessie glared at him. She muttered a couple of choice words under her breath and shook her head.

Orlten said, "Rumor has it *The Death Arrow* is the most notorious pirate ship in the Vrian Ocean."

Jessie pressed her lips into a thin line, "You flatter me. We are glorified smugglers. We make our shipments with *minimal* risk."

Donichello said, "Please, Jessie. I am begging you. Can you please take us there?"

She gave him a hard look. She flicked her eyes between Orlten and Rekasi. She sighed. She jabbed a finger at Donichello's chest, "If we pull this off, you best be singing my praises. And not have me arrested… Ever!"

Donichello said, "Kiro! If we pull this off, I will have you knighted!"

※

Jennica sat on the floor in front of Cypol. He said, "Breathe in now, Jennica. You are doing well. Now, slowly let the water come to your hand."

Jennica let it free. She heard a creaking as the water crystallized. She opened her eyes in surprise. There was a small ball of ice sitting on her hand.

Cheo clucked her tongue in approval, "You have come a long way from when you arrived here."

Cypol smiled at her.

Jennica said, "Thank you, Master."

Sammaria moved to her sister's side, looked at the Hawkaties, and said, "I have a question."

Cypol replied, "Ask it."

Sammaria asked, "Have you any news of the outside world? It's been weeks since we arrived on the Island and we've heard nothing."

Cypol slowly nodded, "Many Dragonians have become refugees where they can. The Resistance is losing the war."

Sammaria covered her mouth in shock, "Master Cypol, I …"

He looked at her expectantly, but not surprised.

"I must return to Dragonia. They need me. I can't let this go on. People are dying and I am the only one that can stop it."

"You are not fully trained. This is a very dangerous time."

"I have enough control to not harm the people around me or myself. You know I have to go back. You wouldn't have told me this news if you didn't think I could handle myself."

Cypol slowly nodded his head, "That is true."

Sammaria said, "Please, sir. Allow me to go back to my country. They need me."

Cypol said, "Very well. I will allow you to return."

He eyed both girls, "You must finish your training. Return here after you have settled this."

Jennica bowed to the circle of Hawkaties that surrounded them. She said, "Thank you for your hospitality."

She climbed up onto Criketchen's back. Sammaria stowed the last of her supplies in the bags. The circle of Hawkaties moved away.

Cricketchen said, "Your Highness, we should be leaving. Treescet is expecting us."

Grumrose shuddered. She settled into Jennica's pack with her locket. Sammaria climbed onto Criketchen's back.

Mokana suddenly materialized in front of Cricketchen, "Your deceit has been discovered."

Sammaria and Jennica exchanged looks. Sammaria said, "Most Honored…"

Mokana waved his shifting hand at her. He spoke directly to the Hawkatie in front of him, "You'd best fly swiftly. I will placate the Patriarch."

Jennica asked, "What is happening?"

Cricketchen took off running. He leapt and spread his wings. Shouts echoed out below them. Mokana's voice boomed over the din. The cacophony silenced.

Cricketchen did not slow until they were well beyond the reach of the Island of the Hawkaties. Jennica asked, "What was that?"

Sammaria asked, "What did you do?"

Criketchen said, "I righted the wrong they committed."

Grumrose popped out of the pouch. She whispered, "Jennica!"

Jennica looked down. She was pulling on a small silver object. Jennica took it from the little creature. She gaped at the sapphire set in the front. She showed it to Sammaria.

Sammaria exclaimed, "You stole the Sapphire of Mytositsa!"

Criketchen said, "You need it more than them. They will see this in time."

Sammaria asked, "What will happen to the Island now? They said the stone was their protection."

Criketchen shrugged, "Hawkaties are strong creatures. They will either use their magic to continue to hide or finally be forced to help with Ethota's problems. As it should be."

CHAPTER XLIII

Jennica and Sammaria dismounted from Criketchen. He folded his wings to his side. Grumrose pushed the air aside to open the arch in Trydid Rock. Jennica entered, followed by Criketchen and an amazed Sammaria.

Grumrose ignored the looks she got from the other Grumpices as they passed. Sammaria, however, felt immensely uncomfortable. She asked, "Why are they glaring at her?"

Jennica said, "She left. They didn't think that their secret should be let out."

Sammaria frowned but quieted. Grumrose turned down a hallway with a sloping ceiling. Soon, it was too short for all but the Grumpice. Grumrose looked behind her, "Perhaps you should stay here."

Jennica nodded, "We can't follow you where you're going."

The ceiling sloped further down the hallway. Grumrose nodded, "That is true. I will be back soon."

Criketchen laid down, "Settle down girls. This could be a while."

As Grumrose entered the room, the other Grumpices stopped as they noticed who it was. Many of them glared at her. Grumrose forced herself not to shrink back. She needed to do this.

Treescet said, "So, you have finally come home to us." Grumrose nodded her little head, not knowing what to do. He said, "Why have you come? If I'm not mistaken, the Elva sit just down the hall."

Grumrose added, "And a Hawkatie."

This caused murmuring among the creatures present.

Grumrose said, "I have not come back home to stay. I have to help the Elvateth."

"Oh, and how are you to do this?"

"Mokana spoke with me," she said. More murmuring erupted in the hall.

Treescet nodded, but continued, asking, "So, I return to the question. Why have you come back?"

Grumrose took a deep breath. It filled her small body. She looked at the leader of her clan, "The force of the O'rult has grown since I was last here. The Elvateth will never defeat them on their own. They don't have the power. We do. I've returned to ask for your help in defeating the O'rult army."

Treescet leaned forward in his chair. He rubbed his long, cottony beard. He didn't say a word. The Grumpice stared at Grumrose with an intensity that mesmerized and frightened the girl. She shifted her river stone eyes to the worried faces of the other Grumpices.

She said, "You think we'll be asked for help every second?" A few faces confirmed this thought. "The rest of you are worried we'll be captured and sold." The rest of the faces confirmed this fear.

Grumrose said, "I was out in the world. They respect the Grumpices. We are the power of old. That is something not to be trifled with. People will ask for our help, yes, but we are in full right to refuse. Jennica and Sammaria have sworn to stand behind us. Whatever our decision, no matter who we refuse. The secret is already out. We can finally come out of hiding. It's time."

Treescet smiled faintly, "You have grown in your time away, Grumrose. I am pleased your travels went well. As for us Grumpices of Trydid Rock, we must now decide."

Treescet stood and looked at the members of his clan. "Are there any objections to this proposal?"

A few people called out. Treescet said, "I understand your concern. There is a risk to every endeavor. Grumrose, we will come to your aid."

She smiled broadly, "Thank you, Treescet."

Grumrose smiled to herself as she closed the door behind her and made her way back to her waiting friends. She said, "Treescet has agreed to help us."

Jennica smiled and picked up the Grumpice, "You are the most wonderful creature, Grumrose."

Sammaria breathed a sigh of relief.

Criketchen said, "Finally, I will be able to see the legendary Grumpices fight. If only my own race would come."

The princesses returned to Criketchen's back. He took a running leap off the cliff and spread his wings. He angled them southwest, heading toward the Kilhatea Mountains. Criketchen flew them quickly over the Dragonian landscape. Sammaria was upset and surprised to find the trail of destruction on the ground below them on the eastern border with Mysticus. She couldn't even fathom what Mestchester must look like.

"Scores of people saw the strange shadow fly over their town. No one alive remembered the famed Hawkaties. Even if there were, they wouldn't recognize the deformed creature for what he was. The people of Likenton say they saw riders resembling the princesses on this strange creature. Many people didn't believe it was possible. They didn't think Sammaria and Jennica could have survived. They had been missing for so long. Even so, it brought hope to the enslaved people."

Rekasi lit the lantern and set it down in the covered nook facing away from the shore. He sat down and stared down at the riding cliff face. It was a little more than a looming shadow in the night. Orlten sat down next to him. He said, "What are you thinking about?"

Rekasi continued to stare at the shadow of the cliffs. He said, "I am worried that we've done all this for nothing. Lady Veron has moved against Dragonia. She has betrayed Gabvand. What if we cannot fix this?"

"That is always the fear, is it not?" Orlten replied. He moved over as Jessie came and leaned against the rail next to them. She eyed the cliffs.

Rekasi looked over at the older man. Orlten said, "You have to have faith. Faith in yourself. Faith in Sammaria."

Rekasi said, "That would be easier if she were here. If I knew she was all right."

Jessie scoffed, "Seriously? She does *not* need your protection.."

Rekasi stared at her.

Jessie sat down next to him. She took a sip of thick, brown liquid and noted his face, "Oh…um. I mean… She is a queen straight out of a fairytale. She is going to be fine."

Rekasi stared back at the cliff, "I suppose I should listen to you. You *are* one of the Keepers."

Jessie took a sip of her drink and made a face, "So you say."

Brother Orlten examined her for a moment.

"What?" she said defensively.

He asked, "You do not trust in your destiny?"

She sat her cup on the deck in front of her. A sweet aroma wafted up to Rekasi's nose. She said, "I believe destiny is something that you make."

Orlten said, "An idealistic view."

She narrowed her eyes. She took another sip and shrugged, "Tell me, Sage. What is my destiny? You seem to know behind those meaningful looks you have been giving me."

Brother Orlten said, "The texts disagree why the Keepers were created. Throughout history, it has been done a handful of times. The roles are varied. However, all agree it is tied to the old magic."

Rekasi said, surprised, "The Draigar?"

Brother Orlten nodded, "The consensus is that the Keepers' destiny is tied to the old magic of some form. Though I have not been given any indication of what their purpose is."

Jessie scoffed, "Even you scholars can't agree. More of a reason to hold onto my idealistic thoughts."

She stood and drained her cup. She asked, "Are you boys ready?"

CHAPTER XLIV

Reness kissed Jessie, "Be careful." Donichello turned away and busied himself with the ropes in the liferaft. Rekasi helped Jessie into the boat. She sat down and gripped one of the oars. She glanced up at her husband and nodded. He nodded back and began lowering the raft into the water. Jessie said, "Remember. No noise."

The boat dropped into the water with a quiet splash. She took the other oar from Donichello. He looked at her, surprised. She dipped the oars in and out of the water, pulling them forward, with hardly any splash. Jessie gestured to her eyes. She pointed ahead.

Rekasi was already scanning the coastline for any sign of danger. Donichello reached out with his Power. He could feel no vibrations in the earth. If there was anyone present, they were not moving.

Jessie continued to pull them forward. She sank the oars into the water silently. Donichello could see her body was tense. Her jaw set, but she kept her strokes steady.

Rekasi held up his hand. Jessie pulled the oars up and let them rest. The boat propelled forward on the current they had made. Rekasi's eyes continued to scan the coast. Donichello felt with his Power. He could still not sense anything. He glanced over at Rekasi. He was squinting into the darkness. He slowly dropped his hand. He nodded to Jessie. She hesitated for a moment before resuming her rowing.

She rowed them close to shore and nodded for them to go. Rekasi slipped into the chilled water. They were swimming from there. Donichello glanced up at the cliff face. He nodded at her. She stopped him and whispered, "If there are survivors, send them down here. We will take them away." Donichello nodded and slid into the water.

Rekasi and Donichello took a deep breath and submerged. They swam until the sand met their bodies. They stood and climbed onto the shore. Donichello looked behind him. Jessie's boat was not visible in the moving waves.

Rekasi looked at the cliff face. It was almost a sheer climb. He looked questioningly at Donichello. Donichello nodded. He stepped forward and took a deep breath, calling on his Power. This was the dangerous part of the plan. There was no way to quietly move earth.

Donichello pulled repeatedly on the cliff face. The ground rumbled. Giant slabs of rock extended from the wall, creating a crude stairway up to the top.

Rekasi began running up the path. Donichello quickly followed behind him. They heard shouts up above them. Rekasi pulled on his Power and Fire came to his hand.

Rekasi breached the top. He stopped, and the Flame dropped from his hand. Donichello followed behind him. He saw what Rekasi was looking at. Several people stood there huddled in terror. Nothing remained of their town.

Rekasi asked, "The O'rult. Are they here?"

A woman in the front shook her head, "They left yesterday."

Donichello said, "Carefully. Down the steps. There is a ship waiting for you."

The woman held a hand to his cheek, "Kiro bless you!"

The small group of people began to make their way down the steep embankment.

Rekasi and Donichello stopped a man leading horses. Rekasi said, "Please let us take those."

The man pulled on the reins and opened his mouth to protest. Donichello shoved a bag of coins into his hand.

Rekasi and Donichello mounted two of the horses. They set the others loose and rode hard toward the Resistance base.

❦

Criketchen landed in front of the entrance to the Resistance's mountain castle. Jennica and Sammaria slid off and took up their packs. Grumrose flitted around behind them as Sammaria pushed the large doors open. She walked into the entrance hall with an air of royalty. As she approached the room where the members of the Resistance were gathered, the people in the hallway began bowing their heads to her in shock. She looked at them all.

The General Tynacar and Olo approached her and said, "Your Highness! Forgive us. We assumed the worst. Is Rekasi with you?"

The men stood uneasily, glancing at the two creatures following the girls.

Sammaria said, "Thank you, General, but no. We were separated." She paused for a moment, steadying her emotions, "Don't ask me where I've been. We have more pressing issues on our hands."

Tynacar bowed to her and said, "O'rult have been advancing throughout Dragonia."

Olo said, "They have already taken over the capitol."

Sammaria said, "I am aware of this. Do you have reconnaissance information on the placement of their troops?"

Tynacar said, "We have scouts out now getting this information."

Sammaria asked, "Are they on foot?"

Tynacar nodded.

Sammaria looked at Criketchen. She asked, "Criketchen can you fly around and tell us the troop positions in this area?"

Criketchen bowed and took flight. He flew from the hall and out the door. Sammaria tapped her chin, thinking. She turned back to Tynacar, "Where are your maps?"

Sammaria pushed a troop line up to the Katart Wood as Criketchen had suggested. Tynacar nodded at her placement. He said, "I didn't know that you had such knowledge in military strategy."

Sammaria shrugged, "I've studied. But I have also been out there. I have seen where the destruction is."

Tynacar nodded and said, "Your Majesty, might I suggest placing a line of troops here?" He pointed to the border between Pilleetain and Dragonia.

Sammaria asked, "From where do you suggest that we take the troops?"

Tynacar said, "We have a reserve of troops in the Draconle Woods."

Sammaria gave him a sharp look, "A reserve?"

Tynacar said, "Yes, you placed it there yourself."

Sammaria said, "That is not a reserve! Did you not listen to a word that Criketchen said?"

Tynacar said, "Of course I did, Your Majesty."

Sammaria said, "Then you *did* hear that there is a unit of O'rult camped there and the report of what has been done to that town. We leave the troops there."

Criketchen said, "Pilleetain is a foolish country, but they aren't so thick as to attack Dragonia while it's fighting the O'rult. That would not only put them at risk, but they know that, if Dragonia doesn't destroy the O'rult, then they will have to. They aren't prepared for that. What if you were to bring other allies, Majesty? You have the Hawkaties, the Grumpices, and a fury of dragons. Your sister can also call the Fraychavae if it is needed."

Sammaria's head whipped up, "Fraychavae?"

Criketchen nodded, "During her search for you, she allied with the Fraychavae. As well as with Anahi, the Immortal."

Tynacar's face turned three shades of red, "The Fraychavae? There is no way in Deildly that my men are…"

Sammaria interrupted him, "You will if I say you will. We could use them. The Fraychavae are cunning strategists. We'll call them if we must. And we must talk to the leaders of our allied countries."

Tynacar nodded his head, "Who do you suggest contacting? We can't travel to any of them quickly enough."

Sammaria cursed inwardly, "Our alliances with Illicus, Griffinia, and Casparia are still strong. We can speak to Pilleetain and Keyinture as well. We have a common enemy. It might be what we need to band the countries together."

Tynacar nodded and called in several messengers. Sammaria gave them their instructions, "A horse is not fast enough for this message. You shall each be taking a dragon. I've summoned my sister. She will be here shortly to explain."

Jennica picked up the map that fell from the book she was reading. She looked out the library window. Her heart longed for Donichello. She missed him.

Jennica tucked the map in her pocket. She fingered the dagger that she had picked up from the table. She heard the soft tread of a foot as Sammaria's message appeared in her mind. She pretended not to hear the footsteps. Maybe if she ignored him, he would go away.

She heard a moan. Jennica started to turn. A hand covered her mouth. She slammed her elbow into their abdomen. It was softer than expected. Strangely, the person did not react to her attack. She spun to face the intruder, pointing the dagger at them with a wild look in her eyes.

Jennica said, "Who are you?"

The man moaned, "Trust me."

Jennica eyed him suspiciously. She said bitterly, "Trust is hard to come by in these times."

Jennica spied the blue sextant on his neck. Her pulse quickened. He was dead! How was he not dead?

Trydexzi.

She said, "How can I trust you now, knowing you are Misseter's puppet?"

The man didn't say anything. He lunged at Jennica. She flicked the dagger up just in time. His body burst into ash. Jennica dropped the dagger, horrified. She retreated from the corner where the remains of the man with the sextant lay. Jennica slammed the door and leaned against it, out of breath.

CHAPTER XLV

Sammaria looked up as the doors were thrown open. Jennica rushed in, out of breath. There was powder covering the front of her dress. Jennica said nothing, and Sammaria didn't push it.

Sammaria met Criketchen's eyes, "This is all for now. I'll have Rekasi check this when he arrives. The two of you can figure out how best to mobilize the few troops we have."

Criketchen nodded and left as Sammaria turned to her sister, "Jennica, I'm sorry, but you must summon the dragons before going."

Jennica nodded weakly.

Sammaria led Jennica to the balcony just off the room. Jennica stood away from the rest of the group. She let out a piercing whistle, resonating with magic laced into every sound wave. She waited. Flying figures appeared on the horizon. As they grew closer, the messengers shrank back in fear. Dratasha hovered over the balcony rail. Jennica said, "We must ask you to ferry messengers across to Keyinture, Pilleetain, Illicus, Griffinia, and Casparia. And, unfortunately, we must also ask you to fight the O'rult with us."

Dratasha said, "We will honor our promise to you, *Aska*."

Jennica cocked her head, confused.

Dratasha replied, "*Aska* is a friend of many. It fits you better than *Kiata*."

Jennica smiled, "Thank you, Dratasha. We appreciate all you do."

As the dragons landed in the field behind the castle, Jennica instructed the messengers on how best to ride them. When she was satisfied that they wouldn't insult their hosts, she sent them on their way. Sammaria broke in before anyone could say anything else, "Now, if you'll excuse me, my sister and I will retire to our room. Anything that needs attention, bring it up with Tynacar who will bring it directly to me if he sees fit."

Sammaria took Jennica's arm and pulled her away. Sammaria sat down in a chair while Jennica sat on the bed. They said nothing, just stared awkwardly around the room. Sammaria was waiting for Jennica to explain the blood on her dress, but Jennica wasn't volunteering any information.

The mountain castle came into view. Rekasi and Donichello reined in their horses. Donichello swung off his horse, and they walked their horses up the unsteady path.

Rekasi burst through the castle's main doors. The horse's reins dropped from his hands as he and Donichello walked briskly to Olo's study. Without knocking, Rekasi entered the room. Startled, Olo dropped his glasses. Donichello picked them up and handed them to the startled Elf. Rekasi said, "Show me the battle charts."

Olo muttered as he walked into the planning room adjacent to his office, "Never a hello."

Rekasi surveyed the charts with an educated eye. Tynacar approached the table, "The scouts have returned. They say that battle is imminent. The O'rult have taken up camp in a field on the edge of the Katart Wood, near Mestchester."

Rekasi absorbed the information. There was no more time to prepare. He commented, "Impressive placement. Well placed indeed. Was this you, Tynacar?"

He retorted, "It wasn't me. I only gave numbers. It was the queen who placed them."

Taken aback, Rekasi asked, "The queen?"

"Yes, sir. Queen Sammaria, sir."

Rekasi said with new urgency, "Where is she?"

Olo replied, "She is in her room, sir."

Rekasi patted Tynacar on the back and said to Donichello, "Stay with the Prime Minister."

Without another word, Rekasi left, sprinting to Sammaria's room. Outside her room, Rekasi hesitated. The door opened.

Jennica emerged and closed the door before turning around. She jumped as she came face to face with him. She smiled, throwing her arms around his neck. Rekasi was surprised. He'd thought she still held some resentment toward him. She stepped out of his way. Rekasi smiled at her and slowly opened the door.

Sammaria stood behind the dressing screen, "Jennica? Back already? Who's there?"

There was no fear in her voice, just a frightening curiosity. Rekasi found he couldn't speak.

Not receiving a reply, Sammaria pulled a robe over her head and stepped out from behind the screen. A man with tangled lengths of dark hair and intriguing eyes stared at her.

Sammaria's breath caught in her throat as she looked past the dirt on Rekasi's face. Sammaria stared at him. Rekasi broke his trance and rushed over to her, pullig her into a kiss.

Donichello moved through the castle like a restless ghost. He was searching endlessly. He knew that she had to be here. Tynacar said the queen was here, and Jennica was always with her. Unless...

Donichello shook his head. Sammaria and Rekasi entered the room. Donichello nodded his head toward them. Rekasi looked over the troops again. He consulted Sammaria as changes arrived. Donichello stood in the background, fidgeting. He could see lightning passing between Rekasi and Sammaria.

Donichello couldn't help but think of where Jennica might be. Sammaria and Rekasi remained oblivious to his worries as they were caught up in their own world. Donichello nodded to them as he left to pen their horses.

Donichello walked into the stables. He shut the two horses into different stalls. He petted the horse that had carried him and mused, "She has to be here, doesn't she? I would know if she wasn't. Wouldn't I?"

A rustling startled Donichello, causing him to draw his sword. He carefully walked around the small stable, looking for the source of the noise. Donichello lowered his sword when he saw Jennica curled up on the straw, asleep. Not wanting to disturb her, Donichello lay down next to her. He held her hand as he too drifted off to sleep.

Jennica awoke, feeling pressure on her hand. She smiled at Donichello's sleeping form. She moved closer to him and laid her head on his arm. She watched his sleeping face. It was so serene. She caressed his cheek. His hand moved to hers as his eyes flicked open. His nut-brown eyes smiled into her blue ones. He said, "How are you?"

Jennica beamed, "I'm all right. A little shaken, but fine."

Donichello said, "Shaken how?"

Jennica said, "Before, it was just everything that has happened. Now..."

She stopped as Donichello sat up. He didn't release her hand. He kissed it. Jennica whispered, "So proper."

Donichello helped her up and said, "Maybe we should go see that darling sister of yours."

Jennica grinned and said, "Don't you mean the queen?"

Donichello nodded. They started back to the main fortress. People rushed past them. Donichello stopped someone. He asked what was going on. They said, "The queen has ordered an audience."

Donichello and Jennica hurried to see what she had to say.

Sammaria stood before them in the main room. Rekasi stood beside her. She said, "We all know why we are here. It's unfortunate, yes, but I know that we can reclaim our country. We have held back the O'rult before, and I know we can do it again. My father was a fool. He thought that the O'rult weren't going to attack this country. He led us into a false sense of security. Now, we must take back what is ours. Rekasi will tell you your positions."

The crowd gave a huzzah to the queen, and she left the floor to Rekasi.

Rekasi asked Tynacar to bring in the maps that he and Sammaria had poured over the day before. He waited a few minutes for the map to arrive. When it did, he said, "There will be many different points of attack. The siege will last just under a week if we execute it correctly."

He pointed to a place on the border of the Draconle Wood, "There, we will have Quarlite's regiment along with Monthe's. The O'rult have their supply house in this area. Capture it, and you cut off their supply. It will hinder them for a while. Then," he pointed to the town called Drannor outside the Katart Woods, "Marquis's group is going to move in on Drannor from the right. Balankey's is going to converge on them from the left. We are sending several regiments to the rest of the land. We have to comb the country and destroy all of them."

Marquis asked, "What about our capitol, Mestchester?"

Rekasi said, "Queen Sammaria, Princess Jennica, Lord Donichello, and I are going to infiltrate the capitol along with the Grumpices and Criketchen. Do not abandon your posts unless your job is completely done. That means O'rult killed, stores captured, citizens saved. I mean it. It will not bode well for those that do not listen."

The generals agreed. Rekasi said, "Get some rest tonight men and women. We have intense training at first light."

Donichello sat next to Caliet. She looked up for a moment, "Could you please stop doing that?" Donichello frowned, "Doing what?"

Caliet dropped her sewing for a moment, exasperated, "Brooding! You're making me mess up."

Donichello said, "Oh yes. You're the girl who senses feelings."

Caliet picked up the pants she was mending. She asked, "So, is it, Jennica?"

Donichello said, "I don't feel comfortable discussing Jennica and myself with someone so young."

She smirked, "Oh all right. Don't talk to the girl who knows the feelings of everyone around her."

Donichello replied, "All right. Yes, that's why I'm brooding. I think I'm losing her."

Caliet snorted, "Fat chance. Why? Did you bed her?"

Donichello stared at her in disbelief. She said, "I'll take that as a no."

Donichello replied, "No we haven't. I didn't. Our relationship…She's young. I'm …It just wouldn't be right. Why?"

Caliet shrugged, "Why do you think you're losing her?"

It was his turn to shrug, "She's been getting distant. She won't come around me. Ever since that first day when we reunited."

Caliet placed the last few stitches into the pants. She said, "You are an idiot. She's not avoiding you – well, she is – but because she's up to something. Not because she wants you gone. Obviously, she's going to do something you wouldn't like."

CHAPTER XLVI

The dragon landed in the court of Keyinture. The messenger swung his leg around the dragon's head and slid to the ground. He wobbled a little as he walked. Bowing before the King, he said, "King Aggravius, Dragonia humbly beseeches you. Dragonia is danger and we ask you to hold to your alliance and aid us in our time of need."

The King sat back in his chair, "And what threat is King Enchardo facing?"

The messenger looked up, "Sir?"

King Aggravius barked, "What?"

The messenger buried his head, "King Enchardo is dead, killed by a dragon. His daughter Sammaria is now fighting for the throne."

The King rubbed his beard, "Who is this girl fighting?"

The messenger replied, "She is fighting the entire O'rult army. She has asked for you to come with haste."

King Aggravius sat for a moment, "Has she a plan?"

The messenger said, "Yes, Your Majesty. She is going to take back Mestchester."

"When is this going to take place?"

"As soon as possible. She isn't going to allow the O'rult to treat her people as they have any longer. They are being slaughtered."

"I shall send three thousand men. Will that suffice?"

The messenger bowed, "Yes. Thank you, Your Majesty."

The messenger mounted his dragon once more and set off, returning to Dragonia.

"The other messengers had more or less the same success as the first. Sammaria and Rekasi added their allies' troops to the map. The training intensified as each set of allies appeared."

"What status can you give me, Tynacar?"

"Three thousand troops came from Keyinture. Five thousand come from Illicus, just under seven thousand from Griffinia, and a surprising eight hundred from Casparia."

Sammaria asked, "Any news from Pilleetain?"

Tynacar replied, "None, my Lady, none at all." Sammaria nodded briskly and continued watching Rekasi work with the Elementals.

She felt Jennica come up behind her. She whispered, "Come with me."

Sammaria half turned and transmitted her thoughts, "What do you need?"

Jennica said, "I'll show you. Come!"

Jennica led Sammaria through the castle and down to the basement where the stream ran through it. Sammaria was overcome by fear. This was the stream into which she had been thrown. Jennica froze a section of the stream, forming a walkway for them to cross. They continued into a black corridor. Sammaria called to her Power, illuminating the walkway. She asked, "Where are we going?"

Jennica replied, "You'll see when we get there." Sammaria followed her sister down the path. She could see carvings on the wall. Jennica was walking much too fast for her to examine them closely.

Jennica said, "Watch your step. It gets wet up ahead."

Sammaria let her Firelight expand, shining up ahead. Water dripped from cracks in the ceiling.

She asked, "What is this place?"

Jennica replied, "We are under the Rivers of Kilhatea, heading toward the plains between the Draconle and Katart Woods."

Sammaria asked, "How do you know this?"

Jennica looked back and smiled, "You'll see."

The darkness up ahead seemed to swallow up the light Sammaria was casting. Jennica said, "It's a large cavern. If you light the chandelier, it helps."

Jennica led Sammaria to the chandelier. Sammaria transferred the Fire from her hand to the candles, lighting the cavern. Jennica turned a wheel and raised the chandelier. Sammaria looked up. The ceilings were uncommonly high. She asked again, "What is this place?"

Jennica didn't reply. She lifted the chandelier higher. Sammaria saw tunnels on every side of cavern, nine in total. Jennica said, "This is a tunnel system."

Sammaria asked, "To where?"

Jennica replied, "Pick a tunnel."

Sammaria pointed to the one on her left.

"That one heads east. It comes out under the Crycra Waterfall in Pilleetain."

"How about that one?" She pointed to one across from the first.

"It goes out into the Rolling Plains."

"And the one next to it?"

"That one has caved in, but it used to lead to the Zephyr River valley."

"Do they all lead to places in Dragonia?"

Jennica shook her head, "As you've already seen, one leads to Pilleetain. The one we came from lets out deep inside the Kilhateas. The one next to it travels all the way into the depths of the Illican mines. They were built long ago. Before the Resistance built their headquarters here.

When they moved in, they just wanted to use the castle. They didn't know about this."

"Who built it then?"

"The Draigar."

Sammaria looked up, "Draigar? You mean…"

Jennica replied, "Yes, the original Dragonians. This was the castle of their leader. These tunnels were his escape routes."

Sammaria touched the stone walls, "How do you know so much about them?"

Jennica rubbed her arms, "I read about them in the library. One of the books had a map tucked into it. It fell out when I was searching for something to calm my mind. Then, when I learned of them, I used the Sight to find out where they were and explore them."

Sammaria asked, "Do any of them come up in Mestchester?"

Jennica said, "Not in. One does, however, come up near the jeweler's in Drannor."

Sammaria asked, "Who owns the shop?"

Jennica said, "A family named Cronson. They have two daughters and a son. Their father was killed by our own father's soldiers."

Sammaria said, "I believe that we've found a way to get to Mestchester without being seen."

Jennica said, "We must send word to them."

Sammaria said, "At once. Do you think we could use this system for anything else?"

Jennica said, "I'm toying with an idea. I will tell you as soon as it formulates further. I have concerns. I might be able to use Sight State to see."

Sammaria said, "Well then, let's go find out."

They returned to Jennica's chambers. Sammaria had guards standing outside her door.

Rekasi and Donichello joined them later. Sammaria stood next to Rekasi and held a chart. Donichello stood behind Jennica.

She said, "Remember, I'm just going to go through and see how it could turn out. This doesn't mean it'll work."

Rekasi nodded. Jennica continued, "And, whatever happens, don't let anyone in this room. And don't touch me. I'll come out of it."

She looked at Donichello who nodded. Jennica faced the wall. She took a deep breath and focused on the tunnels beneath the Plains. She felt a pull on her mind before she was rocketed to the place on which she focused.

The cave network looked similar to the Grumpices', except much larger. Jennica saw troops filling the caverns. They sat nervously on their horses, awaiting a signal. Jennica moved along the lines. The soldiers' faces were young and scared. Jennica felt her resolve falter. She kept herself from uttering a word. The soldiers might be afraid, but they were ready. The sound of a trumpet blaring reached them in the caves. Jennica watched them draw their weapons. The second blaring of the horn came.

General Concha led the charge. They sped ahead toward the end of the network. The men in the back on the outside edges slammed their weapons into the tunnel's supports. They raced on, away from the collapsing ground.

Jennica watched in horror as the back lines were crushed under the stone and earth. She listened to their screams as they waited for help that would never come.

Jennica couldn't believe this had happened. She once again forced herself not to tell Rekasi that this was a bad idea. She had to see what could happen next.

She ran down the tunnel to the exit, coming up behind the attacking regiments. She watched the battle, relaying the information to the people back in the sealed room. Jennica watched as the Resistance and its men were beat back repeatedly. She closed her eyes to the bloody scene. Silence came over the field. She snapped her eyes open.

The leader of the O'rult regiment was dead. The others didn't know what to do. The Resistance had won the battle. Barely. A hundred men of the Resistance lay dead, their blood beginning to pool in the grass. Jennica shook her head and returned to her body.

Sammaria finished marking on the board. Jennica said, "This could work. We just won the battle. But a hundred of our men died in the process. I can't let you go through with this if they die."

Rekasi said, "Some things are for the greater good."

Jennica said, "Were you not listening? We just *barely* won."

Rekasi said, "But we won, did we not?"

Jennica shook her head, "That's what happened as of now. The future is always changing. Bynakst'r might add more free-thinking O'rult to the battle or -"

Rekasi interrupted, "You said we won. We can do it."

Jennica said, "But a hundred men died! It's our fault their lives were lost."

Rekasi said, "These soldiers signed up knowing their lives could be lost. They are ready to make that sacrifice."

Jennica said, "Those soldiers signed up to fight for a free Dragonia! Not to die at the hands of their leader when he has the means to change the outcome."

Rekasi said, "They are ready to do their duty. What's it to you anyway? You don't know these men!"

Jennica shook her head, "It doesn't matter. They are my people, Rekasi. You can't change *that*."

Rekasi stepped forward, "And how do you propose we change the future you have seen?"

"Find a way to attack without having those men die."

Rekasi said, "The plan is solid. Any change we make could unravel it."

"So help me, I'll unravel you if you go through with this. How can you stand the blood of those people on your hands?"

"I'm a leader. As you'll learn, sometimes you have to make decisions that you don't want to make."

Jennica shook her head, "But you can change it. You know what's going to happen. Those men don't deserve to die."

Rekasi roared, "You think I don't know that?"

Jennica stepped forward. Donichello pulled back on her arm. She looked back at him. He shook his head, defeated. Jennica said, "Then fix it. You have all the resources to do it."

Jennica turned her pleading eyes on her sister, "Don't let him kill those people."

Sammaria said, "He wouldn't do that. Not if there was another way, Jennica. Maybe he's right. What other choice do we have? If we can win that battle, we can get that much closer to winning this war."

Jennica said, "This isn't a guaranteed victory. How many times do I have to say this? Any little thing can change the future. This is the most likely possibility now. But what if you go in without those men … we all could die. There is no guarantee."

Rekasi shook his head, "It's impossible."

Jennica's eyes flashed with a fire rivaled only by Sammaria's, "Nothing is impossible. You didn't hear their screams as the rocks crushed their bodies. You didn't hear them cry out in pain, for help. Help that would never come. One hundred men crushed beneath the earth that we ordered to be dropped. It's just too cruel."

Donichello wrapped his arm around her as she buried her face in his chest, waiting for Rekasi's answer. She knew what it would be before he gave it voice. He had made his decision. He said, "It is impossible, Jennica. I'm sorry. I don't want to say so, but it's something I have no control over."

Jennica said, "Then allow me to be there. Allow me to be in the battle so that I might help them when it happens."

Rekasi sighed. Donichello tightened his grip on her. He didn't want to let her do what she had asked, but he knew she'd do it no matter how much he protested. She'd grown so much since she'd left Mestchester. Rekasi said, "I can't let you do that Jennica. We need you in Mestchester."

Jennica said, "Then I leave the Resistance. You have no control over me then. Rekasi, I am going to be in that battle whether you grant me the permission to be there or not. Believe me, I'd really rather not sever my ties with you."

Rekasi said, "Is there nothing I can do to change your mind?"

Jennica shook her head, "I have a duty to those people. That's what having Sight is about. Saving those you can and trying your best to save those you can't."

Rekasi said, "You've seen things no one your age should. You've seen things that *no one* should. Go! We'll make it without you. As soon as that battle is over, ride as quickly as you can to Mestchester. We will need you there."

Jennica nodded, "Thank you, Rekasi."

She walked up to him and kissed him on the cheek. She turned and left the room. Donichello sighed.

Rekasi said, "I'm sorry, my friend."

Donichello said, "There is no quarrel between us. Keep your apology."

Rekasi nodded. Donichello followed Jennica out of the room.

Donichello knocked on the door to Jennica's room. She said, "It's open."

Donichello pushed the door open. Jennica looked over. She saw his face. He looked upset. She walked over and took his hand. She led him to her bed, "What is troubling you?"

Donichello said, "Is this something that you must do?"

Jennica nodded, "It is. I have to help those people."

Donichello kissed her forehead, "I know you do. I just wish that you didn't have to be so far from me."

Jennica replied, "I wish I didn't either. Donichello, sometimes we must sacrifice what we want for what needs to be done. You of all people should understand that."

Donichello said, "It is something that I understand very well. I love you."

Jennica said, "I know you do. I love you too."

Donichello said, "You've been planning this for some time haven't you?"

Jennica looked down, "I suspected something was going to happen. Donichello, they need me. I can't... You know I can't."

"Will you stay safe? I don't think I could handle losing you."

Jennica said, "I couldn't lose you either. I'd rather face the O'rult army for a thousand years."

Donichello gave her a faint smile, "You'll always have me."

Jennica smiled broadly, "Good because I'm not giving you up anytime soon."

Donichello kissed her. She felt pain in his kiss. It was strong and urgent. She said, "I'm coming back. I don't break that easily."

Donichello said, "I know. That's what I'm worried about."

Jennica looked at him. He said, "Even if you were riddled with arrows, you wouldn't give up on what you were doing. Please don't let that happen."

Jennica said, "I won't. I'm still needed here."

Donichello kissed her again, "And don't you forget that."

Jennica kissed the palm of his hand and folded it closed, "Hold that with you and I won't."

Sammaria handed Jennica a sword. Asravi cawed from his spot on her shoulder. She said, "It isn't too late to change your mind."

Jennica smiled, "It is. I'm sorry."

Sammaria shook her head, "Don't apologize. You have to do this."

Jennica smiled, "Thank you for understanding."

Sammaria nodded to her sister. She clucked her tongue and held out her arm. Asravi fluttered from her shoulder down to her wrist. Sammaria said, "Take him. He will watch your back for me."

Jennica said, "I couldn't take him from you."

Asravi cawed stubbornly. He bounced from Sammaria's wrist and settled onto Jennica's saddlehorn. He glared at the both of them.

Jennica said, "I guess it is decided."

Sammaria hugged her sister, "Be careful."

Jennica nodded.

Sammaria stopped in front of Dakota. He bowed from his horse, "Your Majesty?"

Sammaria groaned, "It's still just Sammaria to you, sir."

Dakota smiled, "What do you need, just Sammaria?" He winked to the man sitting next to him.

She rolled her eyes, "Keep an eye on her, please. Don't let her do anything rash. Believe me, she will try."

Dakota looked back at Jennica. She was dismounting. He said, "I'll do my best."

Sammaria smiled, "That's all I ask. Thank you."

Jennica smiled as Donichello crossed to her. She could see him from the corner of her eye as she stroked her chestnut mare's neck. He whispered in her ear, "I'm carrying your love."

Jennica felt shivers go down her spine as his lips caressed her ear. She turned, "Are you?"

He showed her his closed fist.

Jennica smiled, "We are leaving soon."

Donichello replied, "I know. We leave shortly after you. Sammaria needs to get to Mestchester quickly. The Cronsons are expecting us tonight."

Jennica smiled weakly. Donichello looked off, "We will meet again, Jennica."

She didn't reply. She didn't doubt it. Finally, she said, "I'm not the one who needs convincing."

He looked at her. She eyed him. He said, "It's my doubting head."

Jennica said, "You can always change the head. Do you have a doubting heart?"

Donichello shook his head.

She replied, "Turn off your mind and listen to your heart. I'll be with you again soon."

Donichello kissed her. He pressed her against her mare. Jennica felt his urgency. It wasn't as hard to bear this time. He released her and buried his head in her hair.

Asravi squawked from his perch. Jennica pulled herself from Donichello's grip. She smiled at the falcon.

A cry sounded from the front lines as Jennica mounted her horse again. They were heading out. Jennica looked back at Donichello as she kicked her horse into a fast trot. They left the mountainous terrain and headed toward the flat plains.

CHAPTER XLVII

Donichello sat on his horse. Rekasi pulled himself up onto his own. Sammaria turned her horse, taking the lead and heading down the tunnel that led Drannor. The horses' hooves crashed against the stone floor. Sammaria looked back. The map Jennica had shown her through mind speak drifted into view. She kicked her horse into a canter. She felt the cries of every Dragonian, all of their pain. She wondered what form of magic could cause her such pain. Sammaria urged her horse onward.

Light came from ahead. Sammaria slowed her horse. She halted him and dismounted. Slowly, she walked up the path. Rekasi and Donichello were behind her, but she scarcely noticed their presence.

A small face appeared at the end of the tunnel. Sammaria stopped. The girl asked, "Queen? Ma'am? Are you Queen Sammaria?"

Sammaria replied, "Yes. Are you of the Cronson family?"

The girl came into full view. She had long, brown hair and matching eyes. A scar, red against her skin, peeked from the edge of her shirt. She replied, "Yes, I'm Demetria. I'm your guide to Mestchester."

Sammaria asked, "What news have you of the fighting?"

Demetria replied, "Just under a thousand O'rult have headed toward the Kilhatea Mountains. They are expected to pass over the Plains soon."

Sammaria asked, "No fighting as of yet?"

"The skirmishes continue as they always have. Otherwise, there is no fighting."

Sammaria nodded, "Thank you."

Demetria looked behind her, "Damn! Retreat a few yards back into the tunnel, Majesty."

Sammaria could see a shadowy figure lurking just outside of the tunnel's exit.

Sammaria said, "Take the greatest care."

Demetria nodded before covering the tunnel's exit. Sammaria led the horses, Rekasi, and Donichello back into the tunnel and listened.

"Lunan." There was caution laced in that one word. From the sound of her voice, Demetria considered him a traitor.

He said, "Demetria, you should be home. It's not safe on the streets, especially at night. You should know this."

"I do know this."

"Then why do you constantly stay out?"

"What's it to you?" There was bitterness in her voice. The boy didn't reply. Demetria said, "See? You don't care about your people. They killed your brother. Trampled him just because he was in the street. You were one of the first to volunteer for the guard."

He paused, "Is that what you think? That I volunteered?"

Demetria said, "Prove otherwise."

Sammaria wasn't able to see the proof, but it seemed to have silenced Demetria. She said, her voice soft and understanding, "All right, Lunan. I'll go home."

Demetria turned, and they could hear her footsteps retreating. They heard a door open and close and quiet footsteps was heard as Lunan walked away from the hidden tunnel exit.

The screen over the exit was peeled back after a few minutes, "We must hurry. Lunan won't be detained long."

Sammaria led her horse to the exit. Rekasi took her hand. They emerged, flanked by Donichello, into the night. A figure gathered the horses and led them away. Demetria opened a door that looked as if it had been kicked in at one time. She led them through the small house. She said, "My brother is switching out your horses. We leave as soon as you are disguised."

Donichello asked, "Disguised? How so?"

Demetria gave a small smile, "You must be disguised as women. Men don't leave this town. There are hardly any left and certainly none of your skill."

Rekasi and Donichello exchanged looks, "Will we still be able to ride?"

Sammaria looked down at her dress. She said sarcastically, "It's just a skirt, boys."

They said, "Yes. Well, you've had practice at it."

Demetria said, "Queen Sammaria, we must disguise your hair."

Sammaria nodded, "Also, I need another dress. I'm afraid this is too grand for where we are going."

Demetria nodded, "We have everything prepared for you, ma'am."

Sammaria nodded, "Good."

Sammaria helped lace up Rekasi's dress. He murmured, "I'd never thought I'd live to see the day."

Sammaria giggled. He groaned as she lifted the brunette wig he was to wear and placed it on his head, tucking his short hair into it. She pulled it back into a bun.

She said, "You need to stand straight."

Rekasi straightened up, "Why?"

She said, "We have to take care of a certain area and can't while your slouching."

He said, "You aren't …"

Sammaria sighed, "We are. Do you want to make it through the night?"

Rekasi nodded, resigned. Sammaria stuffed cotton down the front of his dress.

He said, "If the situation wasn't so dire, this could be considered highly inappropriate."

She said, "All done. Now, turn around. I must change."

Rekasi turned his skirts, making a bell shape. He groaned. Sammaria gave a small chuckle. He glanced slightly over his shoulder. She was having difficulty with untying her dress. He asked, "Are you in need of some assistance?"

Sammaria said, "It's just that the ties have gotten knotted."

Rekasi said, "I can undo them."

Sammaria said, "Help me, please."

Rekasi turned around. He watched as she swept the hair from her neck, leaving it exposed. Her pale skin still hadn't recovered from the time she had been locked in a single room in the castle. It gave her a milky coloring. Rekasi looked down and saw the knot placed on the small of her back. He set to unraveling it. His hand bumped her back, but she didn't flinch from his touch.

He said, "Done."

She released her hair. It fell back into place, covering most of her back. She said, "Now, turn back around."

Rekasi smiled and did as he was told. She slipped from the dress and pulled on the older one Demetria had given her.

She laced it and said, "Tie it please."

He turned around. While tying the dress, there was a knock on the door. Sammaria said, "We're decent."

The door opened. Donichello walked in, wearing a red wig. Sammaria stifled a laugh. His dress didn't fit his strong build as well as Rekasi's spry one. Donichello complained, "This is unfair! He makes a good woman!"

Rekasi laughed, "What's that supposed to mean?"

Donichello gave him a look of disdain.

Sammaria said, "I wish that Jennica could see you."

He threw her a dirty look. Demetria came in carrying a blonde-brown wig. Sammaria swept her long, bright blonde hair up and Demetria fitted the wig in place.

Sammaria looked up and said, "We need to leave before the sun rises."

Sammaria swung herself onto her horse, showing the others how. They pulled themselves up with several comments about how they were going to tear their dresses.

Sammaria smiled. Demetria looked up at the sky, "We need to leave now. It's a two-hour, hard ride to Mestchester. We have about that much of total darkness left."

Sammaria said, "Let's go then."

The four spurred their horses into a gallop. Sammaria wondered how her sister fared as they headed toward Mestchester.

CHAPTER XLVIII

Jennica stood before General Concha. He shook his head, "That is unfortunate indeed. I will permit you to help the men you have seen die, but you must get to safety afterward."

Jennica asked, "Excuse me?"

He said, "You must get to safety after you help those men."

Jennica said, "I don't think we have an understanding, sir. I am going to be in that battle."

The general shook his head, "I don't want to risk losing you, Jennica. You are too precious to the people of Dragonia."

Jennica said, "That might be, but I am going to fight with my people."

General Concha shook his head, "That is impossible."

She spat, "Impossible! I hate that word."

She curtsied to the general before exiting his tent. She would be in that battle no matter what he said. She needed to find Dakota.

He was sharpening his dagger when she found him. He smiled as he looked up, and the grinding wheel slowly stopped. He said, "Highness."

She shook her head, "Just Jennica."

He laughed, "What is it with the Aeradal twins and not wanting to be addressed as they should?"

Jennica said, "A power-hungry father for one."

Dakota didn't reply. Finally, he said, "What can I do you for?"

Jennica said, "I need your help."

Dakota said, "Ah, help. With what might I inquire?"

She said, "I need to be in this battle. I know a hundred men are going to die in the tunnels before it even begins, and I am here to protect them. I need to be *in* the battle. I can't just sit idly by watching men die for my country. Concha doesn't want to risk it."

Dakota nodded, "I understand his reasoning. If you were killed, what would happen to the morale of every soldier in this army? They couldn't handle it, Jennica. You know you are a symbol of hope, don't you?"

Jennica shook her head, "Why am *I* their hope? Sammaria is their queen, their leader."

Dakota replied, "You have both become living contradictions of your father and embody the legacy of your dear mother. Sammaria is becoming queen, yes, but you are more approachable. People have an awesome love for you."

Jennica said, "All the more reason for me to fight alongside them."

Dakota said, "And it's for that reason that I'll help you."

Jennica smiled, "Thank you, Dakota."

He nodded, "Not a problem."

Jennica stood by the tunnel exit, looking out. This is where they would be cutting off the O'rult army. The air was clear, but she felt an ominous twist in the wind. They were coming. Jennica felt the water flowing close. The burden of what she was undertaking sat on her shoulders. Jennica wished this wasn't the only way. A loud noise startled her from her listless stupor. She looked out carefully.

A man stood in the shadow of the trees, the torch in his hand giving him a dead look. He had an almost serpentine gaze as he turned his eyes, examining the area.

Jennica knew he had spotted their camp. He melted back into the trees. Jennica sprinted back down the tunnel to the General's tent. She relayed the information. He said, "This is dire news indeed, Princess. Now, tell me what were you doing at the mouth of the tunnel? You could have given away our position."

Jennica said defiantly, "I was there to make sure our plan worked. The smoke had already given us away."

Concha looked at her, annoyed. He barked an order to the messenger. The man gathered the people. Jennica said, "They will be here before daybreak."

Concha said, "Thank you, Princess."

She stared out at the people. They looked to her expectantly. She didn't know how they expected her to reassure them.

Concha addressed the soldiers, "The O'rult army is close. We must prepare for their attack."

Murmurs ran through the crowd. Jennica interrupted the general, saying, "I have reason to believe that we can win this battle. I have received information from the queen herself. The O'rult army has fewer than one thousand troops. We have the trees to hide us. We have the tunnels. We have Elementals. We are fighting a defensive war. Now, we must have the right mindset. We can pray to Kiro all we want, but if we don't believe that we can do it ... then they're just words to the sky."

The crowd erupted in cheers.

Jennica turned to Concha. He nodded to her, "Prepare for attack."

Jennica sat on her horse near the back lines, nervous with anticipation. The men next to her looked exactly as they had in her vision: young and afraid. Asravi dug his talons into her leathers. She said, "They are going to knock down those supports. Run that horse like the god of Deildly himself is after you."

They nodded to her.

She whispered, "Kiro let them live."

She waited for the signal. Concha sat on his horse at the front of the troops. The other general sat above them in the trees, watching for the O'rult to come into view. The trumpet blared.

Jennica pulled her sword along with the hundreds of others in the tunnel. She looked at the boys next to her. They shifted their weight as they waited for the second blaring of the horn. Jennica leaned forward on her horse and whispered the Old Elva word for speed. The horse nickered and sent the other horses down the line nickering as well.

Asravi took flight. He cawed, circling the cavern. The soldiers moved nervously. They seemed to be reacting more favorably to the old language spoken by the horses than to anything she or the general had said. The horn echoed through the caverns a second time. Concha raised his sword ahead and yelled, "Charge!"

Jennica kicked her horse into a canter. The men next to her took her Old Elva word to heart and jumped ahead, pressing the people in front of them to move faster. Jennica jumped in line with them as the soldiers ahead began to slam their weapons into the stone pillars. Pebbles fell above her.

She shouted the Old Elva word for speed once more. The horses reacted, shooting ahead of the falling debris. Asravi weaved through the falling rocks. Jennica looked back as O'rult men started marching into the tunnel's mouth. Three men were trapped under the debris behind her. She pulled on the reins, turning her horse around. The horse reared up. The boys around her started to slow their steeds as well, but she shook her head, "Go!"

Asravi cawed and flew forward. They raced up the ramp, following the falcon out of the tunnel network.

The archers near the mouth of the cave loosed their arrows. Many of the O'rult fell dead. Jennica jumped off her horse and calmed him. Moving carefully toward the wreckage, she began whispering in Old Elva, hoping the trapped men understood her words. Someone cried out. Jennica repeated her whisper. The person cried out again. She moved around the body of a dead O'rult and saw the bloody face of a boy. His legs were trapped under a large boulder. She dropped down beside him and said, "I'm here to help."

He didn't seem to listen. He cried out. She held her hand over his mouth, "You must be quiet. There are still live O'rult in here."

The boy nodded and winced from the pain. She placed one hand on his leg and the other on the boulder. The boy bit his lip as she began to push on the boulder. Jennica muttered her apologies. She pulled on water from the canteens of the dead bodies around her. She wrapped it around the boy's legs and set it to work as she pushed the boulder from him. He looked down in fear. She shushed him.

He screamed, "Watch out!"

Jennica looked up as an O'rult lunged at her. She rolled out of the way and snatched up the sword she had left by the boy. The O'rult's long sword whistled toward her, but she knocked it aside and jumped from his reach. She felt the wall coming up behind her, holding up the sword to block his attack. His sword jarred her wrist and shattered her blade.

She backed up. The wall was directly behind her now. She called on the water inside the O'rult's body. He began to choke. Jennica retched at the disgusting noises coming from his throat. She pulled the water from him and he crumpled to the ground.

She put her hand out toward the boy as if offering something. The boy shrank back.

He said, "I'll be thanking Kiro that you're on *our* side."

Jennica smiled and asked, "Can you walk?"

The boy said, "Yes. I feel perfect."

Jennica said, "Go back to camp and rest."

He stood up, "No disrespect ma'am, but I can fight."

Jennica shook her head, "You feel that way now. It will fade, and you'll be left without any strength. Rest. If the battle still roars when you regain your strength, then come back."

The boy nodded, "Yes, Your Majesty." He turned and retreated into the caverns.

Jennica sighed. She called out in Old Elva again. This time, there was no answer. She returned to her horse and looked at the bow tied to it. Pulling the quiver of arrows onto her back, Jennica swung herself up onto the horse. She turned him toward the battle. His hooves clattered on the stone path as they raced from the tunnel.

Jennica nocked an arrow and released it. The arrow hit an O'rult in the neck. Dakota looked behind him and Jennica nodded to him. He said, "We're holding our own."

Jennica nodded and surveyed her surroundings. She saw many dead bodies in the fallen earth near the mouth of the tunnel. The archers loosed volleys of arrows. Jennica was thankful for their accuracy.

She watched as Concha led his men around to where the O'rult were trying to cut them off. Jennica could see they were faring well. For now.

The cry of an O'rult brought her back to her senses. She pulled an arrow from her quiver, but she wasn't quick enough to nock it. The O'rult cut the horse out from underneath her. Her horse reared up, and she fell into the dirt as he kicked and ran off. Jennica snatched up the arrow and threw it at the O'rult.

The arrow lodged in its eye, but the O'rult kept coming. Jennica reached for her bow. A sword whistled above her and hacked the O'rult's head from its shoulders. Jennica looked up. Dakota held out a bloody hand. Jennica allowed him to help her up. She said, "I owe you much. Thank you."

He smiled before attacking another O'rult. Jennica turned a quarter and shot her bow at one of the two O'rult that were now advancing upon her. She ducked as one of the O'rult swung its sword and stabbed the other. Jennica stabbed an arrow through the other's neck. She saw another coming at her. She let instinct take over. She took her bow and shoved it up into the creature's face. The force of the blow pushed the O'rult's serpentine nose into its brain, killing it.

She turned around to the sound of Concha crying out.

The general was surrounded by five O'rult, and the rest of his men were detained by several others. She pulled an arrow from her quiver. She started picking off the O'rult. She screamed as Concha was stabbed through the stomach. He pulled himself up with the sword and snapped the O'rult's neck.

Jennica sprinted toward Concha. The O'rult started to retreat from around him. Jennica crossed her arms over her chest. The water started to leave the four O'rult that had remained close. She felt their lives cease. Jennica shook as the water surrounded her. She sent it into the closest O'rult's lungs, drowning it. Jennica pulled the water out and dropped at Concha's side. He whispered, "You are supposed to be back at the camp."

Jennica said, "You knew I wouldn't be there."

He nodded, "You are capable. I pass my responsibilities to you."

Jennica shook her head, "I can heal you."

Concha said, "I'm too far gone for that."

A trickle of blood ran down the side of his mouth. Jennica watched the light leave his eyes.

She screamed. Her Power reacted to the intense fury. The river running through the meadow began to churn. She let out a piercing, magically-laced whistle and lifted her hands into the air. A giant wave began to rise in the water. It spun like a whirlwind.

Jennica separated the water and sent it rushing into the lungs of several O'rult. Her allies looked at her in fear. She kept just enough control. Someone cried out as they saw spots on the horizon. Jennica said, "Leave them be. They are with us."

She called out in Old Elva, telling the Evfiah Fury what she needed from them. The battle continued, but Jennica took out half of the remaining O'rult single-handedly.

Fatigue set in. She collapsed in the blood-soaked soil beneath her. Dakota was at her side in an instant. He called some other men over to her as well. Jennica recognized the boy from the rubble. He said, "I'm here to protect you, Majesty."

Jennica said, "Take out their leader."

The boy nodded. He set off again. She said, "Someone watch his back."

Another man ran off, following the first.

Dakota said, "Can you stand?"

Jennica said, "Of course I can." She pulled herself to her feet.

Dakota accepted a horse from someone, "Mount up, my Lady."

She shook her head, "You stay. I stay."

Dakota said, "As stubborn as a mule."

Jennica said, "With about as much sense too."

She sought out the O'rult leader. She pulled up her bow and nocked an arrow. The O'rult was holding a crossbow. He pointed it at the boy she had saved from the rubble. She drew her bow, "Oh no you don't!"

She loosed the arrow, and it struck the O'rult in the arm. A bolt exploded from its crossbow. The man following the boy moaned as the bolt stuck in his arm. Jennica reloaded her bow. The boy leaped onto the O'rult and plunged a dagger into the creature's neck.

Jennica sighed as the O'rult fell to the ground dead. Silence fell over the field. The O'rult ran around, trying to continue the battle.

Jennica had already signaled the dragons. They chased the O'rult into the trees. Dratasha breathed fire onto the trees, lighting up the morning sky. The Elvateth army could hear the cries of the remaining O'rult as they burned.

The dragons landed on the field. Jennica walked to their side. Asravi landed on her arm. Jennica tiredly stroked his feathers.

She said, "Thank you once again for aiding us in our time of need. We are forever in your debt."

Dratasha said, "This is not yet over."

Jennica nodded, "I thought not."

Dratasha said, "You are going to need a lot more than dragons to face what's coming next."

Jennica looked at Dratasha, worried, "What do you know?"

Dratasha looked back at the burning trees. The ground was shuddering. She said, "There are more free-thinking O'rult."

Jennica said, "Is there any hope of victory?"

Dratasha said, "There is no telling."

Jennica nodded. She returned to the camp with Dakota. The last general met with her. She said, "There is another wave coming. Dratasha is unsure of the outcome. I believe we can win, but we must be clever. We have to outthink them."

The General, Zike, asked, "How long till they arrive?"

Jennica said, "Only a few hours."

General Zike said, "How many men did we lose?"

They turned toward one of the messengers. He said, "We lost less than a third of our men. We have Princess Jennica to thank for that."

Jennica ducked her head. She wasn't proud of what she had done.

Zike said, "That's good. We need every hand."

Jennica turned to Dakota, "How many Elementals do we have?"

Dakota said, "Rekasi allowed us to have twelve. I don't know how many survived."

Jennica said, "Gather them. Bring them to the tent. Take care to point out the ones with Earth Power."

Dakota bowed and said, "As you wish."

Zike asked, "What do you need them for?"

Jennica replied, "They can buy us time."

"Time, my Lady?"

Jennica nodded.

"Time for what?"

"Time for us to regroup. Time to figure out our next move. Do we have any of our cavalry left?"

Zike nodded, "Most of our cavalry survived the attack. The horses might be short though. What would you have them do?"

"Do you have anything that smokes?"

"Smokes?"

"When you burn it. Anything that causes thick, opaque smoke?"

The general shook his head, "I don't know, my Lady."

"Ret weed would work."

Jennica looked over at who had spoken. It was an older boy around nineteen. She asked, "Your name?"

He said, "I go by Lark." Jennica smiled, giving a short nod. He said, "Ret weed smokes something terrible."

Jennica smiled broadly, "You guarantee this?"

He said, "Of course. I accidentally set a field of it on fire when I was younger. I couldn't see my house that was just down the road."

She turned toward the tent flap as Dakota returned. He smiled. Ten people stood before her. She said, "Please separate into groups by Power. I need to know what I have to work with."

Three moved over by Dakota. They held the Power of Water. Three moved to the corner by Zike. They held the Power of Earth. A girl went and stood by Lark and another boy. They held the Power of Fire. That left one with Air Power. She stood in the center by herself and smiled.

She said, "You have a special mission. You are to detain, stall, and kill the O'rult. As many as you can. I need Lark."

He stepped forward. Jennica said, "This ret weed? Does it grow in this area?"

He nodded, "It's a weed. Grows pretty much everywhere."

Jennica said, "Good. Show the others what we are looking for. I want you to gather it and dry it out."

Jennica said, "Water Enchanters. Use your power to stop the O'rult. I know you know how. Air Enchantress, you're with them." The girl nodded. "The Earth and Fire Enchanters will be joining you shortly afterward."

General Zike said, "I guess I don't understand what you are planning."

Jennica replied, "That's because I haven't explained it."

She motioned for the people to gather around the map. She pointed to the forest. She took a red thread, "This is what has been burned. Dratasha said their camp is just outside the burned area."

She laid the thread around the supposed campsite, "I want you to sneak into the woods on either side of the camp. Wreak as much havoc as possible. Destroy their food. Steal weapons. Kill as many as possible. This is the only time I will ever give you that order."

She looked up at them with a deadly serious face. They nodded to show their understanding.

Zike said, "But the ret weed?"

"I'm getting to it. It is vital that you don't get caught. That you aren't seen."

They nodded again. "Once you are done, the O'rult are going to want to attack us. That's good."

Zike looked worried, "Why would we want to make someone attack us?"

"The O'rult species is very impulsive, even the free-thinking of them. They will want to attack immediately. They won't be making rational decisions."

Zike nodded in understanding, but then frowned in confusion.

Jennica continued, "Ret weed smokes. If we set up patches of the weed and cover it with tar from old barrels and whatnot, we can make a shield for ourselves. A cover. Like night in broad daylight. The O'rult will march into the smoke. Our cavalry will be waiting for them farther back. They charge. In all the confusion we can strike them hard. There is one more thing…"

Jennica picked up her pack that was sitting next to General Zike's table.

Jennica dug into her pack, "Where is that map?"

"Map?"

"Of the tunnel system. The tunnel we are in intersects with another. I want a way for us to retreat if things go badly."

A dull thump sounded on the floor, but she ignored it. Dakota said, "Majesty? I believe you dropped something."

Jennica frowned before looking down at the floor. She picked it up. The object was in the shape of a crescent moon. She gasped, "Of course."

She turned to Dakota, "Do you know what this is?"

He replied, confused, "A whistle."

Jennica nodded excitedly. He frowned. Jennica brought it to her lips and blew. A dull note rang out. She looked slightly disappointed. Dakota asked, "What's it supposed to do, Majesty?"

Jennica replied, "It's supposed to call the Fraychavae to aid us."

Murmurs rippled through the small people gathered there.

Zike asked, "Isn't that just wishful thinking?"

Jennica shook her head, "It isn't just a legend. I was almost killed by one."

She showed them the palm of her hand where an angry red scar moved across it.

Zike asked, "This proves that they exist?"

A man rushed into the tent. He whispered into General Zike's ear. The general looked at the messenger in shock. The messenger whispered something else. Zike whispered something back. Jennica watched them uneasily. General Zike said, "If you'll please excuse me."

Jennica asked, "What is the matter?"

"It is no problem."

Jennica took a step toward him. He started toward the door.

She said, "General?"

The Fire Enchanters moved in front of the door, crossing their arms over their chests. Jennica said, "You wouldn't be running off while we are planning the battle if there weren't something dire. Now, General Concha didn't have much respect for me either, but I believe you are forgetting who I am." Zike stared at her. She said, "Now, what is going on?"

He said, relenting, "There is a mysterious mass heading our way from where the O'rult are supposed to be camped. It makes no sound so the scouts do not believe they are O'rults either."

Jennica swept in front of him and out the door. She grabbed the messenger, "Show me to the scouts."

He led her across the camp. Zike and the others followed.

She looked out to the edge of the camp but didn't see anything moving. Jennica said to one of the scouts, "Show me where the movement came from."

The scout said, "Look at the edge of the burned trees. There is movement there. The bodies are too spry to be O'rult, and they are deathly quiet."

Jennica smiled, "Let's go greet them."

The scout stared at her. She looked to where he had indicated. She could see a tall form with dark hair. His skin was the color of mud. She said, "You silly people!"

Zike asked, "Why are you insulting us?"

Jennica said, "No insult intended, sir. It's the Fraychavae. They'd have to come from that direction. There is no other way for them to reach us from Athers."

She held the whistle and blew it again. She saw them move into a mass, reacting to the whistle. The scout lowered her arm, "What are you doing?"

"They aren't dangerous."

The scout said, "The Fraychavae may have promised you something. Don't count on them honoring it. They are tricky devils."

"You don't know them. Half the people in this country don't believe they exist. The other half is scared to death of them. They are just people."

She blew the whistle again.

The dark forms moved from the trees with lightning fast speed toward the camp. The people surrounding Jennica retreated, scared of the approaching mass.

Jennica stood firm. She smiled as the first blurred mass stopped in front of her. She recognized him to be one of the original Fraychavae that had captured her. She nodded to him as the others started to take form.

Her head was spinning. She stumbled back. A hand steadied her. She smiled as she looked into Se's cat-like eyes. She said, "So, it did work."

Se said, "We always honor our promises."

He shot a look at the scout. He looked back at Jennica. She said, "Thank you. We need your help."

"As I took from the whistle."

"Now that the obvious is taken care of, I must introduce you to General Zike."

In a low voice, she added, "He is stubborn as a mule, and he will be skittish around you."

Se replied, "Wouldn't want it to be any other way."

Jennica nodded and rolled her eyes, "Zike?" He nervously stepped forward.

Jennica said, "This is Se. He is new to the Fraychavae traditions. He will be working with you."

Zike nodded. Jennica dismissed him. Se started to follow him. She said, "Before you go, where is Anahi?"

Se pointed to the blonde at the back of the group of Fraychavae. She seemed to be hiding. There was something on his face Jennica didn't understand.

Jennica nodded, "Thank you."

She moved through the crowd of dark people. Asravi took flight. He landed on Anahi's shoulder.

"Anahi?"

The girl looked up, "Jennica!"

She looked at the falcon. The bird croaked at her. Anahi smiled at him. He bounced off her and back to Jennica.

Jennica kneeled beside her, "Are you well?"

Anahi nodded, "Of course. Why?"

Jennica replied, "It's just when I asked after you, Se seemed to turn to stone. What happened?"

Anahi looked down, "It's just that... Jennica, I'm pregnant."

Jennica looked surprised, "Excuse me?"

She looked down at Anahi's stomach. Sure enough, it was swollen with child.

Anahi said, "It's a miracle!"

"But what does that have to do with Se?"

"I wasn't supposed to get pregnant. That could only mean one thing."

"What?"

"He's upset because I wasn't supposed to fall in love with him."

Jennica said, "What's wrong with love?"

Anahi looked down, "Se is a Fraychavae. He lives for an ungodly long amount of time. I'm Elva."

Jennica said, "I don't understand. You are Fraychavae as well."

Anahi shook her head, "I am adopted into the Fraychavae traditions. I may look it, but I don't have all the same qualities they have. They can still outlive me by hundreds of years."

Anahi stood up and faced away from Jennica. "He didn't want me to love him. He doesn't want me to die."

She turned to look at Jennica, "I don't know how this curse works. When I became like this," She stopped, "When the tree blessed me, there was no indication of what that spell would do. I've lived for almost three millennia. I've finally found someone to be happy with. Jennica, do you understand?"

Jennica shook her head. Anahi continued, "He thinks that by pushing me away I'll fall out of love with him, and I'll live. He's afraid, that if I start to age now, he'll lose me. Jennica, I'm not afraid to die. I have been stuck at this age for two thousand nine hundred and seventy years. I suppose I should be flattered, but -"

Jennica placed an arm around Anahi, "There is a way to fix it. I'll help you. First, can you help me?"

Anahi said, "I would do anything for you, Jennica."

Jennica wished Anahi luck. Anahi nodded, turned her horse, and kicked it into a gallop. She was going to Damask in Keyinture. Jennica was sending her to find the *Death Arrow*. Rekasi believed that Jessie was one of the Keepers of Knowledge. Donichello believed that Jessie would do anything to help this world. Jennica hoped that Donichello was right. These pirates would be able to take the Immortal to the Hawkaties. She would be able to convince them. The Hawkaties respected old power. She wrote up a letter to Jessie and Reness, explaining their predicament and hoping they would be able to help Anahi.

Anahi knew that Jennica had her doubts, but Jennica believed the crew would be sympathetic to their needs. Anahi knew that she had a limited amount of time and that it would be difficult to find the ship and its crew. Jennica had told her that a dragon would be meeting her along Dragonia's border with Pilleetain, and she would continue her journey on its back.

Anahi pushed herself along. She looked down at her stomach. Her baby kicked. She smiled slightly.

The Pilleetain-Dragonian border was still almost a day's ride away. The woods were dark. She closed her eyes for a moment and listened to the sounds of nature. In all her time on this earth, she had never grown tired of the hustle and bustle of the woods. She sighed, feeling calm.

A snap of a branch demanded her attention. She tensed, pulling back on the reins. She surveyed the scenery around her. Everything seemed as it ought to have been. She kicked her horse back into a slow walk. She chided herself for being silly. Anahi started moving quicker. She cried out as something dropped from the trees, knocking her to the ground.

CHAPTER XLIX

Jennica led the Earth Elementals to the edge of the field where it met the forest. She had them lay ret weed there and around the battlefield. She had others follow behind and carefully place tar over the weeds. She smiled when the work was done.

Jennica was examining the map one last time. She sensed something awry. She moved away from the map and walked to the mouth of the tunnel. She stared out at the trees. She could clearly see movement.

She frowned. Why hadn't the scouts picked up on this yet? There was a shout from below. She turned to Zike and said, "It's time." He nodded nervously.

Jennica returned to her tent. She clasped a sword around her waist. She shoved her dagger and a canteen of water into her belt. She pulled her hair up and twisted it into a severe bun as she headed back to her post.

Jennica could hear the pounding steps of the O'rult army. She surveyed her surroundings. Everyone was properly placed. She nodded to Lark. He and his fellow Fire Enchanters sent fire roaring through the patches of ret weed. Just as the boy promised, the ret weed sent up a lovely opaque smoke. Jennica smiled. She was still able to see the O'rult army. They looked confused. The roaring fire had surprised them.

Jennica saw the leader. He held up his hand and grunted. A quarter of the O'rult sprinted forward into the smoke. Jennica bellowed her order to the cavalry. They jumped forward into the smoke. Jennica couldn't see them fighting, but the cavalry returned without a soul lost. No one emerged from the other side.

Jennica brought her attention to the O'rult leader. Their eyes seemed to lock for a brief moment. He flicked his large hand.

She watched as bolts flew at her men from the O'rult's crossbows. She lifted a shield of ice over half the army. She yelled for the Fire Enchanters to burn the rest of the bolts. Jennica sighed with relief as most of the bolts bounced off her ice shield while the rest burned up midair.

The O'rult leader paced, agitated. Nothing was going as he had planned. He sent in another wave.

The cavalry again met them in the smoke. Again, Jennica couldn't see. She kept her eyes trained on the leader. Jennica barked an order down to the men. They relayed the information to the cavalry. It was a few moments before her men emerged from the smoke. This time, a few men were missing, but again no one emerged from the other side. Jennica wondered why the O'rult leader was wasting his men.

Jennica watched as the leader sent a large portion of the remaining army into the smoke, but this time she felt a difference in the coming wave. She said, "He has something planned. He's wasting his men!"

"I have the same feeling," Zike replied. He looked at her with an odd expression. Jennica turned away uncomfortably. She called Lark and beckoned for him to join her.

Jennica asked, "How successful were you on the raid?"

Lark replied, "Fairly, Majesty. We destroyed most of their food. The other Fire Enchanters and I burned the camp to the ground. The Water Enchanters killed many O'rult soldiers. The Air Enchantress did a wonderful job as well."

Jennica asked, "When you were there, did you hear of any plans for this battle?"

Lark shook his head, "I'll ask around and see if the others know anything."

He bowed and left.

Jennica drummed her fingers on the table. "What can he be planning?" she asked, exasperated.

Zike didn't answer. He looked out across the field. The O'rult leader stepped down from his platform. Jennica left Zike to watch as Lark came back to her.

He lowered his voice, "Armanda, the Air Enchantress, heard someone talking to the O'rult leader. Majesty, we have a traitor in our midst."

Jennica said, "Armanda. Does she know who it was?"

Lark shook his head, "She said it sounded like they had to have been in the room when we were planning, or else they were eavesdropping. She says this person gave the O'rult information almost exactly word for word from our planning."

Jennica tapped her chin.

Zike said, "Your Highness should see this."

Jennica turned from Lark to Zike. He was pointing across the field. A boy stood next to the O'rult leader. Lark said, "I've never seen him before, have you?"

Zike shook his head. Jennica didn't say anything. His face turned up in her mind. He was one of the boys from the raid. One of those she couldn't find after the rock had crushed them. Ire sparked inside her.

She said slowly, "I know him. But I don't know his name."

Lark said, "I'll try and find out."

Jennica stopped him as he headed out. She made sure their eyes locked, "Thank you, Lark."

He nodded, "No problem."

Jennica said, "We need an entirely new plan. We keep

the smoke. It's protecting our men. We need to rest our cavalry."

Zike asked, "What are you doing?"

Jennica said, "Formulating a plan."

He said, "You can't just shout orders as they pop into your head. It causes confusion."

Jennica said, "We have to rest our cavalry. The archers can rain arrows on them until the cavalry retreats."

"All right, but who is going to take their place?"

Jennica scanned the field. The O'rult seemed to have caught sight of the tunnel system. Jennica cursed. She saw water pooling on the ground. An idea sparked, "That's it! Zike, bring me the Water Enchanters. I have a plan."

"Do any of you know how to make ice?" the princess asked the Water Elementals.

The boy, Andean, raised his hand. Jennica said, "All right. Girls, make sure we have water at all times. We are going to build an ice cover within the tunnels. This will prevent the O'rults from moving further than this point. We cannot risk them finding their way back to the Resistance."

Lark came up behind her, "No one seems to know the traitor's name. They remember him not wanting a war, but there was never malcontent toward you, Sammaria, or anyone else."

Jennica nodded, troubled, "He was crushed by the rocks, or so I thought. They must have come into that part of the tunnel while we were back at camp and taken him prisoner. Now, they are using him."

"That very well may be."

"Thank you, Lark. Now, I must go."

Lark bowed to her. Jennica ordered all of her men back to camp. She and the other three Water Enchanters walked back through the mouth of the tunnel to begin their work.

She walked slowly beneath the field, moving deeper into the tunnel system. She began the breathing patterns she had learned from Cypol. She had one of the Water Enchantresses place the barrel of water down beside her.

After practicing for a while, she made her way back to the main tunnel, holding her breath. She saw several hundred O'rult begin to enter through the tunnel's mouth. She took a deep breath, knowing the brutality of what she was about to do. She pulled the water from the O'rult and used it as the base layer of the ice cover. She pulled the water again and strengthened her wall of ice. She looked back at the girl.

The girl said, "Andean is almost done as well."

Jennica nodded as she continued building the wall. With her Power wrapped in the ice, she felt something impale the wall. Once she had drained and frozen the water from every O'rult, she returned to the camp to find Zike.

Zike said, "Jennica, I'm glad that so many O'rult are dead, but what exactly are you planning?"

Jennica sighed with exhaustion, "We aren't hiding anymore. That's for sure. The Fraychavae have inhuman speed and strength."

Zike said, "We could send them out to the front line."

"Will they be the most useful there?"

"They'd be useful anywhere. We hope the Fraychavae scare the O'rult into retreating. If that doesn't happen, the Fraychavae should be able to do enough damage to hold them back."

"You are the general. Place them where you believe is best."

"What else?" Zike asked.

"We have twelve Elementals. Place them where needed. Mix the powers."

"No other plan, Majesty?"

"We aren't using trickery anymore. Now, we must stand and fight."

Jennica stood next to Armanda. The Air Enchantress looked frightened but was grimly determined. Jennica raised her hands. She and the other Water Enchanters pulled water from different places and sent the water into the O'rult lines, drowning some and spooking others as the soldiers began advancing upon the O'rult front lines. The O'rult leader smiled, raised his sword, and marched the remainder of his army toward the Dragonians.

CHAPTER L

Anahi opened her eyes. She was staring into the dappled brown hair of a horse's flank. She looked up. Matted hair fell along her captor's back. She involuntarily moaned as she lifted her head. She tried to reach her stomach. The baby mustn't be harmed. The captor spun around. Her green eyes flashed. She dismounted Anahi's horse and said, "So, the strange Fraychavae has awoken has she?"

Anahi looked up in fear. The woman faced away from her, "You are a false Dancer. You don't belong. I am here to remove this abomination from the world."

The woman turned to face Anahi. She seemed to have a cool rage about her. The woman's face contorted with surprise, "You are the Immortal!"

Anahi nodded after hesitating, "How do you know?"

The woman said, "I have heard stories of you my entire life. The hair white as clouds."

Anahi asked slowly, "Why have you captured me?"

The woman replied, "You have entered the territory of the rhiloxes. I am their slave and must do their bidding. I was just now deciding whether to hand you over for my freedom or to leave you outside their territory. Why are you crossing here?"

Anahi said, "I am trying to reach the Pilleetain-Dragonian border where I am to meet my dragon escort to find the ship known as the *Death Arrow*. I am to ask for their help for Jennica Aeradal."

Lilliana looked up, surprised, "You are a messenger from Princess Jennica?"

Anahi nodded, "I am."

She said, "What would you have the *Death Arrow* do? What is her motive for finding them?"

Anahi said, "That is a secret even to me. She's outlined what she wants in a letter."

Lilliana said, "I always liked that girl. She has Power."

Anahi said, "More than you know."

Lilliana said, "I'll help."

Anahi said, "You will?"

Lilliana said sharply, "I said I would."

❦

Jennica released an arrow. The O'rult charging toward her fell to the ground as the arrow stuck in its neck. Another took his place. She didn't reload her bow. Instead, she jammed the bow into the second O'rult's stomach and dropped to the ground. The O'rult stumbled forward and fell to the ground. Jennica seized the first O'rult's sword and plunged it into the second's back.

She looked up. The O'rult army was still being overwhelmed, but they had taken many Dragonians with them. These were the free-thinking O'rult of which they had heard so much. They were harder to kill because they were capable of acting on their own rather than only acting on their leader's will. She cursed herself inwardly for not realizing that the leader wouldn't have wasted his troops if he didn't have better troops remaining.

She shot toward another O'rult coming toward her, but it dodged the arrow. She set her jaw and slowly pulled her sword. The O'rult yelled as he charged. She swung her sword into his gut. He grasped the blade and pulled Jennica toward him. He grinned, and she could smell him rotting teeth. She cringed and dug her nails into his neck. The

O'rult squealed in pain, and she shoved a dagger into its leg. She hit him in the head with the hilt of the dagger, and he fell to the ground.

Jennica stared at the dead O'rult bodies around her. She stepped over them in disgust. She looked up. There, crossing the field was the traitor. He had finally left his protection behind. Jennica's eyes flashed with fury. She swiftly moved across the field. The boy looked at her. His eyes grew wide. She cut him off. Standing in front of him, she held her sword at his throat, "What's stopping me from cutting you from throat to trouser?"

He said, "It isn't what it looks like."

Jennica said, "Really? From my view, it looks like you betrayed your country. You betrayed your entire race!"

He didn't reply.

Jennica asked, "Why'd you do it?"

The boy replied, "What choice did I have? You abandoned me."

Jennica said, "I did no such thing."

He nodded, "In the rubble, I screamed for you. I cried out. But you never came."

Jennica said, "I wouldn't have left you. I didn't hear anything. I found the other boy, but I never heard you. I searched."

He said, "The O'rult found me instead."

Jennica said, holding out her hand, "Come back to the right side."

He said, "I can't. I've been cursed. If I try to leave them, I'll die. Please, kill me. I can't stand to do this. I can't betray my family."

Jennica looked at him with a pained face. She couldn't kill him.

He said, "Please, Highness, have mercy on me. Let me die knowing *I* didn't let the O'rult win."

Jennica nodded, "Are you ready?"

He nodded, "I could never be more ready."

Jennica nodded, with tears burning her eyes. She slit his throat. There was a smile on the boy's face as he died.

Tears jerked from her eyes. She felt like throwing up. She knelt beside him and held his head in her hands. "Kiro, save your soul."

Dakota rushed over to her, "My Lady, they are retreating! We must follow them."

Jennica looked up. The O'rult leader was yelling for his soldiers to retreat. Jennica said, "We have to kill him."

Dakota nodded, "I know."

Jennica allowed him to help her up. She ran with the surviving members of the Dragonian army after the O'rult.

They pursued the retreating army for a long while. The O'rult ran into the trees. Jennica recognized the place.

She suddenly remembered Rekasi and Donichello telling her of being attacked by something. She screamed for the Dragonians to stop. The order was carried on down the line. She said, "We mustn't go on."

Dakota looked into the forest. There were movements, and the branches of the trees cracked. They heard cries of O'rult as they were cut down. Dakota said, "Look!"

Jennica peered into the trees, not moving from where she stood. There was a brief moment when she thought she saw a man with gray skin. The rhilox stepped out from behind the trees, looked at them, and nodded. Jennica stared at him. He said, "Leave the border, Dragonians, or you will suffer the same fate."

Jennica nodded, "Back to the Plains." The army moved away from the blood bath of O'rult and rhiloxes. She smiled to herself. It was a victory.

Back at camp, Jennica turned to Dakota and said, "Are you all right here?"

He said, "We can manage without you."

Jennica replied, "I must get to Mestchester. I'm needed there."

Dakota said, "Ride hard, Jennica."

Jennica smiled, "Finally, someone didn't call me Highness. I like that."

Dakota smiled back, "Take Renai. She will serve you well."

Jennica took the reins of the horse and swung up into the saddle. Jennica smiled, "I shall see you soon."

Dakota said, "I hope so."

Jennica nodded. She kicked the horse and began moving out of the camp. She shouted the Old Elva word for speed. Asravi let out an ecstatic cry. Renai galloped past the exhausted army and down the tunnel leading to Drannor.

CHAPTER LI

Sammaria stepped outside the small house in which they were staying. Rekasi and the others were still asleep. Sammaria sat down on the step. The sun started to rise. Her Power gave her a thrill. She closed her eyes for a moment and imagined that she was on her balcony in Mestchester before any of this had happened.

The sun rose over the broken city. Sammaria looked at the filth that covered the street. She no longer cringed at the sight of the bodies piled along the wall. Sammaria wondered when their blood would wash from her hands. A small sigh escaped her mouth. She looked down the street.

Someone wrapped a blanket around her shoulders. She looked up. Donichello sat down beside her. He said, "It almost looks fake in this light."

Sammaria looked out at her city. She agreed with him. In the new light, the city looked surreal. He asked, "Do you think sometimes everything we've done was for nothing?"

Sammaria replied, looking back down the street, "Sometimes I think that. But then I see the wall of bodies and the broken faces in the city, and I know we're fighting for them. My hope is restored."

Donichello said, "You never give up faith, do you?"

She shook her head, "I give up my faith all the time. I just restore it quickly."

Donichello smiled. He looked off at the horizon, barely visible over the wall. There was a haunted look to him. She said, "I'm sure she's fine."

Donichello said, "I'm sure she is. I just hope she hasn't gone into the spirit realm again."

It took Sammaria a second to realize he was joking. She laughed, surprised.

The sun rose higher over the city. People began walking about, doing their business and trying not to catch the notice of the O'rult guards who all too readily brought out their swords. Sammaria looked up as Rekasi exited the house. He said stoically, "It's time."

He turned and went back inside. Sammaria exchanged looks with Donichello. She got up and followed Rekasi through the door. She asked, "Time for what, exactly?"

He replied, "We are going to enter the castle."

Donichello asked, "What about Jennica?"

Rekasi shook his head, "The battle there is taking longer than anticipated. We must start here soon if we have any hope of succeeding."

Sammaria nodded woodenly. She didn't like the thought of Jennica not being around to watch her back. She didn't like acting without her.

Rekasi said, "We are going to have to split up. A large gathering of people going to the castle would be too obvious. With all of this death, even three people is a large crowd. I have contacted Brother Orlten. He has agreed to let us in through the back gate. We will be posing as servants in the castle. We must wear our disguises."

Sammaria had a feeling in her gut that this wouldn't go as they hoped. She banished the thought. It was only nerves. She said, "So, are we meeting at the gate?"

Rekasi said, "Yes. Brother Orlten will let us in then. Everyone good?"

They nodded. "All right. Get ready. We need to leave soon."

Jennica woke with the sound of a horn being blown. Quickly, she dressed. She looked down the road. She was less than three miles from Mestchester. It had taken her just under a week to arrive here. She moved quietly through the brush and looked out to see the commotion. She saw hundreds of boots filling the road and looked up to the faces of the O'rult.

Jennica moved down to her campsite. She saddled Renai and swung herself up. She traveled through the trees as long as they allowed. She let the horse free in the woods, knowing it wouldn't stay there for long. She crept through the open grass toward the tannery, her heart in her throat. She ducked into the shadow of the building and leaned against it, breathing hard. She slowly opened the back door and slipped inside.

"Princess! Thank Helma!"

Jennica started. Someone stepped into the light. A young girl with a nasty T scar on her throat stood before her. Jennica asked, "Who are you?"

The girl said, "My name is Demetria. I am here to help."

Sammaria checked again to make sure the wig was secure on her head. She tightened her grip on the handle of the basket. The market had been placed near the gate so people entering Mestchester wouldn't travel deep into the city, seeing the death and destruction. Through everything, the people of Mestchester were proud enough to uphold the reputation of their city.

However, not many people went to the market now. The people were so poor, and many preferred starving to facing the O'rult. Sammaria cringed at the thought as she moved into the market plaza.

Weight settled onto Sammaria's shoulders. She sighed. Rekasi in his disguise wandered into view. He bought a loaf of bread. Sammaria smiled faintly. She felt safer knowing he was near.

Sammaria watched the large gate while haggling over the price of some fruit. A large caravan entered the city. They called out, saying they had food and supplies. The O'rult guards pushed the citizens out of the way and unloaded the crates from the caravan, taking them to the castle. They left only scraps for the people of the city. Sammaria shook her head in disgust. "You'd better be careful with that look, Madam."

Sammaria looked up. There stood Antien, eyebrows raised. She looked surprised. He smiled and winked at her. He said, "Be quiet. We're smuggling troops into the city."

Sammaria asked, "Have you seen my sister?"

Antien nodded, "She is heading toward the castle, hidden in one of the supply crates. We found her in the tannery. She about ripped our heads off, thinking we were O'rult troops. You'd better be getting back to the castle."

Sammaria nodded, "I will." She raced off.

She turned down an alleyway she had always used to get to the castle.

She slammed into the firm torso of an O'rult guardwoman. She stared down at the princess with serpentine eyes. The guard grabbed her. She pulled her toward the castle. The muscles in her arms rippled. Sammaria would not be able to pull herself from the creature's grip.

The O'rult tightened her grip and began taking longer strides. The O'rult woman pulled her through the castle's front gate. Sammaria saw Rekasi disappear into the shadows. His face was hard. She realized he was waiting to attack the O'rult, but she slowly shook her head and mouthed, "On my own."

He reluctantly nodded. Sammaria smiled faintly as Rekasi moved inside the servant entrance where she knew Donichello was waiting for news of Jennica. Sammaria was heaved up the steps. She had an eerie feeling as the tarnished doors snapped shut behind her.

Jennica felt the crate in which she was hidden drop to the ground. She listened as the footsteps moved away and waited for the tap. In the silence, her mind wandered. She realized how many things could go wrong. She tried not to dwell on it.

The tap came. She pushed the lid off her crate and stepped out. She looked behind her. Three men stepped out of their own crates. She frowned, "This isn't the castle square."

The man next to her said, "I believe we're still in the outer borough."

Jennica looked around her. The castle was in the most interior borough of Mestchester. The gates had long been removed, but, if the O'rult were smart, they could cut off the different parts of the city from each other.

Jennica spotted a familiar gate, "No. We are in the third ring."

They looked at her doubtfully. Jennica knew that this no longer looked like the place where the rich merchants of the city once lived, but that still didn't give them the right to question her. She snapped, "I know my home."

She shoved her way through them, "This gate belongs in the third ring. It has always been so."

The man who had spoken before said, "You must be mistaken. There are many gates between the boroughs."

Jennica replied coolly, "You'd do well to remember that I grew up here. I have spent many days lost in the city. I know where I am."

Jennica placed her index fingers into her mouth and whistled.

The men around her shushed her, "Do you want to alert the entire city of our presence?"

Jennica replied, "No, only the Dragonians."

Asravi landed on her arm. A cry echoed in the air. Jennica looked up, surprised, "Nyma!"

Asravi chortled. Jennica stroked his feathers, "You clever boy."

Jennica said, "Find Sammaria!"

The birds squawked and took flight.

"This had a greater impact on the Dragonians in Mestchester than Jennica had intended. She was simply alerting them to their presence. What the falcons did was more. Broken people once had hope. Sammaria and Jennica had returned. The people were ready to welcome the rightful monarchs with open arms."

Jennica slipped away from the smuggled members of the Resistance, pulling her hood closer to her face. Her heart hammered in her chest. She held her breath as she moved past one of the guards patrolling the corner. Jennica made it past him without being questioned. She guessed it wasn't uncommon for people to be wandering the streets like she was.

She moved around the corner. A market had been set up here, away from the main market near the gate. She needed to get to the palace as soon as possible, and these people were blocking her path. No one was inclined to move, and she couldn't give away her identity.

Something caught Jennica's eye. She looked up. A sheet was blowing in the wind, drying on the roof. Jennica's eyes were drawn to the line of houses that were close together leading toward her destination. She almost laughed in relief.

She went to the closest house and placed her foot on the ledge of one of the windows. The building was made of stone. She pulled herself up. Clutching the frame of the window, she looked for her next foothold. She inserted her hand between two stones, pressed her foot against the rock face, and pulled herself up.

Her hood fell from her head. Quickly, she pulled herself to the roof and swung one leg over the top. She heard a shout. Jennica started. She looked behind her. An O'rult was calling out for her to stop. She swung her other leg over the ledge and pushed back her hair from her recognizable face. The guard was now attempting to scale the wall after her.

Jennica fell to the ground next to the railing along the roof's edge. Her cloak pulled tight against her neck. She yanked it off.

The O'rult had the cloak in his clutches. She wrenched it from his grip, hoping he would fall to the ground, but he remained on the wall.

She looked at the next roof. She wouldn't be able to jump to it. She had forgotten about the enclosed courtyards between the buildings. The winded O'rult was making his way onto the roof. She looked at the thick poles that crossed the courtyard in equal distances. Running to the other side of the roof, she stopped and eyed the pole nervously. Tentatively, she placed a foot on the top of the pole.

The O'rult had reached the roof and lunged for her. She took a step forward onto the next pole, wobbling. Jennica took a deep breath and moved forward more slowly. She closed her eyes, moving from pole to pole. Looking behind, she saw the O'rult was trying to follow her. She cried out in desperation. The O'rult let out a gruff yelp. Jennica looked back again and saw he was checking his balance.

Jennica saw a rock fly toward him. She looked for the source and was surprised when she saw children. The oldest seemed to be twelve. She had a large stone in her hand. She cried out to Jennica, "Go!"

She let the rock in her hand fly. It hit the O'rult in the temple. He fell, crushing the fountain in the courtyard below. Jennica raced across the rest of the poles before another O'rult could come after her. The other houses didn't have courtyards between them as the first had.

She looked back as she was about three houses away. The O'rult guards had been sent after the children. Her heart pounded in her throat. She watched the children scatter into drains and holes, which the O'rult were too large to gain access.

A voice stopped her, speaking in Old Elva. Jennica looked down. A man sat on the roof. He was elderly with a white beard. Jennica recalled him from her memory, "Aren't you the star searcher?"

He said, "I have been called many names. What you call me is not who I am. What is important is that the O'rult power is being lessened by the hope that you are bringing to the people."

Jennica said, "I haven't brought hope. I was just rescued by children. How can I bring hope when I require the assistance of children?"

The man shook his head, "You cannot feel it like I can, but it's there."

Jennica watched the clouds swirling in the sky. They sparked like lightning. Jennica said, "Thank you for our conversation. I hope I don't seem impertinent, but I must get to the castle. What are you known by?"

He smiled and said, "My name is Jonakil."

Jennica dropped to her knees and said, "Forgive me, sir."

Jonakil touched her shoulder and said, "Rise, Jennica. Open the portals."

Jennica asked, "To the human realm?"

Jonakil nodded, "There will be changes when you do. You mustn't fight them."

Jennica asked, "Why are you asking me to do this?"

The god smiled, "We gods closed the portals out of jealousy. We were afraid of the power that the humans and ancient creatures held. When the portals were closed, Socorro placated us. We didn't realize the effect that it would have on the realms. The realms are dying."

Jennica said, "Dying?"

"We forced nature to bend to our will. It is pushing its way back. Left alone, it will destroy both realms."

Jennica shook her head, "I don't understand. It's been two thousand years."

Jonakil replied, "I am well aware. Time works differently for everyone as you will soon learn. I know that you will find the power to permanently open the portals. To right our wrong."

She bowed and he said, "Close your eyes. They have taken Sammaria."

Jennica obeyed. She heard some old chanting and felt nauseous. She heard his voice inside her head. "Open your eyes."

She opened one, then the other. The door that was so familiar to her was before her. It was the servant's entrance to the castle. So many days Sammaria and she had spent sneaking in and out of that door.

She opened it. An ugly woman looked up. She realized then that it was Donichello. Jennica smiled. He grinned from ear to ear. Jennica felt like embracing him, but both knew the risks involved. They couldn't reveal their identities. He asked, "How did you get here? The guards are everywhere."

Jennica said, "You wouldn't believe me if I told you."

"Welcome back."

The voice had come from behind her. She turned. A handsome woman stood before her. Jennica gasped, "Rekasi?"

He and Donichello shushed her. Rekasi said, "It's Resi. It's good to have you back."

Jennica said, "Hello Resi. My name is Renai."

CHAPTER LII

Lilliana stopped as Anahi stepped across the border into Pilleetain. She looked back, "Aren't you coming?"

Lilliana shook her head, "Long ago, I swore I would never leave the country in which I now stand rooted. I will not leave Dragonia. Not till the day I die."

Anahi said, "Thank you so much for what you've done for me."

Lilliana said, "I feel for Jennica and Sammaria. There are horrors in their past that they don't even know."

Anahi started, "What do you mean?"

Lilliana looked around as if she were making sure no one else was listening, "Enchardo was not who he seemed to be."

Anahi asked, "How do you mean?"

Lilliana said, "I can't say more. Just beware."

With that, she melted back into the trees. Anahi watched her retreat.

A shadow passed over her some time later. Anahi looked up. A green belly was descending over her. She scrambled out of the way as the dragon landed to her right. She inquired of it, "Are you the dragon guide sent by Jennica, the *Aska?*"

The dragon projected his thoughts into Anahi's head, "Yes, I have sighted the *Death Arrow* while waiting for you to arrive. My name is Rathatan."

The dragon kneeled, allowing Anahi to clamber up onto its back. The dragon snapped its wings open, pulling itself into the air. Anahi clung to the spike in front of her. They moved quickly across the ocean. Anahi saw a sail moving in the wind.

She asked, pointing, "Is that it?"

The dragon inclined his head and again projected his voice into her mind, "It is. From the look of the activity on board, they have just spotted us. They don't know quite what to make of it."

Anahi asked, "What are they doing?"

The dragon projected what he could see into Anahi's mind. A man was looking through a spyglass at them. His face was stern with concentration. They were pointing and talking animatedly. The dragon said, "Interesting customs. Hmm."

The dragon swooped over to the right toward the ship. He banked and hovered beside the ship, watching the people and their reactions.

A man with dark hair stared at Anahi curiously. She watched as he signaled to the crew. The cannons were swiveled to face them. Anahi gulped. She tried not to let fear fill her. Anahi said to the dragon, "Are they going to attack us?"

The dragon said, "I don't believe they mean us any harm."

The man who seemed to be the leader nodded toward one of the men in front of the cannons. He placed his torch toward the fuse and a cannonball shot toward Anahi and the dragon.

Anahi's heart jumped into her throat as the dragon weaved out of the way. He said, "Why don't you speak to them before they knock us from the sky."

Anahi nodded, "Good idea."

She climbed up the dragon's green neck till she could stand where they would see her. She raised her voice, "Don't shoot! He will not harm you."

The man said, "Give us one reason not to destroy you at this moment."

Anahi said, "I have been sent by Princess Jennica Aeradal. I beg you not to betray her trust by shooting us from the sky."

The man said, "I am the captain of this ship. I have no allegiance to any monarchy."

Anahi stopped. Jennica had assured her that they would at least allow her to come aboard the ship so she could deliver the message. Anahi looked for the female. She wasn't on deck.

The captain called out, "Who are you searching for? Your eyes are not focused on the cannons."

Anahi said, "The human girl, Jessica."

The man asked, "What need have you of my wife?"

Anahi replied, "I must talk to her. Please, it is of the utmost importance."

The man said, "Send for her."

A man moved below deck. He came back, escorting a blonde girl to her husband.

She said, "Reness, why have you called?"

He said, "Look." He pointed to where Anahi stood perched upon the dragon.

She said, "Lady Jessica, Princess Jennica has sent me to speak with you."

Jessie shrugged, "What's it to me?"

Anahi groaned. She muttered a curse, "Please. Donichello -"

The girl cut her off, "Donichello? What about him?"

Anahi replied, "He's gone to Mestchester to help take down the O'rult, Trydexzi, and Misseter. Please, just allow me to give you this letter. Jennica explains everything in it."

Jessica looked at Reness, "Allow her to land."

Reness said, "Girl. You can board our ship, but your dragon friend cannot. He would sink us."

Anahi nodded, "I accept the terms. Thank you."

She leapt from Rathatan's back. After landing with a stumble, she said, "Thank you for bringing me here."

He nodded and pulled himself into the air currents.

Reness asked, "Now. What about this letter?"

Anahi reached into her pack. She pulled the letter from it and handed it to Jessica. She unrolled it. Reness said, "Read it aloud."

Jessica nodded, "It says…" Her eyes scanned the page. She gasped. Reness asked, "What is it?"

Jessica handed the note back to Anahi, "Do you know what it says?"

Anahi shook her head. Jessica said, "Read it."

Anahi nodded. She looked at Jennica's script.

Dragonia is falling. Jessica, I must beseech your and Reness's help. I fear Donichello is in grave danger. We are separated at the moment. He is in Mestchester while I am preparing for a battle that I might not make it through.

I ask that you take Anahi to the Island of the Hawkaties. Anahi must convince them to come to Mestchester to help the Grumpices, who also have resurfaced, and defeat the O'rult.

Jessica, I know that you understand what we need them for if you are indeed one of the Nine. I wouldn't ask this of you otherwise. Our fates are intertwined.

Please, do this for me as my last request. If you accept, I promise you will be rewarded. If I do indeed die in this fight, please take the note I have hidden on the back of this letter to Se of the Fraychavae. Please, Jessica, I plead that you help us.

Anahi stared at the paper in her hand. She whispered, "The Island."

Jessica took the paper from Anahi's hands. "Reness," she said, "We must help them."

Reness shook his head, "No! We can't get involved."

Jessie replied, "We're already involved. Misseter isn't going to stop with Dragonia. She's already taken over Gabvand and many other southern countries."

Reness shook his head, "We could lose everything. Is that what you want? To chase after some dream that you've had since I met you?"

Jessie said, "A dream? Reness this whole *world* is a dream. Things happen here that no one can explain. The Immaculate, the Immortal is standing before you saying that we have to go to the Island, and you can't believe that it exists. Reness, please. You know that we need to help them. Please. Do it for me."

She smiled at him sweetly.

He sighed. She smiled. He ordered, "East, one hundred and eighteen degrees."

CHAPTER LIII

Sammaria was led to the throne room. It didn't look anything like it had before she had disappeared. The once proudly polished thrones were tarnished and scratched. The exquisite rug was soiled. The paintings were worn and torn and had axes and knives stuck in them. Misseter and Bynakst'r were slumped in the thrones, fast asleep. The O'rult that held Sammaria coughed. Misseter was startled awake. She looked at Sammaria with no recognition.

Misseter elbowed Bynakst'r. He snorted but didn't wake. Misseter looked at her long, sharp fingernails and sank them into his flesh. He jerked awake, growled at her, and began sucking on his arm where she had stabbed him. She glared at him before turning her attention to her guest She asked, "What is the meaning of this?"

The O'rult woman said, "We got an unauthorized newbie. She claims that her name is Sam Aden."

Sammaria pushed her long, wigged hair out of her face. Her amber eyes flashed. Misseter watched her. She said, "Come to me."

Sammaria ignored her. Misseter said, "Come here, Sam."

Sammaria looked around. The O'rult grabbed her and pulled her forward, dropping her at the feet of the false queen. Misseter stood and lifted Sammaria's chin to better look into her eyes. She asked, "Don't you have the slightest fear of me?"

Sammaria's eyes flashed, "I do not. I know that you are just a coward who hides behind the brute force of the O'rult."

Misseter looked long and hard at Sammaria's face and then her dirty hair. She fingered it before ripping the wig from Sammaria's head. Her blonde hair cascaded down her shoulders. She winced. Misseter said, "You fool! This is no peasant. Take her to the dungeons. I shall deal with her later."

She ran her sharp nails softly across Sammaria's cheek, "Such a waste to lose such a pretty face."

Sammaria said, "It's not the face that counts. It's the heart."

Misseter pointed her long nail to Sammaria's heart, "How about we feast on your heart? What then?"

Sammaria replied, "In time, you will regret this, Misseter."

The guard clamped on to her arm again and dragged her out of the room.

Sammaria let the serpent woman drag her through the hallways she knew so well. When they reached a secluded place, Sammaria released the force of her Power. The O'rult was thrown backward and tumbled as her garments caught fire. As the O'rult tried to recover, Sammaria ran swiftly up the stairs. She dashed down the halls. Every time her sandals struck the floor her heart jumped in her throat.

A faint voice echoed through the hall. She skidded to a stop. Sammaria was nowhere near the throne room or the grand entrance. She looked around. There was nowhere to hide. She looked at the ceiling. It was too high and smooth for her to reach. She looked to the right and saw a large wooden door. She whispered, "I wonder?"

She quickly moved across the wide hall and to the door. She put her hand on the knob. The voices were coming closer. Quickly, she put her ear to the door. She heard nothing. She tried focusing. She heard heavy footsteps coming around the corner. She pulled on the doorknob. It was locked.

Sammaria looked behind her. She willed the door to open, but it remained locked. She shook the doorknob once more. Nothing. She slammed her body against it with all her might, and the door popped open. She stumbled in and closed the door behind her quickly. It was too heavy to slam. She held her breath and listened as the people passed. It was someone she knew, maids. The maids walked past. Sammaria turned around and gasped.

She was standing in her father's office. In her rush to find a place to hide, she hadn't realized to what part of the castle she had run.

Sammaria rummaged through the drawers of her father's desk. She needed proof that Enchardo had been killed, that there had been a golem. She had no idea what exactly she was looking for, but she needed to find something. She pulled out a stack of paper. On top was a note written to the King of Ancefra. It was from Morlyn detailing Enchardo's wish to have her murdered.

"No one would suspect a thing," Sammaria said quietly.

The hair on the back of Sammaria' neck stood. She glanced around. Outside the window, she noticed a man wearing a dark cloak. He turned toward her. It was almost as if he had sensed her eyes upon him. He had looked in her direction almost immediately. Sammaria fled, slipping into the closet. She felt her heart beating.

She reached out to Jennica. Their minds touched. She whispered, "Trydexzi is on the grounds. I'm inside Father's office."

Jennica moved toward her room. She needed to find the Elvateth locket. She had the locket that symbolized the

Grumpices. While Grumrose had stolen the Hawkaties' locket, they would still need true aid from them to win the war. Hopefully, Anahi was able to convince the haughty creatures that they were needed.

Grumrose and Criketchen were waiting for their signal. The O'rult guards were spread throughout the castle. She could only hope that her maid disguise would hold.

Jennica looked behind her. She swore she had heard footsteps, but no one was there. She started forward. Power radiated from the locket. It was close. She turned the corner and bumped into someone. Jennica stumbled backward, on guard. The woman looked up at her shocked. She exclaimed quietly, "Princess!"

Jennica shushed her, "Diana! Please. They don't know I'm here."

Diana started to ramble, "Yes, of course. Jennica, I have long awaited your return. There is much I have to tell you and show you."

Jennica said, "Hush now, Diana. Listen my name is Renai. Understand?"

The young woman nodded. Jennica said, "Come. Let us go somewhere we can speak privately."

Diana shut the door of Jennica's old room and said, "When you were born, the Queen tasked me with protecting you and your sister. I thought it was just a simple wish. She was gone and needed someone to watch over you. I didn't realize that you would need so *much* protection."

Jennica frowned. Diana quickly said, "Not that I minded. You are wonderful. The best mistresses I have ever worked for. When you first developed your Power, I knew that I would have to hide all of the accidents you had been causing. With your father's tirade against magic users, you wouldn't have lasted long without our protection."

"Our?" Jennica asked.

Diana shook her head, "It would take too long to explain. We tried to keep you safe. But Sammaria was kidnapped. Is she safe? Please, tell me she is safe."

Jennica nodded, "She is here. She is trying to regain the throne."

Diana shook her head, "The girl. Still in need of protection."

Jennica realized just how much Diana had aged while she had been away. She must have been worried sick.

Diana said, "Your mother did give me something to help protect the two of you, though. I'm not sure exactly what it does. She said it was very important. It has been haunting me for so many years. Please, take it from me."

Diana held out a small silver trinket. A red gem glistened against the torchlight.

Jennica snatched it from her hand gleefully, "Diana! You are the most wonderful person I have ever met! Thank you so much!"

Jennica jumped as she wandered back toward the kitchen. She glanced around. She moved down the halls to where Sammaria was trapped. She entered the room. Something was out of place. Papers were everywhere. She knew Sammaria wouldn't have done something like that. She ducked as a guard passed the window. Jennica said, "Sammaria, open up."

From behind the door came a muffled warning. Jennica slowly reached for the doorknob. It slowly turned of its own will, and she watched the door slowly open. Trydexzi held Sammaria, his knurled hand over her mouth. He smiled wryly.

Jennica stared at the necromancer. He stared back. The face that had plagued her nightmares now faced her. Not only was he stealing her country, but he would end up – in the end - stealing her entire family's lives as well. Hatred and fear boiled inside of her.

Jennica was more than capable of handling him. He held tightly to Sammaria, exposing her still pale throat. He smelled her neck as if smelling her blood. Jennica turned away. He grinned as if he knew what Jennica was thinking. He licked Sammaria's neck, and Jennica felt her fury grow, but she held back her Power. It wouldn't get the best of her. If she let it, Sammaria could be hurt. Trydexzi said, "I've waited for this moment for a *very* long time."

Jennica said, "This moment?"

He replied, "I planned this in my head so many times. I never thought it would play out *exactly* as I had imagined it."

Jennica asked, "What have you imagined?"

Sammaria saw Jennica's eyes turn smoky. She wasn't fully in Sight State, but she was scanning his imaginings.

She pulled back with a gasp and shook her head, "It's not in the stars today."

He replied, "Such a waste to lose so much talent. A talent that could blossom in the right hands. In my hands. Too bad that you are wrong and will soon die."

Jennica could feel Sammaria's heat rising. Trydexzi pulled back from her, clasping his hand. She had burned him. Jennica pulled her over to Sammaria side of the room. Sammaria asked, "How did he find me?"

Trydexzi said, "I can answer that one myself. I've been following you. I can sense your Power. You are close to death. I can feel it. That's how I tracked you. Well, to be honest, I tracked Jennica. She led me to you, Highness."

Jennica felt herself grow weary. Her vision. The one about her death. It was going to happen. Trydexzi saw he had struck a chord with Jennica. He said, "Oh yes, Princess. Your death is very close at hand."

He flashed his hands at her as if casting a spell, "Beware!"

Jennica turned in time to see a bench shattering the window. Sammaria jumped out of the way, the bench narrowly missing her ankle. The stone bench split in half as Trydexzi glided over it. He lifted his hands. The bench raised. He lowered them, and the bench crashed to the floor once again.

Sammaria went around to the front of the desk where Jennica stood frozen to the spot. Sammaria seized Jennica's arm and shoved her toward the door. Jennica's legs started to work again. Sammaria wrenched open the door and shoved Jennica out, saying, "Go. I'll be all right."

Jennica shook her head. Sammaria said, "You listen to me. Save yourself. I'm counting on you."

Sammaria slammed the door before Jennica could argue. The necromancer looked at her. He said in a withered voice, "Such a foolish one. To try and trade one's life for your sister's. She will die. This is a fact she knows well. And such a foolish sister to not listen to her when you had a chance. She will die, and it'll be the ones she loves that will kill her."

Sammaria said bravely, "Not if I can help it."

The necromancer looked at her. He began to cast a spell. With her Power, Sammaria sent Fire surging toward him like lightning.

As the magics combined, light filled the room. Sammaria closed her eyes to the brightness. Trydexzi cried out. Sammaria snapped her eyes open. She couldn't believe what she saw. She was in a stone square. She looked around. Trydexzi wasn't anywhere to be found. Sammaria walked toward the walls. She could see a place to turn up ahead. She was in a maze.

Trydexzi cried out, "Princess. Oh, princess! Come out from your hiding."

Sammaria moved around corner after corner trying to escape the voice. Yet, it still seemed to be just behind her while simultaneously coaxing her forward.

Smoke billowed up with her every step like a beacon to her attacker. Sammaria cried out, "Kiro! Help me!"

She turned to look behind her. The smoke gathered into a human form that rushed in front of her along the maze. Sammaria didn't move. The figure beckoned for her to follow. Sammaria looked behind her, feeling Trydexzi was getting close. The smoke man said, "Follow me."

The voice suggested it was male. The voice was low, warm. It sounded like something out of a dream. Sammaria felt like she had heard the voice before. She couldn't place it. The memory seemed to be just out of reach.

Sammaria took a step toward the shadow. The figure said, "Quickly, Sammaria, quickly."

The smoke man took off running. Sammaria sprinted after it. They moved along the twists and chases of the maze. Never once did the smoke man falter. He seemed to know exactly where he was going.

Sammaria struggled after him. Finally, he stood in front of a gate. Through the bars of the gate, she could see a valley. Across the valley was Mestchester. She asked, "What is all this?"

The man replied, "Do you not know?"

Sammaria shook her head. He replied, "When pure good – you – and pure evil – Trydexzi – allow their magic to touch, the world creates this maze. It's a fair way to decide which should prevail. The one that can successfully navigate the maze shall win."

"You helped me. Does it still count?"

A faint smile seemed to form on the otherwise featureless face. He said, "Those who call for help will be answered. Those who ask for help will win."

She asked, "Who are you?"

He said, "It's me, darling. Do you not recognize me?"

His features began to set into the smoke. The smoke turned to skin and bones.

In just a short time the man who gave Sammaria life stood before her. Immediately, she went on guard, Fire coming to her hand. She said, "Why did you help me?"

The storyteller stopped as she saw the confused faces of the little children. She said, "Possibly we should stop for today."

The little children cried out, "No! Tell us what happened. Please!" The storyteller looked toward the parents.

They shrugged and said, "Continue by all means."

The storyteller said, "All right. Sammaria asked her father to explain his motives."

The King said, "I know you don't trust me. You have every reason not to trust me. I must tell you, though, that your mistrust is not adequately placed."

Sammaria frowned, "Not adequately placed? You were bad. You abandoned me. And why? Were you really so power hungry?"

"No, darling. It is true that when I learned of your Power, I pulled away from you. You scared me. Magic has always scared me. But it was I who brought Orlten to the palace. He secretly trained you, did he not? It was as I had hoped."

Sammaria tried to absorb the news. He continued, "Do you remember when I started acting badly as you said?"

Sammaria shouted, exasperated, "What does it matter? You had innocent people killed! You tried to have *me* killed!"

Enchardo reached out to touch Sammaria's arm. She jerked out of the way. He sighed, "It was after my trip to Ancefra in the fall."

Sammaria shook her head, "You're lying. You never went to Ancefra."

Enchardo replied, "I did. It was a secret trip to negotiate a peace treaty. I was assassinated on that trip. A necromancer possessed my body. The necromancer that is now pursuing you."

Sammaria took a step back in shock. She clutched a hand to her chest. Sounds made their way to her ears. She could hear Trydexzi's muffled cries. He was steadily moving closer. Sammaria looked at her father, panicked. She was running out of time. She asked, "How could this be?"

Enchardo replied, "He's the instigator of everything. He faked my death so that Misseter could take control of the country."

Sammaria could feel that her father was speaking the truth. He couldn't lie to her. She sighed and nodded. Enchardo said, "Hurry now. Pass through the gate."

Sammaria passed through the stone arch. She looked back at her father as the doors swung shut. She waved as he faded away. She turned back around.

Suddenly, she was in the hall outside her father's office. She faintly heard Enchardo's voice whisper, "Run!"

The little blonde girl in the young man's lap asked, "What happened next, Storyteller?"

The young woman said, "Jennica had gone back to the kitchen to get Rekasi and Donichello. As a scream echoed down the hall, she feared she was too late. Jennica moved like lightning and sprinted from the kitchen. Donichello had no choice but to follow her. He raced after her down the hall."

Sammaria looked around her. She was surrounded by foreign creatures. They backed her against the wall. Her Fire was useless against them. One of the creatures bent its body to expose its stinger to Sammaria's stomach. The creatures hissed.

Rekasi entered the hall. He jumped and emitted Fire from his hands. The creatures hissed. Sammaria shielded her eyes from the blast. Donichello and Jennica raced up behind him, Jennica crying out her sister's name.

Trydexzi stepped into the hall and threw his black magic in their direction. The straight line of magic grew as it traveled, and finally it came to wrap around Jennica and Rekasi. The necromancer said, "Does the knight have no love for his fiancé? Or his best friend?"

Jennica opened her mouth in protest. The black magic felt like nothingness as it filled her mouth and lungs. She couldn't breathe. She couldn't force it out. Donichello looked at her. She was suffocating.

Rekasi reached for her. The magic wouldn't allow them to move. Donichello said, "Release them."

Trydexzi asked, "Why should I? It's apparent that you have no love for either of them."

Jennica's hearing faded.

Donichello said, "You are wrong. And you have no right to say that. I know what you are doing. You're turning them against me."

She could just see Trydexzi's mouth twitch. Words passed into her ears, "I don't love Jennica. She means nothing to me. I would die for Sammaria."

She shook her head. This couldn't be true. What about all those times...

She didn't doubt her ears. Jennica felt her heart break as her lungs screamed for air, but she no longer cared. Her mind raced. She couldn't reason her way through this. She closed her eyes. It was better this way.

In her heart, she felt no resentment toward Donichello. He had given her the love of a lifetime even if it had been a false love. Jennica felt her body relax.

Donichello cried out as he saw her face change. Trydexzi opened the cocoon of magic in which she was trapped. Jennica looked at Donichello. It was the most mournful look that she had ever given him.

She heard his cry as she closed her eyes. She wished with all her might that it was truly pain he felt. That he had actually felt something for her.

The black magic smothered her. Her body dropped to the ground. She laid there, crumpled on the stone floor. Her brown hair covered her face. Time itself seemed to stop, waiting for her to awaken.

CHAPTER LIV

onichello called out and dropped by Jennica's side. He lifted her head. The heat was still within her. He held her to his chest. Donichello yelled at Trydexzi, "What did you do to her?"

Trydexzi didn't reply to his demand. He nudged Jennica's leg with his foot. Donichello hugged her closer, "Don't touch her!"

Trydexzi said, "Such a shame. She could have been great. You destroyed her."

Donichello conjured up his Power. He saw how weak it was. Still, he attacked. Trydexzi's chuckle was low and menacing, "Lord Donichello couldn't save his one love. That'll be one for the children's stories."

Donichello took those words and put all the strength that he had left behind them. The shock of her death turned to anger. His heart hardened. Rekasi and Sammaria watched as his kind face turned fierce and his jaw set. His eyes glowed, and the castle trembled. He stepped forward, and the creatures were thrown back as stone spikes impaled their heads. Trydexzi didn't look surprised. His face was as expressionless as ever.

Donichello howled in a voice much deeper than his own, "You! This is your fault!"

He stomped. A wave of rocks flew toward Trydexzi. They hit him, but he didn't move an inch. Donichello sent a swell of raw magic at Trydexzi. Trydexzi sent his own. They connected. Donichello's magic shook and bubbled with fury. Trydexzi's was still and steady. Donichello concentrated, but his mind kept wandering to Jennica.

Trydexzi muttered a few words. Donichello's Power strengthened, and he started to rein in his magic. The black magic was like lightning cutting through the distance between the two duelists. In his head, he heard a horrible scream, "Don't do this. Donichello, you still have every reason to live."

Donichello thrust more Power at Trydexzi to keep the conversation going. He yelled, "What reason? You were my reason!"

Trydexzi said, "Why bother trying? You'll just follow your beloved Jennica."

Donichello wasn't listening to Trydexzi. He knew he had gone mad with grief, but he didn't care. He needed to know why. Her voice said, "I heard what you told Trydexzi. You really were too good to be true. I love you. I really, really love you."

He shot another ripple of magic toward Trydexzi. The voice said, "I thought I could tell a lie from the truth."

Donichello yelled to the air, "Jennica! Has everything we've gone through meant nothing? You were going to be my wife!"

Sammaria looked up. Tears glistened in her eyes. She couldn't stand to see Donichello going mad like he was.

"So this is how it ends."

Donichello turned, trying to see who had spoken. A faint light grew brighter. The spirit of Milamare appeared. Donichello turned white, and his Power wavered. He regained his concentration and shot another burst of Power toward Trydexzi as light spread through the hall.

Trydexzi asked, "What in bloody hell is going on over there?"

Milamare twisted her hand like she was scooping something up. Then, she flicked her hand like she was holding a whip. It shot through Donichello and through the magical connection between him and the necromancer. Light, identical to that which had filled the room, encased Trydexzi.

Milamare flicked her fingers over to where Rekasi floated, and he dropped to the floor. He gasped for air as he was shrouded by the light. Sammaria stayed where she was, still in the corner. Jennica's body lay next to Rekasi. Donichello sucked in the Power that had spread through the room. Milamare said, "Donichello, what is it that your heart longs for?"

Donichello closed his eyes and listened. Finally, he said, "More than anything, more than my life, I *need* her to be alive."

Milamare nodded and disappeared.

Donichello shook his head. She had promised she wouldn't let those horrors they had seen come true. She wouldn't let their son get killed. She wouldn't become suicidal. She would *never* let their love die.

He supposed she'd kept her promise. Now, they would never have a life together. She was gone.

Donichello felt his anger for Trydexzi renew itself. He had not just stolen Jennica's life. He'd robbed their family's lives as well. Trydexzi wouldn't live much longer.

Donichello drew his sword, his face still hard, and walked stiffly over to where Trydexzi was encased. He pointed the sword at him and asked, "Why didn't your magic encase me?"

Trydexzi just spat at Donichello. It went nowhere. Donichello pressed the sword against the necromancer's neck. He said, "Just because you can't get out, doesn't mean I can't get in."

To prove his point, he nicked the skin of Trydexzi's neck.

Trydexzi squealed, "She was weak. She did not deserve to be in power. The Dragon Queen will never rise."

Donichello thrust his sword into Trydexzi's neck. Trydexzi was in the middle of a curse when he breathed his last breath. Donichello turned to find Sammaria and Rekasi staring at him incredulously. He looked at his reflection. His eyes were glowing a brilliant forest green. His once soft face was rigid with excruciating pain. He blinked till the glowing faded and his eyes returned to nut brown. His features softened, but they didn't have the same loving, happy look they had before.

※

A snake writhed along the ground. It slowly encircled the trunk of a tree. Its forked tongue escaped for half a second from its jaw, testing the air. It hissed softly. As it moved around the tree, the snake felt a pull. It fell to the ground and whipped in intricate patterns as if in pain. Slowly, the body of the snake split at the bottom. The sides pulled apart. The body of a man slowly began to form again. The jaw locked and then opened into an intense roar.

Morlyn thrashed about in pain. He opened his eyes to the bright light of the sun. His eyes appeared to be a deeper shade of red than before. His naked body glistened with sweat. He stood, eyeing his surroundings. In his mind, he brought forth his perfectly planned revenge.

CHAPTER LV

Anahi followed her guide through a small door. It wasn't the one Jennica had told her about. She hesitated. The Hawkatie turned, "This way, Immortal One."

Anahi nodded and stepped through the door. The room was as Jennica had described it. A large, male Hawkatie sat on a platform. He said, "Immortal One, we welcome you into our presence. Long have we wanted to meet the one from Across the Waters."

Anahi curtsied to him, "It is an honor, my Lord."

The Hawkatie spread his beak into what Anahi guessed was a smile. He said, "I'm not a lord, but thank you for the flattery."

Anahi smiled nervously. He said, "I'm sensing you were sent for a reason. Pray, what is it?"

Anahi said, "I was sent by Jennica Aeradal." She waited for a moment.

The Hawkatie's face remained passive, "Go on."

Anahi said, "Again, the Aeradal twins plead to you to help them in their campaign against the O'rult."

The female on the large male's right said, "Immortal One, how dire has the situation become?"

Anahi replied, "Jennica has called on her alliance with the Fraychavae, the dragons, and myself. They were preparing for the second half of a large battle when I left them. I am unsure of the outcome of the battle. Sammaria, Donichello, and Rekasi are in Mestchester infiltrating the castle. Jennica remained behind to protect those fighting the battle."

The female said, "It is worse than we feared. If we don't help them, dire consequences shall arise from our inaction."

The lead Hawkatie said, "What have you seen? Please enlighten us."

Anahi said, "They cannot do this alone. Sammaria is worried many innocent lives will be lost. The O'rult are becoming more prevalent and harder to kill. I can't convey properly the helplessness of their situation. O'rult are attacking them from Gabvand and their capitol city. The O'rult are taking over Dragonia. Every male in Mestchester was slaughtered."

The leader snapped his beak, thinking. He said, "We must honor the alliance… I am unsure of this. It doesn't seem like we are following the right path. It's eerie."

Anahi said, "You must. It is what you are meant to do. I can see it in the stars. They are mine to decipher after so many years. You must come."

The Hawkatie stared at her with long eyes. He said nothing for several minutes. Finally, he said, "We'll put it to a vote."

۶

Grumrose flitted through the castle, looking for any sign of Sammaria and the others. She flew up in the rafters to avoid attention, but the weight of the necklace was carrying her lower and lower. Her friends were right below her. She saw them close the door behind them. Jennica wasn't with them. Grumrose didn't see her anywhere. She wondered where she was.

Grumrose felt the air pressure change beneath her wings. She moved them slightly to compensate. It sent her flipping through the air. The necklace flew from the Grumpice's grip. Sammaria looked up. She caught the necklace while whispering her small friend's name.

Grumrose fluttered down to Sammaria and landed wobbly on her shoulder.

Rekasi asked, "Where is Criketchen?"

The short Hawkatie stepped from the shadows. His feathers were turning a more red color. He was ready for battle. Criketchen asked, "And where is the fourth? Where is Jennica?"

Sammaria looked down. Tears were forming in her eyes. Rekasi said, "She's dead."

Donichello dropped to the floor. He pulled up his knees and rested his head on them. His body was wracked with tears.

Sammaria knelt next to him, "This is not your fault. We couldn't save her."

Donichello said, "I never told her how much I loved her."

Sammaria said, "She always knew. She didn't think she was good enough for you. She was ready for this. She knew she was going to die."

A tear fell from his eye. He didn't look at the rest of them. He shook his head. He had known her great spirit since he'd first looked in her eyes. They cast a spell on him every time he had looked into them since. They made his breathing unsteady. The way they lit up her face. He saw into her soul every time he looked into her eyes. She let him in that far. He'd loved her from the moment he'd met her.

Donichello wiped the tears from his eyes. He couldn't cry. Not now. Now, he had to finish what they'd started. He stood. Sammaria took his arm. Rekasi turned to look at him. Donichello looked at Criketchen.

The Hawkatie said, "With or without the Water Enchantress, we have to stop Misseter."

Grumrose asked, "Sammaria, do you know the words?"

Sammaria looked at the locket in her hands. She nodded to the Grumpice. Grumrose said, "You must take Jennica's place."

Rekasi said, "Let's do this."

Donichello said, "For Jennica."

⁂

Jennica sat and waited in a dimly lit room. The wooden floor was scuffed beneath her feet. The chair was hard beneath her. She found it strange that she could still feel. She had always thought that death would be painless. She looked around her. Humans surrounded her, staring. She supposed it was because she was in such disarray. Donichello kept yelling at her. She didn't have to speak to answer him. He was able to hear her thoughts.

She had tried to ask the man next to her where they were. He just growled at her and turned back to his large newspaper dotted with minuscule black print.

She sat nervously, forgetting her etiquette and bouncing her feet. Finally, someone called her name. Jennica looked up. Someone held open a door, waiting for her. Jennica wondered what she'd gotten herself into. Bright light spilled from the open door. Jennica looked around. Was she the only one that could see it? The secretary gestured irritably to the doorway. Jennica looked at the lady uncertainly but walked into the blinding light.

⁂

Rekasi looked around the corner. Three O'rult men were walking alone. Rekasi said, "We can pass them unnoticed if we carry something."

Sammaria asked, "What about me? If anyone recognizes me ..."

Rekasi glanced around. He stacked books over the boxes she already held. He said, "Don't let anyone see your face."

Sammaria held the load above her face. Donichello and Rekasi lifted an end table. They walked around the corner.

The O'rult didn't look their way. "Hey, girl," one of them hollered as Sammaria passed them.

She stopped and turned. The stack was large enough that she could hold it in front of her face without it seeming like she was hiding. He said, "Take those boxes to the Queen's room."

Sammaria bowed to the creatures. She assured them that she would. The O'rult walked away. She breathed a sigh of relief and carried on.

Criketchen swooped into a high-set window. He landed next to Rekasi, "Now, what shall we do. It seems that Misseter is starting her plan. We should begin with ours as well."

Rekasi nodded, "I agree. We need to get close to her. We should infiltrate her guard."

Cricketchen stated, "I could make a suggestion."

They turned to look at him. He said, "I could fly you to your post, Sammaria. I could then fly to mine."

Donichello asked, "Where is Grumrose?"

Sammaria shook her head, "I haven't seen her since she -"

She looked toward Donichello.

Rekasi said, "She'll turn up. She probably went to the throne room by herself. She and Jennica were close. She's probably grieving."

Donichello nodded mutely. He said to the Hawkatie, "Good luck. Until next time."

Donichello started walking toward the throne room, Rekasi and Sammaria following closely. He frowned. Where was everyone? It seemed that the castle was a little too quiet? A loud cheer echoed through the hall. Sammaria ducked into the closest room. Rekasi and Donichello followed.

It was a storage room. The room had been an astrology room. Over time interest was lost in the project, and the room was filled with old furniture and papers. Sammaria looked out the window. It gave them a muted view of the balcony from which kings and queens would speak to the people.

When Sammaria leaned out the window, she could see people on the balcony. Below it was an entire army of O'rult. Each with a bloodthirsty look in their eye. Misseter and Bynakst'r stood on the balcony and spoke in the language of the O'rult, a collection of barks and grunts. Sammaria wasn't able to understand any of it. Misseter turned back and barked the name of some O'rult. A short O'rult boy walked onto the balcony. In his hands was a struggling creature. He was holding it by its neck. Sammaria looked at it carefully and whispered, "Grumrose."

࿇

Jennica looked around the room. A giant man was sitting in the chair in the center of the room. There was a large, brass scale in front of him. In a section of the room to the right, an assortment of about thirty humans and Elvateth was seated.

In the wooden benches behind them were more people looking straight ahead. They were staring at the person Jennica assumed was a judge. Jennica had never been to a trial before. Dragonia didn't hold trials. The King decided the fate of criminals.

The judge looked up. His face was incredibly smooth. It was brown. His eyes were wide-set and large. His lips were full. He had high cheekbones, and his skin was stretched across them. Everything about him was beautiful. Jennica looked down. It was hard to look at him, but she thought he seemed familiar.

He looked straight at Jennica. She was studying the floor. The door flew open and someone walked in. Jennica turned. The man rushing down the aisle was familiar. Jennica realized it was Jonakil. She gave him a weak smile. He had counted on her, and then she had died. He didn't look mad. He glanced at her and gave her a small smile. The judge said, "It's fine, Jonakil. We were just starting."

"Jennica!"

Jennica turned back to the judge and looked upon his face, realizing who it was. She gasped, stumbling backward. She tripped on the chair that had appeared behind her when the judge had said her name. She fell to the ground. He said, "Stand up."

Jennica watched him. She was in the presence of the great god. She said, "Forgive me, great and mighty Kiro."

Kiro said, "Enchantress of Water, stand."

Jennica did so.

Kiro continued, "Jennica Animia Kasiana Aeradal, Sister to Sammaria and Einar, daughter to Milamare and Enchardo, Former King and Queen of Dragonia. This is your trial.

Your life was rather tragic. When you were born, your mother died. When you were two, you almost drowned.

You and your sister injured your father. Your brother was stolen from you and then killed. You witnessed battles full of gore and had your memory wiped. Your father was killed on your fifteenth birthday."

He continue listing off the tragedies of her life, "You almost drowned again at the age of nine. You had your memory wiped a second time as you started to recall painful memories of the bloody battles you had witnessed during the war with Ancefra. The King plotted to have Morlyn murder you, Sammaria, and Donichello."

Kiro noticed she writhed at the sound of Donichello's name.

"You had to run away from home to save your sister, and Donichello found out you were a Water Enchantress. You were attacked by the leader of the O'rult and sirens. You also were taken to the spirit realm to meet the god of the griffins. You were almost killed by pirates. You were almost killed by an elephish. You were attacked by Trydexzi twice, you had your heart broken, and then you died. Is there anything I forgot?"

Jennica said, "There is much you forgot. You only told of the tragic things that happened in my life. You forgot all the good."

The crowd and jury murmured to themselves. Jennica looked down, embarrassed. Who was she to contradict the god of creation?

Kiro said, "In all the years that I have been a judge, only one other person has reminded us of the happy aspects of their life."

Jennica said, "Who was that, sir?"

A member of the audience came from the back. Jennica turned. She saw her mother standing in the back next to this woman. Jennica turned away from her, ashamed.

The woman said, "I did."

She had black hair and green eyes. She had a noble air about her that no one couldn't deny. Jennica kneeled out of respect. She didn't know who this was.

The strange woman said, "Rise, Jennica. Please, is there someone to vouch for your happiness?"

Jennica said, "Only me."

Her mother spoke up, "This is not true. I will speak."

Einar said, "As will I. We were not alive for your life, but that does not mean that we were not present."

Kiro said, "Mestchina, sit."

Jennica looked at the woman, astonished. Mestchina winked at her. Kiro gestured for Jennica to come forth, "I would like to hear from our defendant first."

Jennica said, "It is true what you have said. My life has been tragic. More has happened to me in the last year than happens to most people in a lifetime..."

CHAPTER LVI

Sammaria mulled over the plan in her head one more time, moving along the hallway toward the throne room. She arrived outside the room and watched the guards outside. They didn't move. She hoped that Rekasi and Donichello would hurry. The eyes of the O'rult guards were always searching. Sammaria felt the hair on her neck stand up. She stiffened.

Footsteps echoed down the hall. The O'rult guards, clad heavily in armor, tightened their grip on their weapons. Sammaria watched as another guard approached them. He was considerably smaller than the other two. She assumed it was a young O'rult. He said something in their strange clicking language. The guards looked at each other. The young O'rult repeated his order. The guards roared at him before leaving.

The short guard took their place. It looked around, his eyes always searching. They lighted upon Sammaria. She whipped around the corner, hiding from his view. He hissed, "Sammaria."

She looked around the corner. The guard flipped up his face shield. Donichello was underneath the armor. She asked, "What happened to the original plan?"

Donichello said, "An O'rult page passed by us and we thought stealing his armor and telling the guards to leave was a better plan than trying to fight them."

She returned to the window inside the old astrology room. Misseter spoke of the destruction of Dragonia. The royals had to go. While they survived, resistance always would.

Sammaria heard the call of an owl echo throughout

the air. She responded with the cry of the falcon. The bird called again. She answered back. She listened for Rekasi's reply.

Instead, she heard the crying of a falcon. She searched the sky. Soaring through the air was a brown spot. Sammaria smiled as Nyma became clearer in the distance. Sammaria let out a piercing whistle. The falcon turned and soared toward her owner. Rekasi and Donichello moved to their post outside of Misseter's room.

Sammaria leaned out the window. She could just see Grumrose struggling in Misseter's long-nailed fingers. She watched as Nyma soared above their heads like a buzzard.

An idea crept into her head. Sammaria whistled for the bird. Misseter turned as the bird started to fly away.

Sammaria held her breath, and she leaned against the window ledge. Grumrose looked terrified. Sammaria felt her heart fly out to the small creature. It might be selfish, but they needed Grumrose to finish this.

Sammaria stroked Nyma's beak as she whispered into the falcon's ear. She lifted her arm, and Nyma took flight.

The bird soared back toward Misseter, who watched it carefully. She slowly circled the platform. Sammaria could see her people standing below.

They had been listening to Misseter's speech, but their attention was being diverted by Nyma. Their faces followed the falcon.

Sammaria watched breathlessly as Nyma dove, angling herself so she would hit Misseter's hand. The O'rult army tried to beat the falcon away, but they seemed to not affect it. Nyma's sharp beak pierced Misseter's flesh. She screamed and cursed. Grumrose fell from her grip.

A second brown streak flew in. Asravi snatched Grumrose in his talons. Misseter snatched at him and the

Grumpice. She called for her guard, "Find them!"

Grumrose panted as Asravi sat her down. He preened her viney hair. Nyma cooed. Grumrose said, "They didn't get it."

Sammaria looked at the little creature. She didn't seem to be hurt.

"Get what?"

"The locket of course."

Grumrose opened her mouth. Sitting on her tongue was the locket. Sammaria smiled, "You must go to the throne room now. Grumrose, be careful."

Grumrose smiled, her thorn teeth giving her a sinister look, "I will."

Donichello followed Grumrose into the throne room, shedding the heavy O'rult armor. The room was vacant of all servants and people. Donichello looked across the room at a closed door near the servant entrance. He said, "This is too easy."

There was a chill in the air. A voice cut through it, "I would agree with that statement."

Misseter stepped out of the shadows, "Did you *really* think you could defeat me?"

She peered into Donichello's eyes. They had hardened. No emotion was shining through. She said, "Oh. You did." She laughed, "Did you think this would avenge your dear slut?"

Donichello couldn't control himself. He struck Misseter across the face, "Don't talk about her like that!"

He pulled his sword and pointed it at Misseter.

She smiled. "Anger! Ah, let it fill you."

He heard a loud roaring and turned to see Bynakst'r running at him, chopping the air wildly.

Sammaria and Rekasi headed toward the East Tower. They heard a laugh as they sprinted past the closed ballroom. They stopped. Sammaria held her breath. They heard, "Morlyn is enraged that Sammaria escaped with that man. I think he's going to kill them."

The reply was, "Where did Morlyn go? I haven't seen him in months."

Sammaria looked up at Rekasi. He shook his head. Sammaria sneezed.

The man asked, "What the hell was that?"

Sammaria looked over at Rekasi and silently apologized. Rekasi nodded, "Be ready."

He and Sammaria crept down the hall. They passed the aviary. The drunken guard inside looked out but saw nothing. Sammaria and Rekasi reached the steps of the East Tower.

Slowly, they climbed the steps. Upon reaching the top of the staircase, they stood before the door that led into the tower. Sammaria took a deep breath and opened the door. She had a premonition that someone was in that tower. She waited; there was no one on the steps. Rekasi entered, sword drawn. Sammaria felt an overwhelming sense of insecurity as she stood in the room.

It seemed the fact that she couldn't control her Fire very well wouldn't leave her mind. No, that wasn't true. She had been able to control her Fire so much better since she started training with Cypol. She needed to gain her confidence again. She mentally prepared for her part in the battle.

Sammaria thought she heard movement. She listened closely, trying to hear it again, but she couldn't. She whispered to Rekasi, "Did you hear something?"

Rekasi shook his head. He pulled Sammaria to him, "Just in case... I love you.

Sammaria said, "Don't do that. Don't say goodbye. We're going to make it."

She sent a fireball toward the candelabrum. The room illuminated. They looked around the room as the Fire raced along it to other candelabra. Sammaria walked over to the window. The black clouds in the sky were circling.

Rekasi asked, "Where's the locket?"

Sammaria pulled it out of her pocket. He fastened it to her neck. "What now?"

Sammaria said, "We wait. We wait for the signal." She stared out, thinking of her sister and wondering if she had reached Deildly. Rekasi secured the room and stood next to her.

Sammaria jumped as it started to rain. A series of flashing lights emitted from the West Tower. She was trying to read the signal as the rain started to pour. Sammaria chanted the words that Mokana had told her. She could faintly hear Criketchen's voice coming from the other tower, but try as she might she couldn't hear Grumrose's small but strong voice.

Grumrose had been chanting the words ever since Donichello and Bynakst'r locked blades. The O'rult had forced Donichello to the floor. Bynakst'r threw an overhand strike. Donichello parried his blow and rolled out of the way. He jumped to his feet. He jabbed his sword upward and tried stabbing the O'rult through the heart. Bynakst'r was able to redirect the blow and snapped the blade in half. He laughed and tossed Donichello his broken sword.

Bynakst'r threw an overhand blow. Without thinking, Donichello crossed the broken halves of his sword and lifted them to stop the oncoming strike. Bynakst'r's eyes grew wide as Donichello deflected the blow. Quickly, while he was still shocked, Donichello pulled a dagger and jammed it between the O'rult's ribs. The body dropped like a weight. A gossamer thread of smoke began to rise from the wound. The soul of the dragon that had died to create Bynakst'r had been released. Donichello tossed away the enemy's swords.

Grumrose looked down and stopped chanting. Donichello was unaware that Misseter was still hidden in the shadows. Grumrose shrieked, "Donichello! Behind you!"

He turned and snatched up Bynakst'r's blade just in time to clumsily parry Misseter's blow. She yanked her sword away, and Grumrose started to chant again.

Donichello threw an underhanded blow. Misseter redirected the blow and threw an overhand blow at him. He raised Bynakst'r's blade to block. The two swords made contact and were held there.

Misseter said, "Why challenge me? Eh? Why worry about trying to live? What's the use? You're already miserable with your little harlot gone."

Donichello's eyes flashed a dark green. He blinked, and his eyes glowed even brighter. Donichello knew not what he did next.

"*Later accounts of the battle say that Donichello punched Misseter in the jaw. She fell, and he put all of his raw Power behind his sword and thrust it into her chest. Others say that Misseter threw a magical blow at him, and his Power was weakened considerably. Donichello is said to have then thrown all he had left into the blast of magic and stunned Misseter long enough to allow Donichello to stab her. One person knew the truth. A Grumpice actually. But we'll get to that. For now, I must tell you of Jennica.*"

Jennica wished she could just be alone. She took the long deliberation time as a bad omen. Jennica didn't want to be sent to the breeding grounds of pain, suffering, and evil. They were going to send her to Dunldir, the god of death. She would spend the rest of eternity in Deildly. Jennica heard some shouting in the decision chamber. A few minutes later, Kiro and Milamare came out. Kiro said, "We have come to a decision. You are special. You have passed into the spirit realm and lived."

Milamare looked curiously at Jennica, and Jennica blushed.

Jennica was terrified. Milamare stared at Kiro, waiting. Jennica looked at the carpet under the chair. Mestchina took up Kiro's sentence, "That is why we are letting Jennica choose."

Jennica looked up shocked, "Choose?"

Milamare grumbled, "Choose? That is absurd! Unheard of! Whoever got to choose where they wanted to go? Send her back!"

Mestchina looked at the floor and spoke quietly, "This is the court's final decision."

Jennica asked, "What do you mean, choose?"

Kiro said, "It's your choice. You can choose to stay here or to return to your body, unharmed." Jennica hesitated.

"Poor Jennica. This decision was so hard for her. She hadn't any idea what to do.

Now, back to my favorite hero. So, in reality, Donichello was dying. He was doing badly in his battle against Misseter. She thought he was rash to defend someone who was dead. Donichello was mixing the last of his magic with the attacks, and Misseter was blocking them easily. Donichello was backed into a corner against the window. He was giving up. He couldn't find a reason to hang on to life anymore. The pain was too much."

Grumrose faltered in her chanting as the locket cracked open. A light grew from inside of it. Donichello heard the chant grow, like tens of millions of people were singing in one voice. Misseter turned and exposed her back to Donichello, trying to find the source of the song. Donichello took advantage of this break in defense and plunged his sword into her back. She croaked, "You haven't won yet."

Donichello pulled his sword out, and she laughed, "You actually thought you won, didn't you?"

She touched the hole in her chest, and the skin grew back together. The chants grew louder.

Donichello had knocked Misseter's sword out of her reach. Misseter started to walk away from Donichello, and he noticed a flicker of white and gold in the corner next to Misseter's throne. Donichello saw another one by the doors; it was advancing toward the tyrant. Misseter stopped as the white-gold mist reached her. Donichello ran up and grabbed Misseter by a shoulder, putting his blade to her throat.

Donichello heard Misseter hiss, "Go on do it! It won't bring her back. Nothing will."

Donichello felt his anger building up. She taunted, "That's it, boil! Become a mindless killer."

Donichello's sword dropped. Misseter jammed her elbow into his stomach and lifted her right hand. She clawed Donichello's left cheek. He cried out as he reached up and felt the four parallel lines of blood on his face.

Misseter faced him, "Good try."

In one last attempt to destroy Misseter, Donichello threw one final band of his raw magic at her. Before it hit her, several things happened within seconds of each other.

The chanting grew louder until it vibrated around the room. Then, a flash of lightning came through the ceiling and split the floor in half, cracking the altar Misseter had placed there. Donichello was on one side of the fissure, Misseter on the other. She glared at him. A white flicker shot up from the ground. It bound Misseter's mouth. Another bound her hands, and a third entered Misseter's body. This one spoke through Misseter's mouth.

She said, "Kill her, son of Joromo. She can't regenerate now."

Donichello jumped across the fissure and stabbed her as the last of his Power surged through him. The ground shook.

⁂

Jennica stood at the Gates of Ethota. Mestchina stood beside her. Jennica asked, "Why did you bring me here?"

She said, "For remembrance. You can stay here with your father, mother, and brother. Or you can choose to live and be with your sister and the man who loves you."

Jennica flinched. She turned her head to look at her mother. Mestchina said, "Jennica! Your mother can't make this decision for you. Neither can I. This is for you to decide."

Jennica stared at the earth. It was so green and so blue. It looked so peaceful. She thought about Donichello in the Grumpice cave after he had saved her and then thought about what she had heard him say to the necromancer. Her heart ached, "I'm staying."

She turned and walked back the way they had come. A tear dripped from her eye.

CHAPTER LVII

Criketchen stopped chanting as the castle began to shake. His locket cracked open. A beam of light extended from it to the East Tower. The three lockets made a triangle of light. There was a screech from the skies. Criketchen looked out the window as a flock of Hawkaties joined the fight. The Grumpices squealed with happiness.

A flash of gold filled the sky, and scores of a new creature stood where the Hawkaties and Grumpices had been. The new creature had the legs of a Hawkatie and the torso of a stretched Grumpice. The head was shaped like that of a Grumpice but was beaked like a Hawkatie. These were the Maginaties. Criketchen whispered, "Two become whole, and evil is divided."

The new creatures attacked with renewed vigor as they took down the O'rult. The Maginaties sent light into the hallways, illuminating the castle. They swooped through the stormy skies. The leader let out a high-pitched cry that only the other Maginaties could hear. The other Maginaties began to cry out on and on till all were crying out in one voice. Lightning crackled and thunder boomed with the sound of the cry.

Sammaria looked out at the Maginaties. Her breath caught as a bolt of lightning struck the leader's feathery coat. The Maginatie, however, let out his call like a laugh. It sped toward a small group of O'rult. It beat its wings till its talons were facing the group. It cawed again, and the lightning was sent rocketing down through the O'rult. They shook, and their hair burned. As the Maginatie zoomed back toward the sky, the charred O'rult fell dead.

Rekasi pulled on Sammaria's arm. She turned back to the situation at hand. They raced down the stairs of the East Tower.

One of the Maginaties landed on the balcony just as Sammaria and Rekasi rushed out onto it. Anahi climbed off the creature's back. She looked woozy. She steadied herself on the Maginatie's side. Sammaria rushed to her. Anahi smiled weakly, "Well, that was a fun ride."

She gripped her stomach. Sammaria looked at her. She said, "Sammaria, I'm fine. It's just from being on its back during the transformation. I'm fine."

Criketchen looked from his position. Elvateth were marching into battle. They fought alongside the O'rult, loyal to King Enchardo and Prince Morlyn. The Elvateth Resistance fought their brothers.

Criketchen launched out the window of the West Tower. He flew down toward Morlyn. Criketchen hoped killing Morlyn would stop needless bloodshed.

Morlyn was ready for him. As Criketchen passed above, Morlyn turned his sword up to rip the Hawkatie from chest to navel. Criketchen pulled up as he felt the first prick of the sword. Criketchen roared his outrage.

"It is said that the people in the Kilhatea Mountains heard Criketchen's roar; that his cry was what called the remainder of the Resistance into the battle. Now, we all know that is just a story. The truth is that word that the battle had begun in Mestchester had finally reached them in the Kilhatea Mountains. They knew their orders. Following them, they rushed to Queen Sammaria's aid.

Across the country of Dragonia, the revolution had begun, but our three remaining heroes were just trying to stay alive."

Criketchen banked in the air, swooping down and gouging out one of Morlyn's eyes. He tossed it up to a Maginatie, who gobbled it down. Morlyn disappeared, nursing his empty eye socket. Criketchen flew up to the balcony to watch over the battle. A crash of thunder brought another round of cries from the Maginaties. A female swooped up into the clouds and brought down the thunder on her wings. She cawed out across the battlefield, and many of the O'rult fell dead.

Donichello moved in and slew an O'rult who tried to shoot down the Maginatie. Criketchen turned around sharply as Sammaria moved swiftly across the balcony followed by Rekasi.

Sammaria pushed her hair behind her ear, marching over to Criketchen, "What is the status?"

Criketchen looked onto the streets of Mestchester, "The battle is nearing its end, but there is a new wave of O'rult coming in from an unknown place. The Maginaties are doing well to take them out, though.

Even still, there have been many civilian casualties. We can't risk their lives anymore. We are trying to locate the source of the new wave, but are having no success."

Sammaria nodded thoughtfully. Criketchen continued, "Misseter and Bynakst'r are dead by his hand. But I must ask that you and Rekasi find the source of this wave. Take three Maginaties with you. That should be enough to wipe them out. We can take out any stragglers within the city."

Donichello ducked under the swing of an O'rult's curved blade. The O'rult yelled and shoved his sword toward Donichello. Donichello stepped to the side and cut at the O'rult's back, wounding it. Donichello said, "Going to have to do better than that."

The O'rult turned to face him. His large eyes flashed with fearful anger. Donichello thrust his sword into the O'rult faster than it could react.

Before the O'rult fell, a new one was on Donichello. Donichello slew him easily. Yet another swarmed in to face him. The O'rult smiled as Donichello pulled his sword from the previous O'rult. Donichello held his sword at the ready. The O'rult reacted, swiping at Donichello's legs. Donichello just barely blocked the blow. He thrust his sword toward the O'rult's unguarded stomach. The O'rult jumped back.

Donichello adapted his fighting style. The creature was not fighting like an O'rult. He fought like an elf. As the O'rult parried a blow, Donichello spun and thrust the sword into the O'rult ribcage. The O'rult chopped at Donichello's head as it died. Donichello pulled his sword free and ran toward the castle. He had to tell Criketchen.

Donichello watched as the O'rult tore through the city's homes. His hands twitched on his sword. The Hawkatie next to him shook his head, "Let be what will be."

There were screams. People were dying at the hands of these hybrid creatures. Most were able to conceal themselves into the nooks of their homes. Every scream cost Donichello part of himself. He could stop this. Criketchen again shook his head, "There are too many and they are too strong. Wait for the news."

He said to Criketchen, "We better find where they are coming from fast!"

Criketchen nodded in acknowledgment, "In that, we agree."

The room barely illuminated, Sammaria walked slowly across the floor covered in squalor. She halted for a moment as a large rat scuttled across the floor. She looked back at her companion. The Maginatie seemed unabashed by the condition of the cellar. Sammaria moved deeper into the tunnel. She was thankful that the Maginatie had cast a spell of invisibility on them both.

A unit of about thirty O'rult moved toward the stairs. The Maginatie, Xantica, had enough electricity and thunder stored in her feathers to easily take them out. She shot some of her lightning at the O'rult who dropped dead where they were. The next unit swarmed in to see the cause of the commotion. They looked around as Xantica pulled more thunder from her feathers. Sammaria covered her ears as Xantica let out a high-pitched cry. The unit fell down dead.

Sammaria said to the Maginatie, "I'm going back to see how many more are hiding down here. Thank you."

Xantica nodded and Sammaria moved down the tunnel.

Rekasi called his Maginatie, Komotial, to his side. On the wall was a bright blue frame. Magic swirled in the center. It would charge with white magic, and then a regiment of O'rult would appear. Rekasi nodded to Komotial, and they stepped through the churning magic.

On the other side was a camp with what appeared to be at least six thousand O'rult. Komotial and Rekasi stepped back through the portal. Komotial silently called to two other Maginaties. The two that he called swooped into the sky, collecting the electricity and thunder. They swooped down in a winding pattern, flew through the portal, and released their charges. Half the camp was immediately wiped out.

The portal turned white again, and a unit of nearly five hundred O'rult stepped through. Komotial and the others took that unit out and half of what was left in the camp.

The camp couldn't be the place of origin. Too many O'rult were still spilling through the portal. Komotial swooped into the clouds and took out the remains of the camp. The portal started to swirl with white again. More were about to come through. All Rekasi could do was wait.

Sammaria walked through the passageways in the dark. She ran her hand along the wall, trying to find her way to the light. She dared not use her Fire lest she come across any O'rult. She saw a flicker of light up ahead. She blinked, knowing it was just wishful thinking. Sammaria looked down the tunnel again. The flicker was still there. As she hastened to get closer, it became a steady glow. Sammaria gasped as she stepped into the light.

Surrounding her were the carcasses of dragons and bodies of humans. She stifled a scream. All this time, the O'rult were being created beneath her feet. Sammaria walked forward, trying to avoid touching the bodies. She brushed past a younger boy. She jumped as his pale hand clamped onto her ankle. He looked at her with clouded, brown eyes. His voice was rasping when he spoke, "Don't leave me here."

Sammaria stumbled back from the boy, "I'll come back."

The boy shook his head weakly. "I'm next," he whispered, "I'm next."

Sammaria looked at the boy's pale face. An echoing came from the hallway across from her. Sammaria gave the boy an apologetic face and quickly disappeared back into the dark tunnel from which she had come. The last thing she heard was the boy's muffled screams.

CHAPTER LVIII

Xantica moved past the chamber of death. Her senses flared with the presence of O'rult. Sammaria followed close behind. Xantica moved into the next hallway and followed it to the end. At the end of the hallway was a large room. It held three O'rult units. Sammaria could tell that they were newly created. Before she could see anything else, Xantica attacked. She released some of the lightning onto them entirely obliterating every O'rult in the room.

As the lightning settled back into Xantica's feathers, Sammaria noticed a swirling vortex of blue magic. She silently motioned toward the Maginatie, pointing at the portal. Xantica nodded and moved over to it.

Sammaria asked, "Should we go through?"

Without replying, the Maginatie stepped into the blue magic. Sammaria stared for a moment as it glittered white and returned to the swirling blue. She took a deep breath and stepped through.

Sammaria screamed as the first O'rult caught sight of her. It charged toward her. Then she was soaring over the encampment. She looked up. Xantica was carrying her. Sammaria looked around the land below her. She saw a ruined spire of a castle bursting from the ground. The sun reflected off it like a thousand rainbows. She asked, "Are we in Gabvand?"

The Maginatie simply looked down at her. They flew quickly across the land with the wind pressing against the wings of the magical creature. Sammaria gasped as they crossed the border. The small villages were deserted.

"Sammaria passed out just as they were passing over the city of Montest. The next thing that she remembered was waking up next to Criketchen."

The musk of Criketchen's body was strong. She looked up. The sky was still stormy, but she didn't see any of the Maginaties. Criketchen looked at her, "Sammaria, Rekasi and the Maginaties have traveled to Gabvand. They are destroying the O'rult there. The Resistance has arrived and is finishing off the rest of the O'rult here."

Sammaria stood up. The O'rult were few. Lying thick on the ground was the charred and sunken bodies of their companions who had been destroyed by the Maginaties. Sammaria saw homes and buildings on fire being doused in water. She said, "It's almost over."

Criketchen echoed her, "It is almost over."

❦

Rekasi stood on the cliff overlooking the battlefield. Lightning was still flashing all around him. The O'rult were destroyed. Every last one had been detected by the Maginaties and obliterated. Rekasi watched as the Maginaties and the Elvateth piled the charred remains and bloody bodies of the O'rult. Rekasi said, "Kiro, let this be over. Let the O'rult be gone forever."

The Maginaties yawped as the souls of the dragons drifted from the lifeless human bodies. Xantica and Komotial stood before the pile of disfigured human bodies. They tweeted out a small melody. A mist fell from their mouths to settle on the pile. Two more Maginaties cawed out the melody. Silver wisps came, settling on the humans' mouths.

One last time, the lightning over Gabvand flashed. The wisps disappeared. The wounds healed. The humans sat up, blinking. They looked around them, surprised. Xantica led the song. Slowly, every Maginatie joined in.

The humans' eyelids grew heavy, and they drifted off to sleep. The Maginaties switched to a low and tranquil lullaby. Rekasi watched, amazed as the human forms began to ripple. One by one they disappeared. They would finally rest in peace Rekasi smiled. They flew with unnerving speed back to Mestchester.

Sammaria ran to Rekasi as soon as he set foot on the balcony. She said, "I was so worried. Are they gone?"

Rekasi held her more for support than anything. Sammaria sensed his weariness. She helped him to sit down. He said, "They are all gone. The humans have been sent home. They will rest in peace."

Sammaria said, "The Maginaties are unearthing the last of them. One last unit of them came through after you left."

Rekasi held his hand out to Sammaria. She took it and held it tight, "Should we call the citizens out of their hiding? The Maginaties have driven the O'rult from Mestchester. The war is not won, but the O'rult army has been crippled. Victory will be ours soon."

"The Resistance brought the Elvateth out of their hiding. They rooted through each house in the city. The rescued citizens wept and shouted. They were all elated and disturbed by the happenings within the city.

The Resistance herded them like sheep to the castle square below the balcony. Whatever they expected to see, it wasn't Sammaria. She was standing by the balcony ledge, her hands curling naturally around the rail. She had the crown on her head. It was shining through the still stormy skies. She looked down at them with perfect regal grace."

Sammaria said, "Dragonia is ours!"

A shout went up from the crowd. Sammaria continued, "The man that you have called King for the entirety of this Reign of Terror was not in fact Enchardo. The necromancer Trydexzi stole my father's soul almost a year ago. He shrouded himself with it and impersonated him. Trydexzi is dead by Donichello Laeranil's hand. Misseter and Bynakst'r are also dead by his hand."

A loud cheer rippled through the crowd. She waited for them to be silent, "In my travels, I have seen more than one should ever see. I fought against sirens, O'rult, and elephish just to name a few. But I also found friendship in the Grumpices."

She paused as Grumrose fluttered, heavily bandaged, to Sammaria's shoulder. Sammaria could hear their gasps. "Not only with them but with the Hawkaties as well."

She nodded her head toward Criketchen. He bowed to her. She continued, "I also found the Resistance, and together we won back our beloved county."

She looked back at Rekasi as another cheer went up. She smiled vibrantly at him. He smiled back. Turning back around, she addressed the people again, "Yes, yes. They fought famously. But we never would have been able to succeed without the help of Rekasi."

Sammaria said to their confused faces, "You know him as the person who kidnapped me. However, he did so because the necromancer was going to have me killed. Rekasi was protecting me. He protected me through all that we've been through."

Sammaria looked back at Rekasi again. She was oblivious to the people that were getting pushed aside as one man was trying to get to the top of the stairs. Rekasi smiled at Sammaria. He went to her side, taking her now calloused hands in his. He looked into her eyes saying, "In the past year, I suppose, you have pulled me out of who I was. You brought me into who I am supposed to be. I'm so in love with you."

He pulled a handcrafted ring out of his pocket and said, "Sammaria, my love, will you-"

"Face me, whore!" rang a deep voice.

He gripped a sword. Blood ran down his cheek from an empty eye socket. The Prince of Ancefra had a jealous rage in his remaining eye. He said, "She's mine. And I will not bear the insult that I have been shown here. The price is her death."

Rekasi dropped Sammaria's hand as he reached to pull out his sword. Morlyn smiled evilly as he started to charge toward Sammaria, screaming. His sword was pointed directly at Sammaria's heart.

Sammaria lifted her arm to stop the attack. She flicked her wrist toward him. The flame didn't come. She tried again. Still, nothing would come. She frantically flicked both hands toward Morlyn. She couldn't get her Power to respond. Sammaria let out a small cry of fear.

Rekasi watched Sammaria intensely. He knew she wasn't going to be able to use her Power. She was too frightened. She was afraid of what she might do. He jumped in front of her and stopped Morlyn's sword as Donichello tackled her to the ground. A gasp ran through the remaining people as their new queen was knocked to the ground. Sammaria looked at Donichello in awe, "You saved my life."

Donichello looked at her, "I might not have been able to protect her, but I can still help you."

Sammaria kissed his cheek, "Thank you."

She stood up and turned her amber eyes to Rekasi. He narrowly blocked an attack that Morlyn threw at him. Sammaria gasped and turned away. Donichello hugged her.

Donichello saw movement from the people in the crowd. Donichello bowed to Sammaria and said, "Your Majesty, we need to get you to a safer place."

Sammaria gave him a desperate look. Rekasi slashed a line onto Morlyn's cheek. She said, "I can't leave him."

Donichello said, "Sammaria, forgive me."

She looked at him, "For what?"

He picked her up and headed for the door. She screamed, "Put me down!"

❧

Jennica sat on a parkbench looking down at Ethota. Milamare sat down next to her. Jennica continued to stare at her former home. She asked, "Do you hate me?"

Milamare hugged her daughter and said, "No, I could never hate you."

Milamare wiped a tear from Jennica's cheek, "Jennica, I would like to know why you chose to stay."

Jennica said, "I am too broken. My heart, my hope, my faith, my trust."

Milamare said, "You're running away." Jennica shook her head.

Milamare said, "Let's go home. It'll do you no good sitting here, watching."

Jennica said, "I'm going to stay for a while longer."

Milamare turned to leave. She paused and said, "All Donichello ever asked of you was simply that you loved him. He loved you more than anything."

Jennica's eyes shifted to the gates, tears falling.

❧

Donichello sat Sammaria down in a closet and pulled the door closed. An O'rult raced past as they were chased by a Maginatie. Sammaria said as Donichello turned to lock her in, "By order of the Queen, I demand you release me!"

Donichello said, "I can't."

Sammaria looked at him with disbelief. Before Donichello could react, Sammaria flicked her hand, and a ring of Fire encircled him. It did not burn the surrounding area, but he could feel the heat. Sammaria unlocked the door and left. As she moved out of range, the Fire died down. Two Maginaties came to accompany her back to the throne room. Donichello raced after them.

Rekasi ducked under Morlyn's sword. He slid his sword quickly along Morlyn's cheek. Morlyn pushed Rekasi against the balcony railing. He moved his sword into a hacking position aimed at Rekasi's neck. Rekasi ducked under the sword, and the sword decapitated the neighboring gargoyle.

Two Maginaties walked onto the balcony, momentarily distracting Morlyn. Rekasi kneed Morlyn in the groin and pushed him to the ground. Donichello and Sammaria rushed in. The crown was clutched in Sammaria's hand.

Morlyn hooked his ankle on Rekasi's knee and pulled him down. They wrestled, dropping their swords. During the struggle, Rekasi landed a punch on Morlyn's face. He heard a snap and, as blood spurted, realized that he had broken Morlyn's nose.

Morlyn pinned Rekasi to the ground. His blood fell onto Rekasi's face. Morlyn pulled a dagger from his boot and held it threateningly over his head. Sammaria screamed. Donichello restrained her as Morlyn prepared to kill Rekasi. The dagger moved down swiftly.

As the dagger was a breath's touch from Rekasi's chest, something knocked the dagger from Morlyn's hands. Morlyn knelt up, and his knee pressed down on Rekasi's chest. They heard a handful of cracks, and Rekasi cried out in pain. Morlyn lifted up Rekasi's head and beat it with his own, knocking Rekasi out cold.

Donichello watched as a stream of water retreated from the balcony. To the right of the balcony, the water soared into the window of the East Tower and wrapped around an outstretched hand.

Donichello moved toward the edge of the balcony. Morlyn caught his arm. Donichello turned and punched Morlyn in the face. He jumped, grasping the roof's edge. He pulled himself up and walked carefully across the roof to the tower. He inserted his hand in a crack and began scaling the tower.

He wrapped his hand around the lip of the window and pulled himself up to see in. His breath disappeared as he saw Jennica watching him with surprise. She walked to the window. Gingerly, she placed a hand on his cheek. Donichello placed his hand over hers to hold it there.

Jennica smiled, her eyes tearing, "I'm sorry. I…"

Donichello said, "Don't apologize. I understand."

She shook her head, "I'm not sure you do."

He said, "Then explain it to me."

Donichello roared with pain. Morlyn had caught up with him and had stabbed him in the side with his dagger. Jennica reacted. She sent out a whip of water knocking Morlyn from Donichello.

Jennica pulled Donichello into the tower room. Morlyn cried out as he fell onto the ground below. She didn't stay to see his shattered body splayed on the ground.

Jennica said, "Hold on, I need you to hold on."

Donichello caressed her face. She pulled the dagger from his side as he winced.

She pressed her hand to his bleeding side. The water swirled in and out of the wound, healing it. Donichello's eyes closed and Jennica cried. She hadn't been fast enough. She leaned over, crying on his chest, "No! Donichello! No!"

The children cried out. "Donichello can't be dead! Jennica just came back!"

The storyteller looked over at they. He silenced instantly. The storyteller smiled. They were accepting the story. It was a good sign.

"But wait," she said.

Donichello's chest twitched, and Jennica felt an arm cover her back. Jennica looked up. Donichello's eyes were open.

Jennica said, "Oh, Kiro. Thank you. Kiro, thank you."

Donichello gave her a weak smile, and she pressed her lips to his.

Jennica walked onto the balcony, supporting Donichello. Sammaria was holding Rekasi's limp hand. There were tears in her eyes. Rekasi's breathing wracked his body. Jennica touched her sister's shoulder, and Sammaria moved away automatically. She was confused and scared.

Jennica knelt by Rekasi and placed a hand on his chest. She breathed in and out. A quarter of an hour later, Rekasi opened his eyes.

Sammaria looked at her sister. She couldn't find any words. Jennica said, "Sammaria?"

Sammaria's hand was lingering just inches from Jennica's shoulder. Jennica took her sister's hand, "It's really me."

Sammaria smiled as tears started to fall from her eyes again. Rekasi took Sammaria's other hand. Sammaria turned from Jennica and Jennica dropped her hand. Rekasi lifted his head from the ground and kissed Sammaria. She whispered, "I thought I was losing you."

Rekasi said, "Never."

CHAPTER LIX

She and the other Fraychavae stood before Jennica and Sammaria. Sammaria said, "I thank you for your service during this war. Now, here, in front of all these witnesses, I honor you and your kind."

She placed a medal around each of their dark necks. She smiled. The Fraychavae didn't return her smile, but they were pleased. Sammaria bowed to them and turned to address the people, "The Fraychavae will be forever in our debt. No longer will they be forced to hide their traditions. They are heroes."

Thunderous applause erupted from the crowd. The Fraychavae finally did smile faintly. Sammaria nodded at them. They moved to the side. Sammaria waited for the applause to die down, "There is another group of people to honor."

She gestured to the band of pirates standing to the side opposite the Fraychavae. Jennica walked over to them and escorted them to Sammaria.

Sammaria swept her long robe around and faced the pirates, "Please kneel."

Jessie and Reness knelt along with the other thirteen members of their crew. Sammaria accepted the sword from Zike. Dakota stood slightly behind him. She said, "People of Dragonia. Long have we been menaced by the pirates of the Sea of Mytositsa. But in our time of need, the crew of the *Death Arrow* stepped up to help us. Reness, Jessie, and their crew are responsible along with another for the appearance of the Hawkaties. Therefore, we will honor them."

She turned to them once more. "Jessica Conrad, I knight thee in the name of Kiro. I knight thee for

Dragonia. And I knight thee in the name of the Aeradal bloodline."

She tapped Jessie with the sword three times, "Rise, Lady Jessica."

Jessie stood. Sammaria fastened a pin to her tunic.

She moved on to Reness, "Reness Ornae, I knight thee in the name of Kiro. I knight thee for Dragonia. And I knight thee in the name of the Aeradal bloodline."

She tapped Reness three times, "Rise, Sir Reness."

She fastened an identical pin to the one Jessie had received to Reness's tunic.

Sammaria addressed the crowd again, "Behold. I give you the Dragonian Pirate Knights."

The members of the crew beamed. Reness slipped his hand into Jessie's. She smiled up at him. Sammaria smiled faintly and clapped with the rest of the crowd.

She said, "I would also like to thank everyone who fought with the Resistance and in any of the battles. Please, step forward."

Several people from the crowd moved to the front. Jennica recognized Lark and Armanda in the crowd. She smiled at them.

Sammaria continued, "Everyone shall receive a gift. I'm afraid I don't have enough time to knight everyone."

There was some chuckling from the crowd. She held up a hand for silence, "To conclude our ceremony, we are going to honor one more person. Anahi, please step forward."

Anahi's stomach had rounded further. She moved from the crowd. Jennica watched Se's face turn to stone as she looked toward him. There was sadness in his eyes.

Sammaria said, "Anahi. The girl from across the water. The Immortal. She already has so many titles. It is an honor to give her one more. Anahi went with Captain Reness to the Lost Island of the Hawkaties. She is the one who convinced the Hawkaties to come. Not only that, but she was much help to my sister and many others in her time on this earth."

Sammaria placed a medal of honor around Anahi's dark neck. Anahi smiled at Sammaria, but Jennica could see her sadness. Anahi winced and clutched her stomach. Jennica looked at her, concerned. Anahi smiled at her, reassuringly.

Sammaria said, "The Fraychavae, the Dragonian Pirate Knights, and Anahi are not the only people that we need to thank. During our journey, several alliances were formed. We recognize that Illicus, Keyinture, Mysticus, Griffinia, and Casparia honored their alliances and aided us in our defeat of Misseter and the O'rult.

Without the mighty Maginaties, we would have had no hope of winning this war. As my first act as Queen, I am restoring magical freedom to Dragonia."

She waited patiently for the murmuring to die down. "This shouldn't scare you. There is resentment toward those with Power, Elementals, as they are correctly called. This attitude will no longer be tolerated. People of Power will no longer have to hide."

Jennica smiled, "This is how the gods meant for the world to be. They wished for all beings to live in harmony."

The crowd was silent. Sammaria forged ahead, "Elementals, please step forward."

The Elementals cautiously stepped forward. Sammaria said, "Reach out with your Power."

Jennica reached her hand out. Sammaria walked to her side. She extended her hand with Jennica. She said, "Now!"

Power streamed in a beautiful explosion of light. It spread across the plaza like a blanket. The spectators shifted uncomfortably.

The Maginaties, hovering in the sky, lifted their heads. A light emitted from every one of their chests. The head of a Hawkatie emerged and the two creatures split apart. The Grumpices and Hawkaties squealed with pride. The spectators gasped and began to clap at the spectacle above them. Jennica smiled and left the balcony.

Anahi said, "Jennica, I'm not feeling well at all. Can you please help me?"

Jennica nodded, "We'll go to the infirmary."

Anahi nodded, "Have you talked to Se?"

Jennica shook her head, "I'm sorry, but I haven't."

Anahi said, "I didn't mean to push. I know you've been busy."

Jennica said, "It's not being pushy."

Anahi stopped and doubled over in pain, "I think it could be the baby."

Jennica said, "We must hurry then."

They rushed into the infirmary. Jennica could see blood seeping through Anahi's skirts. She said, "We need to birth that baby now. I can feel it. It's going to die if we don't get it out of her."

The midwife looked at Jennica. She said, "Now!"

The midwife laid Anahi down on the bed, then cut away her skirts.

Jennica said, "Can you see the baby?"

The midwife said, "Aye, I see it. The baby is crowning. This woman has been in labor for a while."

Jennica wondered why Anahi hadn't been in more pain. She remembered hearing Anahi was on a Hawkatie as it transformed into a Maginatie. That couldn't be good.

Jennica was asked to wait outside while the birthing took place. Jennica protested, insisting that they might need her to heal. The woman informed her that they had healers far more experienced than she was. Jennica nodded and left the room.

Jennica went in search of Se. She found him talking to Brother Orlten. She said, "Brother Orlten, do you mind if I interrupt for just a moment?"

Brother Orlten said, "Not at all. Se, do you mind?"

Se shook his headand smiled at her.

She said, "It's so good to see you." She hugged him.

He asked, "What is it that you wish to speak with me about?"

"Walk with me?"

Se held out his arm. Jennica took it. She led him to the garden. They started up a path into the woods.

Se asked, "Where are you taking me?"

"To show you something."

Se nodded. Jennica led them to ruins with trees and vines growing along the walls. She said, "Se, I need to talk to you about Anahi."

Se shook his head, "I am not talking about it."

Jennica said, "Okay, don't talk. Listen to what I have to say."

Se shook his head in the most impertinent way Jennica had ever seen. She said, "Anahi loves you. Just accept it. She is so in love with you that she willingly gave up her immortality."

Se turned to look at Jennica. She said, "Oh, you didn't know. I spoke with the gods when I was dead. She just wanted to be with you. She didn't care if she died. She's been alive so long. The gods gave her a choice. She could retain her immortality and live forever, or she could choose mortality. She chose to live and die with you. Age normally. Bear children."

Se said, "She chose this? She chose to *die*?"

Jennica shook her head. "No, Se," Jennica said forcefully, "She chose to live."

"Well, she chose wrong. I don't love her."

Jennica looked at him, "You don't mean that. I can see your love for her every time you look at her and try to hide it. You think by doing this you are protecting her. Se, what's done is done. She can't go back on it any more than you can change being a Fraychavae."

Se was silent for a time. Eventually, he said, "She wasn't supposed to fall in love with me. I wasn't supposed to fall for her. It just happened."

Jennica said, "Love doesn't do what it's supposed to. It's not something that you control. It always just happens. It's what you do with that love that matters."

Se fell to his knees, "Jennica, I love her too much. I can't do this."

Jennica knelt beside him and placed her hand on his shoulder, "Do you love her too much, or is that just an excuse?"

"I don't think I could handle losing her."

"Everyone thinks that. But you can't do that. Not with your child being born."

Se whipped his head up, "What?"

Jennica said, "Anahi was on the back of a Hawkatie as it transformed. It sent her into early labor."

He jumped to his feet. Jennica looked at him with empathy. Se asked, "Where is she?"

Jennica said, "She is in the palace infirmary."

Se said, "Jennica, thank you."

He took a step and raced toward the castle with all his speed.

Anahi's face was covered in sweat. She screamed as they told her to push once more. She sighed in relief when she heard the crying of the baby. She sank back into the covers, exhausted.

The doors flew open. A flash of brown raced into the room. Se clutched her hand, "Anahi, please forgive me."

She looked up at him. Her eyes were tired, but she looked beautiful to Se. She placed a clammy hand on his cheek, "There's nothing to forgive. You're here now."

The nurse handed the crying child to Anahi. She said, "Oh Se, we have a son. A little boy."

Se looked at the boy. He was small. His large eyes were squeezed shut. He had his mother's lips and his father's nose. He was the most beautiful creature he had ever seen. He asked breathless, "What should we call him?"

Anahi looked up at him. She asked, "Would you like to hold him?"

Se nodded. He took the cooing baby into his arms. Anahi asked, "How about Rasler?"

Se bounced the baby in his arms. The child opened its eyes after a yawn. They were cat eyes. Se laughed at the miracle this baby was. He said, "Rasler. That's a good name. My son. Our son, Rasler."

He gripped Anahi's hand. She smiled at her two men.

Jennica watched them with happiness. She knew they were going to be just fine. After Anahi had fallen asleep, Se handed Rasler off to a nurse. He came over to Jennica, "Thank you. There is no way I can repay you for what you have done for me. There is just one more thing I would like to have done."

Jennica asked, "Hmm. What's that?"

Se asked, "Could *you* marry us and be our child's godparent?"

Jennica smiled, "Yes."

❧

Anahi stepped out from behind the doors as the music began to play. Her chocolate skin looked radiant under the cream wedding dress. Jennica smiled as Se's breath became unsteady. Anahi walked down the aisle. Rasler was carried behind her by a palace attendant. He was sleeping. Anahi reached the altar and took Se's hand.

Jennica said, "We are gathered here to celebrate the marriage of Se and Anahi. Kiro bless."

Jennica read a passage from Kiro's book, "Love is giving. It fills the person so they have to give it away. Love cannot lie. Love rejoices in the truth. Love is patient and caring. It is a gift."

Continuing, she said, "So, here today we celebrate the gift of Anahi and Se."

Se and Anahi turned to face each other.

"Se, do you take Anahi as your wife? To cherish and love for the rest of your life? Do you swear to be faithful and put her well-being before all else?"

Se peered into Anahi's eyes. "I do."

"Anahi, do you take Se to be your husband? Do you promise to be loyal to him and obey his commands? Do you promise to love him and cherish him all the days of your life?"

Anahi shifted so she could look at Se. She smiled, "I do."

Jennica said, "So be it. By the power vested in me as Princess of Dragonia, I now pronounce you husband and wife."

Jennica looped the rope around Se and Anahi's linked hands. She winked at Se, "Kiss her."

Se took Anahi delicately in his arms. She smiled. Se leaned in and gently placed his lips on hers. She brought them closer by pressing harder to him. When they broke apart, they enveloped each other in their arms. Anahi accepted Rasler from Jennica. She looked up at her husband, "Look, Se. Look at our family."

He looked down at them and smiled.

EPILOGUE

Sammaria knelt in front of the priest. He said, "Sammaria, do you swear to the gods that any decision you make will be for the people? Do you swear you shall follow the path that Kiro, the Almighty One, has laid out for you? And do you swear that you will love this country, uphold its traditions, place it before all else, and always hold it in your heart?"

Sammaria said, "I swear."

The priest placed the crown on her head. The crowd in the courtyard rejoiced.

Rekasi escorted her to the gazebo. Sammaria kissed his cheek and addressed her country, "These are the beginnings of better times. This country faced many hardships in my absence and survived because of the strong character of its people. I know that it's hard to have a queen who is younger than most of you, but with your help, we can make it."

The crowd clapped and cheered. Rekasi took Sammaria's hands, "Let me try this again,"

Sammaria grinned faintly "Sammaria, I know I've known you only a little over a year, but I want to live the rest of our lives together. I know that we have what others have found. I know we can be happy."

There were some cheers from the crowd. Sammaria looked out into the crowd. Reness had his arms around Jessie who had a slightly bulging belly. They smiled at her. Sammaria asked, "Rekasi?"

He said, "Would you marry me?"

Sammaria was speechless for a moment and said, "Of course." She hugged him, and he swung her around.

❧

Sammaria walked down the aisle toward Rekasi. Everyone bowed as she passed. She smiled at the sight of Rekasi watching her in amazement. Butterflies were fluttering a mile a minute in her stomach. This was it. She was going to be married to her only love.

The priest said, "Lord Rekasi, will you love and cherish her Majesty Sammaria for your whole life? Will you place her first before your duties? Will you help her rule this fine country?"

Rekasi nodded, "I will."

The priest turned to Sammaria and said, "Your Majesty, will you take this man to be your husband? Will you love him for your whole life? Will you be loyal and cherish him always?"

Sammaria said, "I will." She looked at Rekasi and repeated, "I will." Rekasi kissed her.

"What happens next?" asked the little blonde girl in the young man's lap. The young woman telling the story smiled at the girl. She said, "Well, Margo…"

The young woman looked at the man with a peculiar look, "Averyon!"

The man looked startled, "Ma'am?"

The young woman said, "I'll tell you what happened next, Averyon. But afterward, you must do me a favor."

He stared at her, trying to figure out what type of cryptic message she was trying to send him.

He frowned for a moment before nodding his consent. The man looked at her face intently as she continued with the story.

Sammaria and her husband, Rekasi, moved into the palace. They were happy. They had a daughter who was to become the next ruler of Dragonia, Princess Endellion Tathrina. She is destined, like her mother, to have the Elemental Power of Fire.

Queen Sammaria brought Dragonia back to order. The country was restored to its former glory. She even brought peace with the Pilleetains. She was able to keep all alliances she had created. That is an amazing feat. Sammaria is a great queen.

"Now, you know the rest of the story. You're living it," concluded Storyteller Manaian. The children started to get up and move toward their parents who were sewing and writing quietly along the walls.

Averyon, however, wasn't so easily satisfied. He moved Margo off his lap and stood up defiantly. He demanded, "Oh Storyteller of Infinite Tall Tales, please tell us, oh wondrous one, what happened to dear Jennica and Donichello?"

The room froze. The little children stared at them. The woman's eyes flicked toward the transfixed children. She could see the question was on all their minds now as well. But all the storyteller of Zansetun did was smile. She said, "Please sit, and allow me to explain."

Her hand brushed across her heart as she recalled the tale."

Jennica sat in the chapel of the gods just outside the Queen's chambers. She prayed, "Kiro, help me. Mestchina, help me. Jonakil… forgive me."

Jennica looked up from her lap as three glittering lights floated in front of her. The forms of Mestchina,

Jonakil, and finally Kiro lighted before her eyes. Kiro spoke first.

His voice sounded like a thousand violins. It both hurt and was soothing at the same time.

He said, "Jennica, daughter of Enchardo and Milamare, sister to the Queen of Dragonia, what is the reason for calling us here?"

Jennica looked at each god in turn, "Please leave any children Sammaria or I might have out of any plans you have for this world."

Jonakil said, "What of opening the portals?"

Jennica said, "I'll open them; I just don't want the children to be harmed. I'm not strong enough."

Mestchina laid a hand on Jonakil's arm as he was about to speak, "It takes a large amount of strength to admit you can't do something. And to know that you can't do it. We will do what we can to protect the offspring."

Jonakil opened his mouth. A voice that was not his own protested. It sounded like a roaring fire. Kiro muttered something and Mestchina and Jonakil let out some Power. The voice was calmed.

Kiro said, "Jennica, you will be required to travel to the human realm. That is the only way the portals can be opened. We need to know the portal locations and any resistance to the portals on that side. That is your first task."

The majestic figures swept their cloaks around their bodies, transforming back into the little lights. They floated to the ceiling and disappeared.

"*Jennica returned to the Lost Island of the Hawkaties to train with Cypol. Her sister followed her there after a short time. Jennica traveled the world for awhile after that,* doing Sammaria's bidding as an ambassador to other countries.

Jennica disappeared from the world several times, slipping into Mythral. Donichello remained in Mestchester and aided Sammaria and Rekasi as they saw fit. He wasn't aware of all of Jennica's journeys, but they remained deeply in love.

Jennica returned to Dragonia when she was nineteen. She stayed a year to catch up with friends and family before she was to go into the human realm again. Jennica married her love Donichello the next year, at the age of twenty. She continues to live in both the human realm as well as her native realm. Donichello has followed her on her missions, and they have collected valuable information. Donichello and Jennica have a daughter named Miliama. And I can assure you she is very happy with what she is doing," concluded the storyteller.

The Storyteller of Zansetun said to the leaving children, "Sweet dreams, younglings."

Averyon stayed behind, staring at the storyteller. He asked, "How do we know that story is true?"

The young woman eyed him for a long while. She waited for the last child to leave. Margo protested as her father picked her up. She sleepily waved to Averyon.

The storyteller asked, "Do you know who I am?"

Averyon said, "The traveling storyteller…"

She smiled, shaking her head, "I am sure you are wondering what favor I need from you."

A man came in. He had long hair, and the stern look of a warrior. He smiled at the storyteller and handed her a baby. She cuddled the baby to her, and the man kissed her.

Averyon gasped, "You're her!" His face went white, "Oh, Kiro! Your Highness, I am so sorry!"

Jennica smiled at him, "It is all right, Averyon."

Averyon frowned and asked, "What could you possibly need from me?"

Jennica said, "I need a partner."

His eyes flicked over to Donichello. She said, "I have been watching you for a while. That's why we came here. For you."

Averyon glanced between the two.

Donichello said, "I won't lie to you. This job will be dangerous, and sometimes it will hurt. But you have wit, and you trust your instincts. That's a rare quality these days."

Averyon looked at the little family, "You want me to open the portals with you?"

Jennica nodded solemnly.

His mind showed him visions of glory and people telling his story.

He said, "I'll do it."

GUIDE TO THE WORLD OF ETHOTA

The events of *Rise of the Dragon Queen* take place from 1459-1460.

FAMILIES

AERADAL FAMILY

The Aeradal (er′ ə del) line was established in Dragonia (drag ō′ nē ə) during the Revolution of 1250. This placed King Thirin Aeradal on the throne, removing King Socorro V. The country considered the royal line corrupt. In the current age, King Enchardo (en chär′ dō) reigns. His wife Milamare Deswayze (mil′ ə mer de swāz′) died giving birth to twins – Crown Princess Sammaria (sə mär′ ē ə) and Princess Jennica (jen′ i kə). Their older brother Einar (ī′ när) was killed many years earlier in battle.

DARKEYES FAMILY

The Darkeyes Family is the line of women from which Jennica and Sammaria descend. Their grandmother – Gentra Azis (gen′ trə əz ēz′) – told the girls when they were young they were descended from a long line of women of Power. The woman who gave them this power is Eilvyre (el′ ver) Darkeyes. She is half Elva, half Draigar. All those that have Power in their family have descended from the Draigar.

DE' JENGINALD FAMILY

The de' Jenginald (di jen′ gi näld) Family is the ruling family of Ancefra (an si′ fru). This family was established in 1400. In 1445, they invaded Dragonia to gain more

land. This ended with the death of the crown prince of Dragonia. Relations with Ancefra have been tense ever since. King Malcolm runs the country with an iron fist. His son Morlyn was chosen to marry the heir to Dragonia's throne to strengthen relations between the two countries.

IANHORN FAMILY

The Ianhorn (ē′ ən hôrn) Family is the ruling family of Keyinture. This family was established in 1290. The family took advantage of the chaos that followed the closing of the portals to seize power. King Aggravarius (ag′ rə ver′ ē əs) has a treaty with the Aeradal family.

LAERANIL FAMILY

The Laeranil (ler′ ə nil) Family is headed by Duke Joromo and Duchess Isla. The Laeranils rule over the Myhadry Peninsula on Dragonia's coastal region. The Laeranil family is considered next in line to throne. The Laeranil line is descended from King Socorro V. Donichello (dän ə chelō′) is the first son. He has become a prominent knight in Dragonia.

SILENTREAD FAMILY

The Silentread (sī′ lin tred) Family is a family of farmers that fled from their village at the edge of Dragonia because of fear of magic users. Dakota Silentread revealed his Water Power to save his daughter Caliet (kal lā′) from being drowned. They take refuge with the Resistance where they are accepted.

TATHRINA FAMILY

The Tathrina (tath rē′ nə) Family is headed by Sir Reks and Lady Milamae (mil′ ə mā). The commonality between Milamae and Milamare's names falls within the Ethotan tradition of common born children to be named after nobility. This is seen as a way to aid the child in rising in the ranks of society. Sir Reks low noble from Gabvand. Sir Reks and Lady Milamae were killed in the take over of Gabvand by Lady Misseter Veron. After Rekasi fled to Dragonia, he was adopted by Huor (hōō′ ôr), the founder of the Resistance.

PALACE

ANTIEN

Antien (an′ tē in) is a squire to knights that are in service to the King. He is one of Sammaria's best friends in the palace. He leaves the palace and abandons his knight's service to join the Resistance. He believes this is the best way to protect Sammaria and Jennica.

BROTHER ORLTEN

Brother Orlten (ôr′ əl tin) was hired when the princesses were young to teach the girls. He is a member of the old religion of Dregon. While he is called "Brother," his religion has been banned due to the fear of magic users. Brother Orlten discovered when the princesses were young that they had Power. He was instrumental in hiding their Power from King Enchardo. It is discovered he is a member of the "Order of Inquisition" that helps train and push for religious freedoms.

PRANSHEY

Pranshey (pran′ shā) is King Enchardo's advisor and the master of secrets. This makes him a feared person in the castle. He is kept close to the King at all times.

RESISTANCE

DEMETRIA

Demetria (də mē′ trē ə) helps run a jewelry shop in the town of Drannor (dra′ nor). Her family is attacked and her father is killed by the King. From that point on, she aids the Resistance.

GENERALS

Marquis (mär kē), Zike, Ebiyo (eb′ ē yō), Tynacar (tī′ nə kär), and Concha (kän′ chə) are the generals employed by the Royal Family. Tynacar, Zike, Concha, and Marquis later join forces with the Resistance to remove Enchardo from the throne.

JESSICA CONRAD

Jessica Conrad is a human that fell through a *glaret* (gler′ ā) – a natural portal between the two realms – when she was a teenager. She is considered one of the Keepers of Knowledge. Jessie is a pirate on the Sea of Mytositsa.

MAEOKA

Maeoka (mā ō′ kə) is the name given to Lilliana Krulle by the rhiloxes. It rougly translates to "She who has been forgotten by her people." Lilliana was the fiancé of Einar. She was pregnant with his child when he died. She rejected the Elvateth after his death.

OLO HAMWICH

Olo Hamwich (ō′ lō ham′ wich) is the Prime Minister of Dragonia. He is the senior most member of the cabinet.

He is in charge of appointing positions within the cabinet and advising the King. He aids with the passage of bills.

RENESS ORNAE

Reness (rā nes′ ôr nā) is the captain of the *Death Arrow*. He is married to Jessica Conrad. He uses his ship to smuggle goods and people to places that need it, while also turning a profit.

SE MONKA

Se Monka (sā′ män′ kə) is a member of the Fraychavae. He is the son of the ousted chief, Lunak (lōō′ nak), who saved Jennica and Sammaria's mother Milamare from death.

SUNDRIE CLIPAR

Sundrie Clipar (sŭn′ drē clī′ pär) is an elderly woman that Sammaria meets in the Resistance. Sundrie provides Sammaria with the mother that she never had. She is Dakota's sister and has excellent healing abilities while she does not have Elemental Power.

ISLAND OF THE HAWKATIES

CHEO

Cheo (chē′ ō) is a young Hawkatie that is gifted in Elemental magic. She aids in teaching outcast Elva to control their Power.

CRIKETCHEN

Criketchen (krik et′ chin) is a Hawkatie who was born with a deformity. He is considered an outcast in Hawkatie society.

CYPOL

Cypol (sī′ päl) is an elderly Elvateth that has been accepted on the Island of the Hawkaties. He was a master of Earth Power before it became banned in Dragonia and he fled.

HAWKATIE

A Hawkatie (hôk′ ə tī) is a mystical creature that lives in the Ethotan Realm. They have the face of a falcon, ears of a bat, the body of a wolf, and the tail of a lion. They are known for their ability to capture the wind. It is thought they taught the Draigar how to harness this ability.

KOMOTIAL

Komotial (kō mō′ tē äl) is the nephew of the chieftess Hawkatie and fights alongside Rekasi during the battle for Mestchester.

XANTICA

Xantica (zan′ ti kə) is a warrior Hawkatie that protects Sammaria during the battle for Mestchester.

TRYDID ROCK

GRUMPICE

A Grumpice (gruhmp′ is) is a mystical creature that appears to be made of plant matter and rock. They are able to blend in to the areas surrounding them. Grumpices are known for their ability to harness Earth Power. It is believed these creatures taught the Draigar this ability.

GRUMROSE

Grumrose is a young Grumpice seeking adventure who often finds trouble instead.

TREESCET

Treescet (trē′ skit) is an elderly Grumpice. He is the leader of the Grumpices of Trydid Rock. They look to him for wisdom.

TRUCKLE

Truckle (trək′ əl) is a scout for the Trydid Rock Grumpice community.

TRYDID ROCK

Trydid (trī′ did) Rock is the hiding place of the Grumpices. They hid themselves after the war between the O'rult and the Elva in the year 277.

VINEYEEDLE

Vineyeedle (vīn′ yēdl) is Trydid Rock's lead architect, aiding mostly in the expansion of internal structure. She is very suspicious of outsiders.

DRAGON FURY

ASKA

Aska (ask′ ə) means friend of many. This is the highest honor that can be bestowed on a person by the dragons of Ethota. The title belongs to the person that the dragons have been waiting for to save their race from destruction.

DRACONLE WOOD

The Draconle (drə kä′ nl) Wood was named for the large dragon population that used to live there. These creatures would live in the cover of the trees and in the different rock outcroppings in the woods. Over time, the dragon population dwindled. By the 1400s, the people of Dragonia had thought all the dragons were extinct. However, in 1450, eggs were found while traveling through the Wood. These became a prize awarded to nobility for acts of bravery.

DRATASHA

Dratasha (drə tä′ shə) is a dragon that has been able to survive the extinction of her species. She has been living in the Draconle Wood with a few others of her race. She is waiting for the one who will restore her species to what it once was.

KIATA

Kiata (kē ä′ tə) means friend of dragons. It is a great honor to receive this title especially as a creature outside of the Wygair.

SNIBLEA

Sniblea (snib′ lē ə) is the dragon that hatches for Jennica.

SSNALANBAR

Ssnalanbar (snä lən bär) is the draconic name of the dragons' home, the Draconle Wood.

TSNABLIA

Tsnablia (snäb′ lē ə) was the first dragon to be tamed. This led to the destruction of the dragon line. She believed that, by aiding the Elvateth, the dragons would be seen as friends. However, they were treated as pets, and many were domesticated while the wild dragons were slaughtered.

WYGAIR

Wygair (wī gär) is the ancient name for dragons. The name dragon was given to this group of creatures by the Elvateth. It was believed that Draigar were able to transform into these beasts.

O'RULT ARMY

BYNAKST'R

Bynakst'r (bī nak′ stir) is the leader of the O'rult army. He answers only to Trydexzi, the necromancer that created him, and Misseter, the dominator of the southern countries.

MISSETER VERON

Misseter Veron (mi sē′ tər ver än) is the woman in charge of the O'rult army. She was a minor noblewoman from Arctos, who rose in power and took control of Gabvand. She wishes to continue her conquest, setting her sights on Dragonia.

O'RULT

O'rult (ō rult′) are mystical warmongering creatures created from black magic. They are created by taking a human body and infusing it with a dragon's soul. The creature takes on both humanoid and serpentine features.

TRYDEXZI

Trydexzi (trī dek′ sē) is a necromancer that practices the art of trapping souls. He has become the most feared mage in Ethota. He is the head of a cult obsessed with taking religious freedom by deposing "weak" leaders. He inspired Misseter's grab for power.

DEITIES

ANAHI

Anahi (an′ ə hē) is considered the Immortal. She was born three thousand years earlier in the land across the water, Griceland (grīs′ lənd). When she was young, she defeated the leader of the Rican (rīs′ ən) who were trying to destroy her people - the Ebwae (eb′ wā). In destroying him, she was cursed with immortal life. She has been wandering Ethota ever since. Legends have deemed her the greatest saint that has walked the earth. She married Se and is the mother of Rasler (rās′ ler).

BAIZE

Baize (bās′) is the season of fulfillment and growth. During this time, the Harvest Festival is celebrated. The goddess of the harvest – Omaira (ō mī′ rə) – is celebrated during this time. A good harvest under Omaira will aid the people through the Frez days.

BLESSIM

Blessim (bles′ əm) is the season of renewal. During this time, Dragonia holds a festival called Alban Kiran (äl′ bin kēr′ än) meaning 'The Light of Kiro'. This festival offers the god of creation fruits of his labor. Children conceived during this time are said to have special gifts.

DEILDLY

Deildly (del′ də lē) is the land of the dead. The Ethotan people believe that, when they die, their souls travel to this place. All souls have the same fate. The keeper of this land is Dunldir (dōōn′ əl dēr). His name is not spoken, especially during the Frez days. It is believed he wanders Ethota, looking for souls.

DELFAN

Delfan (del′ fin) was the first being to be considered an Elva. He was a halfling- the child of the god of fire and a human. Elvateth came from across the water, wielding Fire Power and tried to destroy the Draigar.

DRAIGAR

Draigar (drā′ gär) were the early beings that lived in Ethota and settled in the land that became Dragonia. They were known for their peaceful ways and their ability to commune with nature.

DREKA

Dreka (drā′ kə) is the feast of the Blood Moon. This is the time when the Fraychavae can transform new members.

DYUMKL

Dyumkl (dī əm kəl) is the god of the wilderness. He takes the form of a large, golden griffin.

ELVATETH

Elvateth (elvə′ teth) is the race birthed by Namonii. They were a race able to control Fire and sought to take over all of Ethota for their mother goddess.

ERIF

Erif (er′ if) is the season of heat and growth. During this time, the Dragonians celebrate the Festival of Fire, honoring the goddess Namonii. This festival honors the goddess who gave Elvateth life. It also remembers Namonii in her banishment to the Frozen Lands.

FRAYCHAVAE

The Fraychavae (frā′ kə vā) is a secretive society that lives in the town of Athers (ā′ thərs). The place is feared for the sacrifices that the group makes to transform their people into great warriors. The Fraychavae have increased strength, speed, and senses. The price of that is the blood spilled during Dreka. The ban on magic was meant to stop traditions such as this. However, people are too fearful of the Fraychavae to enforce the ban.

FREZ

Frez (fres′) is the season of cold, death, sacrifice, and remembrance. During this time, Dragonia holds a festival called 'The Day of the Innocents' during which they remember the ancestors that have passed into Deildly. Offerings are sent to the goddess Caterine (kat′ ir ēn) and her husband, the god of death.

HAVAE TREE

The Fraychavae have worshipped the Havae (hə vā′) Tree for centuries, and it gives them the power to transform into their fully realized bodies.

JONAKIL

Jonakil (jän′ ə kil) was elevated to god status after he was killed. He was a Draigar who was able to restore peace to the dying race.

KIRO

Kiro (kēr′ ō) is the main god of Ethotan religion. He is considered the father of the world.

MESTCHINA

Mestchina (mest chē′ nə) is the only halfling to have been elevated to god status. She was the savior of the Draigar people and founded Dragonia as a country for religious freedom.

MOKANA

Mokana (mō kä′ nē) is the god of wonder and mysteries. He is also considered a trickster in some stories.

NAMONII

Namonii (nə mō′ nē) is the goddess of fire that birthed the first Elvateth, Delfan. She was banished and killed after the other gods found out that her son was trying to vanquish the ancient Draigar race.

NYMA AND ASRAVI

Nyma (nī′ mə) and Asravi (az rä′ vē) are falcons that Sammaria tamed as pets. The falcon is also a messenger for Kiro and is the symbol of the high gods. Falcons respond to the call of their god and do his bidding.

TEARA

Teara (tir′ ə) – often called the Mother of the Bounty - is the goddess of rain and agriculture. She is often depicted wearing bright colors. Keyinture has claimed her as the patron of their island country. Every year, they host weeks of festivals in her honor.

LOCATIONS

CASPARIA
Casparia (cas pär′ ēə) is the country to the north of Dragonia. They have and maintain an alliance and trade of spices.

DAMASK
Damask (də mäsk′) is a port city in Keyinture. The city is known for its fine markets of wool and linens.

DAYTERRAL
Dayterral (dā ter el) is the largest port in Pilletain.

ETHOTA
Ethota (eth ō′ tə) is the name of the realm in which the Elvateth live.

FLYC-ANTELL PASS
The Flyc-Antell (flik′ an′ tel) Pass is a dangerous path through the Kilhatea Mountains. Most travelers opt to go around the range rather than passing through.

GABVAND
Gabvand (gab′ vand) is a small country to the south. The borders have always been closed to the outside world. It was rumored that the country had fallen many years prior. However, due to the nature and distance of the country, confirmation was never given.

GRIFFINIA
Griffinia (grif in′ ē ə) is Dragonia's counterpart to the east. Its people are known for their devotion to the wild god Dyumkl. Dragonia exports rock to their country.

ILLICUS

Illicus (il i kis) is a country northeast of Dragonia. Dragonia maintains a relationship with them, and Dragonian Elvateth train their medical students.

KATART WOODS

The Katart (kə tärt′) Woods are a vast forest in Dragonia. They border the Kilhatea Mountains to the east, and are the home of the rhiloxes.

KEYINTURE

Keyinture (kē in′ tʉr) is an island country to the southwest of Dragonia. It is known for the fine fabrics that it produces.

KILHATEA MOUNTAINS

The Kilhatea (kil āt′ ə) Mountains is a mountain range that spans from Dragonia to the Sea of Mytositsa. it begin west of Dragonia's capitol and extends to the Vrian Ocean.

LAVINRAC

Lavinrac (la′ vin rak) is a border town between Pilleetain and Dragonia. It is considered one of the largest ports in the world. The place is also considered a natural portal between Mythral and Ethota.

MEADOW OF GAMERANA

Meadow of Gamerana (ga′ mər änə) is a meadow at the edge of Trydid Rock. The Grumpices have enchanted it to put passing travelers to sleep.

MESTCHESTER

Mestchester (mest′ ches tər) is the capitol city of Dragonia. It is named for Mestchina. This city is the home of the royal family and the trading hub of the country.

MYHADRY PENINSULA

The Myhadry (mī′ ə drī) Peninsula is the land controlled by the Laeranil family. It is located in the southern most edges of Dragonia. This land is known for its white, sandy beaches.

MYSTICUS

Mysticus (mis′ ti kis) is a country bordering Casparia to the east. They have and maintain an alliance and trade of sugar.

MYTHRAL

Mythral (mith′ rəl) is the name for the human realm, which collides with the Elvateth realm of Ethota at the port town of Lavinrac.

PILLEETAIN

Pilleetain (pil ē′ tin) is the country that neighbors Dragonia to the west. These two countries have had a tenuous relationship for decades. The Pilleetain people have raided the borders of Dragonia, furthering tensions.

POCCUOTTAWA

Poccuottawa (pä′ kōō ä′ tə wə) is a chain of islands northwest of Dragonia. The Poccuottawan people are known for their pottery and revolutionary fighting styles.

RIAF CANAL

The Riaf (rī′ af) Canal was built in the Port of Dayterral to allow ships to pass between Pilleetain and Dragonia.

SEA OF MYTOSITSA

The Sea of Mytositsa (mī tō sit′ sə) is the sea that creates the eastern coasts of Dragonia and Keyinture.

ZANSETUN

The village of Zansetun (zan sēt′n) is a border town subjected to raids by the people of Pilleetain. It is a major village that is frequented by people leaving and entering Dragonia and Pilleetain

ACKNOWLEDGMENTS

This book would never be where it is today without the help of so many people. While I may not be able to thank everyone, there are a few people I would be remiss not to mention.

First, I would like to thank my husband, Dylan. He has been so supportive through this whole endeavor. Even if that means giving up more then a few evenings with me so I could finish writing. He also was the editor of my first few drafts. He could probably write this story back to me in his sleep.

I would like to thank my sister, Kinley. She has read through this so many times as well. She also has listened to all of my anxious spirals and fears that I am not good enough. She helped me through different aspects of design and just generally supported me on this journey.

I would like to thank my cover artist Marta Dec for the wonderful art and help she provided.

Lastly, I want to thank the many English teachers I have had over the years who noticed me scribbling in notebooks in my spare time. They continuously encouraged me to pursue my interests. Eventually, that led me here. Thank you Miss Sung, Mr. Denton, Ms. Ecryod, and Miss Flax.

ABOUT THE AUTHOR

Darrah Steffen grew up in Ottawa, KS. She lives in Dickinson, ND with her husband, dog Willow, and cat Jasper. When she is not writing books, she works as a fossil preparator at the Badlands Dinosaur Museum. Visit her at www.darrahsteffenwrites.wordpress.com.

If you liked what you read, leave a review on Goodreads and Amazon.

www.ingramcontent.com/pod-product-compliance
Lightning Source LLC
Chambersburg PA
CBHW071728110726
47908CB00006B/1540